The War of the Grail

The War of the Grail

GEOFFREY WILSON

HODDER &
STOUGHTON

First published in 2013 by Hodder & Stoughton
An Hachette UK company

1

A CIP catalogue record for this title is
available from the British Library

Hardback ISBN 978 1 444 72116 4
E-book ISBN 978 1 444 72117 1

Typeset in Minion Pro by Palimpsest Book Production Limited,
Falkirk, Stirlingshire

Printed and bound by CPI Group (UK) Ltd, Croydon CR0 4YY

Hodder & Stoughton policy is to use papers that are natural,
renewable and recyclable products and made from wood grown in
sustainable forests. The logging and manufacturing processes are expected to
conform to the environmental regulations of the country of origin.

Hodder & Stoughton Ltd
338 Euston Road
London NW1 3BH

www.hodder.co.uk

For my London family: Helena, Anita, Blue, Molly,
Jet and little Griff

Prologue

The Evil One walks in these woods.

Noel Miller shivered as he recalled what the old man had said. He'd been trying to forget about it all day, but now that night had closed in and the forest had clenched itself tightly to either side of the road, those words kept worming their way into the back of his head.

The Evil One walks in these woods.

Noel's horse nickered and shook her head. He leant forward in the saddle and whispered in her ear to calm her.

Forester Warwick, riding alongside Noel, snorted. 'Your horse senses her rider's nerves.'

Noel quickly sat up straight again. 'I'm not nervous.' Thinking he might have spoken too abruptly, he added, 'Master.'

Warwick grinned, the silver stubble on his cheeks glinting in the moonlight. Thick lines furrowed his face and his skin was like aged leather. He'd been a forester for nearly thirty years and had spent most of that time living outdoors, battered by the wind and rain. 'Don't you worry, boy. Shawbury's not far off now. Your mother won't have to fret for much longer.'

Noel felt his cheeks redden. Warwick was always making fun of his mother. But she did have a way of embarrassing him. On the very first day of his apprenticeship with the Earl of Shropshire's foresters, his mother had come running after him with a pair of mittens he'd left behind. She'd rushed up to him, puffing and panting, and insisted on trying to push the mittens over his hands herself. Noel still winced at the memory of the other young apprentices bellowing with laughter.

He took a deep breath, circled his shoulders and straightened his back. He might only be fourteen years old, but he was an apprentice forester. He had to make sure he at least acted the part.

But his eyes kept straying to the whorls of shadow and foliage all about him. The wind changed and the trees creaked and rattled. He caught a whiff of rot from the marshes that speckled the countryside in this part of Shropshire. Frogs chirped and cawed and the night insects shrilled.

Hills swept up to his right, only barely visible against the black sky. A ruin crowned one of the summits, the moon casting the ancient stonework pale and spectral. He'd heard the building had once been the fortress of a mad sultan who'd ruled these lands long ago. Now crazed djinns were said to haunt it. Hardly a comforting thought.

There was a rustle in the undergrowth and a dark form shot out of the woods. Noel jumped in his saddle, but then saw it was only a boar. The creature slipped like a sprite across the track and then disappeared into the trees again.

Warwick shook his head. 'God's blood, lad. Calm down.'

'I'm fine.'

'It's just the woods. You telling me you never been out in them at night?'

'Course I have, sir.' Noel hesitated for a moment. Should he tell Warwick what was on his mind? 'It's just . . .' His voice trailed off. He couldn't bring himself to speak about it. He was certain Warwick would only laugh.

'You're not thinking about that old blind fool, are you?'

'No, sir.' Noel heard an owl hoot nearby. 'Maybe.'

'That man was a simpleton.'

'He sounded sure of himself.'

The incident had happened earlier in the day. Warwick and

Noel had been sent to Drayton to investigate a claim of illegal woodcutting. As they were on their way back, the old man had staggered out into the road, babbling that the Devil himself was hiding in the forest.

'He killed a man yesterday,' the old man had said, drool running down his chin. 'I was near, but I hid myself. But the Devil it was.'

Warwick gave a wheezy laugh. 'That old man was blind. How did he even see the Devil?'

'Said he smelt the brimstone on his breath,' Noel replied. 'Said he heard him growling.'

'Boy, the Devil might be at work in these lands. Perhaps his hand is behind our Rajthanan enemies even. But he won't be hiding out in a forest to frighten old men. What purpose would that serve?'

'Suppose you're right,' Noel mumbled. For a moment the darkness seemed less threatening and the shadows less thick. He cast his eye over the branches swaying all about him. Of course Warwick was right. The Devil wasn't lurking in these woods . . .

'Wait.' Warwick stopped his horse abruptly.

Noel's heart quivered and he dragged at the reins to pause his mare. 'What?'

Warwick pointed into the mottled darkness to the right of the path. 'There.'

Noel peered into the blackness. What was Warwick talking about? Then he spotted it – a tiny, greenish light winking in the gloom. 'What is it?'

Warwick pursed his lips. 'Must be poachers.'

'You sure?'

'That light's right in the middle of the forest. There's no track. Only poachers would go out there at night.'

'But . . . would they light a fire?'

Warwick rested his hand on the pommel of his arming-sword. 'They must have made camp for the night.'

'Couldn't it be bandits? Outlaws?'

3

'Haven't been many of them in these parts for a few years.'
Warwick turned his horse towards the light. 'It's poachers. I'm
certain of it.'

Warwick set off along an animal track that wound through the
trees. Noel nudged his mare and followed. The branches knitted
together about him and twigs scratched at his face. Spots of
moonlight lay scattered like coins across the ground. Occasionally,
through the leaves, he caught glimpses of the pallid ruins hovering
on the crest of the nearest hill.

He swallowed hard. If poachers were out here, he and Warwick
would have to confront them. After all, one of the main jobs of
the foresters was to prevent hunting in the earl's woods. In theory,
he and Warwick would have to capture the poachers and take
them to Shawbury for trial. But that would prove difficult if there
were many men and they decided to resist.

Noel had been training hard with his arming-sword, but so far
he'd never had to use it.

He whispered a Hail Mary under his breath. With any luck,
the poachers would scatter and disappear into the night.

The trail petered out and the horses were forced to wade
through brambles and bracken. The ground became uneven as
the base of the hills drew closer.

After perhaps two minutes, Warwick raised his hand to call a
halt.

Noel rode up beside him. 'What now?'

'Quiet,' Warwick hissed. 'They're not more than two hundred
yards away.' He nodded ahead to where the green light glimmered
between the tree trunks. 'We'll go on foot from here.'

They both dismounted and tethered their horses. Warwick drew
a pistol from his belt, flexed his fingers about the handle and then
led the way ahead. They crept through the trees, treading as
silently as they could. Noel winced each time the bracken crackled
beneath his boots.

They passed through moonlit arcades of trees. Vines draped

down from the branches and mosses furred the trunks. The sound of the frogs and crickets throbbed constantly.

Noel's heart beat faster. He found his fingers sliding around the pommel of his sword. He'd sharpened the blade that morning, before they'd set out. He was certain it would do some damage if he landed a good blow. But would he be able to land a good blow? It was one thing to train, quite another, he was sure, to use a sword in a real fight. What if he lost his head and made a mistake? What if he found himself up against a more seasoned fighter?

What would it be like to feel a blade slicing into his stomach?

His heart raced and he panted softly. He had to calm himself. Get himself under control.

He shot a look at Warwick. The grizzled older man had a sword at his side and the pistol in his hand. The firearm's polished metal glowed softly in the dim light and Noel could just make out the ornate designs engraved along the side plate. Not many people had a pistol like that. Although some crusaders had been issued muskets, a pistol was a special prize. It could fire six shots without reloading. You could kill a group of men before they even got near to you. Like magic.

Noel took a deep breath. He was with Warwick, who'd been a forester for years. The old man knew what he was doing. Noel would be quite safe while he was with him.

He squinted ahead and studied the light. Now that the radiance was closer, it looked as though there were in fact two separate lights standing close to each other. Two fires? Was that it?

And something else was bothering Noel. It had been lurking at the back of his mind since Warwick had first spotted the light.

'Sir,' Noel whispered.

'What?' Warwick said without pausing or even turning his head.

'If that's a campfire up there, why's it bright green?'

Warwick muttered something that Noel couldn't hear.

'What, sir?'

Warwick drew to a halt and spun round. His eyes burned in the darkness. 'You listen here, boy. You'd better shut your mouth and start doing what I tell you to.'

Noel gulped. What was Warwick so angry about? 'But, sir, I just meant the fire's a strange colour—'

'I said, shut your mouth.' Warwick grasped Noel's tunic at the neck and twisted the material tight. 'You and your bloody talk about devils.'

Noel's breath was shivery. 'Didn't say nothing . . .' Then he noticed the wild gleam in Warwick's eyes. It was as though the man were crazed.

Or afraid.

Noel's heart quickened. Warwick. Afraid.

He glanced in the direction of the light and then gasped.

The glow had vanished. He could see nothing but the patchy gloom in all directions.

'What the devil?' Warwick had noticed too. He let go of Noel's tunic and scanned the surroundings.

'What happened?' Noel asked.

'Some sort of trap, I'll warrant. Guard my back.'

Noel drew his sword and stood with his back to Warwick, as he'd been taught to do many times before. He gripped the hilt tightly, but couldn't stop his hand from shaking. The moonlight flowed and rippled over the blade as it moved.

He scoured the woods, staring into the caverns and passages formed by the trees. The wind tugged at the branches and sent the shadows shifting and weaving. He kept thinking he saw figures moving in the dark, but each time he concentrated on them they vanished.

There was a soft crunch off to his right. It sounded like vegetation breaking. He jumped slightly and stared into the gloom, but saw nothing but shadows.

'What was that, sir?' he asked.

'Keep watching my back,' Warwick hissed.

Noel nodded. His hand was shaking so much now that the sword was waggling like a silver eel.

There was another crunch, accompanied by a thud. It sounded as though something had struck the earth.

Cold fingers crept up Noel's spine and his scalp crawled. His breathing was short, ragged and so loud it echoed through the forest.

Warwick pointed the pistol towards the source of the sound.

There was another thud. Then the shuffle and rustle of something moving through the undergrowth. Another thud. And then a great cracking, thrashing and groaning, followed by a thump that shivered through the earth. A tree had fallen somewhere in the dark.

'By Saint Mary!' Noel shuddered.

'Keep to my back.' Warwick was breathing heavily and his voice sounded strained.

More threshing in the undergrowth.

Noel's breath came in short gulps. Tears pricked his eyes and he blinked in order to stop his sight becoming completely blurred. He thought of his mother for a moment, pressing the wretched mittens over his hands. He'd been furious with her for embarrassing him. Only now he felt ashamed of himself. He shouldn't have been angry. She'd only been trying to look after him as she'd always done . . .

'Run,' Warwick said hoarsely.

It took Noel a moment to understand the words. The crashing in the forest was growing louder. And now he could see the two green lights again. They were hurtling towards him and Warwick.

Noel's stomach dropped. Something warm ran down his leg and he realised he was pissing in his hose.

Warwick was already charging off into the woods and disappearing through a curtain of vines. Noel spun round and sprinted after the older man, trying to catch up. Behind him he heard a contorted howl that sounded like iron breaking. Sweat ran down his face and tears welled up in his eyes. He was wailing now and couldn't stop himself.

To his left he heard more slashing and crunching. He caught sight of the green lights flickering through the netting of branches.

What was it? The Devil? Could it really be the Devil?

He was sobbing. What else could it be? It had to be the Devil.

Twigs and leaves slapped him in the face. He flailed through thickets of shrubs. He was dimly aware that he'd thrown his sword aside at some point. What a stupid thing to do. Now he had nothing to fight with. Although, what good was a sword against the Devil anyway?

He tripped on a stone, went flying through the air and skidded across the ground. As he scrambled back to his feet, he heard bellowing and roaring up ahead. He paused for a second, squinting into the dark. He couldn't see anything, but he heard more howls and the crack and thump of a tree falling. Someone shouted – he was certain it was Warwick. There was a pop, and a flash lit up the forest for a second. Warwick must have fired the pistol.

And then there was silence.

Almost complete silence.

Noel could hear his own ragged breathing, the sizzling of the night insects and the cackle of the leaves in the wind. But that was all.

'Warwick,' he whispered.

There was no reply.

He swallowed, tasting salt from his tears in the back of his throat.

'Warwick,' he said more loudly, his voice shaking.

Still nothing.

A chill crawled across his skin.

His mind clouded for a moment and he couldn't think what to do. Should he try to hide somewhere? Should he go back the way he'd come? He quickly realised he had to go forward, had to find Warwick. If he could.

8

Cursing the fact that he'd thrown away his sword, he sneaked ahead. The stench of the rot was stronger now and at one point his foot sank into a shallow pool. He must be near to the edge of the marshes.

Then he heard a splash and a slurping sound behind him. Something had dropped into swampy ground.

He froze. He had the strange sense that there was something near to him. He spun round and crouched slightly, panting hard. Who was there? What was there?

He saw nothing but tangled branches dripping with moss.

He waited for a moment, searching the alternating patches of light and dark. Then he sensed a tiny shift in the air, as if a door had closed at the far end of a long hall. Something had moved in the dark. But he couldn't tell whether it was just ahead of him or further away.

And now he noticed a new smell cutting through the scent of the bog. It reminded him of coal smoke mixed with perfume. The hair shot up on the back of his neck. Was that smell brimstone?

Shaking, he turned and jogged ahead. He tried to go quietly at first, but then a metallic wail erupted behind him. His heart spiked and he charged forward, smashing aside bushes that got in the way. He was whimpering involuntarily. Tears smeared his eyes.

A branch smacked him in the face, but he ducked underneath it. He staggered through a mesh of vines and then came out in a clearing. Something lay glinting in the grass. As he ran closer, he saw it was a pistol.

Warwick's pistol.

He grasped the firearm. His hand shook so much he thought he was going to drop the weapon. He'd never shot a pistol before, but he'd seen them used often enough to know what to do. You just pointed the thing at the target and pulled the small lever at the bottom – a 'trigger', it was called.

A roar boomed behind him. He swivelled and pointed the pistol at the shadows. He heard a thump and further crashing through the undergrowth. But he still saw nothing.

Heart smacking hard, he turned again and ran to the far side of the clearing. As he reached the trees, he almost tripped as his foot struck something lying across the ground.

He looked down.

His skin seethed and bile rose in his throat.

It was a human arm, severed from its body and its end a bloody stump. Worse, he recognised the material of the sleeve that still covered it. It was from Warwick's tunic.

Noel stifled a cry.

There was a thud behind him and a shriek so loud it made the air shiver. A blast of hot air scorched the back of his neck and smoke billowed about him.

His heart bashed in his chest.

The Devil was right behind him.

His only hope was to shoot with the pistol. But would that even have any effect? Could the Evil One be harmed by a firearm?

He had to try.

Trembling, crying, he turned round.

A gigantic form towered over him, silhouetted against the moonlight. Two green fires glowed where he imagined the Devil's eyes must be.

He gasped and raised the pistol. But the Devil lunged straight at him.

Piss flooded his hose and his bowels emptied. For a second he caught a glimpse of a monstrous face. He tried to pull the trigger but he'd already been whipped off his feet and swung into the air. Steam and smoke whirled about him. He felt himself being stretched apart. And then a great weight slammed into his chest.

As he slipped away he could think of one thing only – his mother weeping with worry as she pressed the mittens over his hands . . .

PART ONE

1

Jack Casey stood before the great portcullis as it groaned and rattled upwards. The chains and pulleys squealed so loudly he thought they would break and send the ironwork slamming back into the earth. This was the first time he'd seen the portcullis in use since he'd arrived in Clun Valley. Clearly it was in need of repair.

Indeed, much of Lord Fitzalan's castle was in need of repair. When Jack glanced up at the walls and towers, he spotted many broken battlements, chipped turrets and cracked stones. Once the castle would have been a grand fortress, with banners flying above the keep and archers lining the walls. But that was all long in the past now.

The portcullis clanged into place and Jack strode through the arched passage beneath the gatehouse.

Constable Henry Ward stood waiting for him on the other side. The large man had his hands on his hips, and his eyes glinted from within his bearded face. An arming-sword hung at his side and an ornate rotary pistol was stuck in his belt. As always, he wore a white surcoat emblazoned with the red cross of St George – the mark of the Crusader Council of Shropshire. Three guards stood just behind him, also wearing crusader surcoats. Lord Fitzalan had long been one of the Council's staunchest supporters and now few in his service even wore the Fitzalan sign.

Jack raised his hand. 'Greetings.'

Henry narrowed his eyes and looked Jack up and down, his mouth twisting with distaste. Jack and Henry had never seen eye to eye, but over the past seven months, since Jack had returned from Scotland, their disagreements had become even more heated.

'What is it you want, Henry?' Jack held his hands open to show he wasn't carrying a weapon.

Henry's expression soured further. '*I* don't want anything from you. I'd be happier to see you run out of that little enclave of yours. I can't understand how you were ever appointed reeve of that village in the first place.'

Jack raised an eyebrow. 'It was you who summoned me. If I'm not needed—'

'Wait.' Henry scowled. 'It's the master who wants to speak to you. It's urgent.'

Jack followed Henry and his men across the bailey, through a set of double doors and into the great hall. The chamber was silent and all the shutters were closed. A handful of sputtering torches tried feebly to hold back the gloom, but most of the hall remained draped in shadows. Jack could only just make out the lord's chair standing on the dais at the far end of the room.

Henry led the way up a set of corkscrew steps. The silence was so complete Jack could even hear the guards' scabbards tapping against the wall of the stairwell.

When Jack had visited the castle in the past, the place had been bustling with men-at-arms, servants and courtiers. Where was everyone?

Henry reached a landing at the top of the stairs and paused beside a door. He turned to face Jack, his features lit only by a streak of light from an arrow slit in the wall. 'You must not speak to anyone about what you see beyond this door.'

Jack blinked. This was a surprise. 'What?'

'You must not speak of it,' Henry hissed, his cheeks flushing.

His gaze was so intense that Jack couldn't think of anything to do but nod his agreement.

Henry placed his fingers on the ringed door handle and paused for a moment as if deliberating whether or not to proceed. Then he pushed the door open and ushered Jack into a small but richly decorated chamber. The walls were plastered, painted dark red and adorned with tapestries. Two ornate chests stood against one wall and a wooden chair was lodged in a corner. Fresh rushes and herbs lay strewn across the floor, filling the room with a heavy sweetness.

A large four-poster bed dominated the chamber. The curtains around the bed had been pushed back and Jack could see Lord Fitzalan lying within, propped up against the pillows and enveloped in quilts and coverlets. The lord was so thin his cheeks sank inwards and there were deep hollows between the tendons in his neck. His skin was a greyish white and his face was smeared with sweat. His eyes were closed and his chest rose and fell unevenly.

Jack needed no explanation. His wife, Katelin, had died of fever twelve years ago. The memory of her lying on her deathbed, feebly raising her hand to him, was seared in his memory.

Henry closed the door and stood with his back to it, his huge frame seeming even larger in the small room.

'How long has he been like this?' Jack asked.

'Four days,' Henry replied. 'Only a few know. It could . . . upset the people if it got out.'

Jack nodded. In the present climate, news of Lord Fitzalan's illness could cause panic in Clun Valley. The Rajthanans' forces had been massing at the border of Worcestershire for months. Their advance into Shropshire had stalled when troops were diverted to quell an uprising in al-Saxony. But everyone in Clun knew the invasion could come at any time.

'We've tried to treat him,' Henry said. 'One of the monks from Clun Abbey has been visiting. But the fever has taken a strong hold and won't let go.'

Suddenly Lord Fitzalan's eyes sprang open and he began babbling in a weak voice.

'My lord.' Henry rushed to the bedside and placed his hand on Fitzalan's arm.

Fitzalan stared at Jack and grasped at something on the bed beside him. It was only now that Jack noticed the sword lying half hidden beneath the quilts. With great difficulty, Fitzalan managed to grasp the sword's hilt and drag the blade out from under the bedding.

He began speaking agitatedly. 'They're here. I knew they would come.'

'You must rest, my lord,' Henry said.

Sweat coursed over Fitzalan's brow as he tried to lift the sword. 'Bring me my armour. My steed. I will defend this manor.'

'My lord, please.' Henry grasped Fitzalan's arm more firmly. 'It's not the heathens.'

Fitzalan's forehead creased. 'Not the heathens?'

'No, my lord.' Henry eased Fitzalan's arm down so that the hilt rested on the bed once more. 'It's Jack Casey. You called for him, remember?'

Fitzalan's jaw worked silently for a moment. His eyes swam as they searched the room. He seemed uncertain where he was. Then he jolted and pointed at a corner of the chamber. 'The land is cursed! The King is dead and I am fading!'

Jack flicked a look at Henry. The ill news that King John had died had filtered back to Clun a week ago. The King had passed away peacefully in his sleep, it was said. But his heir, Prince Stephen, was barely seven years old. The Raja of All England, General Vadula, had appointed the Earl of Norfolk as regent. However, the earl was almost as hated in England as Vadula. He'd sided with the Rajthanans during the First Crusade and would do whatever Vadula commanded.

Fitzalan's eyes focused on Jack. 'There is pestilence. The animals are dying. It is as in the days of King Arthur. We are sick with enchantment. Only the Grail can free us. Galahad found it long ago. Then Oswin during the war against the Caliph. We must find it once again.'

Spittle foamed from Fitzalan's mouth and he raved unintelligibly, trying to grasp at the sword again.

Henry spoke quietly to the lord, as if soothing a distressed child. Finally, Fitzalan slumped back on the pillows and slipped into an uneasy sleep.

Henry looked across at Jack. 'I don't know how long he can last.'

Jack pursed his lips. 'Looks bad.'

'He's right about the Grail. It's our only hope now.' Henry looked at Fitzalan. 'His only hope. The Grail can cure the sickness sweeping over us. And defeat our enemies.'

Jack took a deep breath. He was starting to understand now why he'd been summoned. 'We've tried to find it. You know that.'

'Not hard enough. We have to go back to Scotland.'

'Sir Alfred said—'

'Alfred's not here now.' Henry's voice was sharp, and he stepped over to Jack.

Jack paused. The expedition he'd led to Scotland had failed. There'd been some talk amongst the Crusader Council about going back, but Sir Alfred had ruled against that for the time being.

But Henry was right. Alfred was now at the front, at the border with Worcestershire, and was unlikely to be back soon.

'There's no point,' Jack said. 'What we found there, it was a meeting point of sattva streams. It was strong sattva, but not much else. I don't know if that's the Grail – and I don't know how we can use it, if it is.'

'We've only got your word for that.' Henry's eyes glinted in the dim light.

'Saleem was there too.'

'That little Mohammedan? He's one of your followers. He'll say whatever you tell him to.'

'Alfred said we can't spare the men. We have to be ready to fight. I agree with him.'

Henry pointed at the prone lord. 'And then he'll die. Is that what you want?'

'He could survive—'

'Look at him.' Henry's eyes glimmered. 'He could go at any time. The whole of Clun will fall apart if that happens. He has no heir.'

'I can see the problem. But going to Scotland won't help. Let's send word to Alfred, or wait for him to come back.'

Henry's face seethed. Suddenly, he lunged at Jack and grasped his tunic.

Jack was caught off guard and knocked back against the tapestried wall.

'You will go.' Henry brought his face close to Jack's. 'I order it.'

Jack gripped Henry's wrist. 'Let go of me.' He didn't want a fight if he could help it. But he'd hidden a knife in his undergarments before entering the castle, and he wouldn't hesitate to use it if he had to.

'You will do it, or I'll march my men into Folly Brook and take it. And then I'll put that Rajthanan witch you have hiding up there to the torch.'

This mention of Sonali made Jack's face go hot. Sonali had been living in Folly Brook village since she'd arrived in Clun. She was under Jack's protection and he wouldn't allow anything to happen to her.

The blood pounded in Jack's ears. But still, he held back. If he fought Henry, the guards on the landing outside would rush in. He couldn't fight against so many with just a knife.

'I said, let go of me,' Jack hissed, staring at Henry. 'Now.'

Henry was breathing heavily and his eyes were wild. He looked like a madman.

Jack removed one of his hands from Henry's wrist and went to grab the knife.

Then Lord Fitzalan groaned. Henry looked back at the bed and eased his grip on Jack's tunic. Jack wrenched himself free and slipped over to the door. As he left, he snatched a look over his shoulder. Henry was standing beside the bed again, and Lord Fitzalan was muttering and reaching up feebly.

Henry lifted his eyes to meet Jack's. 'I'll be coming for you. You're a traitor. Always were.'

Jack eased the door open and slid out on to the landing. The guards looked startled to see him alone, but they parted as he pressed forward. He brushed past them and clattered away down the steps.

He wasn't sure what Henry would do next. In theory Folly Brook was safe. Sir Alfred was the leader of the local arm of the Crusader Council and he'd always sided with Jack. But with Sir Alfred away and Lord Fitzalan ill, there was no telling what Henry might try. Jack hadn't liked the crazed look in Henry's eyes.

Jack reached the bottom of the stairs. It was best he got back to Folly Brook as quickly as he could.

— ◆ —

'It doesn't look good, Jack, sir.' James, a tenant farmer, scratched the stubble on his face.

Jack squatted down beside the dead sheep. Flies were already buzzing about the carcass, although the animal couldn't have been lying there for more than a few hours. Its eye stared up at the overcast sky and its mouth hung slightly open.

'Found her here just a few minutes ago,' James said. 'Came straight to find you.'

Jack rubbed his chin. The ewe looked emaciated, but it was clearly her hind leg that was the problem. The limb was swollen and when he touched it, the skin seemed to crackle beneath his fingers. He'd seen this in sheep and cattle before. One or more legs became infested with disease and the animal soon succumbed.

'Must be the plague they're all talking about,' James said quietly.

'Heard it's all over Clun Valley. Sheep and cattle dying in their hundreds.'

Jack drew back from the carcass. 'Let's not jump to conclusions. It's one dead sheep.'

He didn't want to cause alarm in the village. He'd heard of the animal plague, but so far Folly Brook had been spared. He could only pray it stayed that way.

He stood up. 'Best burn it. And don't spend too much time around it either. The contagion could spread.'

'I'll do that.' James removed his woollen hat and shook his head. 'Pity. She was one of my best ewes.'

A shrill cry rolled across the field from the direction of Folly Brook. Jack frowned and searched the row of white-walled huts. There was another scream, and this time his heart jolted. He recognised that voice. He would be able to pick it out from a busy crowd.

His daughter. Elizabeth.

He sprinted across the recently ploughed field, slipping and sliding in the deep furrows. He reached the edge of the village and skidded round the corner of Elizabeth's cottage. He drew to an immediate halt, James running up beside him.

Elizabeth was standing outside her doorway. She appeared well enough, but her face was red and she was waggling her finger and shouting at Sonali. 'You took them, I know it!'

As always, Sonali was an improbable sight, an Indian woman in the midst of a European village. She wore an English dress and cloak, but this did little to make her blend in. With her tasselled earrings, numerous bangles and dark eyeliner, she was like a being from another world.

Sonali scowled at Elizabeth and drew her cloak more tightly about her. 'I took nothing.'

'You're a thief,' Elizabeth continued. 'Always have been.'

Several villagers began gathering to watch the confrontation.

Jack stepped forward. 'Elizabeth, what's going on?'

Elizabeth turned to Jack and pointed at Sonali. 'There were three eggs missing from my cottage today. She took them.'

Jack frowned. Eggs were highly prized in a poor place like Folly Brook, but stealing was unheard of. A thief would quickly be caught in such a small village. Furthermore, he was certain Sonali wouldn't steal anything. If she wanted eggs, she would ask him for them. If there were no eggs available, she would accept it. If she were tired of living in the impoverished conditions here in the village, she would return to the Rajthanan-controlled lands. She could go back any time she wanted.

'Why would she take eggs?' he said to Elizabeth.

Elizabeth's eyes flashed. 'You know why.'

Jack stood still. The gathered villagers went silent.

You know why. Elizabeth's words had been hostile, said in an icy whisper. She'd never spoken to him like that before. Not in the nineteen years since she was born. He and she had rowed, of course, but she'd never said anything to him with such . . . contempt.

'What are you saying?' he asked.

Elizabeth stared back. 'She makes those potions with eggs, doesn't she? She's always making them.'

'Potions?'

Elizabeth's eyes blazed. She pulled a lock of her hair out from under her bonnet and held it up. 'For her hair.'

'Champoo? You mean champoo?'

It was true, Sonali did make that strange concoction the Rajthanans put in their hair. He'd often seen her stirring together the egg yolks, lime juice and meal before straining the mixture through a piece of cloth.

'I don't know what it's called,' Elizabeth said. 'All I know is she's always brewing up some mischief and you can't see it, Father. You just can't see it. Maybe that's because she's been putting that wickedness in your hair as well.'

Jack hesitated. He sensed everyone in the small crowd staring at him intently. The wind ruffled his long hair. Several strands had broken free from his ponytail and now fluttered about his forehead. He was suddenly aware of how light and clean they were. Sonali had convinced him to let her rub some of her champoo into his hair a few times. But he didn't think anyone knew.

He quickly brushed the hair away from his face. 'Listen, Elizabeth. Sonali wouldn't steal from us. You need to stop this now—'

'She's a witch!' Elizabeth's voice was high-pitched and cracked.

The gathering went deathly silent for a moment and then mutters flickered from person to person.

Witch.

The word hovered in the air, seeming to echo between the walls of the huts.

Jack felt his face go cold and then slowly hot. How could Elizabeth use the word 'witch'? Hadn't he told her burning witches was evil? He'd been certain Elizabeth would never believe in such cruel nonsense.

Elizabeth glared back at him, her eyes burning and her chin raised defiantly. She'd always been a headstrong girl, but never like this. She'd never so brazenly challenged him.

For a second he felt as though he were going to raise his hand to her, something he'd never done, save for the occasional smack when she was very young.

But then Sonali grasped his arm. 'Jack, leave it.'

He swivelled round. Sonali was staring up at him, her eyes moist and her brow tightening into a knot.

'Leave it,' she said again, her voice husky.

Then she spun on her heel and scurried away, holding one hand to her eyes to stop the tears. The crowd parted to let her through and geese honked and scattered as she rushed past.

Jack turned to Elizabeth. 'You. In here.'

He grasped Elizabeth's arm, shoved her into the cottage and

slammed the door shut behind him. It was dim inside – the shutters were all closed and the central hearth contained only glowing embers. Elizabeth stared at him, the ruddy light tingeing her face.

'What the hell has got into your head?' he said. 'How many times have I talked to you about witches? There are no witches. It's just a wicked old custom.'

Elizabeth's eyes shone and her bottom lip trembled. 'Maybe I was wrong to call her that. But she's still a thief.'

'I don't believe that for a second.'

'She's got you wrapped around her little finger, Father.'

'Wrapped around . . . ? I can't believe the nonsense you're talking today.'

'It's like you're in a dream. You can't see what she's doing to you.'

'She's doing nothing to me.'

'Oh really? Then why do you take her side over your own daughter's?'

She brushed past him and fled out of the door, tears welling in her eyes. Her husband, Godwin, rushed over to her. Their child, Cecily, lay cradled in his arms. Elizabeth paused to check the baby for a moment and then led Godwin away from the cottage.

Jack was about to go after them, but stopped himself. His anger was draining away now. But his mind was whirling. What would he even say to Elizabeth if he caught up to her?

He rubbed his forehead as he watched Elizabeth, Godwin and his precious granddaughter disappear round the corner of a hut.

Christ.

Elizabeth was going mad.

2

Sonali wasn't in her hut. Nor was she in the House of Sorcery when Jack put his head in there. Nor was she in the spot on the village green where Jack knew she liked to sit and stare out across the valley.

Jack paused on the edge of the village. There was only one place she could be: down by the brook, where she washed herself every morning. He set off along the track through the forest. Birds warbled high up in the canopy, and hawthorn and honeysuckle flowers swayed in the breeze. Everything was so quiet and peaceful, he could barely believe the argument between Elizabeth and Sonali had even happened.

He paused as he neared the place where Sonali bathed. Ahead of him, a line of boulders obscured the brook, but he could hear the water babbling and rushing. He retied his ponytail and straightened his tunic. He felt somewhat foolish fixing his appearance like this, but he couldn't help himself.

He peered up the path. Would Sonali be washing herself now? Surely not. The Rajthanans were obsessed with cleanliness, and Sonali was no exception, but even they only washed themselves once a day.

On the other hand, how much did he really know about Rajthanan women? Very little. Although he'd spent a lot of time around Rajthanans in the past, Rajthanan women had always been strictly out of bounds. He would have been executed for being so familiar with Sonali if they'd been in a Rajthanan-controlled part of England.

He'd been more than just familiar.

He'd kissed her.

'What are you doing?'

Jack jumped slightly at the sound of the voice nearby. Sonali was walking along the path towards him, still wearing her English cloak and dress. Her face was solemn and her eyes were rimmed with red. Her kohl eyeliner had run, but she'd managed to wash most of the streaks from her cheeks. She stopped about four feet away from him and looked up. Foliage hovered behind her and a shaft of sunlight made her earrings sparkle.

'You all right?' he asked.

She nodded and looked away into the forest.

'I'm sorry,' he said. 'Don't know what got into Elizabeth.'

'She finds it hard to accept me.'

'No, she doesn't. She just had a strange turn—'

'You haven't noticed the way she talks to me. The way she looks at me. She doesn't trust me.'

Jack frowned. He hadn't noticed anything like that. 'She'll come around. All the village will. We've spent years seeing the Rajthanans as the enemy—'

'It's not just because I'm Rajthanan.' Sonali faced Jack again.

'What do you mean?'

'I mean . . .' She gazed at the ground, searching for the right words. 'A daughter might find it hard if her father . . . If he had affections for someone new.'

Jack stood still for a moment. He hadn't considered this before. 'What? You think Elizabeth's jealous?' He cleared his throat. It was strange to be speaking aloud about this. 'Jealous of you?'

'Jealous.' Sonali sounded the word out carefully. Her English had improved since she'd come to Shropshire, but she still struggled with the language at times. 'Yes, I believe "jealous" is the right word. But not just that. Perhaps it's hard for her to see her father showing interest in another woman. Perhaps she sees it as betraying her mother.'

'Betraying?' For a moment, Jack saw an image of his dead wife, Katelin, in his mind's eye. Could Elizabeth really think he would betray Katelin's memory? 'No, that's not possible.'

'Why not?'

Jack spluttered. The conversation had taken a surprising turn and he was struggling to digest everything Sonali was saying. He'd never been good at this sort of thing.

'Look.' He rubbed the back of his neck. 'Elizabeth doesn't even know there's any . . .' His voice trailed off. How to explain himself?

'Any what?'

'Any . . . friendship between us. But we've hardly . . . and we've never let on to anyone.' They'd kissed only a few times and this had always been when no one else was around. 'No one could have seen us.'

'Don't you think a daughter can tell what's in her father's heart? Don't you think she can see the little gestures he makes, the tiny signs that give away his thoughts?'

'You think so?'

'I'm sure it will be obvious to her there's something going on between us.'

Jack breathed out sharply. Could this be true? Did Elizabeth know, or at least suspect? And what was it she would be guessing about anyway? What *was* going on between him and Sonali? Not even he knew. 'You could be right.'

Sonali nodded and brushed back her hair, the bangles encrusting her arm making a jingling sound.

'So, that means there *is* something between us,' he said.

His words seemed to jolt her with their frankness. She looked up and frowned. 'Of course there is.'

'It's just that . . . When we've been together, you've always pulled away. I wasn't sure . . .' Whenever they'd kissed, she'd been quick to stop and rush away, as if she were upset about something.

Sonali pursed her lips. 'Yes. It's true. I have been like that.' She sighed. 'This is so very difficult. I wanted to, but I couldn't see any future for us.' A fresh tear blossomed in her eye. 'That's why I have to leave Folly Brook.'

Jack's shoulders slackened. He felt as though the air had been knocked out of his lungs. This was more of a blow than he liked to admit. 'You don't have to leave.'

'I'll go to my aunt's in Dorsetshire. It's for the best. This thing can never work between us. We can't carry on sneaking around. But Elizabeth will never accept me. Your people will never accept me.'

'That's not true.'

'We're from different worlds.' She stared hard at Jack. 'Maybe we should never have met.'

Tears flooded her eyes and she choked back a sob. She rushed past him and fled along the path in the direction of the village.

Jack didn't even think about pursuing her. First Elizabeth had run away from him. Now Sonali.

Nothing seemed to make sense any more.

⟫⟪

'Alban's done it,' Mark said as Jack rounded the corner of the House of Sorcery.

Jack halted. 'Done what?'

Mark grinned and put his hand on Alban's shoulder. 'He's got the Lightning yantra.'

Jack allowed a smile to slide across his lips. He glanced across the meadow at the back of the house. His other pupils sat cross-legged on the grass, either studying sheets of paper or staring at the Lightning yantra, which was painted on a banner that had been strung up between two trees. The complex, circular design was the most powerful yantra Jack and his charges knew, and it was the only one useful in war. Kanvar the Sikh had shown it to them months ago, and since then the apprentices had been trying to learn it as quickly as they could. To date, ten of them, including Mark, had mastered it.

Alban would make eleven.

'He managed it this morning.' Mark placed the stick he used like a drill sergeant's cane under his arm. He was a few years older than the other lads and had always been Jack's ablest student.

Jack looked Alban up and down. The boy was tall, gangly and probably no older than sixteen. He was one of the many youths who'd come to Folly Brook to learn the ways of the enemy's yoga. It had been Jack's plan for a long time to use the Rajthanans' powers against them.

'So,' Jack said to Alban, 'you're certain of this? You're certain you've learnt the power?'

'Yes, sir,' Alban replied. 'I could show you right now. I reckon I could lightning that tree over there. Reckon I could knock it down.'

'No!' Mark cuffed Alban over the head. 'Don't you listen to anything the master tells you? Never use a power.' Mark looked across at Jack. 'Isn't that right, sir?'

Jack nodded slowly. 'You must hold back, Alban. The law of karma, remember? When you learn a power you'll feel like using it right away. But you mustn't. The moment you do, you'll become blocked. You'll never be able to learn another power.'

Alban rubbed his head where he'd been hit. 'I remember, sir. I just wanted to show you I was telling the truth.'

'That's not the way to do it,' Mark said sharply, then faced Jack. 'But he is telling the truth. I was with him. I sensed him smelting. He's not lying.'

'Good.' Jack trusted Mark's judgement. Mark had learnt well how to detect when a person was truly smelting sattva and on the verge of using a power. He wouldn't have made a mistake.

Jack placed his hand on Alban's shoulder. 'Well done, lad. You are now a siddha, one of the perfected ones. Take the rest of the day off. Then get back here tomorrow and start on the next yantra.'

Alban beamed. 'Thank you, Master Casey.'

As Alban turned and left, Jack drew Mark aside, saying, 'There's something I need to tell you.'

'What's that, sir?' Mark asked.

Jack looked at the ground for a second. This was going to be difficult. 'Don't tell the others yet, but Sonali's said she's leaving.'

'When's she coming back?'

'She's not. She's going for good.'

'Ah.' Mark tapped the cane against his leg. 'Not the best news, sir.'

That was true enough. Sonali had been helping to train the pupils for the past seven months. She'd been instrumental in helping many of them master Lightning. She'd also supplied the group with two minor yantras. But more than all this, the lads had become attached to her. It had bolstered them to know that a real Rajthanan siddha was helping them. Jack had noticed them walking taller and speaking with confidence about facing the army when the time finally came.

'It's not to do with what happened the other day?' Mark said. 'I heard there was some sort of argument.'

'That might have had something to do with it. But it's been building up for a while.'

'You know, sir, me and all the lads back Sonali. Others might think different, but as far as we're concerned, she's one of us.'

'I'm sure she'll be glad to hear that.'

'Perhaps you could talk to her. Convince her to stay.'

'I've tried that. Believe me. Her mind's made up.'

'It would be a pity to lose her.'

'Aye.' Jack looked away into the trees. He felt tired. 'But she's a Rajthanan. This isn't her place. She was always going to have to go back to her people one day.'

Mark nodded solemnly. He was silent for a moment, then said, 'Perhaps Kanvar will come back.'

Jack looked back at Mark. The young man was doing his best to stay hopeful. He was dedicated to the small force Jack had assembled, to the point where he seemed to have no life outside of it at all. He'd once told Jack he was an orphan, so perhaps he

29

really did have nothing else. Perhaps the House of Sorcery and its pupils was all he'd ever had.

Jack rubbed his chin. Kanvar had left nine months ago, saying he would be back soon. He'd never returned and never sent word. Perhaps he'd never intended to come back, or perhaps something had happened to him. There was no way of knowing.

Jack gave Mark a firm smile. 'Yes, perhaps he'll come back. We can only hope.'

———◆———

Jack sat in the dark, his legs crossed, his back straight and his hands on his knees. On the other side of the hut, Saleem shifted on his straw bed and muttered in his sleep. The lad had been living with Jack for the past seven months. Jack had found this irritating at first, but now he was so used to having Saleem around that it would seem strange if the lad moved out.

Jack closed his eyes. Outside, the wind stirred the trees and shook the window shutters. Further away, he heard people talking – it was only ten o'clock at night and some of the villagers were still up.

He took a deep breath, felt the cool air flow down his nostrils, hit the back of his throat and fan out into his lungs.

The Lightning yantra. He would try it one more time. He'd been attempting to use it for months, without any success. Of course, that was understandable as he was a blocked siddha. But on two occasions now he'd broken the law of karma and developed new powers. His guru, Jhala, had told him this was impossible. Kanvar had told him no one had ever done that before. And yet, miraculously, he'd achieved it.

Only he couldn't do it again.

The Lightning yantra wouldn't work. The lesser yantra Sonali had taught him – Find Water – wouldn't work either. He'd memorised both of these designs in the space of seven months, a daunting task.

But he couldn't use them.

He brought the Lightning yantra to his mind's eye. The image circled before him, white on black. He concentrated on each tiny detail, each line, curlicue and angle. He had to hold the entire shape still in his mind, without any other thoughts intruding, in order to use the power.

But his mind was troubled. It was like a rippling pool and he couldn't still it.

Images harried him.

For a moment he saw the dead ewe with the diseased leg, then Lord Fitzalan lying in his bed, then flames and war and hordes of circling crows . . .

Was England truly cursed? Was the land truly sick?

An explosion burst in his mind and he saw Folly Brook burning, saw villagers fleeing. Saw Elizabeth screaming . . .

He quickly forced the visions from his head. But now further memories flooded over him . . .

He was back in Ragusa, standing in the trench with his old friend William. Dawn was hovering on the edge of the sky and the guns and mortars had fallen silent. The conch-shaped horns began roaring. First one sounded far off in the distance, then others responded, the blaring flickering along the trench.

The hair stood up on the back of Jack's neck.

It was time.

Captain Jhala strode along the trench, bellowing at his men. He stepped up on to the fire step and raised his scimitar above his head. He looked back at his troops for a moment, then shouted 'Charge!' and clambered over the top. The men gave a joint cry and swarmed up after their commander. Musket in hand, Jack scrambled over the edge and bolted across the muddy field with his comrades. Gunfire rumbled. A storm of bullets and shot shrieked about him. Men screamed as they tumbled to the ground.

Jack kept running. William was sprinting along to his left and up ahead he could make out Jhala's scimitar glinting in the dawn light. The captain was out in front of the company, leading the way, even as his men toppled over behind him.

Jack focused on the blade. It was like a beacon leading him along a dark path. He would follow Jhala wherever he led . . .

Then the boom of the guns suddenly vanished.

And now Jack was sitting cross-legged in the gazebo at the estate where he worked as head guard. It was four years ago and Jhala sat before him, looking old and tired as he related the news that Elizabeth had been captured for helping the crusade. And then Jhala offered Jack a terrible choice – help to capture William, now a rebel leader, or see Elizabeth hang . . .

Jack felt his breathing quicken at the memory. He'd trusted Jhala all those years, only to be betrayed when the rebellion broke out.

His hands twisted into fists. He opened his eyes and stared into the darkness.

Jhala was in Worcestershire. He'd risen to the rank of general, and was now commanding the forces threatening Shropshire. Jhala was the one who would lead the invasion . . .

Jack forced himself to close his eyes again and drive the thoughts from his head. If he were going to master Lightning he had to forget everything but the yantra . . .

Breathe deeply. Step away from the material world, the world of pain and illusion.

He struggled to hold the yantra steady. Then, finally, it locked into place and burst into dazzling light.

But nothing happened.

Nothing.

He opened his eyes. He was breathing heavily. He'd managed to hold the yantra still, but no power had come to him.

Damn it. Once again, he'd failed.

He rolled on to his back and felt his breathing slowly ease.

He'd learnt three powers during his forty-three years of life. Europa, which he was still able to use. Great Health, which he'd used in Scotland and then discovered could only be used once in a lifetime. And the yantra that held back sattva-fire injuries, which he no longer needed now that he was well.

That, surely, was to be his lot. That was as far as he would progress as a siddha.

He'd spent seven months trying feverishly to gain a new power. Now he had to give up.

3

Jack gazed ahead to where the road curved out of sight behind a hill. They had reached this point so soon.

He gripped his horse's reins tighter. 'So, this is it.'

Sonali didn't reply as she rode alongside him and instead cast a look across the wide, shallow valley. To their left, the hills crowded close to the road, but to their right, open fields stretched away to the more buckled countryside in the distance.

'Once we're round that corner we'll be at the border,' he said.

Sonali clenched her lips and gave him a small nod. There was a knot in the centre of her forehead and her eyes were moist. She was dressed in Indian clothing once more, wearing a red shawl and a green sari that was gathered between her legs to form a pair of loose pantaloons. The sari allowed her to mount and sit astride her horse far more easily than any woman Jack had ever met before. She didn't have to sit sideways or even hitch up her clothing.

Jack had asked her about the sari once, and she'd explained that her ancestors were from the land of the Marathas, a region that bordered Rajthana in India. 'This is how we Maratha women dress,' she'd said. 'Even when we're born and brought up in Rajthana.'

The curve in the road drew closer. The horses' hooves clopped steadily towards it.

Jack and Sonali had ridden along this valley twice in the past few months – the first time to allow Sonali to send a message on the sattva link to her aunt, the second time to collect a package the aunt had sent to the Leintwardine post office. Sonali had been delighted to find powders, oils, perfumes and a bottle of lime juice inside the parcel. Apparently these were necessary for her survival even in the wilds of Shropshire.

Certainly, they were necessary for making champoo.

For a moment, Jack's mind drifted to the last time Sonali had massaged champoo into his head. She'd joked with him about his filthy hair and he'd told her to mind her own business. Then she'd gone silent for a moment as she pressed her fingers more deeply into his hair, rubbed his scalp more firmly . . . He could still feel her fingers even now as he thought about it.

'You know,' he said, 'you don't have to go. You can change your mind.'

'Jack-ji.' Sonali's voice was husky. 'Please. Don't.'

'I'm sorry.' He stared ahead at the road. 'I had to try.'

Sonali wiped her eyes, then fumbled behind her in one of her saddlebags. 'Here. You should have this.'

Jack looked across and saw an envelope in her hand. 'What's that?'

'The letter from Rajiv.'

'You sure you don't want it?'

'It was addressed to you.'

Jack leant across and took the envelope. He studied the coiling handwriting scrawled across the paper. He couldn't understand any of the letter, but Sonali had read it aloud to him.

It was from Captain Rajiv Rao, who'd accompanied Jack on the journey to Scotland. Jack hadn't expected to ever hear from Rao again, but the captain had tracked down Sonali's aunt and had written letters to both Sonali and Jack. Sonali's aunt had included them in the package she sent to Leintwardine.

'Strange fellow, that Rao,' Jack said.

Sonali smiled. 'You remember how that Scottish woman wanted to marry him?'

Jack grinned. It was good to see Sonali smiling again. 'I remember. He was so worried about it.'

Sonali gave a small laugh.

Jack had been pleased to hear from Rao, and even more pleased to learn that instead of going back to Rajthana, Rao had ended up in Andalusia. Apparently his sweetheart, Reena Chamar, had fled Rajthana for Europe. Now Rao and she had met and were planning to marry, in defiance of Rao's father and jati.

The letter had ended on a strange note, though. Rao had hinted that he might soon be travelling to England and that he hoped to see Jack again. He said that he had something of great importance to tell Jack, but he didn't give any indication what it was.

Mysterious.

Jack tapped the envelope against his hand, then folded it away into his side pouch.

And now they were at the bend in the road.

Ahead, the valley narrowed and the hills loomed higher to their left. Several carts and wagons trundled along the road in both directions. In the distance, Jack could make out the smudge of the town of Leintwardine, smoke twisting up from its myriad of chimneys and vents. Closer, about a hundred yards away, a collection of striped pavilions clustered to one side of the road. Pennons bearing the cross of St George and the gold lion of the Earl of Shropshire flickered atop the tents.

Jack frowned. The pavilions would be for those guarding the border with Herefordshire. The last time he'd been here, there'd only been two guards slouching beside a tree. But now he could count perhaps fifty tents.

His eyes drifted up to the hills and he noticed dark spots bristling over the summits. Amongst the specks he made out several flagstaffs and a winking light that could only be a heliograph.

He felt a tremor of foreboding and shot a look across at the far side of the valley. There he spied gun emplacements and a second heliograph blinking back in reply.

Sonali followed his gaze. 'What is it?'

'Troops.'

'Who, though?'

'Not sure yet. Let's find out.' Jack nudged his horse into a canter.

Sonali did the same, and in less than a minute they reached the pavilions. Around thirty soldiers wearing crusader surcoats stood beside the road, eyeing the carts, riders and pedestrians passing by.

'Greetings.' Jack tipped his head as he drew up alongside one of the guards. 'The road ahead safe?'

The guard wiped his nose on the back of his hand. 'Safe enough.'

'Who's that up there?' Jack motioned to the troops and guns massed in the hills.

'Heathens.' The guard sniffed.

'The army?'

The guard grunted and nodded.

'So far west? I thought they were in Worcestershire.'

'Reinforcements have arrived. They're all over the place now.'

Jack felt a line of ice down his back. If reinforcements had arrived, then an invasion of Shropshire could be drawing nearer. And the troops ahead of him were just across the Herefordshire border – no more than a day's march from Clun.

'They're letting through travellers,' the guard said. 'You can pass this way. There's no danger for the present. Wouldn't take that with you, though.' He pointed at the musket hanging across Jack's back.

'Why not?' Jack asked.

'Rajthanans are checking everyone passing in and out. They won't let you through with that.'

Jack rolled his tongue in his mouth as he considered this information. He'd planned to escort Sonali all the way to Leintwardine. But he didn't want to give up the musket. He could leave it somewhere and come back for it later. But he also didn't like the idea of crossing the border now. He could easily find himself stuck on the wrong side of the front line in a battle. How would he get back to Folly Brook if that happened?

'Jack.' Sonali's voice shook. She was staring up at the troops. 'I've changed my mind. Let's go back.'

'No.' Jack spoke more loudly and abruptly than he'd intended. As much as he wanted Sonali to stay, he was now more concerned that she leave. If the army were planning on invading, he wanted her well away from Shropshire. The best place for her to be was in the Rajthanan lands.

Sonali frowned. 'But I—'

'You need to go. You can travel on from here alone. Leintwardine's just ahead.'

It would take Sonali less than ten minutes to reach the town. And from there she could take the train to Dorsetshire. The railhead had reached Leintwardine a year ago.

She would be safe. She just had to get across the border.

Sonali's eyes moistened. 'I made a mistake. I'll stay.'

Jack clenched his jaw. He had to make sure Sonali got into Herefordshire.

'Over there.' He nodded towards a copse just beyond the guards. 'We can talk more privately there.'

They rode across to the trees and drew their horses to a halt beneath the spreading branches.

'My people don't accept you,' Jack said. 'You said it yourself. This isn't your place.'

Sonali's bottom lip trembled. 'I could try again.'

'No. I can't talk Elizabeth around.'

'I know what you're doing.'

'What am I doing?'

'You've changed your mind. Since you saw the army up there.'

Jack studied his horse's mane, picking at a burr stuck in the animal's hair. 'It's for the best.'

'But I could help you fight.'

Jack stared hard at her. 'Fight your own people? You'd do that?'

'It would perhaps be difficult.' Her voice was almost a whisper.

'I can't expect you to do that. And I couldn't live with myself

38

if anything happened to you. Go. Get to safety. I'll come and find you when all this is over.'

She choked back a sob. 'Why don't you come with me? We could start a new life.'

'And leave Elizabeth? And Cecily?'

'Bring them too.'

Jack felt a stone in his throat. This moment was unbearable. And yet he didn't want it to end, because that would mean he and Sonali had parted. Quite probably for ever. 'My family and I can't leave. These are our people. We have to fight for our freedom.'

'Must you? Isn't it better to live?'

'Live as a slave?'

'Not as a slave.' She looked down. 'You remember I said I ran away from home when I was young? I lived with impure jatis. I became an outcaste. I know what it's like to be at the bottom. And as bad as it is, it's better to be poor and alive than dead.'

'You talk as though we've already lost, as though the crusade will fail.'

She went silent for a moment. 'I don't know. It'll be a hard fight.'

Jack was well aware of this. He knew better than she did what any battle would be like. He knew there was little hope of the crusaders resisting a full-scale assault by the army. And yet he had to hope that somehow they would succeed. He hadn't supported the First Crusade. But he couldn't run away now. This was the last stand for his people. Their last chance. If Shropshire fell, the rebellion would be snuffed out.

'We have to try,' he said. 'And you have to leave.'

A tear bled from Sonali's eye and trailed black eyeliner down her cheek.

'I'll be able to fight better knowing you're safe,' he said.

Sonali sobbed and further tears slid down her face. 'I'll wait for you. At my aunt's.'

'I'll come for you.' Jack's voice was thick. 'Now go while you can.'

He slapped the rump of her horse and the animal bolted. Sonali dragged at the reins and quickly got the creature under control again. She circled round and for a moment Jack thought she was going to ride back to him. But then she jabbed with her heels and urged the horse into a gallop, the animal's hooves kicking up chunks of turf. She charged back to the road and rode swiftly away towards Herefordshire.

She didn't look back once.

Jack waited beside the trees for a long time. He wasn't sure how long. Perhaps it was twenty minutes. Perhaps it was longer. At any rate, he was still sitting astride his horse watching the road long after Sonali had disappeared.

Finally, he sighed and massaged his eyes with his fingers.

She was gone. And that was by far for the best.

He'd been a fool. Had he really thought that he and Sonali had a future together?

He must have been mad.

<hr />

It was close to midnight when Jack, weary from the long day of riding to and from the border, reached Folly Brook. He tethered the mare to a tree and was about to walk to his hut when Elizabeth materialised like a ghost out of the dark. She looked sombre, her face taut and her eyes glassy.

He was pleased to see his daughter – of course he was – but he didn't want another argument. Not now. 'Elizabeth, what are you doing? It's late.'

'I need to speak to you.'

'Of course. But we can do that tomorrow.'

'No.' She stepped closer. 'I wanted to say sorry.'

'Sorry?'

'For, you know. How I've been with that woman.' She lowered her eyes. 'Sonali.'

Jack felt warmth bloom in his chest. Elizabeth was his little girl. It had been painful to be at odds with her. Now she was coming back to him.

'Elizabeth.' His voice was hoarse. He opened his arms and she fell into his embrace.

'I'm so sorry, Father.'

'Shush, shush.' He patted her on the back. 'There's no need to say anything more. I understand. I've made some mistakes too. I should have thought about how you'd feel.'

Elizabeth drew back. 'No, I should have thought about how you'd feel. It was just . . . I still think about Mother.'

'I think about her too. We'll always remember her. When all this is over, we'll go to her grave again and leave flowers. Like we used to.'

Elizabeth nodded and sniffled.

Suddenly Jack had an idea. 'I want you to have this.' He reached under his tunic and drew out Katelin's Celtic cross necklace. Katelin had given it to him on her deathbed and he'd been wearing it ever since.

'No. It's all right. You don't have to.'

'Take it. I should have given it to you a long time ago. I always meant to.'

Elizabeth grasped the necklace and weighed it in her palm. She stared at the intricate designs that knotted about the cross. 'I remember her wearing it all the time.'

'She told me it's a family heirloom. Apparently lots of people have them in Wales. It's one of many, but this one is ours. Our memory of her.'

Elizabeth tied the cord about her neck and the cross hung down over her chest. She gave Jack a small, hopeful smile. 'I'll take good care of it. Thank you, Father.'

Jack sat on the rocks and gazed at the churning water. The brook swirled into a deep pool at this point before tumbling away in the direction of the River Clun. Sunbeams filtered through the trees and shattered into diamonds on the water's surface.

This was where Sonali used to bathe. Jack hadn't meant to visit the spot, but he couldn't help himself. He knew there was no point thinking about Sonali, but she kept appearing in his head . . .

Memories clouded his mind.

He saw Sonali in her room in Mahajan's castle, the place where he'd first met her . . . Then on the day she'd begun training the lads at the House of Sorcery . . . Then kneading champoo into his hair . . . Drawing close to him and kissing him on the lips . . .

He had to put her out of his mind. She would be safe in Dorsetshire now. He had to forget her and concentrate on preparing for the defence of Shropshire. He couldn't let himself get distracted.

Perhaps he would see her again one day, but that would be in some distant future that was hard to even imagine at the moment.

He had to let go.

Then suddenly it was easy. The vision of Sonali blinked away and instead he saw Katelin on her deathbed. Her damp hair was plastered to her scalp, her chest was heaving and her pale hand reached up to touch his cheek . . .

He felt a twinge of guilt. Hadn't he been neglecting Katelin's memory? Wasn't his affection for Sonali a betrayal?

'You're not forgotten, Katelin,' he whispered. 'You'll always be with me, and Elizabeth.'

He felt strangely light. Sonali was fading from his mind and being replaced by Katelin.

Further memories tumbled through his head but they didn't trouble him. Mostly he saw happier times, when Elizabeth was young and Katelin was still alive.

And finally his thoughts flitted through all the yantras he'd ever learnt. Without meaning to, he focused on Find Water, the yantra Sonali had taught him. He only held the image in his mind for a second, but somehow he managed to enter the trance and draw in sattva at the same time. He did all this instinctively, almost without being aware of it.

And for the split second that he held the yantra still, it burst into dazzling light.

He felt dizzy. Sweet sattva tingled in his nostrils. He stared at the gurgling water and felt drawn to it, as if the brook were physically dragging him closer.

And then he knew what was happening. He was so shocked by it that he slid out of the trance and stumbled back down the boulder.

He'd learnt a new yantra – Find Water. The knowledge of how to use the power was now lodged in his mind, as if it had always been there.

This new power was useful enough, but hardly remarkable. What was truly incredible, and which still made his head spin, was that once again he'd broken the law of karma. Once again he'd developed a new power when he was blocked.

He shook his head. He was happy but mystified. Why had his strange ability come now? Why not during the previous seven months when he'd been trying so hard? Why now when he was barely trying at all?

He looked up at the sunlight twinkling through the canopy.

Yoga and sattva were still a mystery to him.

James didn't have to explain it to Jack. The sight spoke for itself – four sheep lying dead in a ditch, all of them with swollen hind legs.

Jack couldn't help breathing out sharply. It was hard to pretend now that the plague hadn't reached Folly Brook.

James made the sign of the cross. 'Had to happen. Why should we be spared?'

Jack nodded grimly. 'Best burn them quickly. We might still hold off the contagion.' Even as he said the words he knew they were unconvincing.

Before James could reply, someone called out behind them. When Jack turned, he saw a squire running across the field, stumbling over the furrows. The young man was shouting something, but Jack couldn't make out the words. By the time the squire arrived, he was panting so heavily he was unable to speak.

Finally, he managed to catch his breath enough to say, 'It's started.'

'What's started?' Jack asked.

The squire wheezed. 'The heathens. They've marched into Shropshire.'

Jack felt a chill. He'd been expecting this moment, and yet the news was still a blow. Now it was real. The thing they'd all been dreading for months was finally happening.

James stood up straighter and crossed himself several times.

'Constable Ward's asked to see you,' the squire said to Jack.

Jack mulled this over. Henry wanted to see him? That made sense. He and Henry had to put their disagreements aside and work together now, for the good of Shropshire.

'All right,' Jack said to the squire. 'I'll ride back to Newcastle with you.'

4

Jack walked along the top of the castle wall to where Henry stood alone, staring out at the open fields. The big man held his hands behind his back and his cloak flicked in the wind. He remained impassive and didn't even turn as Jack drew up beside him.

Jack stood in silence for a moment and looked out over the parapet. He found himself gazing at a darkening world. Iron clouds had swept across the sky and the wind carried the scent of rain. In the fields immediately below, five mounds of dead sheep and cattle were burning, sending up columns of black smoke that blended into the clouds. Further away up the valley, more carcasses were smouldering and Jack counted at least twenty cords of rising smoke. To his left, the town of Newcastle-on-Clun crouched behind a line of trees. Just beyond the buildings stretched the cluster of ragged tents and bivouacs that housed many of the refugees pouring into the valley from other parts of England. Vadula's forces had crushed the rebellion everywhere but Shropshire, and those fleeing the fighting and the brutal reprisals had no choice but to come to this native state. There was even a large contingent of Mohammedans in the camp – a strange sight in Clun.

Henry breathed in, his nostrils flaring. 'The land is dying. Just as Lord Fitzalan said. I hear rumours of enchantments. A beast is said to stalk north Shropshire.'

Jack frowned. Enchantments? Beasts? Henry was caught up in Fitzalan's madness and ancient superstitions. But there was no time for all that now. It would only serve as a distraction, when the people of Clun needed to be fighting the enemy.

'What's the news from the front?' Jack asked. 'Your messenger said—'

'My messenger was sent to get you this one last time. In our hour of need, will you now help us?'

'Of course. I'm here to fight.'

'No!' Henry turned to Jack. His mouth was twisted and his eyes blazed. 'The Grail. I have called you here to ask you to find it.'

Christ. Jack rubbed his forehead. 'Look, I haven't come here for another argument. I want to help. But I need to know what's going on at the front. What news do you have?'

'News?' Henry turned back to the parapet and stared into the distance. 'Nothing but ill news. The rebellion in al-Saxony is failing. More enemy troops arrive in England every day. General Jhala's men have marched north from Worcestershire. Our forces have fallen back to Ludlow and for the moment are holding their own.'

'Ludlow. That's only a few miles across the border.'

'Aye, the army have not got far yet. But they are on our lands and many doubt we can hold them back now.' Henry placed his hands on the battlements. 'They are but two days' march from us. At the most.'

'And Herefordshire?'

'The heathens have only a small force there. They have remained where they are.'

'We should go to the front. Our comrades need support.'

Many men from Clun Valley had already been assigned to the front, but there were still plenty who could be rounded up to serve as reinforcements.

'We will go nowhere,' Henry said. 'The Council have sent word that we are to stay here.'

'Stay here? Why?'

'The Lord of the Marches is mustering an army. If his men advance on Shropshire, we will be the only bulwark against them. If we cannot hold them, they will be able to sweep all the way to the earl, in Shrewsbury.'

A gust of icy wind buffeted Jack, plucked at his ponytail. More bad news. The Lord of the Marches ruled the region of Wales immediately to the south-west of Clun. He had long been an ally of the Rajthanans, and his men would no doubt have been told they were free to loot as much of Shropshire as they pleased.

'How long before the Welsh get here?' Jack asked.

'They are not on the move yet. We don't know when they'll come. It's likely to be more than a week before they're ready to march.'

'How big is the force?'

'They are still mustering. They'll probably reach three thousand.'

'How many men do we have left in Clun? A thousand?'

Henry snorted. 'Five hundred more like.'

'Then we'll have to fight with five hundred, if it comes to it.' He looked along the wall. Rajthanan serpent-headed guns had been set up at various intervals. They looked to be only nine- and twelve-pounders, but they were better than nothing. They must have been captured from the army during the First Crusade. 'We have artillery here. Do we have ammunition? How about Clun Castle further up the valley?'

Henry faced Jack, his face seething and his hair whirling in the wind. 'All these questions. That's not why I called you here. Lord Fitzalan is dying. The kingdom of England is dying.'

'Lord Fitzalan's still ill?'

'Worse than ever. The news is out now too. The whole valley will know soon. Only the Grail can save us.'

'Only fighting can save us. We have to prepare—'

'We cannot win if we are cursed. There are ten thousand heathens just south of us. The Lord of the Marches and his men are in the west. Yet another army of men under General Vadula himself are massing to the east, in Staffordshire. Shropshire is caught in a vice.'

'Staffordshire? I hadn't heard.'

Henry stepped closer. The clouds roiled behind his head. 'And all you do is sit in your village toying with your black magic. Still you refuse to do the one thing that could help us the most.'

'I will do all I can—'

'You must go in search of the Grail. Now. I order it.'

Jack tensed. Once again, he'd come to the castle without a firearm but he still had a knife hidden under his tunic. 'We've been through this countless times. I'll wait for word from Sir Alfred.'

Henry gave a wheezy laugh, then stared at Jack. 'Alfred's wounded. Near death.'

Jack went silent. The light seemed to darken and the air grow colder.

Henry laughed again. 'Alfred was caught in the fighting. They say he won't survive.' His eyes gleamed wildly. 'Changes things, doesn't it?'

Jack kept his hand at his side, ready to grasp the knife if he needed to. 'It changes nothing.' He tried to speak firmly, but it was difficult to still the shake in his voice. Henry was right. Alfred's death would change things.

'You keep believing that. If Alfred dies, no one will take your side. I will claim control of Folly Brook myself. That will be the end of your little kingdom up there.'

'This arguing serves no purpose.'

Henry shoved his finger in Jack's chest. 'You mark my words. Your days as reeve are numbered.'

Jack gritted his teeth. He didn't like to back down to anyone, least of all Henry. But he was achieving nothing at the moment by staying.

Without saying anything further, he turned on his heel and

marched back along the wall. He didn't look back, although he listened carefully for any sign that Henry was following him.

But the big man stayed where he was and instead shouted, 'Coward! Traitor! I always knew that's what you were!'

Henry continued bellowing even as Jack reached the stairs down to the bailey. Jack looked back along the ramparts before descending. Henry was a lone figure beside the battlements, his cloak whirling in the wind and his hand raised in a fist.

<hr />

They all went silent. Elizabeth, Godwin and Saleem all stared across the fire at Jack, their eyes wide and their faces wavering in the light from the flames.

Jack had just told them the news from Henry.

Outside Elizabeth and Godwin's hut, the wind moaned and worried the window shutters. Rain hissed in the thatching and gurgled as it trickled from the eaves. A storm had rolled across the village not long after Jack had returned from Lord Fitzalan's castle. It had grown ever stronger as the evening progressed.

'What should we do, Father?' Elizabeth said softly.

Jack stared into the fire. That was a good question. One he found difficult to answer.

Cecily, lying wrapped in a blanket near to him, began whimpering and wriggling. He reached across and lifted her up. She gazed back at him, her eyes shining and her skin traced yellow by the firelight. She reached out to him with her tiny, perfect fingers. When he smiled, her eyes flashed with excitement and she gave him a huge grin.

For a second Jack felt a wave of painful happiness. His four-month-old granddaughter was a miracle. But a dangerous world swirled outside the walls of the hut. How would he protect her? How would he protect any of the people sitting with him now?

He gently placed Cecily back on her blanket. He looked up at the others, who were still watching him, still waiting for his response.

'We have to stay here,' he said. 'With the Lord of the Marches mustering an army, we have no choice.'

Godwin shifted his legs as he sat on the earth floor. 'It seems hard to leave our comrades at Ludlow. We're abandoning them.'

'We won't be helping them if we let the Welsh in through Clun Valley. Henry was right about that. Our friends would be encircled or attacked in the flank.'

'What about this army in the east, in Staffordshire?' Saleem said quietly.

Jack found himself squeezing a clump of rushes that he'd picked up from the floor. That news had been a particularly bad blow. 'There's nothing we can do about that from here.'

They all went silent again. There was little point going over their situation further. Jack knew they could all understand that Shropshire faced foes to the east, west and south. Fleeing to the north was the only way to escape. But where would they flee to? They would be pursued – and, anyway, they would be fleeing back into Rajthanan lands, back into virtual slavery.

'Perhaps the rebellion in al-Saxony will spread,' Saleem said.

'I'd like to hope so,' Jack replied. 'But Henry said it's failing.'

'But it hasn't yet failed.' Saleem looked at his hands and toyed with a piece of straw. 'I was speaking to one of the imams at Newcastle the other day. He's heard others of my faith will rise up in Europe.' Saleem looked up. 'If we join forces with them, we would be stronger.'

'Join forces with Mohammedans?' Godwin snorted, then quickly added for Saleem's benefit, 'Mainland Mohammedans, I mean.'

'We all want the same thing.' Saleem's cheeks reddened and a nervous smile crossed his face. He stared more intently at his hands. 'We all want to be free.'

'Aye,' Jack said. 'Strange as it may seem, the Mohammedans could help us if they rise up. The Rajthanans will have trouble fighting in several regions at the same time. But if the Mohammedans are going to rise up, they'd better do it quickly. Al-Saxony is not enough.'

Elizabeth lifted her chin and said in a clear voice. 'Whatever happens, we'll stand firm and we'll fight.'

Jack managed a tight smile, but there were tears forming in his eyes. Once again, he was proud of his daughter. It was she who'd first sided with the crusade. If it hadn't been for her, he might never have joined the struggle.

The wind continued to wail outside and the rain battered against the shutters. But, for the moment, they were alive and safe – and a faint cord of hope still led off into the darkness ahead of them.

———⊷◈⊶———

Lightning flickered overhead. The flash filtered through the hooded smoke-hole, the cracks in the window shutters and the edges of the door frame. Jack lay on his back in the dark, waiting for the thunder. After a few seconds, the heavy crack split the sky and rolled away across the valley. As the sound faded, he again heard the splatter of the rain on the muddy ground outside.

Saleem snored on the other side of the hut, but Jack lay awake, unable to sleep. His thoughts were as turbulent as the storm outside. He remembered Sir Alfred the last time he'd seen him three months ago, in Newcastle . . . Then Jhala at the battle of Ragusa . . . Then Katelin on her deathbed, reaching out to him with her weak hand . . .

He imagined an army swarming over the green hills of Shropshire. He pictured Folly Brook on fire . . .

Another flash of lightning lit up the rafters for a second. Thunder grumbled shortly afterwards.

Jack shut his eyes. He had to rest.

Then he heard a scratching sound.

His eyes shot open and he sat up instantly. All his senses

quivered into life. He listened intently. The rain pattered and slurped. The wind whined. But there was nothing else.

Had he imagined the sound?

Saleem snuffled and turned over on his bed of straw. Jack eased himself back down. He must have imagined the noise.

But then it came again. He was certain this time. It sounded as though something were scraping lightly against the door.

He crouched and stared into the shadows. Was someone there? Who would come at this hour? If it were someone from the village, they would have knocked more loudly.

Slowly, carefully, he eased himself up. He avoided rustling the straw even slightly – although, with the storm whirling outside, it was hardly likely anyone would be able to hear him.

The scratching sound came again. A slow scrape that lasted for only a few seconds.

He crept across the floor towards the door. Once again, he was a tracker and an army scout, sneaking through the forest behind enemy lines. His eyes searched the dark for any sign of movement. His ears sifted through the sounds of the storm.

He reached the doorway, crouched beside it. He studied the thin gap between the bottom of the door and the ground. The faintest trace of moonlight, like a hint of breath, drifted under the door.

He bent closer, stared harder. And then he saw it – a shadow that was no more than a slight darkening in the centre of the gap.

There was someone on the other side of the door.

He shot straight back up again, his heart beating faster and a light sweat filming his forehead.

Whoever was there couldn't have good intentions if they were lurking outside in the middle of a storm. At the same time, they'd scratched at the door and alerted him. Why would they do that if they wanted to sneak in and attack or steal?

None of this made any sense.

He snatched a look around him, and his eyes locked on the two muskets hanging on the wall. Neither of them was loaded, but he could use their knives. Still, they would be cumbersome and he would have to cross the room to get to them. There was no lock on the door – whoever was on the other side could enter at any moment.

His knife. It was in the chest behind him.

He turned, edged the lid of the chest up and felt around inside. His hand slid amongst the old clothes and blankets and finally touched cold steel. There it was. He felt along the blade and found the handle.

Holding the knife in one hand, he stole across to the nearest window. If he got the shutter open and stuck his head out, he would be able to see whoever was at the door. He might even be able to slip out unnoticed and attack the person.

He paused when he reached the window and glanced back at the door. From this angle he could no longer make out the telltale shadow of the person on the other side, but he could hear, once again, the faint scratching. And there was something else now. He thought he could hear a voice, a whisper.

Was the person outside speaking?

He shook his head. Perhaps he'd imagined the voice. He must have.

He lifted the latch and slid one of the shutters open just a fraction. The dark night was alive with rain. Trees tossed and swayed a few yards away. But from this position he couldn't see the doorway.

He would have to open the shutter wider. That could risk alerting whoever was outside. But he had to do it.

His heart quickened as he edged the shutter open further and inched his head out. The wind howled and blasted rain in his face. The droplets beat in his eyes and ran down his cheeks. Blinking away the moisture, he looked along the side of the cottage . . . and saw a figure hunched beside the door.

So, he'd been right. But what was the person doing? Listening? Waiting for Jack to come out?

Whatever the case, Jack would have to take a closer look.

The figure's head appeared to be turned away, so Jack lifted himself up, swung his legs over the window sill and splashed down into the mud outside. The rain battered him, drenching his night-shirt and plastering it to his back. His hair was stuck to his scalp.

He tightened his grip on the knife and crept forward. The mud squelched and sucked beneath his naked feet, but there was little chance of him being heard over the wind.

The figure didn't move. Good. Jack hadn't been seen. All he had to do now was sneak forward a few more feet and then he could pounce.

He moved faster, the rain pouring over him. A flash of lightning lit up the walls of the huts nearby for a second. More thunder racked the sky.

The figure remained still.

And now Jack could see that the person was sprawled before the door, as if they'd collapsed. They appeared to be wearing an overcoat and some sort of hat.

Jack froze. That was no hat. It was a turban. A scarlet, army-issue, officer's turban.

The figure was a Rajthanan.

Why had a Rajthanan officer sneaked into Folly Brook? A dark thought crossed Jack's mind – had the army already arrived in Clun? That was unlikely. They couldn't have marched from Ludlow in such a short space of time. And in any case, why would an officer come all the way to Folly Brook alone?

Jack couldn't wait any longer for answers. He charged the last few feet, leapt upon the man and held the knife to his throat. The man was strangely limp and offered no resistance. He did nothing other than give a low moan.

'Who are you?' Jack shook the man.

The figure groaned again and slowly turned his turbaned head.

Jack recognised the thin, bearded features through the slanting rain.

It was Kanvar.

The Sikh's face was gaunt and his cheeks were streaked with dirt. But he was unmistakeable. His eyes wandered about, as if he were drunk, before they finally focused on Jack.

Jack dropped the knife in surprise, and it plopped into a puddle. 'What the hell are you doing here?'

The rain beat against the side of Kanvar's face and dribbled down from his beard. He opened his eyes wider, gripped Jack's shirt and tried to speak, but all that came out of his mouth was a hoarse croak. Then his eyes rolled back in his head and he collapsed against the door.

5

Elizabeth placed a blanket over Kanvar's shoulders. The Sikh sat shivering before the flames in Elizabeth and Godwin's hut. His sodden tunic, cummerbund and trousers had been removed and he instead wore a loose nightshirt that Godwin had lent to him.

Elizabeth went to untie his turban, but he raised his hand to stop her.

'But it's soaked through,' Elizabeth said.

'It is all right,' Kanvar said. 'A Sikh must wear a turban.'

Elizabeth raised her eyebrows and flicked a look across at Jack. Jack nodded at her to leave the turban. He knew the Sikhs had as many strange customs as the Rajthanans.

The storm outside had eased, but the rain still rattled on the shutters and the wind still whined through the cracks in the walls.

Jack cast his eye around the fire. The little group that had been sitting about the hearth a few hours earlier – Saleem, Elizabeth and Godwin – had reassembled. Jack hadn't wanted to wake them, but he'd needed help with Kanvar, who'd seemed near death.

At least Kanvar was now less pale and was able to sit upright unaided.

'You're looking better,' Jack said.

Kanvar stared back with his wide, fish-like eyes. 'I'm fine.'

'What happened to you?'

'I became weak. I had to use many powers in order to get here. I had so little strength that I was unable to even open the door to your cottage.'

'You're lucky I heard you out there. And why were you wearing that Rajthanan uniform?'

'A disguise. I can no longer wear the uniform of a Sikh anywhere in England. It has become too dangerous. Vadula's forces are spread too widely. Too many spies . . .'

Kanvar's voice trailed off and he stared into the flames. The fire wheezed and smoked as the green wood burnt.

Jack cleared his throat. 'You took your time coming back.'

Kanvar started, as if he'd been woken from a dream. He gazed at Jack and the others in turn, as if seeing them for the first time. Finally, he said, 'I am sorry it took me so long to return.' He looked down. 'After I left, I faced many obstacles which prevented me from coming back. It was difficult for me to come here even now. But I knew I must.'

'Why? Why have you come back?'

Kanvar frowned. 'I promised that I would. Also, I wanted to know whether you were alive, Jack.'

Jack half smiled. 'As you can see, I am. I managed to use Great Health in the end. It saved me.'

'That is very good. I had been wondering how far you had progressed.'

'Progressed?'

Kanvar glanced at the others, then stared at Jack again. 'Do they know about your special ability?'

'You can talk openly here,' Jack said.

'Good.' Kanvar looked at the fire again, seemingly transfixed. He said nothing further.

Jack shot a look at the others. They were all frowning as they stared at the Sikh. Elizabeth raised her eyebrows at Jack again.

'Kanvar,' Jack said. 'What do you mean about me progressing?'

Kanvar looked up in surprise once more. He licked his lips and then seemed to remember where he was. 'Oh yes. I wanted to know whether you had mastered your special ability yet. Whether you could now use it at will.'

Jack scratched the back of his neck. 'Unfortunately not. I used Great Health in Scotland. Then I used Find Water last week. But every other time I've tried to learn a new yantra, I've failed. I can't control my ability.'

'I see.' Kanvar nodded slowly. 'There is no pattern to it?'

'Not that I can see.'

'Ah. It remains a mystery. I perhaps had hoped for too much. At least you are alive.'

'I'm alive, but we're in a bad situation. The army have invaded.'

'Yes, I know. I saw many English soldiers on the move as I made my way through Shropshire. But I will do all I can to help.' Kanvar patted his satchel, which lay on the floor beside him. 'I have brought more war yantras. For your students.'

'I'm not sure the students will have much time to learn them,' Jack said. 'But thank you. We need all the help we can get at the moment.'

'Indeed. Things are very bad. Unfortunately, I cannot stay long. I must leave by tomorrow night.'

'That's a pity,' Jack said. 'One day isn't much time.'

'I know,' Kanvar replied. 'But I have an . . . important matter to attend to.'

'What important matter?'

Kanvar frowned and stared into the fire. His lips worked, as if he were muttering to himself, although he made no sound.

'Kanvar,' Jack said. 'What important matter?'

Kanvar kept his eyes fixed on the flames and spoke slowly. 'I must go to Scotland. I am looking for something.'

Jack sat back. 'That's strange. Saleem and I were in Scotland just a few months ago. We were also looking for something. The Grail.'

Kanvar looked up quickly. 'That is a strange coincidence.' He rubbed his beard. 'The Grail. An old story, I believe. Did you find it?'

'No. We found something else, though.'

Kanvar stared at Jack. 'What did you find?'

'A place where many sattva streams meet. Many powerful streams.'

Kanvar gave a guttural cry and leapt to his feet, flinging the blanket aside. He moved so suddenly that Godwin jumped, scrabbled for a branch and raised it as a club. Even Jack flinched for a second and thought about grasping a weapon.

Kanvar's eyes were wild, although he looked faintly ridiculous in nothing but a knee-length nightshirt and a turban. 'This is astonishing. Truly astonishing.'

'What are you talking about?' Jack said.

Kanvar stared at Jack with his gleaming, unblinking eyes. 'I believe you have found what I'm looking for.'

'What? The meeting point?'

'Yes,' Kanvar whispered. 'You must come with me to Scotland. Show me where it is. I must know its exact location.'

'Hold on.' Jack raised his hand. 'I can't go to Scotland. The army are coming. I'm not leaving my people at a time like this.'

Kanvar crouched down again, licked his lips and fidgeted. 'I understand. But I must locate the meeting point.' He looked around at the others assembled about the fire. 'It might be our last hope of defeating the Rajthanans.'

Elizabeth frowned. 'So, this meeting place *is* a weapon. Is it the Grail, after all?'

Kanvar looked at his hands. He clenched his fingers into fists and released them again. A frown coursed across his forehead. Finally, he took a deep breath and said, 'I know very little of this Grail. But I can tell you the meeting point is not in itself important. What I need to know is its location. I must mark it on a map.'

Jack gave a small cough. He felt odd, as if everything were unreal, as if he were in a dream. 'If it's a map you want, I might be able to help.'

'What?' Kanvar's voice was a whisper once again.

'I have some maps,' Jack said. 'The meeting place might be on them. I found them when I was in Scotland.'

'Who created them?'

'A Rajthanan siddha made some of them. He was doing some surveying in Scotland. The others are from a siddha called Mahajan. He was using the meeting point for one of his projects. He might have marked it down on his charts.'

Kanvar shivered and his eyes went moist. He stood again, and the blanket slipped to the ground. 'I must see these maps. At once.'

⎯⎯◆⎯⎯

The rain hissed on the roof of Jack's hut. A strong gust of wind made the building's timber frame creak like a ship. Jack paused as he stood before his old, battered chest. His tunic was drenched from the storm and dripped on to the earth floor. He wiped the damp hair from his eyes, then opened the chest's lid and rummaged inside. Finally, he drew out the maps he'd brought back from Scotland, which he'd rolled into a tube and tied with string.

He turned round. Saleem and Kanvar sat before a newly lit fire. Godwin and Elizabeth had stayed behind to look after Cecily and snatch what sleep they could.

Kanvar was a strange figure in his turban, sodden nightshirt and nothing else. He'd been in such a rush to get back to Jack's hut that he'd charged off into the night without even putting on his boots. His bare feet were now smeared with mud. He shivered – perhaps from the cold, perhaps from excitement – and watched intently with his saucer-like eyes as Jack returned to the fireside.

Jack squatted down and handed across the maps. Kanvar looked at the rolled-up sheets as if he were handling a bar of gold. He stroked the paper with his finger, then carefully untied the string and unfurled one of the charts, spreading it out over the rushes on the floor. The yellow firelight throbbed on the white paper.

Jack looked across and noted the dense scrawls of ink. He couldn't understand any of it – he'd never been able to read

Rajthanan maps. He'd meant to take the charts to the library at Clun Abbey but hadn't found the time.

'Can you see the meeting point?' Jack asked.

'Not yet,' Kanvar said. 'But this is promising.'

Kanvar rolled the first map aside, then spread out the second. His eyes flickered over the markings. He traced certain lines with his finger, muttering to himself in a language Jack couldn't understand. He seemed enthralled, as if he were studying a profound mystery.

Jack glanced across at Saleem, but the lad was gazing at the fire, lost in thought.

Kanvar crackled the second map to the side and began studying a third. His eyes widened and he bent closer to the paper, eager as a cat stalking its prey. His spidery fingers flitted from one spot to another.

The fire popped and a spark jumped on to the chart. Kanvar jerked and gave an almost comical yelp. His hand shot out and flicked the spark away before it could leave more than a small black spot on the sheet.

He continued poring over the map.

Then he froze and began trembling. His hand shook as he prodded his finger at a point on the sheet, making the paper crinkle.

A strong squall rattled the shutters on one side of the hut. The door tapped incessantly in its frame.

'What is it?' Jack asked.

Kanvar tightened his jaw and looked up. 'This is it.' His voice was a mere whisper, so quiet Jack could barely hear it.

'The meeting place?' Jack asked.

'Yes. Marked here. Up in Scotland. The exact location. The exact coordinates.'

'Good,' Jack said. 'So, you've found it. Are you going to tell me what the hell all this is about now?'

A frown quivered across Kanvar's forehead. He looked at the ground and mumbled something to himself.

After waiting for perhaps twenty seconds, Jack said, 'Are you going to explain yourself, or do I have to wait around all night?'

'Yes.' Kanvar looked up suddenly. 'Yes, I will tell you. But it will take some time.'

Jack stood with Kanvar in the middle of the glade. A chorus of birds sang in the surrounding trees. Bees murmured and a gentle breeze combed the grass. The storm had passed during the night and the sky was now a sharp blue. The sun baked the wet earth and the scent of the rising steam mingled with the smell of warm grass and wild flowers.

'Look, Kanvar,' Jack said. 'I need some answers now.'

'Yes, yes,' Kanvar said. 'Soon.'

They were about a quarter of a mile from Folly Brook. Kanvar had insisted on coming here before he explained anything further. The Sikh seemed fully recovered now, despite only sleeping for three hours. Jack, on the other hand, ached with tiredness. But he was eager to hear what Kanvar had to say.

'Walk forward,' Kanvar said.

Jack frowned. 'What?'

'Just a few steps.'

What was Kanvar playing at now?

Jack thought about protesting, but he'd gone along with Kanvar's wishes so far. He might as well go along with them for a little while longer.

He took three steps forward and slipped into a powerful sattva stream. The invisible substance swirled about him and sent his skin quivering. The sweet scent tickled his nostrils.

He turned and looked back at Kanvar. 'It's a sattva stream. So what?'

'This one flows back down to Folly Brook and through the House of Sorcery.'

'Thought as much. Never followed it up the valley this far, but I would've guessed that.'

'It flows on after the village, all the way to Clun Valley and even beyond. And there are streams like this all over England, are there not?'

Jack sighed. 'Of course. I know—'

'Let me show you something.' Kanvar crouched on the ground and fished a sheet of paper from his satchel.

Jack walked over to him, sliding out of the stream again. He squatted down and watched as Kanvar unfurled the sheet and flattened it over the grass.

'Looks like a map,' Jack said.

Kanvar gave him a small smile. 'Well done. You are learning. In fact, it is a map of this region.' He pointed at a spot near the centre of the paper. 'This line here is the Folly Brook. These markings here are the hills to either side.'

Jack hunched over the map. He could see a squiggling line which was presumably the brook. He couldn't see anything that looked like hills, though.

'Don't worry about the detail,' Kanvar said. 'Just note this blue line here.'

Jack followed Kanvar's finger to a line that curved gently to the right side of the brook.

'That,' Kanvar said, 'is the sattva stream you just walked into. I marked it down myself the last time I was here. Blue is always used for sattva.'

'If you say so. What's the point of all this?'

Kanvar swept away the chart and retrieved another from his satchel. He laid it out before Jack, saying, 'This map is smaller in scale than the last. It shows an area a mile across. It's of a part of Yorkshire. Take a look. See if you can see it.'

'See what?'

'Look.' Kanvar pointed at the map. 'The sattva streams.'

Jack peered at the map. A blizzard of lines confronted him.

He could make no sense of them. This was ridiculous. 'Enough. I need some answers. Now.'

'Please, try again.' Kanvar flicked away a beetle that had crawled on to the paper.

Jack gritted his teeth and stared again at the confusing mass of markings. Kanvar had told him the blue lines were sattva streams, so he concentrated on those. There were many of them, perhaps hundreds, wriggling all over the chart.

What was he supposed to see?

He was about to give up when he noticed something. He sat still and stared more closely. The blue lines covered only the central part of the map. There were none at all in the four corners of the sheet.

The blue lines were all contained within a circular area.

A circle. Interesting.

And then the design leapt out at him. He'd been looking at it all along, but his mind hadn't been able to put it together. It was like tracking a deer in the forest. At first, you could only see the trees and the branches and the leaves. But if you sat still and concentrated for long enough, you could pick out the tiny details of the animal ahead of you.

A shiver ran up his spine and his scalp crawled.

The blue lines formed a yantra.

6

A smile crept across Kanvar's face. 'You see it?'
'Aye,' Jack said. 'A yantra. Not one I know, though.'
'It is a minor one. Grow Wheat.'

Jack sat back on his haunches. A hundred questions were tumbling through his head. 'So, the sattva streams are in the shape of this yantra?'

Kanvar bowed his head slightly. 'That is so.'

'In some spot in Yorkshire?'

'Yes.'

'Why is that?'

Kanvar hesitated and held his lips together tightly for a moment. 'I am not supposed to tell you. I have already told you more than I am permitted to. A siddha is not supposed to speak of these things to anyone outside his order.'

'I see. This is all part of some siddha secret.' Jack was well aware of the secrecy surrounding much of the siddhas' teachings. Few people were taught the siddha language – and even fewer were allowed to see the yantra designs. Jhala had told him only a handful of people had ever set eyes on the most powerful yantras.

'Yes,' Kanvar said. 'This information is kept secret as far as possible. Although it would mean little to those who are not siddhas.'

'But you're going to tell me anyway, right?'

Kanvar's brow furrowed and he looked down. 'Yes. I feel I must.' He looked up again. 'I only ask that you think carefully before passing this information on to anyone else. Perhaps it should be more widely known. Perhaps not. Whatever the case, I believe the best way to proceed is with caution.'

'I'll be careful. You have my word.'

'Very well. I will explain further. This yantra, Grow Wheat, was discovered around a hundred and twenty years ago by a Rajthanan explorer. He was searching for new yantras in Europe. You see, the thing you are not aware of yet is that all the yantras have been found in this way. The original siddhas discovered the designs in the sattva streams in Rajthana. Since then, yantras have been found outside Rajthana. All over the world, in fact.'

Jack felt a strange sense of unreality again. This had happened several times since Kanvar had arrived. Things seemed to be shifting in his head, or the world was shifting around him, or both. '*All* the yantras are in the streams?'

'All of them.'

'That's a surprise. My guru didn't think to tell me that.'

'No. The Rajthanans don't give Europeans any more than the basic training. You would not be told these things until you rose up further in an order.'

Jack swivelled round and looked back across the glade. For a moment, he imagined he could see the powerful sattva stream rippling as it coursed past. 'It would be difficult to find a yantra, though. There are so many streams.'

'Oh yes. Many people have searched their whole lives and not found one. That is what makes the yantras all the more precious.'

Jack turned back to Kanvar. 'This is all very interesting. But what has it got to do with that meeting point in Scotland?'

Kanvar breathed in and stood up suddenly, as if he'd received some shocking news. He paced back and forth across the glade, muttering to himself, with his hand to his forehead. The silver braid edging his tunic glinted in the sunlight.

After a minute or so, he stopped and squinted up into the sky. Finally, he walked back across the grass and sat down again, crossing his legs as if he were about to meditate.

He stared at Jack, his eyes seeming impossibly wide. 'I will tell you. But this is a great secret. A far greater secret than anything I told you earlier.'

'All right.' Jack shifted into a more comfortable position. This was becoming more intriguing by the minute.

Kanvar gestured at the chart, which was still lying spread out across the grass. 'This yantra has a radius of about half a mile, in European reckoning. Most yantras are this size or smaller. It is rare for any to be larger, and the largest yantra ever found was a mile across. However, for several decades there have been rumours about a very large yantra here in Britain. A yantra far larger than any found previously. In fact, it is said to stretch for many miles, perhaps engulfing most of Britain.'

Jack blinked. This was a strange thought. 'And this thing exists?'

'No one is certain. We Sikhs long suspected it did not. However, several years ago, before the mutiny started, we discovered that the Rajthanans were searching for it. Clearly the Rajthanan siddhas believed in it, so we Sikhs started to think we should investigate as well. You see, the rumours suggested this Great Yantra would give a person some immense power. Something beyond every other yantra.'

'What power?'

Kanvar pursed his lips. 'We do not know. No one knows. Except, perhaps, until now.'

'Now? You've discovered the Great Yantra, then?'

'Sadly not. But we suspect the Rajthanans have.'

Jack sat still. The light seemed intensely bright now and the smell of the flowers overpowering. 'The Rajthanans have the great power?'

'Our spies believe so. We know General Vadula has been determined to get it and has sent his siddhas right across Britain trying to map the yantra.'

Jack's mind was racing now. 'So, we need to map the yantra ourselves. Use it against the Rajthanans.'

'Of course. We Sikhs have been trying our best over the past few years. We have found, we think, parts of the yantra. But we have always faced a major obstacle.'

'What?'

'We have never known where the edge of the yantra lies. Without knowing that, we haven't known the size of the yantra. We haven't known what regions are inside it and what regions are outside it. It has been a huge problem. And the best way to solve that problem would be to find the centre.'

'Why the centre?'

Kanvar leant forward and swept the sticks and dead leaves away from a bare patch of ground. He prodded his finger in the earth, leaving a small indentation. 'Imagine this is the centre of the yantra.' He then drew a circle around the spot. 'And this is the yantra's edge. Obviously, the edge will form a perfect circle about the centre. If we know the location of the centre,' he pointed at the spot, 'then we can look for sattva streams that arc about it in the correct way.' He ran his finger along a section of the circle.

Jack rubbed his chin. This was all a lot to take in at once. 'I think I understand.'

'The important point is that we have needed the centre in order to complete the design. And so far, we have been unable to find it.'

Things were becoming clearer to Jack now. 'So, you think that meeting point I found is this centre?'

'Exactly. We knew we were looking for a confluence point of some sort. The yantra is something like a great wheel with many spokes. All the major spokes meet at that central point.'

'That's exactly what it was like. I stood right in it. I could feel the streams all flowing into that one spot.'

Jack recalled the powerful sattva billowing around him, so strong it almost knocked him off his feet.

He plucked a blade of grass and toyed with it absently. 'If the

Rajthanans have found the whole design, they must have found the centre themselves, then.'

'That is so. Our spies tell us they found it in Scotland, although we haven't known the exact location. My mission was to go to Scotland to seek the centre. But it looks as though you have saved me some time.'

Jack nodded. 'You know, when I travelled into Scotland I was with a Rajthanan expedition. We were supposed to be looking for a siddha called Mahajan. But maybe the Rajthanans were looking for the centre all along. Maybe that was the real reason for the journey.'

'That is possible. That could have been at least one of the reasons for the mission.'

'Right. Here's the thing, though. The siddha who was travelling with us would have been the only one who knew about this centre. But he never made it there. He was killed on the way. That map with the centre marked on it must have been Mahajan's. He'd built his castle on top of the meeting place, so he would have known where it was.'

'I see your point. You don't think the Rajthanans could have learnt the location of the centre from your expedition?'

'Can't see how. The only Rajthanan who made it all the way with me was a captain called Rao. He didn't seem to know anything about the centre. And anyway, I took the only copies of Mahajan's maps.'

'I understand. But perhaps this Rao told his commanders enough for them to mount another expedition.'

'That could be true. I don't think Rao would have meant to help them. He wasn't so happy with the empire by the end of our journey. But he could have said something without realising it was important.'

'Indeed. And in any case, our spies tell us the Rajthanans have sent several expeditions to Scotland. One way or another, it seems they found the centre eventually.'

Jack squinted up at the sun for a moment. It was midday. He was sitting in a glade in a corner of Shropshire. The setting was peaceful. Normal. It was strange to be talking about mysterious powers and great, invisible yantras inscribed across the earth.

He looked back at Kanvar. 'So, now that I've given you Sikhs the centre, you can finish the design.'

Kanvar looked at his hands. 'If only it were that easy. The centre will be a major step forward, but we still have much work to do.'

'How long will it take?'

Kanvar sighed. 'I wish I could tell you. It is a huge task. I and my colleagues have been working on it for years. My every waking moment lately has been devoted to it. It could still be weeks. Months, even.'

'We need it soon if it's going to help with the fight against the Rajthanans. Once Shropshire falls, that's the end of the rebellion.'

'I understand that. We will do our best. I can only hope my comrades have made good progress. I will know more when I meet my commander, Takhat. He has the master copy of the map, the one which contains all of our work. I must leave tonight in order to meet him in Staffordshire at the allotted time.'

'Staffordshire? Why there?'

'We think the edge of the Great Yantra runs through there. Takhat has been working on it. I am to meet him at a small confluence point where one of the spokes meets the edge.'

Jack nodded slowly. He was still trying to arrange all this new information in his mind. 'You're travelling at night?'

'Oh yes. It is too dangerous for me during the day. Some of your countrymen almost killed me when I was on the way here. I only escaped because of my powers.'

'Sorry about that. You do look like a Rajthanan, though.'

'And to a Rajthanan I look like a Sikh.'

'Well, I'm glad you made it here at any rate.' Jack clapped his hand on Kanvar's shoulder. 'Come on. Let's get back to the village. I'm sure the apprentices will be keen to see you.'

⁂

Mark and the other students were overjoyed when they spotted Kanvar walking around the side of the House of Sorcery. They abandoned their studies, crowded about him and bombarded him with questions. Eventually, Mark ordered them to sit down and Kanvar showed them the yantras he'd brought. One by one, he held up the pieces of cloth, each of which had a design embroidered on it.

Later, Kanvar went off to meditate alone and Jack spotted him up on a nearby hill, sitting near the old stone cross that watched the valley like a sentinel. After a few hours had passed, Jack climbed the hill himself. His head was spinning with thoughts and ideas and questions. There were many things he still needed to speak to Kanvar about.

At the summit he paused for a moment and gazed back across the valley. The village lay immediately below him, nestled amongst the trees. He could make out the open space of the green and the clearing that contained the House of Sorcery. The brook coiled through the village and twisted away towards Newcastle.

He turned away and walked over to Kanvar, who sat meditating with his legs crossed and his hands on his knees. The ancient cross towered above him, the stonework mottled with lichens and worn by centuries of wind and rain. On the far side of the hill, the slope rolled down into a landscape of gently buckling hills. Forests rippled across the inclines and flocks of birds twisted like torn flags in the air.

Kanvar was completely still, his eyes closed and his breathing slow and deep. Jack examined the Sikh's face for a moment. Kanvar was only in his late twenties, as far as Jack knew, and yet he seemed to have knowledge beyond his years. It was difficult to know what he was thinking, but to date he'd never betrayed Jack. Whatever was truly motivating him, it seemed he could be trusted.

Jack stood with his hands on his hips. 'Kanvar.'

Kanvar didn't react at all.

Jack tried again, speaking more loudly this time. 'Kanvar.'

Kanvar jumped, leapt to his feet and gave a small cry. He pressed himself up against the side of the cross, panting heavily.

Jack couldn't help grinning. 'It's just me.'

Kanvar passed his hand across his brow. 'Yes, of course. I was in deep meditation. Near the spirit realm.'

'Sorry about that.'

'No. It is all right. It was time I stopped anyway.'

Jack gazed out at the hills. He imagined he could see the sattva streams flowing like veins and arteries across the ground. 'I was thinking. You said the edge of the Great Yantra passes through Staffordshire. Does it go through Shropshire as well?'

'Yes, if our surveys are correct. But far to the north.'

'Nowhere near here?'

Kanvar shook his head.

'So, if I was to travel to the yantra from here, where would be the nearest spot?'

Kanvar rubbed his forehead, then squatted on the ground, drew out a map from his satchel and began studying it. Jack crouched down beside Kanvar.

Finally Kanvar nodded to himself. 'Yes, it is as I thought. The nearest part of the yantra is the place where I will meet my commander, Takhat. It is the most southern point of the Great Yantra, you see. At least, as far as we currently know.'

'Whereabouts in Staffordshire is this place?'

'It is just over the border with Shropshire. Near the town of Drayton.'

'Drayton? That's about two days' ride from here, isn't it?'

'I believe so. Why do you ask?'

Jack rolled his tongue in his mouth. 'I had a strange idea this afternoon. What if the Great Yantra is the Grail?'

Kanvar frowned. 'I am afraid I don't know much about this legend.'

'No, I suppose you wouldn't . . . but think about this. According to the stories, the Grail had some sort of great power that saved England in the past. Galahad used it to free the country from enchantment. Oswin used it to beat the Caliph. What if the Grail and the Great Yantra are one and the same thing? What if Galahad and Oswin found out how to use its power?'

Kanvar paused. 'It seems unlikely. But not impossible. The Great Yantra will have always been here in Britain. Perhaps the native inhabitants could have discovered it. It is hard to imagine how they could have learnt to use it, though. They would surely have had no knowledge of yoga.'

'No.' Jack rubbed his chin. 'I was thinking about that too. You see, in the stories, both Galahad and Oswin are said to touch the Grail to release the power.'

'Touch? I do not understand.'

'Just touch. Put their hands on it.'

Kanvar's frown deepened. 'I have never heard of a yantra being used through touch. The yantras have always been used through the mind. There is no other way.'

'But this is a special yantra, isn't it? Maybe it works differently. Maybe you have to actually touch the sattva streams that make up the design.'

Kanvar shook his head. 'I am sorry to say, it seems improbable.'

'But worth a try.'

Kanvar stared out across the valley. 'Perhaps anything is worth a try in these troubled times. I will attempt it when I get to Staffordshire. I will touch the edge and see if I can achieve anything.'

'You do that. But I reckon I'll give it a try myself.'

Kanvar's eyes widened. 'You want to come to Staffordshire?'

'Is that a problem?'

Kanvar lowered his gaze and paused for a moment. 'You are welcome to come. But, in a way, have you not already touched the Great Yantra? You stood in the centre, after all.'

'True. But I didn't know as much as I do now. I didn't know to try to use it.'

Kanvar bowed his head. 'Very well. I have many doubts about your plan. But if that is your wish, I will take you to the meeting point.'

'The Grail?' Elizabeth dropped the ladle she'd been holding. 'You're going looking for the Grail again? I thought you didn't even believe in it.'

Jack cleared his throat. 'I'm not sure whether it's real or not. But I have to try. It could be our last chance.'

The fire was crackling in Elizabeth and Godwin's hut. Jack and Saleem had stopped by – as they often did – for dinner. A large iron pot stood in the hearth but Elizabeth had abandoned stirring it. Instead, she stood with her hands on her hips, and glared at Jack. 'I don't understand. You're going to another meeting point. How do you know this one's the Grail?'

Jack stalled. It was going to be difficult to explain his reasoning without telling the others about the Great Yantra. And he didn't want to do that. He didn't feel especially bound to keep it a secret. But still, Kanvar had said to be careful whom he told, and somehow this seemed the best advice. The Great Yantra was unreal, a mirage. He would wait until he knew more about it before mentioning it to anyone.

He took a deep breath. 'I don't know for certain this meeting point is the Grail. But I've been talking to Kanvar, and I think it could be. It's a complicated matter and I don't understand it all fully yet myself. You'll just have to trust me about this.'

'You told Henry you *wouldn't* look for the Grail,' Elizabeth said.

'I know. But he wanted me to go all the way to Scotland. This spot is closer.'

Elizabeth huffed and fired a look at Godwin, clearly expecting her husband to say something.

Godwin shuffled, looked furtively at the ground, then raised his chin and said, 'I thought the Grail was some sort of goblet.'

'That's how it looks in the drawings,' Jack said. 'But how many people have seen it? Galahad, Oswin and not many others. Who's to say what it really looks like?'

Elizabeth scowled. 'In the stories only a pure knight could ever touch the Grail. You sure you're pure enough?'

That made Jack pause for a moment. 'I don't know what it'll take to use the Grail. I don't know if I'm pure enough. I'll just have to try my best.'

'Is it because Kanvar thinks you're special?' Elizabeth said. 'You think that's why you can use the power?'

The thought had crossed Jack's mind. He'd quickly dismissed it, but it was still hovering at the back of his head. He had a special ability. An ability, according to Kanvar, no one had ever had before. Couldn't that mean he would be the one to find the Grail again? 'I don't think I'm anything special. You know that, Elizabeth. I'm just an old soldier with a few tricks up his sleeve. All I can do is try to use the Grail and hope for the best.'

Elizabeth's eyes glistened. 'It's dangerous. What about the army? You said they're in Staffordshire now.'

'They're still in the east of Staffordshire. Kanvar and I are heading to the north-west, near the Shropshire border. We'll be safe enough.'

Elizabeth's voice turned hard. 'And you'll leave the rest of us here? To face the enemy without you?'

Jack felt a flush of irritation. He'd come here to explain where he was going. He wasn't here for an argument. Elizabeth was upset and clearly worried about him, but all the same, she was his daughter and should show him some respect. 'I'll be back in four days. The Welsh won't be ready for a week, and Jhala's forces are stuck in Ludlow. I'll be back before any of them get here.'

He was less certain than he sounded. There was a chance Jhala's troops could defeat the crusaders in Ludlow and advance within days. The men commanded by the Lord of the Marches could assemble sooner than expected. Jack was even worried that Henry might try something. He was taking a risk, but on balance he thought it was for the best.

Four days was all the time he needed. Just four days.

He looked around at the small gathering. 'This is my final decision.' His voice came out harsher than he'd meant it to. He sounded like a captain commanding his troops. He tried to soften his tone as he said, 'It's getting late. I leave in a few hours. I have to get ready.'

He stood quickly and brushed the rushes from his tunic. Saleem scrambled to his feet and stood beside him.

Jack glanced at Godwin and then Elizabeth, who now had a tear crawling down her cheek. Jack had upset her and argued with her, but he'd had little choice.

He couldn't think of anything further to say, so he shoved the door open and strode out into the night, Saleem scurrying after him.

His thoughts whirled as he trudged back towards his hut.

Saleem pattered along beside him. 'I'll come with you.'

Jack sighed. He should have expected this. Of course Saleem would want to come.

'Look,' Jack spoke without turning. 'You can't come this time, all right?'

Saleem went silent for a second, but still kept up with Jack's long strides. 'Why not?'

'Because it's dangerous.'

'Scotland was dangerous. London was dangerous.'

'It's different this time. You need to stay here to look after your mother and sisters.'

76

Saleem's mother and five sisters were still living in the village. A hut had been built specially for them a few months ago.

'My family?' Saleem said. 'Why would I need to look after them? You said the enemy won't be here until you get back.'

'I know what I said, but I also know I could be wrong.' Jack stopped suddenly and turned. 'You can't follow me everywhere. This is a desperate measure. It might not work. I might not make it back. I have to know there's someone I can rely on back here – and you're one of the few people I can rely on now.' The words tumbled out of his mouth, but as he was saying them he realised he meant it.

This wasn't just an excuse to get Saleem to stay. The lad was hardly a lad any more. He was twenty years old and had proved himself in a tight spot several times before. With Saleem here and Mark in charge of the acolytes, Jack could leave with a relatively clear conscience. He wouldn't have abandoned the village . . . or Elizabeth.

Saleem gave his usual shy smile and gazed at the ground. Then he frowned slightly, stuck out his chest and lifted his chin to meet Jack's gaze. 'You mean that, Master Casey?'

'Aye. I do.'

Saleem breathed in sharply. 'Then I'll stay.'

———◆———

It was ten o'clock by the time Jack and Kanvar were ready to leave. They stood beside their horses near the edge of the village. In the darkness, Jack's pure-black mare was almost invisible, but Kanvar's white charger shimmered in the moonlight.

Only Saleem had come to say farewell. Jack wasn't expecting to see the rest of the village – he hadn't told anyone he was leaving as he didn't want to cause any more alarm than he had to. But he had expected to see Elizabeth and Godwin at least. Clearly Elizabeth was still upset with him.

But he and Kanvar couldn't wait any longer. They had to go.

Jack was about to mount his horse when he heard footsteps. Elizabeth and Godwin slid out of the darkness, Elizabeth cradling Cecily in her arms.

Jack felt his throat tighten. Elizabeth had come, but her face was grim and her mouth was held firmly shut. It didn't look as though she'd forgiven him yet.

He didn't want to part like this. Not now, when enemies were pressing in from all sides.

He fought back a rising tide of emotion. He had to stay strong now. Had to look as though he were sure he was doing the right thing.

He strode across to Saleem, patted the lad on the shoulder and said, 'You take care of everyone here in the village, all right?'

Saleem nodded, looked down and smiled slightly. Jack could tell, even in the dark, that the lad's cheeks were reddening.

Jack then moved on to Godwin, who stood with his chest puffed out, his chin raised and his oversized longsword attached to his belt.

Jack shook Godwin's hand. 'You're reeve while I'm away.'

'Yes, sir.' Godwin sniffed and drew himself up taller. 'I won't let you down.'

Finally, Jack turned to Elizabeth. Her features had softened now and there was a tear in the corner of one of her eyes.

'Elizabeth,' Jack said, his voice breaking.

'Father. Don't you remember the stories about Galahad and Oswin? They were both taken up to heaven when they touched the Grail.'

'I remember, but—'

'What if the Grail kills you?'

He gripped her shoulder. 'I'm not going to die. You still have Mother's necklace?'

Elizabeth handed Cecily over to Godwin and drew the necklace out from under her dress. The metal was dark with age, but it still glinted as it caught the moonlight.

'Good,' he said. 'Mother will protect you and Cecily, I'm sure.'

He turned to where his two army-issue muskets were leaning against a tree. He grasped one and handed it to Elizabeth.

She frowned. 'But you always said no.'

Elizabeth had, for many months, been trying to get Jack to teach her how to use a musket. So far, he'd refused. It was normal for a woman to learn to use a bow and arrow so that she could hunt. But a musket was a weapon of war. He'd been against her learning how to use one.

Until now. He was leaving, and he wanted her to be able to protect herself in any way she could.

'Take it,' he said. 'I know what I said before, but I was wrong. Saleem will teach you how to use it. Start practising.'

She nodded seriously, grasped the musket and gazed at the gleaming barrel.

Jack stepped away from her. He felt as though he were dying. He had to leave now or he never would.

'Right, then.' He tried to speak confidently, but there was a shake in his voice. 'I'll be back in four days.'

He slung the second musket across his back, turned to his mare and swung himself into the saddle. Kanvar had already mounted his white charger.

Jack gave Elizabeth a final glance. Then he circled his horse round and set off down the path, Kanvar riding at his side. He looked back only once and saw the specks of his family and Saleem standing in front of the white huts.

He turned away and spurred his horse into a gallop.

'Please God,' he whispered under his breath. 'I know I haven't always been a good Christian, but keep my family safe. Protect them until I get back. That's all I ask.'

PART TWO

7

———◆———

Jack heard the jingle and clop of horses coming from the road ahead. He yanked at his reins, drew his mare to a halt and peered into the darkness. In the moonlight, he could see the path curving away through the forest and disappearing into the shadows.

Kanvar stopped his horse beside Jack's. 'What is it?' Despite his many powers, Kanvar couldn't match Jack's uncannily good hearing.

'Someone's coming,' Jack said.

Kanvar frowned and drew out his pocket watch. 'It's nearly midnight. Who could be out so late?'

'Don't know. We'd better get off the road.'

Jack angled his mare down an embankment to the left of the path. Kanvar followed and they rode across to a row of trees at the base of the slope, where they dismounted, tethered the horses and crouched down in the undergrowth. They sat still, watching the road.

The clatter of the horses' hooves grew louder. Listening carefully, Jack made out eight or nine animals, plus the grating of cartwheels and now footsteps as well. It was a large party.

Strange. A large party was moving along the road in the middle of the night.

For a wild moment Jack thought it might be the army. But he quickly dispelled the idea. He and Kanvar were still in Shropshire, just north-east of Shawbury. It was unlikely the army could have made it here so quickly from either Staffordshire or Worcestershire.

And in any case, the approaching people weren't marching in time. They weren't organised troops.

Jack rubbed his eyes and blinked a few times. He was tired. Since leaving Folly Brook, he and Kanvar had ridden hard across a landscape haunted by war and pestilence. They'd travelled at night, to avoid Kanvar being seen, but as they'd camped during the day they'd seen numerous English crusaders marching south towards the front, and many more women and children fleeing to the north. Columns of black smoke from the pyres of dead livestock had darkened the sky . . .

Jack shook his head and shrugged off his weariness. He had to stay alert.

Now, figures materialised on the road. First came two men on horseback, then men and women on foot, then more riders and four mule carts. They all looked English, and most were dressed in ordinary peasant clothing – except for the riders, who wore surcoats bearing an emblem that Jack couldn't make out in the dark. The carts were laden with furniture, barrels, sacks, rolled-up tapestries and what appeared to be several glass windows in frames.

Jack stared harder. This looked like a wealthy household on the move. Windows were rare in Shropshire and so expensive that lords would cart them along if they moved home.

The final vehicle carried a man who was sitting on top of an ornate chest. He wore a red, fur-trimmed cloak and his fingers were covered in rings that glittered in the moonlight. Clearly he was the lord.

But why was he travelling with all his possessions in the middle of the night? And where was he going? The group were travelling west, away from Staffordshire. Were they heading for Shawbury? Or Shrewsbury, even?

Jack stood up. 'I'm going to speak to them.'

Kanvar frowned. 'Are you sure? Is it safe?'

'They're English. They won't harm me.'

He pushed through the undergrowth and scrambled up the embankment. He reached the side of the road, waved his arms above his head and called out. One of the riders peeled away from the others and trotted his horse across to Jack.

The man looked down from his saddle. 'What do you want?'

'Just news of the road east,' Jack replied.

The man narrowed his eyes and looked Jack up and down. His surcoat was emblazoned with a sign Jack didn't recognise. 'To the east? I advise you not to go that way.'

'Why not? The Rajthanans?'

The man snorted. 'The heathens are still many miles away.' He licked his lips. 'No. It's the Devil you need to worry about.'

'The Devil?'

'Aye. The Evil One. He stalks the land here. We're leaving this forsaken place.'

Jack blinked. This was all very hard to believe 'You're sure of this?'

'Aye, I'm sure. You can choose to believe or not, as you wish. But I warn you, don't carry on up this road.' The man nudged his horse with his feet, and the animal trotted away after the rest of the group.

The small party was already disappearing round a bend in the road. Jack could just make out the lord sitting on top of his chest, bouncing as the cart juddered over the uneven ground.

Jack slid back down the embankment and pushed his way through the bushes to Kanvar.

'Just heard something strange.' He began unhitching his horse. 'The man up there said the Devil's walking around this place.' He paused and looked over his shoulder at Kanvar. 'You know who the Devil is?'

'The adversary of God in your religion.'

'That's it. I can't understand it. The people here are superstitious. But this?'

Kanvar stroked his beard. 'It is strange indeed.'

85

They swung themselves into their saddles, rode back up the embankment and pressed on down the path. They spurred into a gallop, the horses' hooves thudding on the soft earth. The black trees flickered past to either side and the wind streamed over their faces.

For a moment, Jack thought of Elizabeth and the others standing on the edge of Folly Brook as he rode away. They looked so small and frail, as if the night were about to swallow them up.

Had he made the right decision in leaving them? Had he risked abandoning them to the enemy for no good reason? He had no idea whether he would really find the Grail, let alone be able to use it. The whole idea was mad. Perhaps, after living in Shropshire for so many years, he was becoming as superstitious as his fellow countrymen. And yet, after he'd heard about the Great Yantra, he'd started to believe anything was possible.

It was just over a day since they'd set out from Folly Brook. Staffordshire lay ahead of them to the east. Before the night was out, they should reach the meeting point on the edge of the yantra. And then Jack would find out whether he could use the great power, whether he could save England in its hour of need.

The trees dispersed and the road snaked off across open marshland. Thousands of frogs croaked across the plain. The scent of rot hung in the air. Occasionally, the road itself turned boggy and the horses splashed through shallow pools. Overhead, the stars trembled in the clear sky and the full moon turned the landscape silver.

After they'd ridden for around two miles, the marshes receded on the right side of the road. Fields of wheat and barley rolled past and Jack spotted a few scattered cottages in the distance.

Around five minutes later, a village about twice the size of Folly Brook loomed ahead up the road. The huts – which included several longhouses and a tiny stone church – were spread out along the edge of a forest.

Jack drew his mare to a halt and stared at the cottages. No

lights flickered in the village and there were no other signs of life. He couldn't even see a trace of smoke rising from any of the roofs. All the same, he and Kanvar couldn't risk riding straight through the hamlet. The villagers might be asleep – but if any of them rose and saw Kanvar riding past, there could be trouble.

'We'd better go round it,' Jack said.

He guided his horse off the road to the left, Kanvar following immediately behind. They'd avoided all the towns and villages along the way, making a wide detour round the city of Shrewsbury in particular.

The swamp slurped beneath the horses' hooves. The stench of rotting vegetation floated up from the ground and the frogs chirped incessantly. At one point, Jack's mare almost slipped over when her leg plunged into a deep bog. But she thrashed with her other legs and managed to scramble to safety.

'The ground is too treacherous,' Kanvar said. 'Perhaps we should go another way.'

Jack peered ahead. The line of the woods was less than a hundred yards away. Once they made it to the trees, and past the village, they could strike back to the road.

'No. We'll carry on. We're almost there.' Jack spurred his mare ahead again, and she waded and slipped through the deepening water.

Kanvar followed behind for a few more paces, but then called out, 'What's that?'

Jack glanced over his shoulder and saw the Sikh pointing towards the ground in the direction of the village.

'What are you talking about?' Jack called back.

'There's something there.'

Kanvar circled his horse round and splashed towards the huts.

Jack cursed under his breath. What was Kanvar up to? They'd given the village a wide berth, but they couldn't risk going any closer. And they needed to get into the cover of the trees as soon as they could. They were completely exposed in the open ground.

Kanvar reined his horse in. 'Jack, you'd better come and have a look at this.'

Jack shot a look at the village. The huts remained dark. For the moment, he and Kanvar were safe. But for how long?

Still muttering to himself, he rode over to Kanvar, the mud sucking at his horse's legs. The Sikh was staring down at a pool. The reflection of the moon hung in the black water, but it shattered into pieces as ripples moved across it.

At first, Jack couldn't see what Kanvar was staring at. But then he noticed a pale shape draped across one side of the pool.

He felt a tremor of nerves. Was that what he thought it was?

He leapt off his horse, splashing in a puddle, and floundered across the boggy ground, holding his arms out to steady himself. He heard Kanvar dismount and wade after him.

As he reached the edge of the pool, he saw that he'd guessed correctly.

The shape was a corpse.

'Waheguru,' Kanvar whispered.

The body lay partially on the bank and partially in the water, held in place by clumps of reeds. It was a man, perhaps in his twenties or thirties, with chalky white skin and eyes that seemed to stare in terror at the heavens. Jack couldn't tell how the man had died, but one of his arms had been cut off at the shoulder, leaving only a bloody stump behind.

Jack crossed himself and crouched down for a closer look. The body hadn't begun rotting yet. The muscles hadn't even gone stiff. The man must have died only a few hours earlier.

'There is something not right about that village.' Kanvar was standing and gazing at the darkened huts.

Jack stood up quickly. 'What?'

Kanvar pointed. 'That cottage there appears to have collapsed.'

Jack followed Kanvar's finger. Now he noticed that the roof of one of the closer huts appeared to have caved in and one wall had crumbled. He rubbed his eyes and stared harder. To the left of the damaged hut, he spotted another that had been half reduced to rubble. Further off, he saw more huts in a similar state of disrepair.

That was odd. Very odd.

'The village has been attacked,' Kanvar said.

'Maybe.'

'What else could have caused all that?'

Jack sucked on his teeth. Kanvar had a point. Why would several huts have collapsed in the village? Why was there a body floating in a pond nearby? 'We'd better take a look. But we'll go on foot. We'll make less noise that way.'

They hitched their horses to a twisted willow tree that sprouted like a scarecrow from the swamp. Jack plucked a cartridge from a pouch on his belt and loaded his musket. Although Kanvar carried a rotary pistol in a holster, he didn't draw it. No doubt he preferred to fight with his formidable powers.

They crept towards the village, doing their best to avoid slipping into the deep pools and sinkholes. Jack's whole leg shot down into the mud at one point and Kanvar rushed across to help him out.

The huts drew closer. Now Jack could see that about a third had either been partially or wholly destroyed. He gripped the musket more tightly. He didn't like the look of this.

They clambered over a low embankment, reached dry land again and scurried across to the rear of the closest hut. They both stood with their backs to the wall, breathing heavily. Jack flexed his fingers about the musket and listened for any sign that anyone had heard them. But the only sound was the endless creaking of the frogs and the sizzle of the night insects in the forest along the side of the village.

The cottage behind them appeared to be undamaged. At least, the back wall and the roof were still intact. The thatching on the neighbouring hut, however, had fallen in, and one of the walls had been ripped apart, leaving only parts of the timber frame and a mound of wattle and daub.

Jack glanced at Kanvar. The Sikh's eyes were wide and shone in the moonlight.

Jack gestured towards the smashed hut and whispered, 'Let's take a look.'

They stole to the edge of the wall and Jack poked his head round the side. He saw nothing, save for the silent cottages and the stone church on the far side of the village. Still no light. Still no sign of people.

He waited for a moment, weighing the musket in his hand, then scurried across to the neighbouring hut. He skidded to a halt beside the shattered wall and Kanvar ran up beside him. They both peered into the shadowy interior and Kanvar caught his breath.

Lying just inside the hut were two dead bodies. One, a woman, lay face down on the ground, both her arms and legs torn off. The other, an elderly man, was draped across the remains of the wall and had been sliced in half just above his waist. Congealed blood and entrails disgorged from his abdomen and drooled over the daub.

Jack hissed and made the sign of the cross.

Kanvar looked up and around at the edge of the hole in the side of the cottage. 'Whoever did this came through the wall. But why not the door?'

Jack mulled this over. Kanvar was right. It was hardly an impossible task to rip your way through a wattle-and-daub wall. But why bother, when even a locked door was easier to kick in?

He shot a look over his shoulder. The village remained silent, still and washed with moonlight. The hair crawled up the back of his neck.

Something was very wrong here.

They crept across to another of the broken huts. Here they found two walls had been smashed and a whole family lay slaughtered inside. Jack squeezed the musket hard when he saw three children, all hacked into bloody pieces.

Who would do something like this?

They slipped across to another hut, which had been reduced to little more than a mound of timber, daub and thatching. A man lay nearby in the grass. He'd been chopped in two, his top half dragged a couple of yards away from his bottom half. Sticky blood and gore formed a puddle about him.

Further off, towards the centre of the village, Jack saw more smashed buildings and more corpses.

His throat went dry. 'They're all dead. The whole village.'

'It appears so,' Kanvar said softly.

'I can't think who would do this. It makes no sense. It can't be the army. They're nowhere near here yet.'

Kanvar gazed into the darkness. 'Perhaps this explains why that lord was fleeing.'

'The Devil? You think the Devil did this?'

'Not necessarily the Devil, but at least someone those people *believed* was the Devil.'

'Who?'

'I have no idea.'

Jack felt a chill pass over him. The shrilling of the crickets beat in his ears and the trees lining the side of the village swayed and shuffled. These people had all died only hours earlier and he couldn't get the nagging thought out of his head that whoever had caused all this carnage was still around . . . waiting.

He did his best to push the idea aside.

'We should make sure there's no one still alive,' he said, 'then get out of here.'

Kanvar nodded.

They ran from cottage to cottage checking, as best they could, that there was no one still around. A few times, Jack risked calling out, but no one replied. They found further corpses, but not a single person appeared to have survived.

Finally, they reached the small stone church. The building seemed entirely intact, except for the entrance, where the double doors had been thrown aside and the stonework around the edge smashed. Jack approached the opening and peered inside. The interior was pitch black, all the shutters closed.

'Anyone in there?' he called out.

Thick silence was the only response.

He didn't want to go in, but he had to.

He clicked the musket's latch and the knife clacked out at the end, just below the barrel. He steeled himself, stepped over the broken doors and rubble, then strode into the darkness. He heard Kanvar follow behind him.

After a few paces, he stopped and waited for his eyes to adjust. But even when they did, the gloom was so complete that he could barely see a foot in front of him.

'I'll get a shutter open,' he said.

He plunged further into the darkness, striking off towards the wall to his left. The stone floor was sticky. Twice, his foot struck something lying on the ground, but both times he couldn't make out what it was.

He smelt salt and iron – the scent of freshly butchered meat. He had a bad feeling about this church now.

When he gauged he'd gone far enough, he waved one of his hands before him, groping for the wall. He stumbled forward a few more steps and then his fingers touched stone. He felt his way along the wall until his hand struck a window frame. He found the latch and drew the shutter open.

Moonlight fell across the floor.

And then he saw what was spread out on the paving stones in front of him.

8

The mutilated body of a woman lay sprawled across the floor. All her limbs had been lopped off, her torso had been slashed open and her head had been severed and lay about a foot away from her body. Her eyes stared lifelessly at Jack and her mouth hung open in a scream. Dry blood and entrails smeared the ground about her.

Jack had seen countless soldiers dead on the battlefield, but it was still hard to see an innocent civilian slaughtered so brutally.

'What is it?' Kanvar was still standing in the middle of the church, although Jack could now see his outline in the moonlight.

'More dead,' Jack mumbled.

He strode along the wall and swung open the next shutter. As the light dropped into the chamber, he saw further dismembered corpses dotted across the floor. He walked to the next shutter and opened that. At the same time, Kanvar opened several shutters on the far side of the church.

A scene of grotesque carnage was revealed piece by piece. Scores of smashed bodies lay scattered over the paving stones. In some places they were piled several feet high. Jack saw men, women and children, all hacked apart. Blood covered the ground and clung to Jack's boots as he walked.

'They took refuge here.' Kanvar's voice rang in the silence.

'They must have thought God would protect them,' Jack said. 'God and the stone walls.'

Kanvar paused for a moment, then said, 'We must go. There is nothing more we can do here.'

Jack nodded. There was no point staying. And whoever had killed these people might still return.

They strode out of the church, began walking across the village and then jogged. Neither of them wanted to spend another moment in that cursed place.

They stumbled and slipped across the marsh, unhitched the horses and rode towards the trees. The animals continued to slide in the mud, but they finally reached the line of the forest.

Jack and Kanvar directed their horses through the woods, heading back towards the road. The ground was still boggy here and the trees formed islands that twisted up out of the water. Sinewy roots clutched at slime-covered ponds. The sound of the frogs and night insects was a dense wall of clicking and sawing.

After ten minutes, they finally reached the road and then headed east, away from the village. After they'd ridden for about a mile, the forest fell away from either side of the road and they found themselves travelling across open marshland interspersed with fields. A few cottages were dotted about the plains and Jack spotted lights twinkling from some of them, along with smoke coiling from roofs.

He relaxed his shoulders. He was back amongst the living, it seemed.

He glanced across at Kanvar. The Sikh looked the same as ever and was seemingly untroubled by what they'd just witnessed in the village. Once again, Jack found it impossible to know what Kanvar was really thinking. Did Kanvar care about the dead villagers? Did he care about the English in any way at all? Was he helping Jack out of friendship, or was it simply to further the Sikhs' struggle against the Rajthanans?

They rode in silence for a further two miles and then entered another stretch of forest. Trees and shadow knotted together next to the path, and heavily wooded hills swept upwards to the left. A pale building appeared at the top of one of the slopes, encircling the summit.

Kanvar frowned. 'What is it?'

Jack squinted up. He made out walls, arched entryways and thin turrets that looked like minarets. In many places the stone-work had crumbled, leaving large gaps in the outer wall. 'Must be a ruin left over from the days of the Mad Sultan.'

'The Mad Sultan?'

'A Moor. He used to rule parts of Shropshire a few hundred years ago.' Jack tried to recall what little he knew about this period of history. There were plenty of legends in Shropshire about the Sultan, but Jack doubted many of them were true. 'The English Caliphate never reached this far. But a sultan did rule this place for a while. You can see some of the buildings he left, here and there. That thing up there will have been one of his fortresses.'

'And this Sultan was mad?'

Jack shrugged. 'So the legends say. Who knows what the truth is?'

'I did not realise Shropshire had never been within the Caliphate.'

'No. Too far away. Too wild, I guess. That's why this place is more like the England of ancient times. You won't see many Mohammedans around here.'

They were interrupted by a deep roar that seemed to emanate from the earth itself. The sound coursed through the forest and bounced between the hills. Jack's horse whinnied and reared up on her hind legs, although he quickly got her under control again.

The roar came again, so loud it shook the trees and sent stones trickling down a bank beside the road.

Jack glanced across at Kanvar. 'You have any idea what that is?'

Kanvar stared ahead without blinking at all. 'No. I do not.'

Jack leapt off his horse, crouched down and placed his ear to the ground. At first, he heard nothing. But then the roar sounded again, this time trailing off into a shriek. The noise vibrated through the soil and tickled his ear. It was coming from some-where up ahead, to the north-east.

He stood again. 'Whatever's making that noise, it's directly ahead of us.'

'It is very strange . . .' Kanvar's voice trailed off and he gazed into the distance, as if he were in a trance.

'Reckon we should get off the road,' Jack said.

Kanvar shivered and seemed to wake from a dream. 'Indeed. That would be wise.'

They rode down the bank to their left and slipped into the cover of the trees. They tethered their horses and stood watching the road. Jack became more aware of the musket hanging across his back. The firearm was still loaded – he would be able to sling it from his shoulder in a second, should he need it in a hurry.

The crickets trilled and the leaves hissed in the wind, but otherwise there were no sounds. Jack kept expecting to hear the roar again, or to see people moving along the road, but nothing happened.

After around five minutes, Kanvar said, 'How long shall we wait here?'

'What time is it?' Jack asked.

Kanvar drew out his pocket watch. 'It is nearly two o'clock by European reckoning.'

'Two o'clock. We're still miles from the border. We'd better keep moving.'

But as Jack turned to mount his horse, the roar came again – except this time it was more of a growl, which then contorted into a screech.

It sounded closer than before.

Jack scanned the surroundings and spied an animal track leading off into the woods, running parallel to the road. 'We'll go along that. We'll be out of sight of the road, and we should be able to hear anyone coming.'

They swung themselves into their saddles and guided their horses down the path, with Jack leading the way. The trees and the branches arching overhead formed a colonnaded tunnel. The moon peeked through the foliage at times, but often the shadows were so thick that Jack could see no more than five feet in front of him.

He kept glancing to his right, to make sure he could still see the bank that led up to the road. So long as he could make it out, he knew he wouldn't get lost. But after ten minutes, the path curved away to the left and headed towards the hills. He pressed on, hoping the track would loop back to the road eventually. But after around five minutes, he stopped his horse. The woods were a dense tangle all about him. If he and Kanvar continued along the path, they were bound to lose their way in the dark.

He looked back at Kanvar. 'Wait here a moment. I need to check the way ahead.'

He leapt to the ground and scrambled up the largest tree he could see. It was a difficult climb in the dark. Twigs scratched his face and arms, and he had to keep groping up blindly in order to find a purchase amongst the branches. Finally, he was high enough to see over the surrounding trees. He sat astride a branch and gazed out over the moonlit sea of foliage. The woods were so thick he could barely make out the path he'd just travelled along. Looking closely, he noticed a slight gap in the trees that showed where the track was. But when he followed the line, it bent away towards the hills and disappeared into the night.

Damn. The path was leading them in the wrong direction and there was no sign that it arced back at any point. They would have to return to the road.

He was about to climb down when the growling started up again, so loud he could feel it shivering through the branch beneath him. He noticed movement out of the corner of his eye. When he swivelled round, he spotted a patch of trees about a hundred yards away thrashing from side to side.

His heart lurched. Something large was shaking the trees. Something powerful.

His mouth went dry as he clambered down. He could hear his

heart pulsing in his ears. He jumped the last few feet and almost toppled over when he hit the ground.

He caught his breath and looked up at Kanvar. 'There's something in the forest just ahead.'

Kanvar sniffed. 'Can you smell it?'

'What?'

'Sattva.'

Jack frowned. They weren't in a strong stream at the moment. There was no reason for him to be able to—

He froze. He could smell it, a trace of perfumed sattva. It was faint, perhaps coming from a distance. But it was unmistakeable.

Another howl blasted through the forest, this time so close the air itself seemed to quiver. The horses neighed, stamped their feet and rolled their eyes.

Jack swung himself up into his saddle. 'Back to the road. Now.'

This was all he could think to do. They couldn't stay in the forest, and they couldn't continue along the track. On the road, they would be out in the open and exposed. But at least they would be able to move at a gallop and hopefully outrun anyone or anything they encountered.

They turned their horses and rode back the way they'd come. Jack took the lead again – he could see better in the dark than Kanvar. Moonlight speared through the canopy ahead of him, but this did little to force away the shadows. Caverns of darkness loomed in every direction. He urged his mare to move faster, but the undergrowth grasped at her legs and she tripped on tree roots and potholes.

Christ. They had to get back to the road as quickly as they could. The howling had stopped, but the quiet was almost worse. In the silence, Jack had no way of knowing whether whatever had been making the noise was moving away from him . . . or getting closer.

He heard a threshing in the woods to his right. Twigs snapped and bushes rustled, as if something large were moving through the trees. He stared into the blackness but could see nothing, no sign of any movement at all.

The path widened slightly and the undergrowth thinned, so he urged the mare into a canter. He stared into the branches to his left, searching for the bank along the side of the road. But he still couldn't see it.

Damn. Where was the road? It should be close now.

A great bellow rolled through the forest.

Jack's heart raced. The sound was close. Perhaps just yards away.

He looked back over his shoulder and saw that Kanvar was around twenty feet behind him now, the Sikh's turbaned head only just visible in the gloom.

There was a cracking sound, followed by a thrashing of foliage and a thump that sent a shudder through the earth. A tree had fallen somewhere. What could be strong enough to knock over a tree?

Jack glanced wildly to either side of him but could make out nothing through the interlaced branches. He jumped when something slapped him in the face. But then he realised it was only hanging vines.

Where was that damn road?

Then a shattering roar erupted nearby. A giant, shadowy form smashed out of the woods and stood blocking the path ahead of him. He caught a glimpse of segmented legs and claws, and two green lights that hovered close to each other. The thing gave a metallic scream and a wall of sattva, hot air and coal smoke blasted Jack in the face.

The mare squealed and reared up on her hind legs. Jack grasped at the reins, but they slipped from his fingers. For a moment, he managed to stay in the saddle, but then he was flying backwards through the air. He landed hard on his back and the wind was punched from his lungs. A wave of pain surged down his spine.

He heard his horse whinnying and crashing away through the greenery.

He tried to sit up, but a tide of blackness whirled over him. He couldn't move. He was slipping into unconsciousness.

He heard a deafening shriek and a great blot of darkness passed over him. The smell of sattva and coal was overwhelming. He glimpsed iron plates, rivets, tubes and pistons . . .

And then purple spots spun before his eyes and he felt himself drifting away.

His last thought as he fell unconscious was that he knew now what had been making the sound, what had been pursuing him and Kanvar through the forest.

An avatar.

———◆———

He woke a moment later. He was certain it was only a moment. He'd barely shut his eyes, when the avatar gave a roar that rippled through the earth and jolted him back to consciousness.

He was still lying on his back on the path. Branches arched above him and the moon, bright as polished metal, glinted through the mesh of leaves and twigs.

He sat up, wincing at the streaks of pain running down his back. He looked around and couldn't see the avatar anywhere. His musket seemed to have slipped from his back when he'd fallen. He fumbled about for it and finally spotted it glinting on the side of the track. He scurried across, lifted it up and examined it in a shaft of moonlight. It appeared undamaged. Thank Christ.

The avatar bellowed behind him. He spun round and scanned the darkness. He felt faint for a second, but shook his head to keep himself from passing out. The path snaked off into the gloom, but he could see no sign of the avatar, his horse . . . or Kanvar.

Where *was* Kanvar?

Musket in hand, he jogged back along the track, keeping low and sticking to the deep shadows on the side of the path. Ahead, the avatar continued to shriek and slash at the woods. But Jack could still see nothing.

Someone shouted. A bolt of dazzling green lightning streaked through the trees. The glare lit up the forest, and for a second Jack could see Kanvar standing in a clearing on the edge of the track, his knees bent and his mouth open as he cried out the words of some mantra.

The lightning vanished instantly and darkness slammed over the woods again. Jack stumbled forward, partially blinded for a moment by the flash.

Kanvar shouted again and a second burst of lightning blazed from his fingertips.

This time, Jack almost tripped over when he saw what the green glare had lit up. On the far side of the clearing, opposite Kanvar, stood a beast that was straight out of a nightmare. It was larger than three or four elephants combined and was something like a spider and something like a crab. It was covered in iron armour and its head was a mass of feelers, stalks and whirring mandibles. Smoke puffed from its sides and a red fire burnt deep within it, just visible through the gaps in its carapace. It snapped at the air with a pair of monstrous claws, and two green mounds – which appeared to be eyes – glowed on top of its head.

The lightning struck the creature in the face, making a clanging sound. The avatar roared and stepped back.

When the lightning blinked out, Jack staggered on through the darkness and reached the edge of the clearing. In the moonlight, he made out the dim figure of Kanvar, who still stood directly in front of the beast. The avatar screeched, its eyes throbbing a brilliant green.

Kanvar held up his hand and barked the words of a mantra. A speck of gold fire shot out from his palm and smacked the avatar just below the eyes. The beast shrieked and shook its head, but it didn't retreat.

Jack was about to call out to Kanvar, when the Sikh suddenly collapsed, a marionette whose strings had been cut. He lay still on the ground, but his chest was rising and falling. He was alive. But what was wrong with him?

The avatar growled and lunged forward. It was about to strike the prone Sikh with its claws.

Jack's old army training took over. In a single, fluid movement he lifted the musket to his shoulder and, without thinking or pausing for even a second, pulled the trigger. The firearm flashed, kicked and coughed smoke. The bullet tinged against the creature's abdomen. This seemed to do no damage, but the beast paused and turned its head. Its eyes glowed more brightly as it appeared to notice Jack for the first time.

But it only halted for a moment before it swung back towards Kanvar, screamed and raised its claws.

No.

Kanvar would be crushed to death instantly within those pincers.

Jack had no time to reload the musket and he had no other weapon with which to fight the creature. Sweat poured over his forehead and his heart battered in his chest.

He had to do something.

Now.

Without thinking, without planning, he gave the loudest shout he could, waved his arms above his head and ran out into the glade.

He charged straight at the beast, with no idea at all what he would do once he reached it.

9

The avatar remained poised, its head a great blot of darkness against the night sky. It didn't react to Jack's shouting, but it didn't attack Kanvar either.

Jack bellowed more loudly, paused for a second, plucked a rock from the ground and hurled it at the creature. With a sound like a gong, the rock struck the side of the beast. The avatar gurgled and, with a metal creak, turned its head to face Jack again.

Jack continued running, but he slowed his pace. He still held the musket in one hand, but he hadn't even clicked out the knife and his palm was sweating so much he thought he would drop the weapon at any moment.

The creature's mouth concertinaed open, the layers of mandibles peeling back to reveal an array of steel blades within. Its eyes blazed, it drew itself up taller and then it blasted Jack with a scream so loud that it made his ears ring. A pulse of hot, coal-scented wind smacked him in the face.

He skidded to a halt.

The avatar sat back on its haunches and swung its claws up above its head. It gave another shriek, and then sprang forward, lurching towards Jack on its spindly legs. It moved fast. Faster than he'd thought possible. Within seconds, it would be upon him.

He whirled round and charged back the way he'd come. He sprinted to the edge of the glade and plunged into the woods. He didn't look back. He didn't have to. He could hear the creature's legs thudding on the ground and the cracking sounds it made as it smashed through twigs and branches. It couldn't be more than ten yards behind him.

And it was getting closer.

He darted this way and that, leaping over tree roots, rabbit holes and clumps of bracken. In the dark, objects loomed suddenly before him and he had to make split-second decisions in order to avoid them. A shrub might leap up in front of him, or a boulder block his path, and he would have to either jump or dodge to the side without a moment's hesitation

He couldn't afford to make a mistake. If he slipped over, the beast would pounce on him.

His heart flew and his breath was like fire in his lungs. Sweat streamed over his face.

He had no plan. His only aim had been to draw the avatar away from Kanvar and now he had no idea which way to run. At first, he headed towards the path that led back to the road. But he soon realised he must have struck off in the wrong direction as the path didn't appear. Nor could he see the road.

He was lost.

A fallen tree appeared ahead of him, blocking the way. The ancient trunk was far too high for him to jump over. He could run round it, but from a quick glance he could see it stretched for at least ten yards in both directions. The beast would set upon him before he managed to get to the other side. His only option was to slide underneath, through the small gap between the trunk and the ground.

But it would be a tight squeeze. The gap was only about a foot high, and he wouldn't have much time to get through.

He flung himself to the ground and slid into the cramped space. Damp earth and rotting leaves pressed against his face. With his head turned to the side, he could see back the way he'd come.

And he could see the avatar.

The creature bounded out of the darkness, moving more like a giant dog than an insect, despite its six legs. Moonlight streamed over its black iron surface, its maw flickered open and its myriad feelers danced about its head. It gave a shriek, which then mutated into a roar.

Christ. The thing had almost reached the fallen tree. He had to get through the gap right now.

He pressed himself hard against the ground, hauled himself sideways . . . and then he was stuck.

His heart shuddered and his head reeled. The space was too tight. He couldn't get through.

The avatar was less than five yards away. It was so close he could smell the coal smoke and sattva billowing about it.

He scratched frantically at the ground with one of his hands and cleared away some of the earth and debris. He jammed himself further into the gap, praying he would be able to fit through.

The beast's face rushed towards him . . .

But now there was enough space for him to move. He wriggled to the other side just as the beast shoved its maw up to the tree trunk.

He shot back upright, whispering a Hail Mary. But the creature was large enough to reach right across the tree. It was already leering over the trunk and jabbing at him with one of its claws. The pincers were wide open and he could see the serrated steel along the inner edges.

He danced to the side and the claw slammed into a branch protruding from the tree trunk. The pincers snapped shut and sliced the branch clean off, despite it being thicker than a man's waist.

The creature immediately swung its other claw down at Jack, using the outer edge like a mace. Jack stumbled back from the tree as the claw smacked into the trunk. Bark and splinters flew into the air and a crack snarled right through the wood.

The creature had almost cleaved the trunk in two.

Jack spun round and bolted into the forest. But he only managed to go a few paces before a tree root snaked out in front of him and tripped him up. He flew through the air, hit the ground and skidded along the forest floor. He dropped the musket and it spun away into the undergrowth.

The beast howled behind him.

He flipped himself over in time to see the creature leap over the tree and swing its claw at him again. He cried out and rolled to the side. The claw whistled through the air and thumped into the earth a few inches from his face, dashing soil in his eyes. He could feel the heat from the metal on his cheek.

He rolled into the bushes to his left and scrambled to his feet. He heard another whistle and ducked instinctively. This was just as well, because the claw whisked past above his head – the wind of its passing ruffling his hair – before thumping into the tree beside him. Chunks of wood went flying and fissures fanned out through the trunk.

Jack lurched forward and glanced over his shoulder. The beast towered above him, smoke and steam haloing its head. It whirled its claw at him again, smashing through a branch that blocked its path.

Jack staggered backwards and the claw bashed apart a shrub just in front of him.

He turned to run, but he found his feet skidding on a slope of damp leaves and soft earth. He flailed with both arms but could do nothing to stop himself toppling forward, crashing through a thorn bush that tore at his skin, then rolling down a short incline. He struck a tree, which sent pain shooting up one arm, before he hit the ground at the bottom of the slope.

The avatar screeched and flung itself down after him, battering through the bushes that clung to the scarp. Jack leapt to his feet, ready to run, but something punched him hard in the back. He flew forward and landed on the ground. Pain welled where he'd been struck. He tried to blot it out, gritted his teeth and spun himself over.

The beast stood poised above him. One of its legs hovered in the air inches away from him – the creature must have used the limb to knock him over.

He went to roll away, but the avatar slammed the base of its foot into his chest and pinned him to the ground. He grasped at the leg, struggling to move it aside. But it was locked in place.

He was trapped.

The avatar pressed down harder. Jack gasped. Pain racked his body and he felt as though his ribs were about to crack. He could barely breathe, could only gulp tiny strands of air into his lungs. Sweat dribbled into his eyes and he fought away a tide of darkness that threatened to sweep over him. He wriggled and kicked, but he couldn't free himself.

The avatar's head lowered until it was no more than a foot from his face. With a steely ring, its layered mandibles peeled open and a trickle of oil ran out of its mouth and pattered on to Jack's neck. A gust of air issued from the maw, as if the creature were exhaling. Jack smelt ancient coal and sattva so strong that it made his nostrils burn.

The creature's eyes glowed more brightly now. He could see they were made up of hundreds of beads, like the eyes of a spider. He had a strange sense for a moment that he was being observed by . . . what was it? A mind? That seemed impossible. An avatar was a living machine, but it was no more intelligent than an animal.

And yet this avatar seemed to be studying him.

He knew enough about these creatures to know that this one was different. The way it had pursued him, the way it had hunted him and attacked him, suggested a beast that was capable of more thought than the lumbering creatures he'd seen in the past.

The avatar observed him for what seemed like a minute but must have only been seconds. Then steam wheezed from somewhere along its abdomen and smoke welled from gills on either side of its face. It drew its head back and raised one of its claws. The pincers creaked open.

Jack stared up at the giant claw. Those pincers would be able to shear him in half without any effort.

The leg pinning him to the ground pressed down harder. His chest screamed with pain and all the air was forced from his lungs.

He could see no way out of this now. He was trapped, and all the strength was draining from his body. Black pools expanded before his eyes. He made one last attempt to free himself, gritting his teeth and straining to shift the ironwork holding him in place.

But his efforts had no effect at all. The beast was immensely strong. There was no hope.

With his eyesight fading, he took one last look at the massive claw. Soon it would strike. And that would be the end of it.

He wouldn't reach the Great Yantra and he wouldn't find the Grail . . .

He saw Elizabeth for a moment, standing on the edge of Folly Brook with Godwin, Saleem and Cecily. What was worse than the pain in his chest, and the fact that he would soon be dead, was that he wouldn't be there to defend his family, or the village, if the Rajthanans came. He'd let Elizabeth and Cecily and everyone else down. They were waiting for him to return, waiting for him to come back with the answer to all their problems . . . and he wasn't going to reappear. Not this time.

He saw Jhala striding down the trench at the battle of Ragusa, drawing his scimitar and stepping up on to the fire step . . .

Elizabeth as a child running towards him across a field, her long black hair flowing behind her . . .

Katelin on her deathbed, reaching out to him with her weak hand . . .

Hundreds, perhaps thousands, of memories flickered before his eyes. He seemed to have been lying there for hours, when in reality it must have been less than a second.

The avatar squealed and whipped its claw down towards him. Though he could barely see through the black mist floating in front of his eyes, he could make out the shining steel of the pincers.

An Our Father tumbled unbidden from his lips . . .

And then suddenly a brilliant light burst in his head. He jolted. He felt as though he were rushing up into the stars.

The Lightning yantra was burning in his mind. Somehow he'd thought of it without meaning to and . . . it had worked. The knowledge of how to use the power flooded into his mind.

All this happened in an instant, even as the pincers were plunging towards him. The metal was less than two feet away from him. In a second he would be dead.

He reacted with incredible speed. He raised his hand, barked words in a language he didn't understand and shuddered as a pulse of lightning forked from his fingertips. His hand went numb and his arm tingled. The lightning shot up, smacked the avatar in the head and formed a sizzling web about its face for a second. The creature jerked backwards, dropped its claw and slipped its foot from Jack's chest. It lifted its face to the sky and howled, as if in agony, the sound so loud it shook the leaves and sent dirt trickling down the slope behind it.

Jack's mind was ablaze. His skin rippled with a strange energy. The pain in his chest was gone and he could breathe freely once more. He clambered to his feet, took one last look at the bellowing avatar, and then sprinted off into the forest.

Avenues of trees led off in every direction and he had no idea which way to go. He just ran straight ahead and hoped for the best.

The avatar stopped wailing and he heard its feet drumming on the forest floor. He risked glancing back and saw the beast bowling towards him again, crashing through branches that got in its way. Its mouth was wide open and its eyes burnt in the gloom.

Damn. The lightning had only stopped the beast for a few seconds. He might have broken the law of karma again, and he might have learnt a war yantra for the first time, but the avatar now seemed entirely unharmed. If anything, it appeared enraged and more determined than ever to hunt him down.

Sweat poured down his face and his breathing became laboured again. His lungs felt as though they were about to burst.

How long could he keep running? How long would the beast keep chasing him?

The ground turned boggy beneath his feet. Water seeped up through the earth and reeds sprouted everywhere. He found himself floundering through increasingly deep ponds.

He shot a look over his shoulder and saw the beast was gaining on him. It splashed through the pools without slowing its pace at all. He could hear the creaking of its joints, the rasp of the iron plates as they shifted about its body. A jet of steam screamed from its side and smoke frothed from its head.

He tried to will himself to move faster.

But the weed was snaring his legs and the mud was clotting on his boots so that it was as though he were shackled in irons.

The beast sloshed through the water right behind him. A cloud of smoke from it whirled about him. He could feel the heat of its breath on the back of his neck. It was so close now that it would surely be able to strike him with its claws at any moment.

He was considering whether to dive to the left or right, when he suddenly shot out of the forest and found himself charging across open marshland. The moon hung in the sky directly ahead of him and traces of mist clung to the ground.

He battled his way forward, but the pools were even deeper here than in the woods. He was wading through water that came up to his knees.

He couldn't run fast enough. The beast was going to catch him.

Should he turn round now? Try to use Lightning again in order to buy himself some time?

He was still thinking about this when he slipped, fell forward and splashed into a pond.

10

Jack flailed about in the water. He was certain the avatar would strike him at any moment. He tried to stand, skidded over again and finally dragged himself onto an island.

Gasping for breath, he spun round, flicking water from his sodden tunic. He held his hand out, desperately tried to recall the Lightning yantra and prepared to voice the command to activate the power.

Only the avatar wasn't there. He'd expected to find the contorted mass of iron towering over him, but instead he saw the reeds and ponds of the marshes, all veiled by tendrils of mist.

He was panting heavily, but he was catching his breath. He looked around him in every direction.

And then he saw it. The avatar had only made it a few yards out of the forest. It was so heavy it had sunk into the marsh up to the bottom of its abdomen. It stood still for a moment, smoke wafting about it, but then it screeched and thrashed its legs. It tried to haul itself out of the mud, but that only served to make it sink further. The water hissed, bubbled and steamed as it touched the creature's hot metal carapace.

Jack whispered a Hail Mary. The avatar appeared to be trapped – but for how long? If it managed to haul itself out, he was certain it would waste no time in pursuing him again. He had to get as far away from it as he could. And find Kanvar.

Wincing at the pain streaking down his back and the aches from the numerous bruises covering his body, he waded back towards the line of the forest. The hills swelled up to his right, and from this angle he could see the fortress of the Mad Sultan clinging to the summit of the nearest slope.

The avatar lifted its head and bellowed at the sky. It struggled more vigorously, the water frothing about it, but it remained trapped.

Jack scrambled more quickly. He slipped over a couple of times and was covered in filth and slime by the time he reached the trees. He scanned the way ahead, staring into the whorls of leaves and shadow. If he were going to make his way back, he would have to find his own tracks and follow them.

He was about to walk along the edge of the forest towards where he'd first burst out of the trees, when he heard footsteps. Twigs snapped and leaves crackled as boots tramped across the forest floor.

He dashed behind a clump of brambles and scoured the woods. Who could be walking about in the forest at this time of night? He'd been wondering whether the avatar could really be acting alone. Perhaps there'd been a siddha nearby giving it commands.

He listened carefully. The person wasn't walking ahead confidently, or even creeping stealthily. They were shuffling and dragging their feet.

Strange.

Then he saw Kanvar limping out of the shadows. The Sikh seemed on the verge of death. He was so weak he had to keep stopping and leaning against trees in order to rest.

Jack scurried out from the brambles. 'Kanvar!'

Kanvar paused, put his hand against a tree trunk and raised his head. 'Ah,' he managed to say in a feeble voice.

Jack rushed to his side. 'What happened?'

'I am all right. Just tired. I have used too many powers in a short space of time.'

'You fell over. I saw it.'

'Yes, that is so. I used all of my strength against the avatar. It was too much for me.'

As if in response, the avatar roared, gargled and splashed about in the pool.

Jack could just see the steaming outline of the beast through the trees.

'We'd better get out of here,' he said.

Kanvar lifted his hand to his forehead. 'Indeed. I have retrieved the horses. They are back at the pathway.'

'You found the horses? That was quick.'

'I had just enough strength to use a power. Call Animals.'

Jack gave Kanvar a wry smile. Call Animals sounded like a useful yantra. How many powers did the Sikh know? He was full of surprises. 'Right, then. Let's go.'

Jack and Kanvar rode through the night, their horses' hooves thundering on the dirt road. The forest paraded past to either side and eventually fell away. The hills and the Mad Sultan's fortress receded into the distance and they found themselves racing across rolling farmland.

Jack kept an eye on Kanvar. The Sikh slumped forward in his saddle and seemed barely able to keep hold of his reins. He constantly looked as though he were about to fall off, but he somehow managed to cling on.

Several times, Jack glanced back over his shoulder and scanned the dark landscape. He half expected to see the avatar bounding down the lane towards him. But the creature didn't appear.

After they'd ridden for two miles, Jack noticed his horse was growing tired. Her legs were trembling and white sweat was encrusting her shoulders and withers. Kanvar's charger was a cavalry steed and could gallop for miles, but Jack's mare was an ordinary country road horse. She couldn't keep going for much longer.

'We'd better stop for a while,' Jack called across to Kanvar.

The Sikh managed to nod his agreement. They slowed to a

walk and then halted beneath a stand of trees. With great difficulty, Kanvar swung himself down from his saddle, then collapsed against a tree the moment his feet touched the ground.

Jack went to his side to support him.

Kanvar raised his hand, saying, 'I am all right. I just need to rest.' He slumped to the ground, breathing heavily, as if he'd just run a mile.

Jack squatted down. 'You sure you can carry on?'

'I will recover in time. It is always like this when I use too many powers.'

Jack glanced back along the road, which tumbled away across the dismal plains. 'You reckon that avatar will get out of the marsh?'

'I do not know. It was strong. It might be able to.'

'It might follow us, then.'

'Possibly. But I have seen no sign of it.'

'Or heard it.'

Kanvar nodded, trying to catch his breath.

Jack was silent for a moment. He had a lot of questions, but he wasn't sure whether Kanvar was strong enough to answer them all. 'What the hell was that thing doing there? In the forest.'

Kanvar gazed across the silent landscape. 'I do not know. It is very strange. And disturbing.'

'Disturbing? You reckon the army must be near?'

Kanvar shook his head. 'They cannot have reached here yet.'

'How else could that thing have got here?'

'It is puzzling, I agree. But what concerns me more is that I have never seen an avatar such as that before.'

Jack frowned. He'd seen plenty of avatars, and even been attacked by them a few times, but the one in the forest had been large, strong and agile. He'd never seen anything quite like it either. That said, he'd lived in Europe all his life. He'd never been to India, where he'd heard there were many more of the miraculous creatures. 'It's not some sort of transport avatar?'

'It was far larger than any transport avatar. It was clearly designed for war. And war avatars are normally very small. Also, its armour was strong. My powers were weak against it. There are no yantras for creating such an avatar – that I have heard of, at any rate.'

Jack thought quickly. 'That you've heard of? You think this could be to do with the Great Yantra?'

'That is exactly what I fear.'

'You reckon that's the power of the Great Yantra? It creates an avatar like that thing we saw?'

'Perhaps. Whatever the case, it is of great concern to me that the Rajthanans have been able to build such a machine.'

Jack sighed and rubbed his forehead. His people were facing not only the forces of the largest army in the world, but now also huge fighting monsters. How could the English hope to win against such a foe? 'At least we know what killed those villagers now. And what that lord was running from.'

'Yes. The avatar must have been terrorising this whole region.'

Jack nodded, then paused for a moment. At least one positive thing had happened in the past hour. 'You know, I used the Lightning power. The yantra came to me.'

Kanvar stared at Jack with his unblinking eyes. 'I know.'

'You know? How?'

'I sensed you use the power. That is how I found you. It is good news. Remarkable news. Do you know how you did it?'

Jack picked up a stone and toyed with it. 'No.'

'You cannot recall anything that might have triggered your ability?'

'Not that I can think of.'

'Ah. It is good nonetheless that you have been able to do it. We can take heart from that.'

'Aye.' Jack stood. He still had many questions. But he also didn't like the idea of waiting around any longer. Not only might the avatar reappear, but he and Kanvar also still had a lot of ground to cover before they reached the Great Yantra. 'Are you strong enough to carry on?'

Kanvar hauled himself upright, leaning against the tree to support himself. 'Yes. We can go.'

They rode for a further four miles across the open farmland. Scattered huts appeared in the distance, but all of them were dark. Even this far from the lair of the avatar, there were no signs of life.

A line of light bled into the sky to the east, directly ahead of them.

Kanvar called across to Jack, 'We will have to make camp soon. I cannot travel once it is light.'

Jack sucked on his teeth. He didn't like the idea of stopping now. They were supposed to be at the Great Yantra already, but the avatar had slowed them down. 'How far away is the border?'

'I will check the map.'

Kanvar drew his horse to a halt and climbed down. He'd recovered somewhat and appeared less exhausted now. He took the map from a saddlebag, spread it out on the ground and studied it closely in the growing light. Jack dismounted and stood watching.

Kanvar consulted a brass instrument in a wooden case. Jack recognised it as a compass – he'd often seen Jhala using one as the company navigated their way through the wilderness.

Jack gazed towards the horizon for a moment. He couldn't help recalling all those times he'd tracked the enemy in the wilds, back when he'd been an army scout. Back when Jhala had been his captain and William his comrade. When his army oath had still meant something to him. When he'd still meditated before his regiment's standard.

When he'd still trusted Jhala.

He found himself clenching his hand into a fist. Now that he and

Kanvar had left the avatar behind, his thoughts were turning again to the threat his people faced. Jhala's men were in Shropshire already. They were mere days away from Clun Valley and Folly Brook.

God's will was strange and unfathomable. Why had He chosen to put Jack and his guru on opposite sides of a war? What purpose could that serve? It was impossible to understand.

Kanvar folded the map and stood up. 'We are only a mile from the border.'

'And how far from the Great Yantra?'

'Once we reach the border, we will have a further six miles to go.'

Jack squinted towards the east. 'We'd best keep moving, then.'

'We will never make it to the yantra before daybreak.'

'We'll just have to keep travelling during the day in that case.'

'If we camp now, we can travel overnight to the yantra. It is not far, and Takhat will wait for us.'

'I can't waste any more time. The Welsh army could be marching on Clun any day now. I have to get back.'

Jack's voice came out louder and harsher than he'd intended. But he knew this wasn't due to anger. It was worry.

Kanvar's eyes widened and he licked his lips.

Jack sighed and ran his fingers through his hair. He tried his best to soften his tone. 'Let's just ride as fast as we can and see how far we get.'

'Very well. We will do as you wish.'

❦

They pressed on along the road, spurring the horses into a gallop once more. Dawn seeped across the land, picking out fields, byres, a watermill and a village, all of which appeared to have been abandoned.

After they'd ridden for a mile, a forest appeared ahead of them, spreading out across an area of gently rolling downs. The trees shone emerald and jade in the morning sunshine.

'If my bearings are correct,' Kanvar said, 'the border is up ahead where that forest lies.'

Jack studied the surroundings. He and Kanvar were clearly visible in the bright light. They hadn't seen a single person since they'd escaped from the avatar. But all the same, they couldn't count on that continuing. And there could easily be guards on the other side of the border. Staffordshire was ruled directly by the Rajthanans, who could be wary of rebels passing through from Shropshire.

'We'd better head through those trees.' Jack nodded towards the woods. 'We'll be safe enough in there.'

They rode up the lane and then veered off towards the forest. As they approached the trees, Jack spied a goat track, which he followed into the woods. Birds sang high up in the branches, greeting the sun. Bees hummed and dog-rose flowers fluttered in the breeze. The strange horror of the night before seemed like a dream to Jack now. He could almost imagine it had never happened.

After about ten minutes, Kanvar said, 'We must be at the border now.'

Jack stopped his horse and looked around. He could see nothing but trees in every direction. 'You sure about that?'

'Yes, I have been estimating the distance. This is it.'

Jack noticed the ground was sloping gently upwards to their right. He nodded towards the incline. 'We'll go up there. Should be able to see something.'

They left the track and began to weave their way through the trees. When they reached the summit, they saw that the far side of the hill fell away sharply. Below them, at the base of the slope, the road coiled through the woods.

'The border crosses that stretch of road,' Kanvar said.

Jack squinted in the glare. The lane was empty. As before, not a single person travelled along it in either direction. And there was no sign of any guards. No sign of life at all.

But when Jack looked to the east, into Staffordshire, he noticed numerous cords of smoke twisting up into the sky. To get a better view, he rode along the ridge to a clearing. As he came out in the sunshine, he found he could see over the tops of the nearest trees and all the way down to the patchwork of fields spread out below. In the distance, perhaps two miles away, a collection of dark buildings smeared the ground. Chimneys jutted up from the structures and pumped smoke into the air.

Kanvar rode into the glade, gazed through his spyglass and then handed the instrument across to Jack. Jack peered through the glass, but he already knew what he was looking at – mills. Dozens of them.

Through the glass, he made out brick walls, smokestacks and gigantic warehouses. Carts and wagons came and went through arched gateways, and tiny figures walked across courtyards. It was a sight he hadn't seen in years. He could be in no doubt that he was gazing back into Rajthanan lands, back into the heart of the empire's stronghold in England.

It was strange. He'd lived most of his life in areas under the direct rule of the empire. Since leaving Shropshire to join the army at the age of sixteen, he'd spent little time in the native states. At first, he'd travelled back when he was on leave to see his mother and the rest of his family. But after his mother had died and his family had scattered, he'd never returned. Over the years, the native states had come to seem far away, foreign . . . backward.

But now it was as though he'd crossed over to the other side of a looking glass. He'd been living in Shropshire for four years. Even when he'd travelled up to Scotland, he hadn't passed through lands where there were mills or large numbers of Rajthanans. Now he was looking back at the world he'd come from, the world that had been torn apart by the First Crusade. It was as if he were looking back at his younger self from four years ago.

'Look.' Kanvar pointed to the open ground just across the border. 'Down there.'

Jack stared downhill and spied shapes moving along a lane. He raised the glass again and saw that, as he'd expected, the shapes were horsemen. He couldn't make the figures out clearly, but he could see turbans and russet tunics – the uniform of the Rajthanan cavalry.

He scanned the rest of the plains. He spotted a few peasants working in the fields, but he also saw further cavalrymen patrolling along a network of small roads. Some appeared to be Rajthanans. Others wore European Army uniform – they were most likely French or Andalusian. Most English regiments had been disbanded after the First Crusade.

He swivelled and checked to the north. The forest ended about half a mile away, and beyond it lay open ground where further figures patrolled. He saw the same when he checked to the south. There were guards all the way along the border for as far as he could see.

He lowered the glass and rubbed his forehead. This was a problem. Although Vadula's troops hadn't reached this area yet, there were clearly plenty of army units in the region already.

'We cannot travel through there during daylight,' Kanvar said. 'I look like a Rajthanan from a distance, but if we are questioned I am certain to be exposed. What is more, you yourself might come under scrutiny.'

'I'm just an Englishman. I'm not even carrying a musket any more.' Jack hadn't been able to retrieve his firearm after losing it in the forest. The only weapon he now carried was a knife in his belt.

Kanvar stroked his beard. 'That is true. But you are not from these parts. A stranger could still attract attention in these troubled times.'

Jack gripped his reins tighter. He didn't like the idea of a delay, but he could also see that Kanvar was right. There was no point in taking an unnecessary risk.

Damn it.

'All right,' he said. 'We'll wait until nightfall. But the moment it's dark we have to get down there and get to the edge of that yantra. I can't wait any longer.'

11

They made camp near a brook that wormed through the forest. Jack sat beside the stream and did his best to wash the mud out of his hair and clothes. Kanvar stripped off his tunic and carefully unwound his turban, which he handled with great reverence, as if it were a holy relic. He released his hair from its topknot, removing a small wooden comb that had been stuck in the back. His locks were so long they tumbled down over his shoulders and reached to his waist.

Jack had noted Kanvar's hair before, but only at night, in the dark. Now was the first time he'd had a good look at it.

Kanvar seemed to notice Jack's gaze, because he paused and said, 'We Sikhs do not cut our hair.' He touched his beard. 'Nor do we shave.'

Jack snorted and shook his head. The Sikhs, like the Rajthanans, had many strange ideas.

Kanvar half smiled. 'Perhaps this custom is strange to you. But it is our way. It is one of the symbols of being a Sikh.' He tapped a steel bracelet about one of his wrists. 'This too is important. It is the Kara. It must be worn at all times.' He held up the comb he'd removed earlier. 'And this is the Kangha, for straightening the hair.'

He next picked up a curved dagger in a small, ornate scabbard. Jack had noticed him wearing it before, but had never seen him use it.

'This is the Kirpan.' Kanvar held the dagger in both hands, as if bringing an offering to an altar. 'Like all weapons, it is to be used only in the service of the will of God, of Waheguru.'

'A noble sentiment.'

'Indeed. One that I live by.' Kanvar placed the dagger back down again and, still wearing his boots, stepped into the brook. He splashed water over his face and body, cleaning away the dirt encrusting him.

Jack thought he might as well take advantage of Kanvar's current talkativeness. 'You Sikhs have been at war with the Rajthanans for a long time, right?'

Kanvar paused for a moment, then continued cleaning himself. 'We have fought wars with the Rajthanans, that is true. But at the moment it is perhaps what you would call a rivalry. A battle for influence.'

'Influence? Over what?'

Kanvar stepped, dripping, out of the brook. He grasped an undershirt and used it to dry himself. 'Influence over different parts of the world.'

'Like Europe?'

'Exactly. Europe is the jewel in the turban of the Rajthanan Empire. The Rajthanans rule almost every part of it. And they control the powerful sattva streams. Especially those here in Britain.' Kanvar walked across to his horse and retrieved a clean undershirt from one of the saddlebags. 'Of course, the Rajthanans also have access to any yantras they find in Europe.'

'And have they found many?'

Kanvar pulled on the shirt. 'A few. That we know of, at any rate. There is the Europa yantra, for example.'

Jack sat back. Of course. He hadn't considered this, but it made sense that the Europa yantra – the yantra that was taught to the native siddhas – would be found in Europe. 'Where was it discovered? Which country?'

'In al-Francon.'

Jack mulled this over. France? The Europa yantra lay in France? It was a strange thought. But then, he'd learnt many strange things over the past few days.

He picked up a stone and tossed it into the brook. 'So, you Sikhs are trying to get influence here in England. That's why you want the rebels to win.'

'Of course.' Kanvar wrapped his hair up in a thin piece of cloth and then sat down near Jack. 'We would very much like to see you succeed, Jack. You and your people.'

'And if we do, then what?'

'What do you mean?'

'If we kick the Rajthanans out of England, what would you Sikhs do then? Take over? Make us part of your empire?'

Kanvar frowned and stared at the burbling water. 'I do not know what to say. I do not think that has ever been the intention of the Sikhs.' He looked at Jack with his wide eyes. 'I am not an important person. I am not a leader or a general. I am just an ordinary Sikh. If there is a grand plan to annex England, then I know nothing about it.'

Jack could see Kanvar was becoming uncomfortable with the discussion. And this was interesting. Kanvar seemed genuine – honest, even. It was probably true that he knew nothing about the greater plans of the Sikhs' empire. And in any case, all this talk was hardly important at the moment. Jack was speculating about a future that might never happen. It was the present that was the problem.

'It's all right,' Jack said. 'We English will take any help we can get, from whatever quarter. You Sikhs have your own aims. I understand that. It's natural.'

Kanvar stared intently at Jack. 'My aims are always to do what is right. To follow Waheguru's will at all times. That is why I do what I do.' He looked away. 'Even when that is difficult.' His eyes moistened slightly.

Was he upset?

Jack was about to ask Kanvar what was on his mind, when the Sikh quickly composed himself, stood and walked towards the small patch of grass where they'd decided to rest. 'I must meditate.'

Jack rubbed the back of his neck. So, Kanvar didn't want to talk about his motivations. That was his choice and Jack wasn't inclined to press him further. Jack had meant what he'd said. He was happy to get any help he could from Kanvar, regardless of what the purpose behind that help was.

'Meditate?' Jack stood and walked across to Kanvar. 'You should sleep. I'll take first watch.'

Kanvar was already sitting with his legs crossed and his back straight. 'No. I must restore the sattva in my mind. It is greatly depleted.' He shut his eyes and took a deep breath.

Jack squatted down. He'd heard before how using powers drained the sattva in a siddha's mind. The sattva apparently returned over time, but that process could be quickened through meditation.

'You know,' Jack said, 'I've noticed something strange since I used the Lightning power. I feel . . . stretched out. Thin. It's tiring even thinking about yantras.'

Kanvar's eyes sprang open. 'You are certain this feeling started *after* you used Lightning?'

'Aye.'

'And you have never noticed this before?'

Jack shook his head.

'Interesting.' Kanvar gazed into the distance. 'It is as I thought.'

When Kanvar said nothing further, Jack asked, 'What is as you thought?'

Kanvar stirred from his reverie. 'What you describe is familiar to me. You must have depleted your store of sattva after using Lightning.'

'You reckon that's what it is? That's why I feel like this?'

'Yes. What you describe is the beginnings of depletion. You must have a great store of sattva and you only used a single power, so you have not been greatly weakened. But you have used up some sattva. That has inevitably had an effect.'

Jack frowned. 'Never noticed this before, though, and I've been using powers for years.'

'But some powers need more sattva than others. You have mostly used the Europa yantra in the past. That requires little sattva. Lightning is of a different order. It is a powerful yantra and requires much sattva.'

'I see. But my guru told me native siddhas don't use up their sattva.'

'I have heard this theory. But I believe it to be false.'

'My guru lied to me, then?'

'Possibly. Or he might have believed that what he was saying was true. You see, the Rajthanans believe native siddhas are inherently inferior.'

'That's what I was told.'

'Indeed. And because of this belief, the Rajthanans have seen the native siddhas as somehow different. A special case. But I have not believed this for several years now. I believe native siddhas are in many ways simply ordinary siddhas – except for the fact that they have a larger than normal store of sattva.'

'You think that's all there is to it?'

'There are other differences between native and ordinary siddhas. But I believe the differences are not as great as many suppose.'

Jack rubbed his eyes. He was tired, and he was sure Kanvar was exhausted. But now that they were talking, he was hungry to know more. 'Right. But why do native siddhas have this big store of sattva in their minds?'

'I do not know. But it is not necessarily so strange. Some Rajthanan siddhas are like this too. And some Sikh siddhas. Every siddha is different. Everyone has a different level of sattva. I think, on average, European siddhas must have more sattva within them than most. That is perhaps unusual, but it is not so unusual.' Kanvar put his hand to his forehead. 'But now I must meditate and we must both rest. We still have a difficult journey ahead of us tonight.'

'Aye. That's true enough.' Jack stood and slapped the dust from his tunic. He could talk to Kanvar for hours, but now was not the time. 'You meditate and then sleep. I'll take first watch.'

Despite his tiredness, Jack had little trouble staying awake. So much had happened over the past few days, and he'd learnt so many new things, that his mind whirled and wouldn't settle.

He found himself thinking about Sonali. By now she should be in Dorsetshire. Far away from any trouble. But what would she do next? Perhaps she could return to Rajthana. That would surely be the best thing for her to do. Or she could at least travel to a more stable part of Europe, such as Andalusia. England was being torn apart, and she would be better off well away from it.

He shook his head and snorted at himself. Why was he even thinking about Sonali? She was gone. He would never see her again. All those words they'd said at the border, the promises they'd made, were simply to make the parting easier. Both of them had known they would never meet again. It had just been easier to pretend otherwise.

He found his thoughts drifting to other memories.

For some reason, he remembered the day he left the army. Jhala had come to the European section of the camp to see him off. It was unusual, and unnecessary, for a commander to do that.

Jhala had looked serious and grey. Jack was sure his commander was sorry to see him leaving.

'You have been my best disciple,' Jhala had said. 'Farewell, Casey . . . Jack.'

The words still rang in Jack's ears.

He'd never forgotten them.

At midday, Jack woke Kanvar and took his turn to sleep. He drifted off the moment he lay on the ground and only stirred when Kanvar shook him.

He sat up, rubbing his eyes. It was completely dark and the crickets were chirping incessantly. It was time to go.

They rode through the forest, not following any track, but picking their way between the trees and over the low hills. Within half an hour they reached the edge of the woods and found themselves looking out across the fields of Staffordshire. The mills lay less than two miles ahead, virtually invisible in the gloom save for the twinkling of a few red fires.

Jack saw no sign of guards or cavalrymen. But, on the other hand, the sky was overcast and only a trickle of moonlight filtered through the cloud. It would be impossible to spot anyone more than two hundred yards away.

He noticed the road snaking into the gloom, heading straight towards the mills. He and Kanvar had originally planned to follow it east all the way to the Great Yantra. But that would be far too risky now. They couldn't go through the middle of the mills, and they had to spend as little time as possible in the open.

He scanned the way ahead and his eyes soon settled on a series of low, forested hills lying to his left, half a mile from the mills. 'We should head through those trees over there.'

Kanvar searched the woods with his spyglass. 'I can see no one in the area. Your plan seems a good one. Once we get past the mills, we can continue east.'

They set off across the plains, riding through fields of wheat. Jack kept a watchful eye on the surroundings, searching for any sign of movement, any sign there was someone nearby. But he saw nothing.

As they passed closer to the mills, the fields vanished and were replaced by grassland. This, in turn, thinned to dry ground that was covered in soot and ash. Jack caught the scent of coal and sattva on the wind.

He shivered as he slipped into a powerful sattva stream. A railway line slithered across the ground to his right and an octagonal sattva-link tower rose up in the distance. The Rajthanans had been busy building in this region. Clearly they'd wanted to take advantage of the strong sattva.

The hills and the forest drew closer. The first slope was only three hundred yards away now.

Then Jack heard a shout to his right. Ten riders emerged from the shadows. They were barely visible save for the puffs of dust kicked up by their horses' hooves. Jack stared harder and spotted the russet tunics and turbans of the Rajthanan cavalry.

Damn it.

One of the riders shouted again and a horn blared.

'They've seen us,' Jack said. 'We have to get into those hills.'

He and Kanvar spurred their horses and shouted at them to gallop faster. The wind streaked over Jack's face and his long hair fluttered behind his head.

But the cavalrymen veered towards the hills as well.

Jack's heart shivered. The Rajthanans were riding hard across the plains. They might reach the hills first and cut off his and Kanvar's escape route.

But Jack knew he and Kanvar had little choice but to press on as they were. If they turned and fled back towards Shropshire, the cavalrymen would almost certainly catch up to them. He and Kanvar could beat the Rajthanans in a fight, but that would mean using powers, which would risk alerting any other guards nearby. The area could soon be swarming with soldiers.

The hills juddered closer. The first of the slopes, a spur that swung out from the main cluster, was completely barren. There would be nowhere to hide on it. But next to it lay a gully that curved into the hills and towards the woods.

Jack glanced across at the cavalrymen. They were gaining fast. His and Kanvar's only hope was to get into the gully and then

ride into the forest. There, amongst the trees, they could hide –
and, with any luck, escape. Without dogs, the Rajthanans would
find it difficult to track them in the dark.

He waved across at Kanvar and pointed towards the gully. The
Sikh nodded to indicate he'd understood.

Their horses' hooves battered the dusty ground. The shadowy
gully loomed closer. It was less than fifty yards away now and
the Rajthanan riders were still around eighty yards to the right.

Jack clenched his reins tight. He and Kanvar were almost there.
They could do it.

Then a shot cracked, the sound rolling across the plains. Jack
saw that the first of the riders was holding a pistol.

Christ. Should he use Lightning now to fight back? How much
longer could he hold off?

But when he looked back at the hills, he saw the gully was now
mere feet away. The lead Rajthanan fired again, and Jack heard
the bullet whistle past. But he and Kanvar were already charging
into the tiny valley. For the moment, the cavalrymen were out of
sight.

Jack led the way down the gully, plunging into a web of shadows.
The ground was uneven and the scarps to either side turned rocky.
Ahead, he could just make out the forest bristling across the
further slopes within the knot of hills.

The horn blasted behind him. The sound of hooves echoed
between the slopes. The cavalrymen must have made it into the
gully. But when Jack glanced back, the gloom was too thick for
him to make anything out.

The valley twisted to the right. Jack's mare whinnied and rolled
her eyes as she scrambled round the corner.

And then suddenly Jack yanked at his reins to curb his animal.
The mare spluttered, reared up and finally skidded to a stop.
Kanvar's horse stumbled to a halt nearby.

The gully ended in a sheer cliff face. There was no way up
without climbing. Furthermore, both sides of the gully were steep

and rocky. It would be difficult for the horses to scramble up – and in any case, the slopes beyond were barren, providing nowhere to hide.

Jack and Kanvar couldn't go forward and they couldn't go back. They were trapped.

12

Jack circled his mare round to face back up the gully. The horn blared again and the hooves clopped closer. Soon the riders would round the corner and then, despite the thick shadows, they would be able to see Jack and Kanvar.

'We'll have to fight.' Jack was already calling the Lightning yantra to mind.

Kanvar raised his hand. 'No.'

'There's no other way.'

'Wait.'

Jack was about to ask Kanvar what the hell he was talking about, when the gully suddenly darkened even further, as if a lantern had been snuffed out. Jack glanced around. Everything appeared as if it were behind dark gauze.

He looked at Kanvar, but the rising scent of sattva told him what he already knew. Kanvar was sitting in his saddle, his eyes closed and his mouth whispering a mantra. He was using a power.

The cavalrymen clattered round the bend in the gully. Despite the dim light, they were close enough for Jack to make out their moustached faces, their pristine uniforms and the pistols glinting in their belts.

'Quick.' Kanvar leapt from his horse. 'Over here.'

Kanvar led his charger across to the side of the gully, out of the way of the approaching Rajthanans.

Jack frowned. What was Kanvar up to?

But then he noticed that the cavalrymen had come to an abrupt halt. Their horses whinnied and stomped. One of the animals reared up on its hind legs and kicked at the air.

'Over here,' Kanvar hissed and gestured frantically for Jack to join him.

Still confused, Jack dismounted and led his horse over to the Sikh. His mare snorted and tossed her head, and Kanvar quickly patted her on the neck to calm her. Kanvar stared at Jack with his moon-like eyes and placed his finger to his lips.

Jack was beginning to understand, although he found it hard to believe what was happening. He glanced back down the gully and saw that the Rajthanans were now trotting their horses forward, frowns on their faces.

The lead rider paused, gesturing to the others with his hand, then dismounted and drew his pistol. He stared ahead, his moustache rippling on his top lip. From the gold bands woven into his turban, Jack could tell he was a captain.

The captain studied one side of the gully and then the other, gazing straight at Jack for a second before looking away again. It was impossible for him not to have seen Jack – or Kanvar and the horses, for that matter. Kanvar's white charger, in particular, glowed in the dim light.

'Come out!' the captain shouted in English. 'Come out, or you will be shot!'

Now Jack was certain. He, Kanvar and the horses were invisible. Hidden by Kanvar's power.

He'd never heard of anything like this before. He wouldn't have believed it was possible.

He turned to Kanvar and saw the Sikh press his finger emphatically to his lips again. They might be invisible, but apparently they could still be heard.

The cavalrymen dismounted and stood watching as their captain advanced further into the gully. The captain's gaze darted about the rocks. He would know his quarry couldn't have fled uphill. Not in such a short space of time. And he would also know there was little chance of two men and their horses hiding in the narrow confines of the gully.

The captain's eyes narrowed and his moustache twitched. His finger rested against the pistol's trigger.

He obviously knew something was wrong. And he didn't like it.

He crossed to the side of the gully opposite Jack and Kanvar and investigated the shadows draped between the rocks. After a few seconds, he seemed satisfied that no one was there and trod slowly towards the other side of the gully, towards Jack and Kanvar.

Jack's mare nickered, and both Jack and Kanvar seized her jaw and managed to silence her. The captain stopped for a moment and stared directly at Jack, but it wasn't clear whether he'd heard the horse or not. After a second, he advanced again, holding his pistol pointing up at the sky. His boots crunched on the ground.

Jack's mouth went dry. He stood immobile, barely daring to breathe. The silence in the gully was almost complete and any sound at all would alert the captain to the fact there were people hiding in the shadows.

The captain halted about two feet from Jack. His eyes scanned the rocks and the gloom.

Then he took another step forward. He was so close now that Jack could smell the perfumed oils he was wearing.

Jack held his breath. His heart spiked. The captain was staring straight into his eyes.

Jack remembered being out on a dark night as a child. He recalled being able to sense his friends without being able to see them. Had that been due to some supernatural sense? Some sattvic power? Or had it just been tiny shifts in the air?

Whatever the case, the captain was so close now he could surely sense Jack, could surely tell there was a presence right before him.

The captain's fingers tensed about the pistol.

Jack bunched his hands into fists. If he had to, he would attack the man.

Slowly, the captain lowered his pistol until it was pointing straight at Jack's chest.

Jack's heart thrashed.

The captain's eyes narrowed to tiny slits. His nostrils flared.

Jack would have to do something now. He couldn't just stand there and be shot. He was about to lunge forward, when the captain suddenly shoved the pistol in his holster, spun briskly on his heel and marched back towards the other cavalrymen.

'Come on,' the captain said. 'There's nothing here.'

One of the cavalrymen said, 'But we saw—'

'There's nothing,' the captain snapped. 'They got away.'

Jack breathed out as he watched the horses clop back down the gully, turn the corner and disappear into the night. He realised now that he was still holding his breath and a layer of sweat was covering his face.

Kanvar gave a gasp and slumped forward, as if his legs had been shot out from under him. He clung to a rock to support himself, and his horse whinnied and gouged at the earth.

The veil of darkness vanished and Jack could see clearly again.

'You need to rest.' Jack put his hand on Kanvar's shoulder. Clearly the Sikh was exhausted after using the power.

Kanvar nodded and swallowed. He seemed to be struggling not to vomit. 'I will rest. But first we must hide.'

Jack glanced around at the rocky slopes looming about him. Kanvar was right. The Rajthanans could come back at any time. He and Kanvar would have to scramble up to the forest as best they could, dragging the horses along with them.

Then suddenly he felt hot breath on the back of his neck and a hand slid over his mouth. His heart shot into his throat. He went to grasp for the knife in his belt, but stealthy fingers were already slipping it away. He brought the Lightning yantra to mind, but whoever was behind him held a dagger to his throat and whispered, 'Try anything and you're dead.'

Jack let the yantra slip away.

Figures flickered from the shadows ahead of him. Five European men emerged from the darkness, two of them carrying ancient flintlock muskets on their shoulders. They all wore peasant clothing that was tattered and worn, and their faces were gaunt, their grey skin hanging from their scalps. There was a look of grim desperation in their eyes, a look Jack had seen plenty of times before.

The men were starving.

One of the group strode up to Jack. He was a tall man who must have been a powerful giant once, but now he was a thin wraith. Much of his hair had fallen out but several long clumps remained clinging to the back of his head.

He stared at Jack. 'Keep your voice down. We won't harm you.'

He then nodded to the person standing behind Jack, who lowered the dagger and stepped away. Jack glanced back and saw that his assailant was another haunted-looking man in ripped clothing.

Kanvar was coughing and leaning against a boulder. He appeared too weak to even raise his head.

The tall man gestured towards the far end of the gully. 'The heathens could be back any time. We'll get you out of here.' He turned to leave. 'Follow us.'

'Hold on,' Jack said. 'Who are you?'

The man looked back over his shoulder. 'No time to talk. You come with us or stay here and get shot by the heathens. Your choice.'

Jack turned to Kanvar. 'Can you walk?'

'I will try.' Kanvar pushed himself away from the boulder and managed to stand upright.

Jack took the reins of both of the horses and led them up the gully, following the group of peasants. Kanvar stumbled along beside him, continually swallowing as if he were fighting off nausea.

After they'd gone about ten yards, the tall man, who appeared to be the group's leader, gestured to the slope to his left. Jack peered into a knot of shadows and now noticed a thin gap between two rocks. Beyond this lay a track that led up the empty scarp towards the forest.

The peasants slipped between the boulders and jogged up the path. Jack and Kanvar scrambled after them. The track angled steeply uphill and the horses skidded and slipped in the sandy soil.

The dark line of the woods rose ahead. The peasants were almost there already, but Kanvar was panting, wheezing and sweating heavily. He could barely walk.

'Can you keep going?' Jack asked.

Kanvar nodded, trying to catch his breath.

As they pressed on towards the forest, Jack glanced to his right and saw that he was high enough now to get a good look across the plains. The fires of the mills glimmered about half a mile away.

The peasants melted into the woods, but their leader stood on the track and waved frantically at Jack and Kanvar.

'Hurry!' he shouted down. 'The heathens are coming back.'

Jack's heart battered in his chest. Damn it. He and Kanvar had almost reached safety and now the bloody cavalrymen were returning.

He dragged at the horses and urged Kanvar on. The Sikh found some reserve of strength and clambered up the track on all fours. They made it into the trees, where Kanvar collapsed and lay panting on the ground.

The peasants crouched in the undergrowth and stared downhill. Jack squatted next to their leader and followed the tall man's gaze. Ten riders were galloping past along the edge of the hills. Jack only noticed them because of the pale dust billowing behind them.

'You reckon it's the same men?' Jack asked.

The leader nodded slowly, but didn't speak.

A horn blared and the Rajthanans disappeared round the side of the hills.

Jack relaxed his shoulders. It looked as though he and Kanvar had escaped.

The group's leader went to stand, saying, 'We have to go.'

But Jack put his hand on the man's shoulder. 'Wait a minute. Are you going to tell me who you are now?'

The man's eyes darkened. He gripped Jack's wrist and shoved the hand away from his shoulder. 'Who are *you*, stranger? You show up in our manor with those heathens after you. Then you vanish right before our eyes.'

Jack sat back on his haunches. 'You saw that?'

'Aye, we did. And we're not too sure about you and your Rajthanan friend there.' He nodded at Kanvar, who was now sitting propped up against a tree. 'We were thinking to slit your throats. But we reckoned you can't be all bad if the cavalry were after you.' He sat forward. 'So, again I ask. Who are you?'

The rest of the group gathered in a circle around Jack and their leader.

Jack sucked on his teeth. These men had helped him and Kanvar. He owed them some sort of explanation and he didn't want to get into an argument, or worse. He held his hand out. 'Jack Casey.'

The man narrowed his eyes and sniffed. Finally, he took Jack's palm in his. 'I'm Elias.' He nodded at his comrades. 'We're all from around here.'

Elias's eyes then strayed over to Kanvar.

Jack cleared his throat. 'This is Kanvar. He's not a Rajthanan.'

Elias grimaced. 'Looks like a Rajthanan.'

'He's a Sikh. That uniform's just a disguise.'

Elias shot a look at his colleagues. They all frowned and leant closer to get a better look at Kanvar.

Eventually, Elias turned back to Jack, 'Whoever he is, he's no friend of the Rajthanans. That much is clear.'

Kanvar bowed his head slightly, pressed his hands together and said in a weak voice, 'Truth is God.'

Elias snorted and spoke to Jack as if Kanvar weren't there. 'He's a sorcerer of some sort, then?'

Jack tensed. He and Kanvar could be in trouble if these men accused them of black magic. 'He's not a sorcerer. Just a yogin.'

'Don't you worry. We're not out here hunting witches or warlocks.' Elias rubbed his face with his hand. 'We've seen a lot of terrible things anyway. If you and your friend are against the Rajthanans, we won't give you any trouble.'

'We're grateful for your help. We won't delay you any longer. We'll be on our way.'

'And which way is that?'

Jack paused and glanced at the men congregated about him. Should he tell them where he and Kanvar were going? 'We're heading east.'

'East? If you go that way, you'll only come across more heathens. Staffordshire's crawling with them. And the army are on their way. Led by Vadula himself, they say.'

'We'll have to take our chances.'

Elias studied Jack closely. 'Why are you going east?'

Jack thought quickly. These men weren't enemies. But, at the same time, he didn't like the idea of giving away too much information. 'We're . . .' He couldn't think of anything to say and flicked a look across at Kanvar.

'We are meeting a colleague of mine,' Kanvar said. 'He has information that should help us fight the Rajthanans.'

Jack wasn't sure it was a good idea to mention fighting the Rajthanans. He still didn't know who these men really were.

But Elias simply nodded slowly, looking between Jack and Kanvar. 'You're fighting the Rajthanans? You're crusaders, then? From Shropshire?'

Jack paused for a moment. How much more should he say? 'Aye. We're from Shropshire.'

Murmurs of approval rippled around the gathering.

Elias gave Jack a grim smile. 'You're crusaders. Then you're among friends. We support your cause. Although I don't like your chances. You're facing a tough fight.'

'We'll do our best,' Jack mumbled.

Elias scratched his balding scalp. 'If you're sure you want to head east, you'd best stay off the road. There are heathens and spies all over the place. Where exactly are you going?'

'To a circle of stones,' Kanvar said. 'About six miles from here.'

Jack was surprised to hear this. Kanvar hadn't mentioned that the meeting point was in a stone circle.

'I know the place,' Elias said. 'A circle of stones. Put there by the ancients, they say. I can show you a better way to get there. There's a path through the forest. The heathens don't go along it. You'll be safe. Safer than the road, at any rate.'

Jack glanced at Kanvar, who shrugged and nodded.

Elias's offer was a good one. But Jack didn't want more of a delay. He and Kanvar had already wasted valuable time fleeing from the Rajthanans and hiding in the hills. 'How long will it take us to travel along this path?'

'By horse?' Elias eyed Jack's mare, as if she could somehow provide the answer. 'Two or three hours, I'd say.'

Jack weighed all this up in his head. Elias's route would take longer than the road, but there would be less risk of being caught. 'All right. We accept your offer.'

'Good.' Elias stood up. 'We'll take you—'

But before Elias could finish his sentence, one of his comrades grasped his arm and hissed, 'Look. It's here again.'

The peasants all scurried to the edge of the forest, squatted in the undergrowth and stared out at the plains. Jack clambered across to join them, while Kanvar crawled over on all fours.

At first, Jack couldn't see what the men were looking at. But then he spotted it – a dark patch moving across the dark ground. He stared harder and made out angular metal and glints of fire. He traced a rounded abdomen, a head, segmented legs and claws.

It was the giant avatar from the forest.

Either that, or a creature exactly like it.

13

Jack felt a tremor of nerves. The creature was three or four hundred yards away at least, but he still found himself worrying it would somehow see them up on the hill and launch an attack.

The peasants all whispered, muttered and made the sign of the cross.

Jack looked across at Kanvar. 'You reckon it's the same avatar?'

Kanvar gazed through his spyglass. 'I suspect it is. I can see several broken stalks on its head. I destroyed them with my powers.'

Jack clenched his jaw. 'It's come all this way. You reckon it was following us?'

'I do not know. Perhaps.'

Elias turned to Jack. 'You've seen this beast before, then?'

'Aye,' Jack replied. 'Just last night. Over the border in Shropshire.'

Elias stared back at the creature. 'It comes past here often. Always at night. Some call it the Devil.'

Jack frowned. 'It comes here often?'

'Every few days. It comes and it goes across the border.'

'Where does it go in Staffordshire?'

'Couldn't tell you. I've heard rumours it walks all the way to the army camp in the east.'

'Vadula's camp?'

'Aye. That's what they say. It walks for miles back and forth, spending a few days in the camp and a few days in Shropshire.'

Jack shot a look at Kanvar. 'What do you make of that?'

Kanvar sat forward. 'Strange indeed. It has undoubtedly been built by the Rajthanans. Perhaps it has been constructed by Vadula himself.'

'And they've been sending it into Shropshire?' Jack said. 'Why?'

Kanvar pursed his lips. 'I can only think to soften up the rebels. Perhaps to prepare the way for the army's advance.'

'That must be it.' Jack tensed his hand into a fist. 'So, they'll be marching into Shropshire soon.'

'It appears that way,' Kanvar said quietly.

There was no need for either Jack or Kanvar to say more. It was obvious what the advance of Vadula's forces would mean – the complete destruction of the crusade. There was no way the rebels could withstand combined attacks from the armies under Jhala, Vadula and the Lord of the Marches.

Jack knew he had to get to the Great Yantra as soon as he could. Even if he failed to use the yantra's power, he might at least still have a chance of getting back to Folly Brook before any invasion.

But he was running out of time.

The giant avatar gave a screech, the sound sailing across the empty plains. The beast strode past the hills and disappeared into the darkness. It still had a long way to go, if it were going to walk all the way to the other side of Staffordshire.

Elias stood up, his knees clicking. 'We must go. It's not safe around here.'

The peasants marched into the woods, following a track that was so overgrown even Jack wouldn't have been able to spot it in the dark. Jack walked his horse, while Kanvar, still too weak to stand for long, sat slumped in his saddle, his white charger faintly luminous in the gloom.

For a moment, Jack wondered whether he should trust Elias and the others. He knew nothing about them. He didn't even know why they'd been lurking in the hills in the middle of the night. On the other hand, they'd helped him and Kanvar avoid the Rajthanans. And they hadn't slit his throat when they had the chance. That had to count for something.

He looked up at Kanvar. 'That was quite a power you used before. Back in the gully.'

Kanvar nodded feebly. 'It is called Night. It enables you to hide within shadows. But it takes a heavy toll. It cannot be used for long.'

'You've used it to get in and out of Shropshire, then?'

'Yes. On this latest visit I had to employ it several times.'

Elias led the group on through the forest. Arcades of trees receded into the darkness in all directions. The path almost vanished and they often had to push their way through clouds of leaves and grasping brambles.

After around twenty minutes, they left the hills and reached the edge of the woods. The peasants stood in the shadows and gazed across fields of wheat and barley.

Elias turned to Jack. 'We have to move quickly now. There could be heathens or spies about.'

Elias and his men struck off into the open, staying close to the ground as they ran. Jack swung himself into his saddle, and he and Kanvar rode across the fields. They were more visible riding their horses – but, on the other hand, they could travel more quickly.

The peasants were heading towards a further stretch of woodland less than half a mile away. Jack and Kanvar overtook them and reached the trees first. Elias jogged over with his men, and then led the way into the forest. Jack dismounted and marched along at the rear of the group, but Kanvar was still too weak to walk and stayed in his saddle.

The woods were even thicker and more tangled here. Vines hung across the track and mantled the trees. Thorns snagged at Jack's hose as he waded through the undergrowth. Without Elias and his men to follow, Jack was certain he would be lost already.

After around twenty minutes, a tiny light appeared in the distance, winking like a star through a mist of leaves and branches. Elias left the track and led his men towards the glow, cleaving his way through bracken and nettles. As the glimmer drew closer, Jack saw that it was a small fire.

The party came out in an area that had been cleared of brush and debris. A campfire flickered in the centre of the space and about thirty peasants huddled in a circle close to the flames. The group included women, children and the elderly, and they all looked as gaunt and grey-skinned as Elias. Several of the children appeared weak, their arms thin and their stomachs swollen. Further away from the fire, half hidden in the shadows, stood bivouacs and simple huts made of branches, leaves and earth.

Many of the peasants stood and watched warily as Jack and Kanvar emerged from the shadows.

Elias raised his hand and said to the group, 'We can trust them. They won't do us any harm.'

The peasants sat down again, but still shot furtive glances at Kanvar.

'You live here?' Jack asked Elias. 'In the middle of the woods?'

Elias squinted at Jack. 'What choice do we have?'

'You're outlaws?'

Elias wiped his nose with the back of his hand. 'You could say that. Though I don't agree with the laws that put us here.'

'What happened to you?'

'What happened?' Elias grimaced. 'The heathens is what happened. They said everyone in this manor was helping the crusaders over in Shropshire. Even the lord was guilty, they said. They confiscated all the land, clapped the lord in irons and knocked over our villages to make way for those mills. They said us commoners were all guilty, so we had to go to work in East Europe.'

Jack frowned. He'd heard many similar stories. General Vadula's rule had been brutal. Many people had been killed or sent to work in the mines and farms in East Europe, where the empire was expanding into lands captured from the Slavs.

Elias hawked and spat at the ground. 'I wasn't going to East

Europe. I wasn't going anywhere. So, me and the others you see here, we turned outlaw. We came to live in the forest. We forage and hunt as best we can. Sometimes we have to go raiding.'

'You raid the Rajthanans?'

'We stole from a few estates. But then more soldiers came in. It's too dangerous to rob the Rajthanan houses now. We stick to the railway villages. But even that's risky.' He looked towards the figures clustered about the fire, and his eyes moistened. 'We do the best we can.'

Jack understood why the peasants would target the railway villages – they housed the gypsies and half-castes who were the only people prepared to work with train avatars. Railway workers were shunned by both Europeans and Rajthanans. But since the First Crusade, they'd had little choice but to side with the empire.

'You were out raiding tonight, then?' Jack asked.

Elias wiped his eyes. 'Aye. Had no luck, though.'

'I would give you food, if I could,' Jack said. 'But we only have a few army biscuits. Just enough to last two days or so.' This was true – Jack and Kanvar had almost finished their supplies and would have to start hunting and foraging themselves, if they didn't reach their destination soon.

'It's all right,' Elias said. 'You're crusaders. We have no argument with you.'

'Why don't you join the crusade yourselves? You could go across the border at night.'

'I've thought about it many times. But I don't see the point. Soon Shropshire will be no better than here. The army are on their way. I'm sorry to tell you this, friend, but you can't win.'

Jack went silent for a moment. He also doubted the crusaders could win. He could hardly encourage Elias to support a rebellion that might very well fail.

'I understand,' he mumbled, then looked up at Kanvar, who still sat astride his charger. 'We should carry on. Can you keep going?'

'I am all right,' Kanvar said.

'Right, then.' Elias adjusted the ancient musket on his shoulder. 'I'll take you to the track myself. You can make your own way from there.'

Elias told the villagers he would return soon and then led Jack and Kanvar away from the campfire. Jack guided his mare by the reins, while Kanvar rode behind on his charger.

As they approached the edge of the encampment, Jack spotted a sheet of white cotton strung up between two trees. On it was a picture painted in vibrant ink. There were several holes in the cloth and an arrow jutted out from the centre.

Jack frowned. What was a painting doing out here in the middle of the forest?

As he drew closer he made out, in the wavering firelight, a portrait of an Indian man with a wide, fleshy face and an elaborate turban adorned with jewels. Jack recognised the man. He'd seen paintings of him before.

'General Vadula.' Elias spat at the picture. 'We took it from one of the Rajthanan mansions. Use it for archery practice.'

Jack stared at the glowering portrait. This was the man who'd enslaved England for the past four years. The man responsible for so much suffering. And yet it was hard to imagine ever over-throwing him.

Elias led them on through the gloomy woods, and eventually, after half an hour, they came to a wide, reasonably clear pathway.

Elias pointed at the track. 'Keep following that. It turns a few times, but it keeps going east. There's forest most of the way, but you'll go through a few open patches. Careful when you do that. There could be heathens about. In a few hours, you'll see the circle of stones in front of you.'

Jack held out his hand. 'Thank you. God's grace to you and your people.'

Elias took Jack's hand. 'God's grace to you.' He nodded at Kanvar. 'And your sorcerer there. I'll pray you crusaders win your fight.'

Elias then turned and slipped away into the darkness, stepping so quietly that Jack couldn't even hear his footsteps.

———•◆•———

The first trace of dawn smouldered in the eastern sky as Jack and Kanvar finally emerged from the forest. They stopped their horses and gazed across uncultivated grassland studded with gorse bushes. About a hundred yards away, on a slightly raised piece of ground, stood a circle of stones. Each rock was taller than a man, and two of them, placed next to each other, were higher still.

The ride along the track had taken Jack and Kanvar longer than expected – they'd lost their way on several occasions and had had to retrace their steps.

But now, at least, they were here. And Kanvar had almost completely regained his strength.

Jack blinked in the growing light. He scanned the area, but saw no sign of life.

'Takhat is late,' Kanvar said.

Jack gestured towards the stones. 'So, that's it? That's the edge of the Great Yantra?'

'That is what we Sikhs suspect. There, at the stones, is where one of the spokes meets the outer edge of the yantra.'

Jack sat up straight in his saddle. Now it was time for him to try to use the Grail. Now was the last chance for him and his people.

He dismounted and handed his reins to Kanvar. 'Keep a lookout. I'm going in there.'

'What will you do?'

'Anything I can think of.'

He strode across the grass. The sunlight was slowly peeling back the darkness and the stones cast long shadows across the ground. Birds came alive in the trees, crying at the dawn.

About halfway to the circle, he slipped into a powerful stream.

The sattva churned about him and scratched at his eyes and nostrils. The sweet scent was overpowering, almost sickly, as if he were drowning in honey.

He must be in the Great Yantra now, within the outer rim.

He strode on and paused at the edge of the stones. The sattva was even stronger inside the circle – he could feel it billowing out and stroking his face, like the spray from waves breaking on a beach.

He glanced back at Kanvar, who was still sitting astride his horse. Then he turned back to the circle and took a deep breath. He recalled the stories of Galahad and Oswin. Galahad had been sent, along with the other Knights of the Round Table, to find the Grail. After travelling through the great forests of ancient Britain, he'd finally discovered it. The stories described it as being in a castle. But how accurate were the tales, really? Perhaps Galahad had simply come to a place similar to the one Jack was standing in now. Or perhaps he'd gone to a castle, but one that lay in the path of one of the Great Yantra's sattva streams.

Then there was Oswin. The army of King Edward had been defeated by the old Caliph of England and had retreated to the top of Garrowby Hill. The Caliph's forces had surrounded them and had come marching up the hill. But, at the same time, the knight Oswin had discovered the Grail once more and touched it. The power of the Grail defeated the Caliph and freed England.

Now England faced danger once again. Would it be Jack who would save his country? The idea seemed mad. But he still had to try.

Even if he failed, at least he would have tried.

He took another deep breath, shut his eyes and stepped into the circle.

14

⟫◆⟪

The powerful sattva boiled about Jack, so strong it burnt his skin and stung his eyes. He rocked back slightly at the force of it. Here two giant streams collided and churned, forming an enormous whirlpool.

He held his hands out, felt the sattva rushing through his fingers. When he breathed in, the perfumed scent flooded his lungs.

He stood still for a moment with his arms raised.

Now what? He was in the meeting point. If the Great Yantra were the Grail, then surely he was touching it now.

But nothing had happened. He'd received no great power, no weapon he could use to fight the Rajthanans.

He lowered his arms and looked back at Kanvar, who was still watching from the edge of the forest. The Sikh did nothing other than bow his head slightly in Jack's direction.

Jack knew Kanvar couldn't help him. No one could. He would have to somehow discover the secret of the Grail by himself.

The sun was rising and the light was filling in the detail around him. He was right out in the open. Anyone approaching would see him instantly.

But what more could he do? He bent down and touched the ground. Perhaps that would help. When nothing happened, he touched one of the standing stones. Still nothing.

He went round the circle, touching each of the stones in turn. Nothing happened. Nothing at all.

He rubbed his face with his hands. He'd come all this way and now he had no idea how to use the Great Yantra.

149

Then he had an idea. He sat down, crossed his legs, straightened his back and put his hands on his knees. He took a deep breath and shut his eyes.

He would meditate. Perhaps if he went into the trance and got himself close to the spirit realm, he would unleash the Grail's power.

The growing light reddened his eyelids. He felt a trace of heat from the sun on his face. He tried to shut it all out – the sun, the slight breeze, the sattva storming about him. He had to leave this world of pain and illusion behind and see himself as he truly was, a spirit that had dwelt for ever in the purusha realm, which the English called heaven.

Memories, as always, tumbled through his head. He saw, in quick succession, Katelin, Elizabeth, Cecily, Jhala, William . . .

But then he managed to calm his mind. The ripples across its surface stilled.

He drifted far away from the material world. Silence settled over him. He was touching the purusha realm now.

And then nothing happened.

Damn it. He opened his eyes and slipped out of the meditation. Damn it.

He grasped a clump of earth and dashed it across the ground. He couldn't fail. Not now, when his people needed the Grail so badly. Kanvar seemed to think the Rajthanans were already using the Great Yantra. There was no reason why he, Jack, shouldn't be able to as well.

He shut his eyes again and breathed in. Now. He must find a way to gain the power of the yantra now.

But then Kanvar called out.

Jack opened his eyes and saw the Sikh waving at him and shouting, 'Someone's coming!'

That was all Jack needed.

He scrambled to his feet and ran back to Kanvar and the horses, slipping out of the sattva stream again.

'Where?' he asked Kanvar.

The Sikh pointed to his right, to the south.

Jack squinted. At first he saw nothing, but then he made out the faint form of a rider coming over a ridge.

He swung himself up into his saddle. 'We'd better get back into the trees.'

They guided their horses into the woods, where they waited, watching the approaching figure.

'Did anything happen?' Kanvar asked. 'In the meeting point?'

Jack gritted his teeth. 'Nothing.'

'Ah. I did make clear I had doubts—'

'Just shut it.' Jack felt his face growing hotter and he fought to control himself. Kanvar hadn't meant anything by what he'd said. But all Jack could think about at the moment was the destruction of Shropshire.

He slowly calmed himself as the rider drew nearer. The figure was a man who wore Rajthanan cavalry uniform, although he hardly looked like a Rajthanan. He was Indian, but he had a huge, bushy beard that reached down to his chest. Jack had never seen a Rajthanan officer with a beard like that.

'It is Takhat.' Kanvar smiled slightly. But, at the same time, moisture was building in his eyes.

Jack frowned. Why was Kanvar reacting like that? 'You sure it's him?'

Kanvar nodded, then rode out to meet his commander. Jack nudged his horse into a trot and followed.

Takhat spotted Kanvar immediately and wheeled his horse round to meet him. He was a short, stocky man with thick eyebrows that flicked up at the ends. Judging by the flecks of silver in his beard, he was at least Jack's age, or older.

When Takhat noticed Jack, his eyes narrowed and his expression soured. He looked Jack up and down slowly, before returning his gaze to Kanvar.

Both Sikhs dismounted and Kanvar showed his respect by

bending down and touching Takhat's feet. The Sikhs spoke to each other in their own language, which Kanvar had told Jack was called Punjabi. Although Jack could make out a few of the words, which were similar to Rajthani, he found it impossible to follow the conversation.

Takhat's tone seemed sharp, and he glared at Kanvar with apparent displeasure. But then, after Kanvar had spoken at length, Takhat's face suddenly lit up, his eyes widened and a grin spread across his lips.

He shot a look at Jack and said in broken English, 'You have found the centre of the Great Yantra?'

Jack glanced at Kanvar, who responded with a nod, confirming it was all right to talk.

'Yes,' Jack said. 'I found it.'

'We thank you for your information, Englishman,' Takhat replied. 'You have done well. Now, you will leave us. I must discuss this with my apprentice in private.'

Apprentice? Takhat was Kanvar's guru? Jack looked at Kanvar and was surprised to see the Sikh's eyes welling up with tears again.

Kanvar sniffed and quickly got himself under control. 'Yes, please could you leave us for a moment, Jack? There is much we need to discuss, and we must transfer information between our maps.'

Jack stalled. His horse danced sideways for a few steps before he calmed her. He didn't understand maps or Punjabi. But all the same, why was he being ordered away? 'Why in private?'

'That is what Takhat wishes,' Kanvar said. 'Please, Jack.'

'You must leave us now, Englishman.' Takhat's voice was harsh and his expression had turned serious again.

Jack sucked on his teeth. He didn't like being ordered about, not least by someone he'd never met before. Takhat might be Kanvar's guru, but Jack owed him nothing.

At the same time, Jack very much wanted to get back to the

meeting point. He couldn't give up on the Grail yet. He had to keep trying. For the present, he would have to trust Takhat and Kanvar. They were the only ones who could find the design of the Great Yantra, and there was no point in arguing with them at this stage.

He looked at Takhat and then at Kanvar. 'Very well. I'm going back into the stone circle. Keep a lookout.'

Jack swung himself down from his saddle and handed his reins to Kanvar. He looked Kanvar in the eye for a second. 'You tell me if anything important comes up during your talk.'

Kanvar took the reins. 'Of course.'

Jack strode across the grass towards the circle. The light had brightened further and the sun had almost completely risen.

He didn't understand what was wrong with Kanvar. The Sikh seemed worried about something – upset, even. And also, what were Kanvar and Takhat discussing? And why did it have to be in secret?

But none of that mattered. As soon as he could, he would question Kanvar further. But right now he had to get back into the Great Yantra and try as hard as he could to use the power.

He slipped into the stream again and the whirling sattva buffeted him. He stopped for a second outside the stone circle, then strode in, the powerful sattva blasting him once more.

He shut his eyes for a moment. The sattva made the insides of his ears itch.

What now? Here he was again, touching the Great Yantra – or the Grail, or whatever it was. But nothing was happening.

He sat on the ground in the middle of the circle and crossed his legs. Did he have to accept that he wasn't the new Galahad? That he wouldn't be the one to find the Grail? Or even accept what he'd long suspected, and what Jhala had told him, which was that there was no Grail? The old stories were myths. Fantasies.

The Great Yantra might be real, but it would only be used

through recalling the design and smelting sattva, in the same way as all the yantras. Anything else was nonsense.

And yet he couldn't give up. Not yet. Because that would mean returning to Folly Brook with nothing. Kanvar had said it would still take weeks – months, even – for the Sikhs to discover the Great Yantra's full design. Shropshire would be crushed long before then.

He looked across at Kanvar and Takhat, who were now sitting on the ground, hunched over their maps. Takhat was brandishing a pen and making marks on his chart.

Jack shut his eyes. There was still time for him to try one more time. He took a deep breath and concentrated on the cool air flowing down the back of his throat and into his lungs. He quickly managed to calm his mind and slip into the trance. Slowly, he inched his way closer to the spirit realm. The material world fell away, as if he were soaring above it like a bird.

But still nothing happened. He kept trying for around fifteen minutes. Still nothing.

The problem was, he didn't know what he was supposed to be doing – or even what would happen, if he were successful.

Then he heard shouts.

His heart jolted and he flung his eyes open, instantly sliding out of the trance. Was someone coming? Was Kanvar trying to warn him?

But what he saw was puzzling. Takhat and Kanvar were standing facing each other. Takhat was pointing his finger at Kanvar and barking loudly. Kanvar stood with his head bowed and his hands behind his back. He replied only softly, his voice too quiet for Jack to hear from where he was sitting.

Takhat's bellowing became even more heated.

Was he going to attack Kanvar?

Jack stood and jogged across to the Sikhs. 'What's going on?'

When Kanvar turned to face him, Jack saw the Sikh's eyes were bloodshot and glassy. Takhat scowled at Jack, shouted a few further words at Kanvar, then marched over to his horse and rode away, without looking back even once.

'What the hell was that about?' Jack asked.

Kanvar's eyes brimmed with tears. 'It is not really important.'

'Not important? You don't look happy about it.'

Kanvar stared at his boots. 'I have been discharged from the army, cast out of my order and disowned by Takhat, my guru. If I return to my homeland, I will immediately face a court martial.'

Jack blinked. 'Why?'

Kanvar looked up. His face was long and serious. 'I disobeyed Takhat's orders. I should not have gone to your village and I should not have told you about the Great Yantra. Takhat specifically instructed me not to do these things.'

'Why would he do that?'

'The Great Yantra is a secret. We siddhas are bound to keep the secrets of our orders. Also, Takhat believed I was becoming . . . too close to you rebels. He said to me months ago that my judgement was clouded. I was not to see you again, Jack, and I was not supposed to even go into Shropshire.'

Jack's eyes bored into Takhat's receding figure. He hadn't liked Takhat much when he'd first met him, and he liked him even less now.

He returned his gaze to Kanvar. 'You went against your commander's orders to help me and the rebels?'

Kanvar nodded solemnly.

'You've risked everything?'

'Indeed, that is so.'

'I don't know what to say. I didn't realise.'

'No, it is all right. There is no need for you to say anything. It was my choice and my choice alone. I was quite clear about what I was doing.'

For the first time, Jack believed he had some insight into Kanvar's thoughts. The Sikh had seemed caught up in some internal battle over the past few days. It must have been a painful decision to come to Folly Brook, to tell Jack about the Great Yantra and to bring Jack along to this spot.

Jack scratched the back of his neck. 'Why did you tell the truth to Takhat? Why didn't you make up some story?'

'That would be wrong. I could not lie to my guru. And in any case, he suspected something when he saw you here with me.'

'I see. I still don't understand, though. Why have you done all this? Why help me when you didn't have to?'

'I try to always follow Waheguru's will. Your struggle against the Rajthanans is a just one. Your lands have been taken by a powerful foe and you wish to get them back. The right thing for me to do is to help in whatever way I can. It was a difficult decision, because one should also follow one's commander's orders.'

'You couldn't win either way.'

'Exactly. Whatever I did would be both wrong and right. It was a dilemma.'

'Well, I'm glad you made the right decision in the end.'

'There was only one decision I could make. I hesitated many times. That is why it took me so long to return to your village. But, in the end, after considering it carefully, I realised it was Waheguru's will that I help the English.'

Jack nodded slowly. He knew well enough what it was like to make a difficult decision. When Jhala had ordered him to capture William, four years ago, he'd had to decide whether to do as he was told, or risk Elizabeth being hanged. He'd been faced with an impossible choice.

'What will you do now?' Jack asked. 'Where will you go?'

Kanvar frowned. 'I will come with you, of course. Back to Folly Brook – I assume that's where you're going. I said I would help in the fight against the Rajthanans. I will not abandon you now.'

Jack felt a surge of warmth in his chest. Kanvar might be odd, but he was undoubtedly an ally – and the English needed as many of them as they could get now.

Jack was humbled for a moment. Kanvar had given up every-thing to help the crusade.

Jack put his hand on Kanvar's shoulder. The Sikh jumped slightly, looked at the hand and frowned.

'You're a good man.' Jack patted Kanvar's shoulder firmly. 'I can't thank you enough.' He lowered his hand again. 'All the same, I can't ride back yet. I still can't get the Great Yantra to work. I can't go back empty-handed.'

'I am afraid I think you will have to,' Kanvar replied.

'I must try again. At least once.'

'There is little time. Takhat told me something else. Something you should know.'

Jack frowned. 'What?'

Kanvar's eyes widened. 'Takhat received news from one of our comrades yesterday. The army have attacked Ludlow and appear to be overwhelming the rebels there. It seems they will soon take the city.'

Jack shivered, despite the fact that the sun was warming his skin. 'If the army take Ludlow, they'll be able to march on to Clun Valley.' His voice was hoarse. The early morning light seemed intensely bright now. 'When did the army attack?'

'Takhat said three days ago.'

'Three days? That was the day we left Folly Brook.' He felt dizzy. 'They could be in Clun already.'

Kanvar raised his hand. 'They might not have defeated the rebels in such a short space of time.'

Jack clenched his jaw. 'But they might have. And even if it took them longer, they might still be on the march right now. They could reach Clun at any time.'

'That is so.'

Jack looked over at the stone circle, which was now bathed in sunlight. He'd wanted to try to use the power again, but he had to admit defeat at some point. The longer he delayed leaving, the longer it would take him to get back to Folly Brook. He'd planned to return within four days. Thanks to all the obstacles he and Kanvar had faced, they'd already spent three days just getting to the Great Yantra. How long would it take them to get back now, when war was spreading through Shropshire?

But he would be returning without a weapon he could use to fight the Rajthanans.

No Grail.

No Great Yantra's power.

Damn it.

He nodded at Kanvar. 'You're right. I can't waste any more time. We have to get back to Folly Brook. As quickly as we can.'

15

A flock of crows wheeled in the sky above Clun Valley. Jack halted his horse and stared at the birds. His countrymen believed crows were a portent of evil – of the Devil, even. But he'd learnt long ago from Jhala that this was just a superstition. He no longer believed in witches and omens and the evil eye. But crows were still a sign, a true sign, of at least one thing – death. Wherever there were corpses and carrion, there would be crows.

Kanvar rode up beside him. 'What is it?'

'Not sure.' Jack rubbed his face and looked first to the east and then to the west. He and Kanvar had approached the valley from the north and had come out of the hills a few miles west of the town of Clun. In both directions he saw pillars of smoke spiralling into the overcast sky.

A chill ran down his back. He didn't like the look of this. The smoke could be from burning livestock, but it appeared too thick for that. A pyre would have to be enormous to produce that amount of smoke.

It looked more like burning buildings.

'Let's get down there.' His voice was cracked.

He angled his mare down the incline and into the valley. It was two days since he and Kanvar had set off from the circle of stones. They'd ridden hard across Staffordshire and Shropshire, stopping only to rest the horses and avoid Rajthanan patrols along the border. Jack's eyes burned with tiredness and every muscle in his body ached. But a feverish alertness was overtaking him.

They reached the base of the valley and struck off along the main road to Newcastle. Three columns of smoke rose ahead, and further crows swarmed in the air. Jack spurred into a gallop, his mare's hooves battering the dry ground and sending up a plume of dust in her wake.

His heart thudded hard in his chest. Bile rose in his throat, leaving a sour taste in the back of his mouth.

Fears gnawed like rats at the back of his mind, but he did his best to brush them away.

He mustn't think the worst. He must hold on to hope.

A crowd of people appeared on the lane ahead. Without a moment's hesitation, he sawed at his reins to turn his horse, left the road and charged towards the nearby woods.

Kanvar followed, calling out, 'Did you see who they were?'

Jack shook his head. He hadn't been able to make the figures out clearly, but he didn't want to take any chances.

He raced down a track that wound between the trees. The path curved away from the main road, but then circled back until he was close enough to be able to spy on the crowd of people through the greenery.

He halted his horse and stared. He could see around forty men carrying a mixture of muskets, swords and bows. Some seemed to be standing guard, while others were lounging on the side of the road. Several appeared to be throwing stones at what looked like a tree stump.

Kanvar handed over the spyglass. Jack gazed through it and shivered slightly at what he saw.

The stump was in fact a man buried in the ground up to his waist. Worse, Jack recognised him. He was a peasant from Newcastle – Jack had seen him several times at the Cock-in-the-Hoop Inn. From time to time, the other men threw stones at the trapped man and laughed, as if they were playing a game.

And now Jack realised something else. Several of the stone-throwers wore surcoats bearing the mark of the three boars' heads.

'They're Welsh,' he hissed. 'That's the sign of the Lord of the Marches.'

'Waheguru,' Kanvar whispered.

As Jack watched, a Welshman hurled another stone at the buried Englishman. Jack could see blood on the Englishman's face and hands. The man was struggling to free himself, but the earth held him fast.

Jack felt his face reddening. His hand shook slightly as it held the glass.

For a second, he seriously thought about charging down to the road and trying to fight off the Welsh. But he knew he couldn't do that. There were too many men for him and Kanvar to kill quickly – even with Lightning. And a fight was bound to attract the attention of any other troops in the area.

What was more important right now was getting back to Folly Brook.

'Let's go.' He handed the glass back to Kanvar and spurred his mare into a gallop, fears whirling in his head.

He had to stay calm, had to stay focused.

Black smoke rose directly ahead, above the trees. He was sure it was coming from Newcastle now.

He slowed his horse and called across to Kanvar. 'I don't think it's a good idea to ride straight into town.' He nodded towards a slope to his right. 'We'll take a look from up there.'

He directed his horse up a steep track, rode through a stretch of woodland and eventually came out on a bare summit.

He leapt from the saddle and tethered his horse. 'We'd better go carefully. There might be more Welsh about.'

Kanvar nodded and followed Jack on to the open ground.

They crept ahead, crouching low in the long grass. The smoke swirled up from the far side of the hill, but Jack still couldn't see the town from this angle.

They drew up to a gorse bush on the brow of the hill. The wind changed direction and Jack caught a whiff of soot. The town was directly below them now. He only had to part the branches of the bush and look down in order to see it. But he hesitated. He didn't want to do it.

Didn't want to confirm what he already knew.

He gritted his teeth and forced aside a thorny branch with his arm. Kanvar drew his breath in sharply, while Jack felt giddy for a moment.

The town below was a smouldering ruin. The larger buildings in the centre had been decimated and smoke coiled up from the husks that remained. The inn was nothing but a pile of timbers and the smaller cottages about the perimeter had all been torched, their thatched roofs burnt away and the walls smeared with black soot. All that was left of the refugees' camp was a muddy field.

The crows circled overhead, giving grating squawks.

Kanvar stared through his spyglass for a moment before handing it to Jack. Jack swept the glass across Newcastle and spotted several corpses, all covered in crows. Troops of Welshmen marched through the streets and searched the debris, no doubt looking for loot.

He moved the glass over to the castle, which rose from a field about half a mile from the town. The walls still stood firm and the keep still thrust up from the bailey. But as he scanned the battlements, he saw no sign of any men-at-arms. And there was no sign either of the old Rajthanan guns that normally poked out from the embrasures.

When he moved the glass down, he saw that the portcullis lay in the overgrown ditch that had once been the moat. The gate had been smashed open and lay in pieces just beyond the gatehouse.

He lowered the glass. His skin crawled and he felt the bile stinging the back of his throat again.

'We have to get to Folly Brook,' he said, his voice cracking.

Still crouching, they scrambled back to the horses and rode downhill. Instead of taking the route through Newcastle, Jack struck off along a little-used track that led through the hills and intersected the valley of the Folly brook.

The day was hot. Jack sweated profusely and his mouth prickled with thirst. His mare was growing weary from so many days of hard riding, and she tripped and stumbled at times on the uneven path. But Jack didn't stop to rest or even slow the pace. He kept spurring the mare into a gallop despite the treacherous ground.

His mind was on fire. His head felt hot and full of blood.

After half an hour, the mare clambered up the final slope and then the thin valley snaked away below him. He saw the trees at the base of the incline and the brook snaking into the distance. But his eyes fell instantly upon the village. His village.

And then he found himself jumping from his horse and sinking to his knees.

Tears pricked his eyes.

Folly Brook was burning. Smoke trailed from the thatched roofs and many of the huts had been completely smashed. He could tell all this even from a distance, even without the spyglass that Kanvar was now offering to him.

Folly Brook was gone.

PART THREE

16

The trees flitted past to either side of Jack as his horse thundered down the track. He caught glimpses of branches and greenery, but it all seemed far away – unreal, even. All he could think about was getting to Folly Brook and finding the answers to the questions battering his head.

He heard Kanvar's horse galloping behind him. Kanvar hadn't spoken a single word during the ride downhill – it seemed he'd wisely decided to maintain a respectful silence.

For a moment, an image of Katelin lying dead flashed into Jack's mind. Then he saw the corpses lying in the streets after the Siege of London. And then more bodies scattered across the battlefield outside Ragusa. So many dead people. All piling up in his mind, as if he were being buried beneath them.

His mare reached the bottom of the slope, skidded to the right and galloped down the main road towards the village. The forest and hills were intensely familiar to Jack now. He'd lived here for four years and had come to call this place home. He'd worked the fields spreading out to his left. He'd taken Elizabeth hunting with him in the woods rippling past to his right.

He spotted the ancient stone cross standing on the side of the road and the two old elms with their branches meshing into an arch over his head.

He shivered. In a few seconds he would be in Folly Brook. And then he would know . . .

Would there be Welsh soldiers still in the village? He didn't care at that moment. If he saw any, he would fire lightning at them, kill as many of them as he could. If he ran out of strength or sattva, he would draw his knife and keep on fighting until he was slain . . .

The first huts appeared. The thatched roofs were burnt, soot streaked the walls and the doors were kicked in. The destruction was so recent, the ruins still smouldered and cast traces of smoke into the sky.

He saw his own hut. It had been completely demolished and was now nothing more than a pile of timbers, daub and charred thatching.

Was Saleem lying dead in there? The boy couldn't have survived if he'd been inside when the hut was torched.

But Jack didn't stop. He had to get to Elizabeth's cottage. He couldn't let anything else distract him.

Tears misted his sight. His throat was so tight he could barely swallow or even breathe.

He snarled at his mare, urging her to gallop faster. Kanvar followed immediately behind him. The burnt-out huts reeled past to either side of the village's main street. Several chickens scurried across the road. A mournful dog skulked between the smoking timbers. But otherwise Jack saw no sign of life.

Elizabeth's hut came into view at the end of the road. The roof had been partially destroyed and the walls and door were scorched. But the walls were still largely intact.

Blinking away tears, Jack leapt from his horse. He felt a howl of rage building inside him. The blood roared in his ears.

He took a deep breath and kicked open the charred door. Inside, it was lighter than usual due to the wide holes in the roof. Ash and cinders coated the floor. The smell of soot was strong. He saw overturned pots, smashed chests, several tunics and blankets scattered across the ground. But otherwise the hut was empty. There was no one, living or dead, in there.

Jack took a breath. He realised he hadn't been breathing for some time. He wiped the tears from his eyes and quickly composed himself. Elizabeth wasn't in the cottage. But then where was she? Captured? Taken somewhere else and killed? The possibilities spun wildly in his head.

The door swung open and Kanvar stepped in. 'There are no bodies.'

'What?' Jack said.

'I have seen no bodies. I saw none when we rode into the village. I have just checked two other huts. There seem to be no bodies anywhere.'

Jack's heart quivered. Was this news some cause for hope? Or was he simply clutching at straws?

He drew the knife from his belt. 'We'll check every building. We have to be sure.'

They both slipped outside and split up, Kanvar taking one side of the village and Jack the other. It would have been safer for the two of them to stay together, but Jack was in a rush now and had no interest in being cautious. He had to find his little girl. He had to know what had happened to her.

He gripped the knife tightly as he marched into the destroyed huts. He half expected to come across Welshmen still busy looting. But in each cottage he found only the scattered remains of household objects.

He met Kanvar on the village green.

Kanvar shook his head. 'Nothing.'

Jack flexed his fingers about the knife. 'There's only one place left to check. The House of Sorcery.'

They marched across the green, splashed through the ford and wound their way through the trees. Jack's thoughts were red with blood by the time he and Kanvar reached the glade at the end of the path. The House of Sorcery stood serenely on one side of the clearing. Strangely, there was no damage to it.

Jack strode across the grass, Kanvar loping beside him. He stopped outside the door.

What would he find in there? Elizabeth, Cecily, Godwin and

Saleem all huddled safely inside? Or their dead bodies strewn across the ground?

He took a deep breath. He was about to kick in the door but decided there was no point. Instead, he twisted the ringed handle and nudged the door open. It was dark inside. There was no fire in the hearth and all the window shutters were closed. He smelt the familiar scent of smoke mingling with the sweet perfume of the powerful sattva that rolled through the glade.

He blinked a few times until his eyes adjusted to the light. The banner of the Lightning yantra was still strung up across the wall. The sand trays the students used to practise their yantras still stood stacked in one corner of the room. Everything was as it had been when he'd last been here.

There was no one in there. No one, alive or dead.

Christ. Now he didn't know what to think. He stepped outside and squinted at the forested slopes sweeping up at the edge of the valley. His eyes trailed along the spine of the hills, which tumbled away towards the larger valley of the River Clun. The old stone cross watched him from the nearest summit.

He saw no sign of life anywhere. Were the villagers hiding up in the forest? Had they been captured?

Damn it.

He punched the wall in front of him, putting a deep dent in the daub. His fist stung. But that didn't stop him thumping the wall again.

Where the hell was Elizabeth? What had they done to her?

He'd been a fool. Why had he gone with Kanvar? Why had he believed he could find the Grail? Why had he believed – and this amazed him now – that he would be the one to save England?

Kanvar placed his hand on Jack's shoulder. 'We will keep searching. We will find them.'

Jack was about to reply when he heard horses' hooves clopping on the far side of the brook.

A quiver ran down his spine. 'Someone's coming. Let's take a look.'

They sprinted into the cover of the trees, clambered through the undergrowth and then crouched behind a blackthorn bush on the edge of the brook. Jack stared across the water and over to the village green. He saw no one, but now he could hear voices. People were shouting.

He listened intently and made out two voices. One was a man's and the other was a woman's.

That was strange. A woman might travel with a Welsh army as a follower, but it was unlikely she would stray far from the camp. Why would she come out to a village like Folly Brook?

Then he caught the word the two people were shouting – 'Jack!'

He stood up quickly. The woman's voice wasn't Elizabeth's. But still, these people, whoever they were, knew him. They were looking for him.

'Let's get over there,' he said.

'It could be a trap,' Kanvar replied.

'I'll have to take a chance.'

Jack strode into the brook, splashed across to the far bank and stepped up on to the green. Two figures on horseback appeared from the huts and rode towards him.

His head reeled and he rubbed his eyes several times to make sure he wasn't seeing things.

It was Sonali and Captain Rao.

Sonali wore her usual green sari and red shawl, while Rao was dressed in the uniform of a Rajthanan officer.

Warmth stirred in Jack's chest for a moment. Sonali was alive. And Rao appeared well. Jack hadn't expected to see either of them ever again.

But then a shadow crossed his thoughts. Why were they in Folly Brook? And how had they got here? They couldn't have come on their own – that would have been far too dangerous. They must have arrived with the enemy.

And after all, weren't they the enemy? They were both Rajthanans. Could he even trust them now that there was a war on?

Kanvar crossed the brook and stood beside Jack. He closed his eyes, raised his hand and began muttering a mantra.

He was going to use a power against Rao and Sonali.

'Wait.' Jack shoved Kanvar's arm down.

Kanvar's eyes shot open. 'We must fight—'

'I know them. Let's see what they have to say.'

Kanvar's eyes widened. 'You know them? These Rajthanans?'

'It's a long story.'

There was no time for Jack to explain further, because Rao and Sonali had already arrived. Sonali leapt from her horse, ran across to Jack and threw her arms about him.

'Jack-ji.' Sonali's voice was husky. 'I was so worried about you.'

'I'm all right.' Jack's voice had a hint of coldness to it, and he didn't respond to her embrace beyond patting her lightly on the back. He was pleased to see her. But, at the same time, he didn't know what was going on.

Sonali frowned and stepped back. 'What's wrong?'

Jack was about to reply, but Rao was already bounding across to him, beaming and saying a namaste.

Rao extended his arm. 'Jack, it is such a pleasure to see you again.'

Jack hesitated for a moment.

Rao's smile widened and he waggled his hand. 'Come on. You shake hands. It's your custom, isn't it?'

Jack smiled tightly. Rao's greeting was so enthusiastic, it was hard for him not to take the captain's hand and shake.

Rao put his hands on his hips. 'It's such a relief to see you.' He glanced across at Sonali. 'Isn't it?'

Sonali nodded slowly. There was still a frown on her forehead. She knew something was wrong. She bit her bottom lip and looked across at the ruined village. When she faced Jack again, tears were brimming in her eyes. 'I'm so sorry this has happened. Is everyone . . . safe?'

'Don't know,' Jack said. 'There was no one around when I got here.'

Her frown deepened further. 'You just got here?'

'I've been away for a few days.' He motioned to Kanvar. 'With him.'

Rao stared at Kanvar. 'Are you Rajthanan?'

Kanvar pursed his lips, squared his shoulders and said something in Punjabi.

Rao's eyebrows shot up. He clearly knew enough of the Sikhs' language to understand. 'A Sikh? What are you doing here?'

'He's a friend,' Jack said. 'He's been helping me.'

Rao rubbed his moustache. 'That is unusual. You always manage to surprise me, Jack.'

Jack sighed. 'It'll take a long time to explain, and I don't have a long time. I have to find my daughter.'

'Ah,' Rao said. 'We might be able to help you there.'

Jack eyed Rao closely. 'What do you mean?'

Rao cleared his throat. 'We have some information. Let me explain. Sonali and I have travelled up with the baggage train from Worcestershire.'

Jack felt a tremor of foreboding. 'Worcestershire? You've come up with General Jhala's troops?'

'That's right.'

'The troops are here now?'

'Yes, but they've taken the east end of the valley. The Welsh have moved in from the west.'

Jack tightened his jaw. 'And Jhala? He's here, then? In Clun Valley?'

'No, the general has taken a force to Shrewsbury, including a siege train. The troops were split at Ludlow, you see.'

Jack sucked on his teeth. This all made sense. Jhala had only sent some of his men to Clun, as he must have known the Welsh would advance into Shropshire from the west. The attack was coordinated. It must have been planned weeks, or even months, in advance.

And now, with Clun Valley captured, Jhala was marching on Shrewsbury, the stronghold of the Earl of Shropshire. Once Shrewsbury fell and Vadula's army swept in from the east, that would be the end of the crusade.

It might all be over within days.

But none of this mattered much to Jack at the moment. He had to find Elizabeth and Cecily. Once he'd done that, he would work out what to do next.

'You said you had some information,' he said.

'Ah yes,' Rao replied. 'I heard from the army scouts that many of the people in this area escaped before the Welsh got here. They've fled to the north. In quite large numbers, I'm told.'

Jack hesitated. 'What about this village? Did they all get away?'

Sonali stepped forward. 'I think so. I spoke with one of the scouts. He said he'd been up this valley. I described the village and he said he thought everyone had escaped. Rajiv and I came here to make sure. But I was thinking you would have gone with them.'

Jack felt his throat tighten. Could it be true? Could Elizabeth still be alive?

He blinked away a tear. He had to focus his mind again. Concentrate. He didn't have much time now. Elizabeth and the others might have got away, but that didn't mean the army or the Welsh wouldn't go after them.

'I'll find their tracks.' He spun on his heel and marched across the green. 'If they went north, they'll have gone this way.'

He reached the edge of the green, the others jogging to catch up to him. He crouched down. The grass was a morass of footprints and hoof marks. Numerous people had crossed it over the past few days and he couldn't spot the tracks of any fleeing villagers amongst the markings. On the other hand, the ground to the north was covered in scrub and knots of trees. He saw no sign of any trail there at all.

He stood and faced Kanvar. 'Get the horses. I'm going to have to search around more.'

As Kanvar strode back towards the village, Jack paced along the edge of the green, scouring the ground. There was a storm in his head. Sickness was bubbling in his stomach. He wasn't concentrating properly.

He paused and shut his eyes for a second.

Your mind is a rippling pool. Still it.

He opened his eyes again and crept forward. And then he spotted a set of boot prints just outside the green. He squatted down, parted a clump of nettles and looked more closely. Judging by the moistness of the prints, and how clear they still were in the ground, they couldn't be more than a few hours old.

He stood and scanned the ground ahead of him. His eyes seized upon another set of prints. He trod gingerly across to them – he didn't want to disturb any other tracks that could be nearby. This second set of marks was much smaller than the first and had to have been left by a child. Nearby he saw further footprints, the scalloped indentations left by horses' hooves and the ruts of carts.

As many as a hundred people could have passed this way.

This had to be the trail.

He stood and gazed into the distance, searching the hills. The overcast sky was silver and the light gave everything a mysterious sheen.

Where would the villagers have gone? Did they have a plan? Was Elizabeth with them?

He heard a neigh, looked back and saw Kanvar approaching with the horses, along with Rao and Sonali, who had fetched their own steeds.

Jack motioned to the tracks. 'This is it, I reckon. I have to get after them.'

'Look,' Rao said, 'before you go, there's something very important I need to discuss with you.'

'More important than finding my daughter?' Jack asked.

'No . . . well, in a way, yes. It's important for the future of your people.'

Jack turned to mount his horse. 'All I care about right now is finding Elizabeth.'

'Please.' Sonali grasped Jack's arm. There were fresh tears in her eyes. 'Just listen for a minute.'

Jack searched her face and felt his resolve melting. This was still the same Sonali he'd met in Scotland, the same Sonali he'd come to care about.

He sighed and turned to Rao. 'What is it?'

Rao pressed his lips together firmly. 'The Maharaja of Europe stands poised to grant England independence. Your people will be freed.'

17

Jack felt light-headed for a moment. 'What the hell are you talking about? Is this a joke?'

'I assure you, it is not,' Rao replied. 'Let me explain. Since we parted, I have given the things you said to me much thought. I have investigated Vadula's rule of this country as best as I've been able to. And I have to say, I'm shocked by what I've found out. Shocked and appalled. Vadula has ruled this place like a tyrant.

'Anyway, I became firmly of the view that something must be done about it. As you know, I met Reena Chamar in Andalusia. While I was there, I also made contact with the Raja of Granada. He happens to be a member of my clan and a personal friend of my father—'

'Of your father? I thought your father would have disowned you by now. Because of your lady friend.'

Rao cleared his throat and looked at his boots for a moment. 'I have not yet told my father about Reena. I will – but only when the time is right. At any rate, that is not important at the moment. My point is that I spoke to the Raja and I was very surprised to learn he was sympathetic to my views. It seems many in the European Civil Service are. There is something of a power struggle going on, you see, between the priest and army jatis. The priest jatis are on Vadula's side, while the Raja and others draw support from the army jatis. At any rate, even the Maharaja of Europe has become concerned. With the uprising in al-Saxony looking as though it will spread, the Maharaja wants the English Question resolved quickly. And it looks as though he wants Vadula out.'

'That's all very well,' Jack said. 'But if Vadula goes, we'll just get some other raja sent over here, won't we?'

'Not necessarily. The Maharaja is prepared to grant limited autonomy to England.'

'What does that mean?'

'It means England will be able to rule her own affairs, but would remain a protectorate of the empire. The King of England would still owe allegiance to the Maharaja, but could rule England's internal affairs as he saw fit.'

'Don't listen to this, Jack,' Kanvar said. 'If England is a protectorate, it will hardly be free. It will be like one large native state.'

'That is not true.' Rao's voice was sharp. 'The English will be free to run their own affairs with no interference from the Maharaja. This will be set out in a treaty.'

Jack stared at Rao. 'Right, but we'll still be part of the empire. It's not complete freedom.'

'That is true,' Rao replied. 'But you have to be realistic. This is by far the best deal the English are likely to get. It is only because of the current circumstances in Europe that it is even being offered. If the English don't take up this opportunity, another might not come around.'

Jack pointed his finger at Rao. 'You sound like all the other bloody Rajthanans. This is my country. I don't expect you or anyone else to tell me what to do in it.'

Rao frowned. 'I am only trying to help. I thought you'd be pleased.'

Sonali grasped Jack's arm again. 'Please at least think about it. The war could be over and Vadula could be gone. Think of all the lives that could be spared.'

Jack sighed. Sonali had a point, and perhaps he'd spoken too harshly to Rao. He turned to the captain. 'All right. I'll think about it. But you're talking to the wrong man anyway. I'm not a nobleman or a leader. I'm just a commoner.'

'But you can take a message to your leaders,' Rao said.

Jack ran his fingers through his hair. 'I can try. But first, I have to find my daughter.'

'Of course,' Rao said. 'I will return to Leintwardine. I'm waiting for a message from the Raja of Granada on the link. If all has gone well, the Maharaja should have agreed to the treaty and Vadula should have been ordered to step down.'

'And I will come with you, Jack-ji,' Sonali said softly.

Jack's throat tightened. Sonali looked so forlorn that all he wanted to do at that moment was put his arms around her. But he held back. 'You go with Rao. It's not safe here.'

'I can look after myself,' Sonali said. 'You know that.'

'There's a war on. Even with your powers you'll be in danger.'

Sonali frowned. 'You don't want me to come. Why?'

Jack rubbed the back of his neck. He didn't have time for all this. 'You could end up fighting against your own people. You can't do that.'

'I will defend myself. And you and your family, if I need to.'

Rao cleared his throat. 'Jack's right, you know, Sonali. You should ride back with me and wait for the message. Once we have it, we'll come and find Jack and sue for peace.'

'No.' Sonali's voice wavered. 'Jack-ji, I made a mistake. I never should have left Shropshire. I told myself that, if I found you again, I wouldn't make the same mistake.'

Jack clenched his jaw. He had no time to argue about this.

On impulse, without considering it any further, he said to Sonali, 'All right. You can come. So long as you understand we could all be dead in days. I can't guarantee to protect you.'

Sonali wiped a kohl-stained tear from her cheek and nodded.

'Jack, I strongly advise against this,' Kanvar said. 'We should not—'

'No,' Jack snapped. 'We're going. Now.'

Kanvar's eyes widened and he bowed his head slightly. 'If that is what you wish.'

It wasn't particularly what Jack wished, but there was no point in debating it further. He swung himself up into his saddle, and Kanvar and Sonali did the same.

Rao remained standing on the ground, holding his horse's reins. He managed a smile, but his voice was cracked as he said, 'It has been so very good to see you again, Jack, despite the circumstances. You must talk to your leaders and tell them to surrender immediately. I will come with word as soon as I can.'

'Surrender?' Jack said. 'Doubt I could convince them – even if I wanted to.'

'You must try. You will save so much bloodshed. In days, I should receive word about the treaty. Then I will come to find you.'

'Not sure how easy I'll be to find.'

'I will do it.'

Jack cast his eye across at Sonali and Kanvar. They both nodded back at him to show they were ready to ride.

He stared at Rao again and raised his hand. 'Farewell.'

'Farewell.' Rao turned to take in Sonali and Kanvar as well. 'To all of you. I very much hope you will be safe. Praise be to Lord Shiva.'

Jack gave Rao a firm nod. Then he circled his horse round and set off along the trail, with Kanvar and Sonali riding beside him.

He glanced back once and saw Rao standing next to his charger, still waving. Jack raised his hand a final time, before he turned away and spurred his horse into a gallop.

⸻

Jack stopped his mare at the top of a rise. Kanvar and Sonali drew to a halt beside him. They'd been riding for three hours and now misty drizzle cloaked the landscape, turning the scene murky and dreamlike. Immediately ahead of them, the slope tumbled down to a heath dotted with skeletal trees and withered scrub. Beyond this, perhaps two miles away, rose a lone hill that appeared to be the tallest peak in the area. A dark fortress sprawled across the summit. The building looked ghostly in the rain, as if it were an illusion that would vanish at any moment.

'What is it?' Sonali asked.

'They call it the Fortress of the Djinns,' Jack replied.

Kanvar raised his spyglass. 'Another of the Mad Sultan's constructions?'

'Aye,' Jack said. 'I've never been up this way before. But I've heard of it.'

Everyone in Clun knew the stories about the fortress. Supposedly it was haunted by djinns and the spirits of the dead Mohammedans who'd once lived there.

Jack accepted the glass when Kanvar handed it across to him. He wiped the specks of rain from the lens and gazed up at the building. Through the drizzle, he glimpsed walls, bastions, minarets and Moorish arches. The stonework had crumbled and in some places the outer wall had collapsed completely. The weathered battlements were like a row of rotting teeth.

He swept the glass across the ruin and spied the specks of figures moving along the ramparts. What looked like guns protruded from several embrasures. Through holes in the masonry, he spotted the ruby glints of fires within.

He lowered the glass. 'There are people up there.'

'Who?' Kanvar asked. 'The villagers? The rebels?'

'Could be.'

Jack looked down. The ground ahead of him had been pummelled and slashed by booted feet, horses' hooves and cartwheels. The tracks he'd been following since leaving Folly Brook had swelled in number, and now he guessed more than five hundred people could have passed this way. The trail coiled down a series of ridges and then rolled away across the heath, heading in the direction of the fortress.

'Let's get over to that hill and take a look,' Jack said.

They rode down the incline and set off across the flat ground. Jack blinked in the feathery rain. Was Elizabeth up there in the fortress? Was she safe? He'd seen no sign of the Welsh or any army forces during the journey here. If the villagers had left early enough, there was no reason why they couldn't have made it this far.

He shut his eyes for a second and whispered a Hail Mary.

He called a halt when they reached a copse near the base of the hill. From this angle he could see why the Mad Sultan had built his fortress here. The hillsides were steep and, in places, rocky and virtually impassable. The villagers' trail climbed the gentlest slope, the only route that horses or carts had any chance of travelling up.

Jack asked Kanvar for the spyglass and again searched the fortress. He was close enough now to see the gatehouse clearly. No gates had survived, but the towers remained solid. The giant outer wall grinned with guns.

Faces watched him from over the parapet. European faces.

'Looks like they're crusaders.' He handed the glass back to Kanvar. 'I'm going up. Alone.'

'I'll come with you,' Kanvar said quickly.

'And me,' Sonali said.

'No,' Jack replied. 'You two are Indian. The people up there might shoot you before I have a chance to explain. Wait for me here.'

Sonali and Kanvar both opened their mouths to protest, but Jack spurred his horse away towards the hill. He knew there was no other option. And as neither Sonali nor Kanvar followed him, it seemed they accepted his decision.

He reached the slope and zigzagged up. Hundreds of people and animals had climbed the scarp before him, and the ground had been reduced to churned mud. The mare skidded and almost fell over several times, but the animal battled on and reached the top of the initial incline. Ahead, the ground levelled off to a plateau. This swept across to a further slope which, in turn, led up to the fortress.

Jack rode across to the base of the second slope and squinted up through the rain. Scores of figures now watched him from the ramparts and the arched entryway. About twenty yards to the left of the gatehouse, part of the wall had crumbled. Figures also stood there, staring down from the breach. Several of them wore surcoats bearing the cross of St George.

Jack waved his arm. 'Greetings! I'm a crusader! I'm on your side!'

None of the figures responded.

The second slope was too steep to easily ride up, so he tethered the mare and plodded uphill. He slipped in the mud a few times and had to hold out his arms to steady himself.

When he was halfway up, a voice shouted, 'Halt!'

He paused and raised his head. The sour face of Constable Henry Ward glared down from the gateway. Henry wore his usual black cloak and the surcoat bearing the St George cross. But his clothes were streaked with dirt and his hair was wild and awry. There was a mad glint in his eyes.

'Get out of here, traitor, before I shoot you,' Henry said.

'What?' Jack opened his arms. 'It's me. Jack Casey.'

'I know who you are, and you're not wanted here. You're lucky I'm sparing you.'

'What are you talking about? I'm a crusader. You know that.'

Henry narrowed his eyes and pointed down the hill. 'Is that why you brought those Rajthanan spies with you?'

'They're not spies. They're friends. They're here to help.'

Henry snorted and looked at the figures congregating behind him. 'He says he's friends with the Rajthanans but he's not a traitor. How can anyone believe the lies that spout from this man's foul mouth?'

Jack's hands tensed. Henry was an idiot, and Jack would gladly have left at that moment. But he had to find Elizabeth. Henry wasn't going to stop him doing that.

Jack thought quickly. 'Let me speak to Lord Fitzalan.'

Henry's face twisted and reddened. 'Lord Fitzalan? He is dead.

He is dead, because you would not look for the Grail – the one thing that could save us. He died of the fever. Just as our whole land is dying. And you,' Henry drew his pistol and pointed it in the air, 'you stood by and did nothing.'

'Wait, Constable Ward,' a voice called out from the parapet nearby.

Jack looked along the wall and saw Mark, one of his apprentices, leaning over the battlements. Jack's face split into a grin. If Mark was here, that surely meant Elizabeth was here as well.

'We can trust him,' Mark called down to Henry. 'Everyone from our village will vouch for him. They'll vouch for those Indians down there too.'

'Silence!' Henry's beard bristled and he tightened his grip on the pistol. 'I am in command here, and I say this man must go.' He turned to face Jack again. 'That's right. I'm in charge now. Lord Fitzalan's gone. Sir Alfred died of his wounds. The Earl of Shropshire made it here. But he has appointed me leader of this fortress.'

'Wait there a moment, Master Casey,' Mark called down to Jack.

Mark disappeared from the ramparts and then reappeared moments later in the gateway.

Henry glared at Mark. 'You leaving too, are you?'

Mark stared back for a second but said nothing. Instead, he plunged down the slope, slipping in mud. He was out of breath by the time he reached Jack. His hair was damp from the rain and his skin was speckled with dirt. But otherwise he looked well.

Jack gave a tight smile. 'It's good to see you. Thank God you're safe.'

Mark's face remained drawn. 'We made it here, Master Casey. Most of us from the village. But we're still waiting on Elizabeth.'

'What?' Jack shivered. The light seemed to darken slightly. 'Where is she? What happened?'

'She was with us up to the last five miles. But then we got word the lepers in a colony near here were stranded. Most of them were too ill to travel. She went with a cart to get them and bring them here.'

Jack gritted his teeth. It would be typical of Elizabeth to put herself in danger to help others. But why couldn't she have sent someone else? Why did it have to be her?

'She went on her own?'

'No, sir. Saleem and Godwin went too.'

'And Cecily?'

'She's here. Safe and sound.'

'Good.' Jack took a deep breath and scanned the surroundings. 'Are there any Welsh soldiers around?'

'We've seen none so far. But we've had word they're on the way. Could be here any time.'

'And Alfred's dead?'

Mark looked down. 'I believe so, sir.'

Jack crossed himself. 'But the Earl of Shropshire is here?'

'Yes. Arrived from Shrewsbury just an hour ago.'

Jack squinted up at the fortress. 'This the best place around here to make a stand, you reckon?'

Mark wiped his forehead with his sleeve. 'I wouldn't know about that, sir. Never been a soldier. Constable Ward sent word to us at Folly Brook that everyone was to retreat here. We just followed everyone else.'

Jack stared at the outer wall of the fortress. Aside from the few places where the stonework had collapsed, it appeared sturdy enough. He gazed out at the open heath and the low hills massing a little under a mile away to the east. He could see nowhere better in the area to mount a defence.

There was no point in running further north. The army would pursue the rebels wherever they went. The only other option would be to split up, hide and eventually dissolve into the countryside. But that was fraught with risk. The rebels could easily be hunted down and killed before they got far enough away from Shropshire.

The crusade would have to make its stand here. For better or worse.

'Where's this leper colony?' Jack asked.

'I was told it was over to the south-east.' Mark pointed towards a series of ridges. 'Over that saddle.'

Jack stared hard through the drizzle and spied the saddle nestling between two slopes. 'Right, then. I'll go and find Elizabeth and the others, and bring them back here.'

Mark drew himself up taller. 'I'll come with you.'

'No. You stay here.'

Mark opened his mouth to object, but Jack raised his hand to silence him. 'I need you to look after the rest of the village. In case something happens to me.'

Mark took a deep breath. 'Very well, Master.'

Jack put his hand on Mark's shoulder for a moment. 'Keep an eye on Cecily.'

'I will, sir.'

Jack glanced back at the fortress. Henry, who still stood scowling in the gateway, grimaced and spat at the ground when he noticed Jack looking at him.

Jack gave Mark a final nod, then skidded back down the slope, a blizzard of thoughts whirling in his head. Was Elizabeth safe? Would he find her before the Welsh arrived?

His heart was beating wildly by the time he reached the bottom of the scarp. He unhitched his horse, rode across the plateau and picked his way down the slope beyond. At the bottom of the incline, he spurred the mare into a gallop and charged over to where Kanvar and Sonali still waited beneath the trees.

He quickly explained the situation to the two Indians, and both of them insisted they would accompany him to find Elizabeth.

'No.' He shook his head. 'You need to leave. Now. The rebels up there aren't going to let you into the fortress. If the Welsh come here, you could find yourselves in trouble.'

'You'll have to explain to the rebels who we are,' Sonali said.

'I doubt that'll make much difference. The commander up there is an enemy of mine. He doesn't even want to let *me* in. If you leave now, you'll be long gone before there's any fighting.'

'We can talk about this later,' Sonali said. 'We have to find Elizabeth, then worry about what to do next.'

'I said I would help you,' Kanvar said. 'I will not run away now.'

Jack stalled for a second, his horse stepping sideways and tossing her head. He couldn't waste any more time arguing with Sonali and Kanvar. They both seemed determined to come with him – and, in truth, he was pleased for their help.

'All right,' he said. 'Let's go.'

They drove their horses hard across the plains, heading towards the saddle between the hills. The drizzle continued to drape the countryside. Jack repeatedly cast his eye over the surroundings, searching the groves and hillocks for attackers.

At one point, he noticed Sonali looking at him.

'Elizabeth will be safe,' Sonali said. 'I'm sure of it.'

Jack managed a half-smile in response. It was good of Sonali to ride with him now. Very good, given the way Elizabeth had treated her.

They neared the edge of the heath. When Jack looked up, he saw figures appearing over the top of the saddle. He stared hard at the blurred shapes and made out twenty or so people gathered about a mule cart. They were moving quickly and were already slipping and sliding down the slope towards the plains.

Jack reined in his horse.

'Spyglass,' he shouted to Kanvar.

Kanvar handed over the glass and Jack swept it across the hillside until he found the figures. They were Europeans – peasants, judging by their clothes. Several were running alongside the cart, while the rest sat huddled and slumped in the back of the vehicle. The group included men and women of various ages – he spotted a tall man in a woollen hat, and a woman in dark robes who limped as she ran. And then he spied a figure in a white tunic, with pale hose and a skullcap. The man had a thin ginger beard that was unmistakeable.

Saleem.

Jack's face split into a grin. He searched further and saw that Godwin was driving the mule cart. And then he made out Elizabeth sprinting down the incline, with the musket he'd given her still slung across her back.

There was a stone in his throat. Thank Christ Elizabeth was safe.

'Jack,' Kanvar said in a thick voice.

'What?' Jack asked, without lowering the glass. He couldn't take his eyes off Elizabeth.

'Jack, you should look at this.' Kanvar's voice was more insistent now.

Jack lowered the glass. Kanvar was pointing to the top of the incline, his face drawn.

Jack peered up the scarp again, and a chill crossed his skin.

He saw a swarm of men running over the saddle. There were hundreds of them, and more were appearing all the time. They poured down the slope, heading towards Elizabeth and the others.

Jack shoved the glass to his eye.

The men were a motley collection of soldiers bearing a mixture of swords, muskets and bows. They wore ragged peasant clothing, but most had three boars' heads emblazoned across their chests.

They were the army of the Lord of the Marches.

Jack's heart shot into his throat.

Elizabeth and the others were about halfway down the hill. But the Welsh were moving far more quickly.

In a few minutes, they would reach Elizabeth's group.

Jack's daughter was about to be captured or killed.

18

———⋗◆⋖———

'Elizabeth's up there.' Jack tried to still the shake in his voice. 'We have to do something.'

Kanvar stared uphill. 'They are out of range of my powers. We must get closer.'

'We only have a few minutes,' Jack said.

But Kanvar didn't wait to reply and instead spurred his horse into a gallop. Jack and Sonali set off after him. The three of them charged across the open ground and over to the base of the hill. Elizabeth's party was still scrambling down the scarp. Behind them, the Welsh forces were a dark tide spilling down from the saddle. Jack could make out the guttural cries of the men and the wailing of several horns.

Kanvar zigzagged up on his charger, with Jack and Sonali following closely behind. The horses squealed and whinnied, their hooves sliding in the mud.

Jack peered up through the drizzle. He shivered. The first of the Welshmen were only around a hundred yards from Elizabeth's group now.

Kanvar suddenly drew his horse to a halt. He closed his eyes, a look of intense concentration on his face. He seemed to grow brighter and sharper, as if he were coming into focus through a spyglass.

Good. Kanvar must be close enough now to use his powers. But Jack wasn't going to wait around to watch. He was continuing up the slope until the Welsh were within range of his lightning.

'You wait here,' he shouted to Sonali.

Sonali tightened her jaw and shook her head.

Jack was about to argue with her, but then realised that was pointless.

The two of them urged their horses up the incline. Jack's mare skidded several times and almost slipped over at one point.

He could make out Elizabeth and Saleem ahead of him now. They were sprinting as fast as they could, but the Welsh were less than a minute behind them. The mule was stumbling and the cart was bouncing and swaying, tossing the people crowded on the back up and down.

Jack wasn't close enough to use Lightning yet. He wasn't going to reach Elizabeth in time.

Sweat streamed down his face. He screamed at the mare to move faster.

The Welsh were only fifty yards away from Elizabeth now. There was nothing he could do to save his daughter.

Then a gust of sattva-tinted wind brushed the back of his head. He heard a pop, then a shrill whistle. Looking up, he saw a speck of golden fire arc overhead, sizzling through the rain. It flew past Elizabeth's party and slapped into the ground amidst the first rows of Welshmen. There was a sound like a thunderclap and then a deafening rumble shivered through the ground. A bright explosion punched the hillside, kicking up a cloud of soot and earth. Welshmen screamed as they were flung in all directions.

Jack's horse reared up and kicked the air. He thought he was going to slip off for a moment, but then managed to steady the animal. At the same time, a second speck of fire curved past above him and thumped into the earth in the middle of the Welsh. A second blast of red and yellow flame jetted into the sky.

Elizabeth and the others slowed their pace for a moment as they looked back, but they soon pressed on. The Welsh held back in obvious confusion. Many lay motionless on the ground, or writhed in agony. Their cries and screams floated down on the wind.

Jack wiped the sweat from his eyes. Thank Christ Kanvar had managed to use his powers. That had granted them a moment's reprieve, but it wouldn't last long.

He glanced across at Sonali. Her eyes flashed and she looked just as determined to save Elizabeth as before.

The two of them rode on up the scarp. Now Jack could see Elizabeth clearly, and she must have recognised him as well. She waved her arm and ran even faster, stumbling over the uneven terrain.

He leapt to the ground and she hurtled into his arms.

'Father,' she gasped. 'I thought we'd lost you.'

He squeezed her tight. 'Don't you worry. I wouldn't leave you.'

She stepped back and glanced up at Sonali, who still sat in her saddle. Elizabeth's features went stony and she narrowed her eyes, but she didn't say anything.

And now the rest of the party was arriving. Saleem grinned and hugged Jack. Godwin, who sat driving the cart, half smiled and bowed his head in Jack's direction. Behind Godwin slumped ten figures in torn tunics and robes. A further ten people limped along beside the cart. Jack couldn't help wincing at the sight of them. Most of their faces were disfigured by blisters and boils, and one woman's features were so swollen Jack could barely make out her lips and nose. Many of the lepers had filthy rags wrapped about their hands and several had fingers missing. They still wore castanets on their wrists, although they hardly needed to warn anyone of their approach at the moment.

Jack had no chance to say anything further, because he now heard a familiar hissing sound. He looked up just in time to see a dark swarm of arrows plummeting from the sky.

'Move!' He slapped the mule's rump. 'Now!'

The group lurched forward as the missiles whistled about them, thick as rain. Arrows skewered the ground, skipped off rocks and slithered through the grass. One of the lepers gasped and fell off the back of the cart, an arrow in his face.

'Keep moving!' Jack bellowed.

He grasped Elizabeth and ordered her up on to his horse. She sat behind him, clinging to his waist, as he circled the mare about and charged downhill.

Saleem climbed up behind Sonali, who then urged her own horse down the scarp.

Another wave of arrows fell about them. Missiles whispered in Jack's ears and hammered the ground ahead of him. The shafts impaled the earth or danced about like hail.

He saw Kanvar further down the slope. The Sikh was still sitting astride his horse, his eyes closed. He held up one hand, bunched it into a fist, then opened it again. A dot of flame burst from his hand, zipped like a fly into the air, and arced away towards the Welsh. A boom shuddered through the earth shortly afterwards.

The arrows stopped falling, but then Jack heard a dense crackling behind him. He knew instantly what it was.

Muskets.

In a split second, the bullets were whining all about him. He felt one pluck his sleeve. Others slashed the cart's sideboard. One of the running lepers cried out and collapsed. The mule screamed. For a second, Jack thought it had been hit, although it appeared unharmed.

Christ. The Welsh weren't giving up.

Kanvar raised his palm and muttered the mantra again. Another spot of fire shot from his hand and shrieked overhead. There was a further deep rumble.

And then the muskets stopped.

Jack looked over his shoulder and saw, through the curtains of rain, that the Welsh had lowered their weapons and fallen back. Many of them lay squirming on the ground. Several large craters had been gouged into the hillside by the explosions.

Jack drew up beside Kanvar. The Sikh's forehead was bursting with perspiration and his face was hollow.

'You all right?' Jack asked.

Kanvar swallowed and nodded. 'I am just drained.'

Jack cast his eye over the ragged group of lepers, and said to them, 'Right. We have to get to that fortress on the hill over there. Run as fast as you can. The Welsh could be back at any time.'

Godwin cracked a switch across the mule's back and the cart rattled forward. The group managed to weave its way down the remainder of the slope and struck off across the heath. Progress was slow. The lepers were weak and exhausted, and many were limping. Jack would have ordered them all up on to the cart, but the vehicle was already overloaded and the mule was struggling.

Jack kept glancing back, thinking he would see the Welsh pursuing them. But he saw no one.

The ancient fortress loomed ahead. The party was now just a hundred yards from the base of the hill.

They were going to make it.

Then a single war horn wailed across the open ground. This was followed by a second, then a third. Jack spotted figures swarming over the saddle again and pouring down the slope. From amongst them rose a standard that snapped in the wind. He couldn't make it out clearly from this distance, but the black on white of the device was unmistakeable – it belonged to the Lord of the Marches.

There were hundreds of men. Perhaps thousands. The previous force must have been a mere advance party.

He shouted to urge the lepers on.

Finally, the party reached the hill. He led the way up the slope, Elizabeth still clinging on behind him. Kanvar and Sonali's horses bounded up, but the mule plodded slowly, skidding in the mud and straining to haul the heavy load.

The roars of the Welsh sailed across the plains. Jack saw that the mass of men had already reached the heath and were sprinting across the open ground, like a wave rushing in across the shore.

The mule was moving too slowly. The cart was only halfway to the top of the first slope and there was still the second, steeper incline to go.

The Welsh were going to catch them.

'All of you who can walk, get out!' Jack bellowed at the lepers in the cart.

A couple of the lepers jumped to the ground but the rest stared at Jack in confusion.

'Get down and run!' Jack waved his arm at them.

Finally, they seemed to understand. All of them, except one old man who appeared too weak to even stand, leapt off the cart and clambered uphill. Several of them were blind and had to be guided by the others. Some were so ill they could only hobble, but they were still moving faster than the mule.

Jack reached the top of the scarp, where Kanvar, Sonali and Saleem were already waiting for him. He looked back down and saw the cart and most of the lepers were nearing the summit.

But now the first of the Welsh had reached the edge of the plain and were swilling about the bottom of the hill. They began swarming up the slope.

The mule cart rattled over the top of the incline and the party pressed on across the plateau. The fortress rose ahead. They only had to make it up the second slope, and then they would be safely within the walls.

Jack spotted hundreds of figures along the battlements. They appeared to be waving and cheering him and his small band on.

But he could also hear the horns and the shouts of the Welsh horde. He glanced over his shoulder and his skin crawled when he saw figures surging over the top of the first incline. He could make out their grim faces, wild hair and surcoats emblazoned with the boars' heads. Some brandished swords, others held muskets, although none as yet were preparing to fire.

Jack's party was less than halfway to the fortress. The Welsh would reach them in minutes. There was no hope . . .

Then Jack heard a loud clap. There was an orange flash at the top of the fortress, and smoke jetted out of an embrasure in

the outer wall. A round shot screamed past overhead. Further bursts flickered along the ramparts and more balls shrieked through the air.

Jack turned his horse sideways and saw the shots streak through the drizzle, smack into the earth and bounce into the Welshmen, spraying steam and water from the wet ground. Balls knocked off heads, cut bodies in half, bowled over whole columns of men. Clouds of blood spurted into the air. Stray shots bounded over the edge of the plateau and plunged down towards the plains.

Jack whispered a Hail Mary. The crusaders had decided to help him after all.

Several of the lepers slowed their pace and stood gaping at the carnage.

Jack waved his arm at them. 'Keep moving!'

The gunfire might be slowing the Welsh but it hadn't stopped them completely.

The lepers reached the final slope and began scrambling up to the gate. Jack and Elizabeth both leapt from the mare and guided her up by the reins. Godwin abandoned the cart and helped a group of lepers haul the sick man up the incline, simply dragging him through the mud as if he were already dead.

The guns roared, kicked and belched smoke. Balls howled away from the wall. The rebels began firing shells topped with sparking fuses. When Jack snatched a look behind him, he saw the bombs slapping the ground and blasting up plumes of fire. Bodies were smacked apart and limbs sent cartwheeling through the air.

The first lepers reached the gatehouse. Henry was no longer standing in the entrance, but scores of crusaders were waiting to greet the new arrivals. Several of the men recoiled when they saw the lepers' disfigured faces, but Godwin yelled at them to help.

Jack heard shouts behind him. His heart jolted when he saw that bands of Welshmen had already reached the bottom of the second slope and were beginning to scrabble up.

There seemed to be no stopping the Welsh.

Still dragging the horse, Jack raced up with Elizabeth and ran into the fortress. Just as he made it into the gatehouse, he heard whistles slice the air about him. One of the crusaders nearby collapsed to the ground with an arrow in his neck.

Jack grasped Elizabeth and dragged her to the left, away from the gateway and behind the wall. Arrows whined through the entrance, skipping across the flagstones and splintering on masonry.

Jack crossed himself. That had been close. At least two crusaders had been hit and lay writhing on the ground.

Panting heavily, but catching his breath, he turned to Elizabeth. Her eyes were wide and shining, and dirt speckled her face. But when she saw him looking at her, a smile rolled across her lips.

He embraced her, held her close.

Thank God his little girl was alive.

He let go of her again and glanced around. Kanvar, Sonali, Saleem and Godwin were standing nearby. They were all unharmed.

He was about to speak to them, when he heard a shriek behind him. He whirled round in time to see a Welshman charging through one of the gaps where the wall had crumbled. A crusader jabbed the Welshman with a knife-musket, and the man vomited blood before tumbling back out of the breach.

But now further Welshmen were hurling themselves at the hole. And others began attacking the gate. Crusaders stood beneath the gatehouse, fighting off the assailants and then firing their muskets, the weapons popping and coughing smoke.

Jack motioned to the musket still hanging across Elizabeth's back. 'That loaded?'

She nodded.

'Give it to me.'

She slung the weapon from her shoulder and handed it over to him.

He paused for a moment, gripped her arm. 'Wait here.'

He glanced at both the breach and the gateway. The breach looked less well defended, so he ran across to this. Crusaders carrying muskets were already taking up positions behind the chunks of fallen stonework.

He slipped behind a slab of masonry that was just taller than him. He looked round the side, but snatched himself back as an arrow whispered straight at him. He felt the wind of the missile's passing on his cheek. He peered round the side again and saw a wave of Welshmen charging at the breach. He raised his musket, stared along the sights and pulled the trigger. The weapon cracked, the butt kicked into his shoulder and a puff of sulphurous smoke blotted out the view for a second.

He didn't wait for the smoke to clear. There was no time to check whether he'd hit anyone. Instead, he grasped a cartridge from his pouch, bit it open and began reloading.

The other crusaders were also firing now, stepping out from their hiding places and blasting at the oncoming Welsh.

Jack raised his musket again and pulled the trigger. The men around him continued to fire as well. A few stray bullets and arrows flew up through the breach. But for the most part, the Welsh seemed determined to run at the walls rather than return fire.

Jack reloaded and fired. Reloaded and fired. He'd practised this so many times during drills in the army that he did it without thinking. His mind was empty. Still. He was certain he could have loaded a musket in his sleep.

Musket smoke welled about the breach, and soon Jack couldn't see more than five feet in front of him. A few Welsh attackers made it as far as the wall, materialising like phantoms from the murk, but the crusaders managed to batter or stab all those who got close.

Suddenly the guns on the wall stopped. The muskets fell silent. The smoke in front of Jack frayed and tore apart, and then he could see the marauders were retreating. Many Welsh lay dead or dying on the slope and the rest were skidding away. Several horns blasted and the mass of men began to withdraw from the hill.

A man near Jack raised his fist and cheered. Almost instantly, the others around the breach did the same. The sound flickered along the wall, and soon hundreds of people were cheering, whooping and whistling.

Jack muttered a Hail Mary, then slipped back along the wall. He found Elizabeth and the others all safe and waiting beside the horses. Godwin had drawn his longsword, but didn't seem to have put it to any use.

Then the cheers subsided and Jack heard the slow crunch of booted footsteps behind him. Everyone nearby went silent. It was now so quiet that Jack could hear the wind whining through the broken stonework and the faint moans of the Welshmen dying on the hillside.

Even before he turned, he knew who it was.

Constable Henry Ward was pacing slowly down a set of stairs from the battlements. His face was twisted, his brow dark and his black cloak whipped about him. The rotary pistol in his belt gleamed softly in the grey light.

Everyone in the vicinity stood watching. No one moved or spoke.

Henry halted on the last step and glared down at Jack. 'I told you to leave.'

19

Jack wiped the sweat from his forehead with his sleeve and adjusted the musket on his shoulder. 'I've come here to defend our people, not fight with you. We need to work together. We should leave anything else in the past.'

Henry narrowed his eyes. 'That would be convenient for you, wouldn't it? Leave it all in the past.' He pointed his finger at Jack. 'You want us to forget how you succoured witches? How you gave aid to the heathens?'

People were beginning to gather to watch the unfolding scene. Several muttered approval at Henry's words. One man, to Jack's right, slung his musket from his shoulder and held it at his side, as if he might need it in a hurry.

'I have never given aid to the enemy,' Jack said. 'I have always served the crusade. You know that well enough.'

Henry scowled. 'Served the crusade? You refused to go in search of the Grail. The one thing that could have saved us, that could have saved Lord Fitzalan.'

'I did look for the Grail. Eventually. I've just come back from the search.'

'Is that so? You refused before. Now you say you went. So . . . where is it, then?'

Jack paused. How was he going to explain this? 'I'm not certain that we found it. If we did, I don't understand how to use it.'

'You speak in riddles.' Henry waved his hand theatrically towards the crowd. 'Are we just supposed to take your word for all this?'

'No. The Sikh came with me.' Jack motioned to Kanvar.

Kanvar's eyes widened as the gazes of the gathered people fell upon him.

Henry clapped his hands slowly. 'An Indian is your witness. You expect us to trust the word of one of the enemy.' He pointed his finger at Jack. 'You damn yourself from your own mouth, Jack Casey. You have consorted with the enemy for many months – years, no doubt. You've always been their servant.' His face reddened and his eyes blazed. 'I should shoot you and your heathen friends on the spot.'

'Wait, sir.' Mark pushed his way to the front of the throng. 'Master Casey is a loyal crusader.' He looked at the faces of the men and women around him. 'I've seen with my own eyes all he's done for the crusade. He's taught me and the other lads how to fight the heathens. Using their own powers against them.'

Many of the apprentices from the House of Sorcery emerged from the crowd and stepped forward to stand beside Mark.

'I can vouch for him,' Mark continued. 'And anyone from Folly Brook village will say the same.'

'That's right,' someone called out.

Jack looked over the heads of the first few rows of people and spotted James, the tenant farmer. Beside him stood several more apprentices, who also shouted out their support for Jack.

Henry scowled at the gathering. 'Casey has you all bewitched. You're fools if you can't see it.'

'We can't send them out there now, sir.' Mark motioned towards the gate. 'The Welsh will slaughter them.'

Henry's face contorted. His eyes bulged and he took in a deep breath, as if he were about to bellow.

But then a man up on the battlements shouted, 'Look over there!' He pointed out at the plains. 'There're more of them coming.'

Henry's chest deflated. He spun round and charged back up to the parapet. All along the ramparts men began to talk and gesture towards the enemy. Jack shuffled forward with the rest of the crowd to gaze through the hole in the wall.

Drapes of rain swept across the landscape. The light greens of the countryside were darkened to deep jade. The Welsh had retreated to about a mile and a half away, out of range of the guns. Further figures were spilling over the distant hills and swirling down towards the plains. Jack stared hard through the drizzle. There were hundreds, perhaps thousands, of Welshmen arriving.

And now they were spreading out across the open ground. Keeping out of range, they marched to the left and right, bearing their standards, which included the red banner of war to the death.

Jack found himself gripping the strap of the musket tightly.

The Welsh were surrounding the hill. They were laying siege to the fortress.

※

Henry didn't say that Jack, Sonali and Kanvar could stay. But neither did he return to speak about it further. So, Jack and the others simply remained in the fortress.

The lepers were assigned to an uninhabited section of the fortress, while Mark led Jack and the other new arrivals to the place where the remaining members of Folly Brook had made camp. James and the lads from the House of Sorcery walked alongside Jack, eager for news about where he'd been and why it had taken him so long to return.

Jack found himself being drawn into a labyrinth of crumbling facades, arches, passages and halls. The stonework was smothered by vines, but traces of carved arabesque designs peeked out through the foliage. He walked across chambers and galleries where the paving stones had long ago sunk beneath the earth and the roofs had melted, leaving the interiors exposed to the sky. He crossed open spaces that must once have been courtyards or formal gardens, the ponds, fountains and flower beds all now overgrown with grass. Cracked domes, shattered gazebos and rotting towers surrounded him. Columns stood alone, attached to nothing. Huge arched windows looked out into empty space.

The drizzle was easing but still cast a trembling veil over the ruined buildings.

A whole city of people seemed to have fled into the fortress. They hunched over campfires, clambered in and out of tattered pavilions, and sheltered from the rain beneath those roofs that were still relatively intact. Numerous children ran, shrieking with delight, through the tunnels and hallways – they had no idea there was a war on. To them, it was all an adventure, a game.

People's faces dropped when they saw Kanvar and Sonali, and many tripped over in their haste to get out of the way.

Mark explained that more and more refugees had poured into the fortress over the course of the day. He'd heard there were now two thousand people sheltering within the walls – a large number, but one that the vast fortress was still able to accommodate. Many people from Clun Valley, including some from Folly Brook, had chosen not to retreat here. A few had decided to stay in Clun. Some had decided to flee to their relatives' homes in other parts of Shropshire. Others had said they would try to escape to Wales or other regions in England. Jack could hardly blame them for trying, although he wondered how far they would get.

Finally, after meandering for about fifteen minutes, Jack's party arrived at the Folly Brook camp. The villagers had found a spot in and around what might have been a palatial residence long ago, but which was now a jumble of collapsed masonry ensnared by ivy. Five cooking fires stood near what appeared to be the building's main entrance. And about the flames were arrayed the inhabitants of Folly Brook.

When they saw Jack and the others, the villagers leapt to their feet, cheered, clapped and rushed across the grass. Jack greeted each person in turn and Mark lined up the apprentices for him to inspect. Jack counted off the lads and found that two were missing. One of them was Alban, the last to master Lightning.

Mark coughed and looked at the ground. 'Alban and David didn't want to stay here. Said they had to protect their home villages.'

Jack nodded. The two lads had made an understandable decision, but that meant there were now only ten apprentices who could use the Lightning yantra. Still, at least Jack had the power himself now. And they had Sonali and the formidable Kanvar on their side as well.

Jack heard crying and wailing behind him and instantly knew who it was. He turned and saw old Mary, the village wise woman, emerging from the entryway with Cecily in her arms.

Jack grinned, crossed himself and took the baby from Mary. Cecily looked up at him and smiled. He gazed at her perfect features, tiny fingers, impossibly smooth skin. She was alive and well. He silently thanked God. Somehow, it seemed there was still hope while the child was alive.

Without thinking, caught up in the moment, he held Cecily above his head and turned slowly in a circle, displaying the child to the villagers congregating around him.

'This is what we're fighting for,' he said. 'The future. A better future.'

'I thought you were gone.' Elizabeth brushed a lock of hair from her face. 'I thought I wouldn't see you again.'

Jack put his arm around her shoulder for a second. The two of them were sitting on a stone slab to the side of the Folly Brook encampment. Cecily lay gurgling in Elizabeth's arms.

'I'm sorry I left,' Jack said. 'I thought I might find the Grail. I was wrong.'

'I understand. You had to try.'

'Just remember, though, no matter where I go, I'll always come back for you.'

Elizabeth smiled slightly. 'I remember how you used to be gone for so long when you were in the army.'

Jack nodded. Back then, he'd only had a few weeks' annual leave and sometimes he could go for more than a year without seeing Katelin and Elizabeth.

'People used to start talking, you know,' Elizabeth continued. 'They'd say you wouldn't be coming back. That you'd been killed in battle. But then you'd suddenly be there, walking through the door.'

Jack remembered these scenes well. In his mind's eye he could still see the young Elizabeth running across the room as he opened the cottage door, racing into his arms. The memories seemed so vivid, but also so long ago. They were from another time, another world, when Katelin was still alive and he still served the Rajthanans. Before the crusade. Before Jhala had betrayed him . . .

Cecily grizzled and Elizabeth jiggled her up and down to calm her.

Jack rubbed his eyes. He was exhausted, but the relief of finding Elizabeth alive had filled him with unexpected strength. 'You still have Mother's necklace?'

Elizabeth smiled. 'Of course.'

She drew the necklace out from under her dress and held it up. The ancient cross twirled slowly as it dangled from the string.

'Good.' He patted her on the shoulder. 'You made it here safely. Mother must be watching over you.'

His eyes strayed across the camp. Blue dusk was falling across the fortress. The rain had finally faded and the villagers could sit outside without getting wet. Saleem was talking to his mother and sisters on the far side of the camp, while Mary was discussing something with several other women. Mark and the lads from the House of Sorcery were helping to peel and cut turnips and parsnips for the pots that stood in the cooking fires.

But there was one person Jack couldn't see. In fact, he hadn't seen her for more than an hour. Sonali.

He'd better look for her.

He said farewell to Elizabeth, walked across the camp and ducked through the entrance to the ruin. He found himself in a gloomy chamber that was more like a cave than something man-made. The upper storeys of the building had fallen in long ago and now the large slabs of the ceiling lay less than a foot above his head. Several villagers squatted in the darkness or lay on blankets. A collection of barrels and sacks stood against one wall. The villagers had brought a few carts of food with them when they escaped, enough to last for several days at least.

He couldn't see Sonali, so he pressed on through an arch and made his way through a warren of further rooms formed by the collapsed stonework. The only light came from the numerous holes in the ceiling or the occasional tallow candle stuck in the ground. He saw more villagers huddled here and there, but still no sign of Sonali.

Finally, he pushed aside a curtain of vines and came out in a larger hall where the ceiling had almost completely disintegrated, revealing the blue-black sky beyond. A row of pillars paraded along one side of the chamber, although they now supported nothing.

Kanvar sat cross-legged in the shadows, still as a statue.

Jack crouched down. 'Kanvar.'

He half expected Kanvar to leap up in alarm, but the Sikh merely opened his eyes slowly and murmured, 'Ah. Jack.'

'You seen Sonali?'

Kanvar stared into the gloom, pondering the question carefully. 'I have not seen her. I have been restoring my sattva for some time.'

'You all right now, then?'

'I am better. Just troubled.'

'Troubled? Why?'

'I have been trying to think of the solution to our current

predicament. We are trapped within the Fortress of the Djinns, as you call it. We are surrounded by the enemy and cannot escape. And more of the enemy are bound to arrive soon.'

'Aye. I agree. General Jhala will send troops here once he finds Shrewsbury abandoned.'

Kanvar passed his hand across his brow. 'Indeed. And the army of Vadula will march into Shropshire too. Perhaps they will come here as well.'

Jack sat back. It was a bleak thought, but it was hard to argue with.

Kanvar looked down, his eyes widening further. 'There is something else. I told Takhat about the giant avatar we saw in the forest. And he said he'd heard other reports about the Rajthanans growing very great in power.'

Jack narrowed his eyes. 'What do you mean?'

'According to Takhat, the Rajthanans appear to have many more siddhas in England than before.'

'They've brought more in.'

Kanvar shook his head. 'They couldn't – not in such great numbers. That would leave other parts of the empire too poorly defended. And in any case, it is not just that there are more siddhas. Takhat also told me the siddhas have new powers. Powers that have never even been heard of before.'

Jack went silent. 'You think this is something to do with the Great Yantra?'

'I fear so.'

'The Great Yantra is giving the Rajthanans all these new powers?'

'That is what Takhat believed.'

Damn it. Not only were the rebels facing the most powerful army in the world, they were also confronted with siddhas with unbelievable powers.

Jack took a deep breath. 'How far away are you Sikhs from finding out the design of the yantra?'

Kanvar looked up. 'It will still be some time, I'm afraid. We have made much progress, and I have transferred all the information from Takhat's map to my own. But still, even with the centre now identified, it will take weeks at the very least, I would think.'

'We haven't got weeks.'

'Indeed. And in any case, I have to say, there is little chance of me ever being shown the design now.'

'Now that you've been cast out of your order?'

Kanvar nodded solemnly. 'If Takhat and the others discover the design, they will hardly come to find me to show it to me.'

'We're on our own. It's just us, up here on this hill.'

'It seems so.'

Jack rubbed his face. 'Then we'll just have to do our best and fight with what we've got.'

─────

Jack finally found Sonali standing alone on the outer wall of the fortress. She was leaning against the parapet and staring out into the pitch-black night. She looked serious and thoughtful – the way she'd appeared when he'd first met her in Mahajan's castle.

'It's cold,' he said.

She nodded and hugged her shawl closer.

He leant against the battlements beside her and gazed into the darkness. A wide arc of campfires twinkled in the distance. They seemed to float like stars in the void.

'There are so many of them,' she said softly.

Jack nodded. More Welsh had arrived as dusk had turned into night, and there were now perhaps three thousand men encircling the hill. The Welsh had made camp out of range of the rebels' guns and, with no artillery of their own, they seemed to have decided to keep their distance for the time being.

Jack cleared his throat. 'Look, sorry if I was . . . cold when you first came back.'

Sonali kept her eyes locked on the lights. 'I wasn't sure if you were pleased to see me.'

'Of course I was. It was just a shock seeing the village destroyed.'

She nodded but stayed silent.

'Thank you,' he continued. 'For everything you've done. You didn't have to come all the way here. You didn't have to help me find Elizabeth. You didn't have to come back for me at all.'

'Of course I had to come back.' She gave him a small smile. 'I had to give you this.' She drew something out of the folds of her sari and opened her hand to reveal two paans wrapped in gleaming gold leaf.

Jack gave her a warm smile. He'd missed paan since living in Shropshire. Tobacco of any sort had been in short supply in the years after the First Crusade, and paan had never been common in the native state. But he'd chewed it often when he was in the army, as did many others who lived in the Rajthanan-controlled lands. He remembered he'd complained to Sonali several times that there was none available in Clun.

He took one of the small packages and turned it around in his fingers. 'Never had any this fancy.'

'It's real gold. I took it from my aunt's house.'

'Real gold? Your aunt must be rich.'

'She married a wealthy man.'

'Lucky her.'

Sonali smiled slightly. 'She's been very good to me. She's the only one in my family who stuck by me when I ran away . . . But never mind that. Have your paan.'

Sonali popped her packet into her mouth. Jack did the same, biting through the betel leaf and into the sharp mixture of spices and tobacco within. The taste was luxurious. He munched slowly, enjoying the sensation.

'You bring any more of this?' he asked.

'I might have one or two pieces left.' She smiled mysteriously.

They chewed in silence for a few more minutes, then Sonali turned and discreetly spat her paan out over the parapet.

When she faced Jack again, her expression was more sombre. 'You know, you must talk with the rebel leaders about what Rao said.'

'Rao's treaty?'

'Yes.'

Jack chewed the paan. 'Henry's in charge here. I don't think he's going to listen to me.'

'I thought the Earl of Shropshire was your true leader?'

'He is. But he's an old man. Frail, they say. Henry's been given command of the fortress.'

'But still, you must try.' She gazed out at the throbbing lights again. 'It is our only hope.'

Jack turned away and spat out the paan. 'This story of Rao's. It's a bit hard to believe.'

Sonali frowned. 'Why would he lie?'

'Maybe there's some mistake. A misunderstanding.'

'Rao seemed very certain about this. When I got to my aunt's house, there was already a letter from him waiting for me. He said he was coming to Dorsetshire to find me. When he got there, he was very excited. He told me the Maharaja was close to offering the treaty.' She stared straight at Jack. 'Rao is from a powerful clan. His father has connections in high places. This is not a fantasy. I'm sure of it.'

'You could be right. But still, Rao wants us to lay down our arms. I doubt I can talk anyone into doing that. I'm not sure it's a good idea myself.' He gestured to the distant army. 'Those Welsh won't know anything about a treaty. All they'll know is that they're here to kill us. If we surrender, they'll probably still kill us.'

'Some Rajthanans must come soon. Some officers. We could talk to them. Reason with them.'

Jack snorted. 'We could try. Don't know how far we'll get.'

'We must do something. To stop the bloodshed.'

He stared into the distance. 'I'll see what I can do.'

Rao's story seemed incredible, unbelievable to Jack. But Sonali seemed convinced by it – and there was no reason for Rao to lie. It was true that the Rajthanans would be keen to end the war in England if there were a risk of further uprisings in the rest of Europe.

Perhaps it could be true. Perhaps it could be a way out.

But he didn't want to hope too much.

He heard the sound of singing, drums and lutes sailing up from behind him. He tore himself away from his thoughts, turned and looked back down into the fortress. Sonali did the same, shivering slightly at the cold wind whipping across the hilltop.

Below them, the ruins were a tangled maze, almost invisible in the dark. Jack could see traces of walls, roofs, courtyards and broken minarets. Hundreds of campfires adorned the fort like scattered jewels.

The sound of drums and lutes grew louder.

'It's strange to hear the music,' Sonali said.

'It keeps the people's spirits up.'

'It's beautiful in a way. That they can sing and make music even now.'

Jack nodded. He was proud of his people at that moment. Proud of the fact that they were still determined to keep the dream of a free England alive.

The wind blew stronger, the cold pressing through Jack's tunic all the way to his skin. 'We should get back. We should eat.'

Sonali's eyes strayed down and she nodded slowly. As she turned to walk back with him, her foot slipped on a loose stone and she fell against him, giving a little yelp. He caught her – although there was no need, as she'd already steadied herself. But then both of them froze. She was pressed against him, and he could feel her chest rising and falling. Her face was close to his. He smelt the heady scent of her perfume.

He leant forward slightly. She leant forward a little. Their lips were close and they were about to kiss.

But then she pulled away, frowned and pattered down the stairs.

The fleeting moment they'd had together evaporated as quickly as it had appeared.

'Come quickly.' Saleem tugged at Jack's sleeve.

'What is it?' Jack asked.

'The army are here.'

Jack's skin rippled. Christ. Already.

He followed Saleem round the shattered buildings and across to the vast east wall. He saw many people moving forward, like him, to see what was happening. Most of them had nervous looks on their faces.

It was a clear morning and the sun beat down on the ruins. Jack's legs felt stiff – he'd slept uncomfortably on the hard earth. He'd also continually woken during the night, thinking there were enemies prowling nearby in the dark.

He and Saleem reached a hole where the wall had collapsed long ago, but the area was already crowded with crusaders looking out. Saleem led the way over to a bastion tower, where he and Jack clambered up the stairs all the way to the walkway along the top of the wall.

A bustling crowd, including a contingent of Mohammedans, had already gathered on the ramparts. At first, Jack saw nowhere to stand. But then he spotted Kanvar waving to him. The Sikh – along with Sonali, Mark and several apprentices – had taken up a position on the wall. Jack and Saleem pressed themselves in amongst the group and peered out over the battlements.

The Welsh forces still surrounded the fortress. Jack could see them spread out across the plains and the closer hills. But now a column of what appeared to be reinforcements – men and animals – was marching from the open ground to the north-east.

Jack took the spyglass from Kanvar and studied the approaching figures.

It was the army – the European Army.

At the head of the column, riding five abreast, were European cavalrymen. They carried their lances pointing up at the sky, the steel tips glinting and the pennons twisting in the breeze. Behind them strode European foot soldiers in blue tunics, cloth hats and puttees. Rajthanan officers rode alongside their men, their turbans either silver or green, indicating Andalusian or French regiments respectively.

Next came horses drawing light artillery carriages, and then teams of elephants strung together with chains and hauling large siege guns. Further back lumbered more elephants with armour on their heads, spikes on their tusks and standards jutting from their backs.

Finally, the ramshackle line of the baggage train and the camp followers snaked across the countryside. The motley collection of men, carts and animals seemed to roll endlessly into the distance.

'How many men, do you think?' Saleem said softly.

Jack lowered the glass. 'Four thousand, perhaps.'

'It is not Vadula's army in that case,' Kanvar said.

'No.' Jack nodded. 'They are too few.'

But it was still a large enough force. The crusaders now faced a combined army of around seven thousand men. There were only two thousand people in the fortress and Jack knew many of them were too old, young or weak to fight.

The mournful wail of an army horn sailed across on the breeze. Jack lifted the glass again and saw that the column had come to a halt. A solitary elephant ambled forward. A glittering covered howdah swayed on the animal's back and a mahout sat astride its neck. Two soldiers strode in front of the beast, blowing horns moulded into the shape of conches. At the back of the party, a rider beat time on a pair of kettledrums strapped to his horse.

The elephant reached the front of the column and the mahout drove his crook into its head to command it to stop.

The howdah glimmered in the sunlight. The drapes and tassels hanging over it swung in the wind.

The elephant knelt and all the troops nearby suddenly dropped to the ground and prostrated themselves. A soldier rushed across to the beast and placed a small ladder against it.

A hand emerged from the howdah and swept the curtains to one side. Then a figure climbed out. He was wearing the ordinary uniform of a European Army officer, but his tunic was festooned with silver braiding and embroidery, and his turban was a blaze of intersecting gold bands.

The man was a general. A *senapati* in Rajthani.

The figure stepped slowly to the ground, put his hands on his hips and turned to gaze up at the fortress.

Jack felt strangely dizzy, as if he were looking at a ghost.

It was Jhala.

20

Jack let out a small hiss and lowered the glass.

Sonali frowned at him. 'Are you all right?'

'Of course,' he muttered. But there was a storm in his head now. His fingers gripped the glass so tightly he thought it might break.

Jhala. Why did it have to be Jhala who was sent to crush the rebellion?

And yet, wasn't it also inevitable? Ever since Jack had learnt that his old commander was still alive and leading the forces in Worcestershire, he'd somehow known it would come to this.

It was always going to be Jhala.

'What's that?' Saleem pointed across the plains.

Jack squinted and saw five riders on caparisoned horses emerge from the mass of troops. One of them was carrying a white flag.

'They want to talk,' Jack said. It was standard practice to at least make the offer of a truce before a siege. But it was unlikely the terms would be anything the crusaders could accept.

Sonali put her hand on Jack's arm. 'You could talk to them.'

Jack frowned. 'Me?'

'About what Rao said.'

Jack went silent. Kanvar, Saleem and the others were looking at him now, obviously wondering what he and Sonali were discussing. Other crusaders were watching as well. This wasn't the place to talk about the treaty – especially as Kanvar was unlikely to be happy about any deal with the Rajthanans.

'Down there.' Jack nodded towards the bottom of the wall.

He set off along the walkway and then headed down the stairs, Sonali pattering after him in her red slippers. They walked together into the ruins and paused beside a line of weathered pillars.

Sonali took his arm again. 'Now is your chance. Surrender, and the rebels will be spared. Then, when the treaty is ready, you'll be free.'

Jack sucked on his teeth. 'It's not that simple.'

'It could be. If you want it to be.'

Jack sighed. 'I'm not sure the Rajthanans will spare us – even if we surrender. Not all of us, at any rate.'

'But the treaty—'

'Those Rajthanans might not know about a treaty. And in any case, there is no treaty yet. There might never be.'

Sonali's brow knitted. 'We can trust the officers. They will do the honourable thing, surely.'

Jack looked up at the wall. 'I used to think that. Now I think differently. You didn't see what happened during the First Crusade.'

Sonali was silent for a moment. 'I only ask that you try. What harm can it do for you to speak to the officers? There is nothing to lose.'

Jack ran his fingers through his hair. Sonali was making some sense. The rebels were in a desperate situation. Two thousand people could die. If there were any chance of him preventing that, he had to act.

'There is one thing,' he said. 'The general down there – it's Jhala himself.'

'General Jhala is leading the troops?'

'Aye. And the thing is, he's my old captain. And my guru.'

Sonali's eyes widened. 'General Jhala was your guru?'

Jack nodded.

She gripped his arm more tightly. 'Then you must talk to him. Convince him to spare your people.'

'I don't know . . .'

'Please. You must try.'

Jack rubbed his forehead. There was so much to think about and so little time. Was there really any point in him trying to talk to Jhala? Would that really make any difference? Would Jhala be more lenient with the rebels just because Jack was amongst them? That seemed unlikely.

And yet, as Sonali had said, what did he have to lose by trying? He couldn't make the rebels' situation any worse.

'All right,' he said. 'I'll see what I can do.'

He marched back to the wall and headed towards the gate. Sonali scurried beside him, trying her best to keep up.

Henry was standing beside the gatehouse, just as Jack had expected. The constable was talking to three heralds on horseback, who were evidently preparing to ride out to meet the enemy. One of the men carried a pole with a piece of white linen tied to it.

Jack strode across to the entryway. 'Henry!'

Henry paused, then turned slowly. He narrowed his eyes and looked Jack up and down. 'What do you want?'

'Let me go out there. I'll talk to the enemy.'

Henry's face twisted. 'Send you out there? So you can betray us?' He waved his hand, as if brushing away a fly. 'Leave.' He turned back to the riders.

'I know the general down there.' Jack stepped closer. 'I might be able to reason with him.'

Henry spun round, his eyes glinting. 'I told you to leave. I've no time for this.'

'If you'd just let me—'

Henry roared and drew his pistol from his belt. He pointed the weapon at Jack's chest. 'Leave, before I shoot you.'

Jack's heart beat faster. He'd known this would be a difficult conversation, but he hadn't expected this.

He searched Henry's face. The constable was enraged, his cheeks bright red. Jack wasn't going to get any sense out of him. There was no point trying to talk about it further.

Jack raised his hands and stepped backwards. 'All right, I'm leaving.'

He walked back to Sonali. Her lips were bunched and a deep frown cut into her forehead.

'Is there some other way you can get a message to your guru?' she asked.

'Not easily,' Jack said.

'There must be something you can do.'

Jack rubbed his chin, his mind racing through various options. 'There is one thing I could try.'

'What?'

'Come with me. I'll show you.'

* * *

The Earl of Shropshire had set up residence in a ruined palace not far from the east wall of the fortress. It must once have been a grand building, adorned with turrets and domes, but now it was a pile of weathered masonry. The stonework was porous with age and mottled with lichens. The intricate geometrical designs that would have encrusted the walls had long ago worn down to vague lines and bulges.

Jack stood with Sonali before what was left of the arched, Moorish entrance. Two men-at-arms stood guard outside.

'I wish to speak with the earl,' Jack said.

One of the guards – a bearded, stocky man – shook his head. 'The earl is resting.'

'It's urgent. It's about the army.'

The guard frowned. 'I said no. Now leave.'

Jack was considering searching for another way in, when a thin man with long dark hair appeared from inside the palace. He walked with a limp, dragging one leg behind him.

Jack recognised the man – he was a member of the Crusader Council. Jack had met him once at Lord Fitzalan's castle.

What was his name? Jack thought quickly, and then he remembered it – Sir Levin.

'What's going on?' Levin asked the guards.

'Just telling this man to leave, sir,' the bearded guard replied.

Levin raised his head and his eyes flickered when they noticed Jack. He wagged his finger. 'I know you, don't I?'

Jack bowed his head slightly. 'Jack Casey, sir. We met at Newcastle. I led the expedition to Scotland.'

Levin nodded slowly. 'That's it. I remember now. I'm glad to see you made it here. Not many did.'

'You too, sir.' Jack looked down for a moment. 'I heard about Sir Alfred.'

'Ah yes.' Levin stared into space. 'It is a great tragedy. But then there are so many tragedies these days.'

'Sir, if I may, I need to speak to the earl.'

Levin studied Jack closely. 'Why is that?'

'I know the general leading the enemy troops out there. Jhala. I might be able to strike a deal.'

Levin raised an eyebrow. 'A strange idea.' He rolled his tongue around in his mouth. 'But I remember our discussion now. You told me then you knew General Jhala.'

'That's right, sir.'

'Very well. You'd better come in.'

Levin stepped aside to admit Jack, then held his hand out to stop Sonali. 'Not you.'

Jack looked back. 'She's a friend.'

Levin raised his chin and eyed Sonali haughtily. 'We will not have a heathen in this hall. Not at a time like this.'

'It's all right,' Sonali said to Jack. 'You go. I'll wait here.'

Jack nodded. 'I'll be right back.'

Sir Levin led the way down a wide passageway, hobbling as quickly as he could with his bad leg. Jack couldn't recall Levin having a limp previously. Perhaps he'd been injured in the recent fighting.

They came out in what must once have been a grand hall, but which was now a roofless courtyard. The paving stones were cracked and largely overgrown with grass. Vines hung like streamers over the walls. Arches, niches and windows encircled the chamber, but they were now so worn they appeared to be melting.

On the far side of the room, an elderly man was slumped on a large, carved chair. He wore a red robe, trimmed with ermine, and a grey cloak was draped over his shoulders. His silver hair was lank and his face was pale and drawn. Several page boys were bustling about him, but he waved them away as Jack approached.

Jack went down on one knee. 'My lord.'

The earl flicked his finger in Jack's general direction and said in a cracked voice, 'Stand up. There is no need for ceremony now.' He took a rasping breath. He appeared to be having trouble breathing. 'Who are you?'

Jack stood up and put his hands behind his back. 'Jack Casey, sir.'

'I can vouch for this man.' Levin stood near to Jack. 'He was well thought of by Sir Alfred.'

'Oh.' The earl's eyes glazed over. 'If only Alfred were with us now.' He went silent for a moment, then drew himself up straighter in his chair. 'Very well. What is it you want?'

'It's about General Jhala,' Jack said. 'I used to serve under him. Before the First Crusade. I'd like to meet with him to discuss terms.'

'Terms?' The earl licked his lips and took another rattling breath. 'What terms can we possibly expect? We are viewed as traitors by the heathens. I have broken all the treaties my ancestors signed with them. We cannot expect fair treatment.'

'I understand, sir. But I believe—'

'Stop!' someone shouted from the entrance to the palace.

Jack turned and saw Henry striding into the room with an entourage of two soldiers. His jaw was clenched and his eyes glittered.

Henry bowed to the earl. 'Forgive me for bursting in here,

my lord.' He pointed at Jack. 'But when I heard this man was here, I had to come quickly.'

'What is the meaning of this?' Levin said sharply.

Henry glanced at Levin and then back at the earl. He opened his mouth and then closed it again, seemingly uncertain what to say. Although he'd been put in charge of the fortress, Levin and the Earl of Shropshire were still his superiors.

Finally, he said, 'This man, Casey, is a liar and a traitor. He is a secret servant of the heathens – and has been for a long time.'

Levin narrowed his eyes. 'That is a strange allegation. Jack was always praised by Sir Alfred. And we all know it was Jack who was chosen to lead the expedition to Scotland.'

'And we all know he failed in that expedition,' Henry snapped, then quickly seemed to realise he'd spoken too abruptly. He said in a softer tone, 'Sorry, sir. I just meant that I have reason to believe Casey cannot be trusted.'

'What is your evidence for making these claims, Constable Ward?' the earl said.

Henry ground his teeth, shot a look at Jack and then faced the earl again. 'He consorts with the enemy. There is one right outside here at the moment. A witch.'

'She's been helping me train apprentices,' Jack said. 'She is Rajthanan, but she's proven herself to be loyal. We can trust her, and we need all the help we can get at the moment.'

The earl's eyes flicked across to Levin, as if he were expecting some answer.

Levin cleared his throat. 'It's true, my lord, that Casey has been training apprentices in the heathens' arts. Sir Alfred explained it to me. There is no reason to doubt what he says.'

Henry's face was now so red it was almost glowing, and his eyes shone a brilliant white. He looked as though he were about to explode, but he managed to keep himself in check.

The earl took a long, uneven breath and nodded at Jack. 'Very well. You were about to tell us something. Continue.'

Jack paused for a moment. Should he mention Rao's treaty? It would take quite some explaining, and he was hardly convinced about it himself. He decided not to mention it – unless he had to. Not yet, at any rate.

'My lord,' he said. 'I think there is a chance, a small chance, I might be able to reach some sort of agreement with General Jhala. I was his sergeant at one time.'

'You being his sergeant once can't count for all that much,' the earl said.

Jack paused. 'We were close, you could say. He was my teacher, my guru. Let me at least talk to him and find out his terms. He might be more willing to listen to me.'

The earl paused for a moment, pondering this. His shoulders eased back and he suddenly looked very tired. This was an elderly man, torn from his comfortable home, who'd lost everything and now faced probable death.

'Very well.' The earl sighed. 'Why should you not try, Jack Casey? I hold out little hope. But nevertheless you will be our negotiator with these Rajthanans. Go, see what terms they have and then report back to us here.'

⸺◈⸺

Jack sat on his horse just inside the gateway to the fortress. The mare stomped and tossed her mane. She'd recovered from her previous exertions and now looked strong enough to gallop for miles.

Jack glanced to his side and saw Henry standing in the shadow of the gatehouse. The constable glowered back for a moment, then hawked and spat at the ground.

When Jack looked over his shoulder, he saw Sonali, Kanvar, Elizabeth and many others from Folly Brook watching him anxiously. And behind them stood a crowd of weary, dishevelled crusaders who all gazed at him like lost souls seeking salvation.

So much was resting on Jack. And there was so little he could do.

He wasn't the pure knight who would find the Grail. He was nothing special. As he'd always said, he was just an old soldier. But now he had to somehow find a way to convince the Rajthanans not to slaughter his people.

Hooves clopped behind him, the gathering parted and Sir Levin rode out on a chestnut horse. He'd slung a cloak over his shoulders and his long black hair whipped about his face in the wind. The earl had commanded him to accompany Jack to ensure the negotiations ran smoothly.

Levin nodded at Jack. 'Let's go.'

Jack took a deep breath and nudged the mare forward with his legs. He and Levin rode out through the gatehouse, zigzagged down the scarp and then set off across the plateau. The corpses from yesterday's battle had been cleared away, but several shell craters still gouged the earth. Scraps of twisted metal from the shell casings lay scattered about in the grass.

They angled their horses down the second incline and then spurred them into a gallop. In the distance, about a mile away, the three heralds sent by Henry and the five cavalrymen sent by Jhala had already met and were discussing terms. Two of the men, one from each opposing side, still held their white flags aloft.

Jack and Levin raced across the heath. The Welsh army seemed alarmingly close to Jack now. He could make out the mottled line of figures, bivouacs, campfires, sheep, cattle and a handful of pavilions. Guards stood at regular intervals, holding spears or muskets at their sides.

Directly ahead, to the north-east, loomed the elephants of the European Army and the forest of lances belonging to the cavalry, who still sat in formation on their chargers. Jhala's forces looked even more imposing from down here on the plains.

After around five minutes, Jack and Levin slowed their horses to a trot and drew up to the negotiators. Jhala's cavalrymen frowned in puzzlement. Four of them were Europeans, but one, who appeared to be the leader, was a young Rajthanan with a thick moustache that gleamed with wax.

Levin addressed the Rajthanan. 'We have a request.' He gestured to Jack. 'Our man here is a comrade of General Jhala's. He wishes to speak to Jhala directly to discuss terms.'

The Rajthanan's features soured. 'The general has assigned me to this task. You will speak to me, or you will speak to no one.'

'Please, sir,' Jack said in Rajthani. 'I served with General Jhala for many years. He was my captain. He'll want to speak to me. I'm certain.'

Jack was far from certain, but he had to say something.

The Rajthanan narrowed his eyes. 'If what you say is true, then you have betrayed your oath. Why would General Jhala lower himself to speak to you now?'

'He will.' Jack still spoke in Rajthani. 'Please tell him I'm here. My name's Jack Casey. He can decide whether he wants to meet with me or not.'

The Rajthanan rolled his tongue in his mouth, his moustache bobbing on his top lip.

'Jhala won't be happy if he finds out I'm here and you didn't give him my message.' Jack knew this was an audacious thing to say and it could backfire. But he had to try.

The Rajthanan sniffed. Jack's words must have convinced him, because he nodded to one of the European cavalrymen and ordered him in Arabic to pass the message on to the general. The cavalryman instantly wheeled his horse about and charged back across the plains towards the line of elephants.

Jack shot a look at Levin, who was fidgeting with his reins. The stakes were high. Unbelievably high. Jack thought of all the people huddled up in the fortress. He couldn't let them down.

He stared back towards the elephants. The cavalryman had already disappeared into the mass of soldiers near to the beasts.

But what now? Would Jhala really come out to meet him? Jhala was a general and Jack was a traitor. Now that Jack thought about it, the whole plan seemed crazy. Of course Jhala wouldn't come. Jack must have been mad to let Sonali talk him into this.

But then the cavalryman came charging back across the heath. He raced up to the group of riders, drew his horse to a sudden halt and spoke quickly to the Rajthanan officer.

The officer turned to Jack, his moustache stretched rigidly across his top lip. 'It seems the general will speak to you.'

Jack felt a wave of both relief and nerves. He thanked God that Jhala would meet with him. But now what? What could he say to his old commander to convince him to spare the rebels?

The officer faced Levin and the other three crusaders. 'You will leave now. The general will meet this man alone.'

'Wait,' Levin said. 'It will be best if we discuss this together.'

The officer shook his head. 'It's this man or no one. Leave now.'

Levin opened his mouth to protest then shut it again. His horse danced skittishly beneath him as his eyes flicked across to meet Jack's.

'It's all right,' Jack said. 'You go.'

Levin was clearly reluctant to leave. No doubt the earl had instructed him to keep an eye on Jack, and now that wasn't going to be possible. But Levin had little choice.

Levin pursed his lips and nodded to the three heralds. All four of them turned their horses and rode away across the plains, heading back towards the fortress.

The officer watched the four figures dwindle into the distance, then turned to Jack. 'Get off your horse.'

Jack did as he was told and dismounted.

The officer swung himself down from his own saddle and frisked Jack for weapons, checking carefully even around Jack's ankles for concealed blades. When he was satisfied that Jack had followed protocol and come unarmed, he climbed back on to his horse and looked towards the army.

Two riders were now approaching, trotting their horses side by side. One of them, a batman, was holding a parasol above the head of the second man, a Rajthanan wearing a glittering turban. Jack couldn't see the second man's face yet. But it could only be Jhala.

Jack felt another ripple of nerves.

It seemed unbelievable that he was going to see Jhala again.

But then a cold, steel fist seemed to clench itself tightly inside him. He'd trusted Jhala, but his commander had betrayed him and threatened to hang Elizabeth.

He shut his eyes for a second, gritted his teeth.

Your mind is a rippling pool. Still it.

The two riders drew closer. And then Jack could make out Jhala's features. His guru looked much the same as four years ago. The lines on his face were deep and there were purple bags beneath his eyes. His eyebrows and what was visible of his hair poking out from under his turban were silver. He was in his late fifties now, and it was hardly surprising he looked old. But despite this, he appeared fit and well. The old injury in his chest seemed not to be troubling him at all at the moment.

Jhala halted his horse beside the small group and gave Jack a smile, his eyes twinkling. He folded his hands in front of his chest and bowed his head slightly. 'Namaste, Jack. It is such a pleasure to see you again.'

21

For a moment, Jack felt as though he were choking. He couldn't speak. His mouth was as dry as if he'd stuffed it with salt.

It was strange. Simply seeing Jhala before him now seemed to have paralysed him.

Finally, he managed to reply, 'Namaste.' But his voice came out strained and slightly cracked.

Jhala raised an eyebrow for a moment, but then smiled again. 'I had no idea you were here, Jack. It's been such a long time. Three years? Or is it four?'

The strange paralysis was slowly falling away from Jack, but now a new sensation began to throb like a wound inside him. His fingers curled into fists, his neck muscles went taut and he could hear his heart beating in his ears. A single thought pounded in his head like a hammer on an anvil – he wanted to kill Jhala. He wanted to rush at the man, drag him from his horse and murder him with his bare hands.

Jhala deserved to die for what he'd done.

But now was not the time. Jack had come here to plead for mercy, and he couldn't let his people down. The fate of everyone in the fortress was resting with him.

With a supreme effort he swallowed down his rage and said curtly, 'It's four years.'

Jhala studied Jack carefully. 'You are not pleased to see your old comrade?'

'I'm here to discuss terms.'

'But we can at least be civil, can't we?'

Jack felt his face reddening but managed to calm himself. 'Of course.'

Jhala nodded slowly. Finally, he swung himself down to the ground and gestured to his right. 'We shall talk in private. Come.'

Jack walked with Jhala across the grass, leaving the group of cavalrymen behind. Jhala held his hands behind his back and strode quickly. He seemed surprisingly spry – strong, even. It was easy to see why he'd been a champion Malla wrestler when he was younger.

'I understand, you know,' Jhala said.

'Understand what?' Jack said stiffly.

'The difficulty of this situation. Here we are, old friends but on opposing sides. It makes me very sad.'

Old friends? Jack couldn't believe he'd heard the man who'd threatened to kill Elizabeth call himself a friend. Was Jhala serious, or was this some game? 'I thought you were dead.'

Jhala's expression turned grim. 'I was betrayed by my own men. They mutinied. Can you believe it? I was reported dead, but in fact my loyal servants smuggled me to safety. They hid me in the forest, and I eventually made my way back to Poole.'

Jhala stopped suddenly and turned to face Jack. 'But enough of that. It's not important now.' He inhaled deeply. 'What are we going to do?'

'What do you mean?'

Jhala waved his hand vaguely. 'About this situation we find ourselves in. You with your people up on that hill. Me and my men down here.'

'Perhaps you and your men could turn round and go back home.'

Jhala half smiled. 'You don't know how glad that would make me. If I could leave right now, I would. I never wanted any of this, Jack. You know that.' His eyes misted. 'I love this country. It breaks my heart to see what's happened to it.'

Jack was taken aback by Jhala's words for a moment. This wasn't what he'd expected. But, at the same time, he'd heard Jhala say similar things in the past. Jhala was born in England and had studied the history and culture of the country in great detail. He spoke English as well as any Englishman. And he'd been closer to his men than any officer Jack had ever known. But all the same, none of that had counted for anything once the rebellion started. Jhala was a Rajthanan and would always be loyal to the empire.

'You know,' Jhala said, 'when I was sent to school back in Rajthana, the country was completely foreign to me. I used to dream every night of the green hills of England. I wanted to be back here. Did I ever tell you that?'

'No.'

'You know what they called me in school over there? Outcaste. I was from the colonies, you see, and had travelled over the wide open sea – the black water, as they call it. All that makes you impure. I wasn't a proper Rajthanan in their eyes. Strange, isn't it? It's almost as though England were my true home.'

Jack felt a flush of irritation. Why was Jhala telling him all this? What was the point? 'As I said, I'm here to discuss terms.' His voice came out harsher than he'd intended.

Jhala frowned and his eyes flickered. 'You disappoint me, Jack. I expected better from you.'

Jack breathed in deeply and held his emotions in check. He mustn't risk angering Jhala until he'd done his best to get a deal for his people.

Jhala sighed and rubbed his forehead. 'This is all such a great pity. Nevertheless, we will have to make the best of things, won't we? You want to discuss terms? Then I will do as you wish.'

He looked into the distance, towards the fortress. 'Now, let's see.' He walked a few paces to his right, clicking his tongue as he surveyed the hill. 'Yes, very good. A good place to take refuge. High walls. About forty feet in European reckoning, wouldn't you say?'

'Something like that,' Jack mumbled.

'Yes, and the hillsides are steep. Nothing but rocks and crags on this side. Skirmishers would have trouble getting up that. Wouldn't fancy it myself, would you?'

Jack clenched and unclenched his hands. What was Jhala playing at?

'No,' Jhala said. 'Wouldn't fancy it.' He frowned and paced back towards Jack, deep in thought. 'On the other hand, that slope there,' he pointed at the edge of the southern slope, just visible from this angle, 'the gradient's much gentler there, isn't it? A force could get up it. But then there's that plateau. Those guns in the fortress could pick off anyone crossing the plateau. Any attackers would have a tough fight getting up that second slope and inside the walls, wouldn't they?'

Jack remained silent. How long was this going to go on for?

Jhala scanned the countryside to the south. His eyes fell upon the range of low hills just under a mile from the fortress. He gestured towards the peaks. 'What about those? A good place to put artillery, wouldn't you say? Put some guns there and the fortress would be within range. You could wreak havoc on anyone inside. Perhaps knock out all those guns on the wall too, or at least make life difficult for the gunners.'

'I wouldn't know,' Jack said. 'I'm not an artilleryman.'

'No, of course you're not. Neither am I. But you and I, we've been in enough battles, haven't we, to be able to pass judgement? You and I have seen enough, faced enough together, to know where to place artillery.'

'I suppose so,' Jack said sullenly.

'Yes.' Jhala waved his finger towards the hills. 'With the guns there, they could soften up the opposition. The people up in the fortress would be sitting ducks. Wouldn't matter so much about the hillsides and the walls then, would it? I mean, they would still present a challenge. But a force of seven thousand could certainly storm up there and defeat a much smaller force already weakened by gunfire, couldn't they?'

Jack clamped his jaw tight. Rage was bubbling in his chest once more and he had to fight to suppress it. 'I understand the situation well enough.'

'Good.' Jhala paced back to stand before Jack. 'I'm glad you understand. So, here's what we'll do. You tell your people to lay down their arms and surrender. If they do that, I will be lenient. Everyone will be spared, save for the Earl of Shropshire, who must hang. The rest will be sent to East Europe to work in the farms and mines. And you, Jack,' he pointed at Jack's chest, 'you I will let go. That's right, you can go free – so long as you leave England and never come back. Return, and you'll be executed. But stay away, and you can live your life in whatever way you see fit.'

Jack blinked. In many ways this was an extremely good offer – especially for him personally. But nevertheless, how could he, or anyone else, accept it? It would mean the end of the crusade. Shropshire was the last stronghold of the rebellion. And the last people willing to fight were probably those up on the hill.

But, on the other hand, what could the rebels expect? Jhala was right, they couldn't hold out for ever. They faced too strong an opposition.

'Listen.' Jack cleared his throat. 'I heard about a treaty that's on the way.'

Jhala smiled quizzically. 'A treaty?'

'Someone told me about it. Apparently the Maharaja of Europe is considering it.'

Jhala's smile broadened, and then it faded again and his eyes clouded slightly. 'You are holding out for this treaty, then?'

'Perhaps,' Jack muttered.

Jhala sighed. 'I'm sorry, but there is no treaty. I have heard nothing about it, received no orders regarding it. I think someone may be playing games with you.'

Jack had always had doubts about Rao's claims, but this news was still a blow. There was always a chance the treaty could still come about – perhaps Jhala simply hadn't been told about it. But it was seeming more and more likely that the whole thing was a dream.

'No,' Jhala continued. 'I'm afraid there is no other way out of this. You and your people must agree to my terms.'

'I can't see how my people can agree to be sent to East Europe. They'll be slaves.'

'They will be alive, at least.'

'How about you just let us all go? We'll all leave Shropshire. You won't hear from us again.'

Jhala snorted. 'No.'

'You can take the fortress, eventually. I agree. But it will cost you many lives and may take quite some time. The people up there will be fighting for their lives. They'll defend themselves with everything they've got. Do you really want to waste all your men on that? What's the point? The mutiny's over. You've won. You might as well let us go.'

'You know I can't do that,' Jhala said softly. 'Even if I wanted to, Mahasiddha Vadula would never agree to it. I'd face a court martial.' He sighed. 'Look, you can't win. It's not just a matter of the men I have here. There are thousands more mopping up parts of Shropshire at the moment. Once they're finished, they'll make their way here. Then there's also Vadula's army in Staffordshire. They will be here in days. In all we could have forty thousand men here, if we choose. You cannot possibly withstand that number . . . I have made a fair offer, and you would do well to accept it.'

Jack pursed his lips. 'I'll pass your message on to my leaders.'

'You should do more than that. You should actively persuade them. You need to understand how truly powerful the army have become. We are much stronger than you could imagine. *I am much stronger.*' Jhala took in a deep breath, his chest expanding. 'I have more powers than you would believe. My abilities have increased tenfold.'

Jack frowned. What was Jhala talking about? Jhala was a blocked siddha, one who'd used a power too early and so been unable to progress. Jhala had never learnt any war yantras.

But now Jack felt a shiver cross his skin as he recalled what Kanvar had told him the day before. The Sikhs believed the Rajthanans already had the Great Yantra and were now deriving unimaginable powers from it. Was Jhala hinting at something like this? Is this what he was driving at?

'I'll do my best,' Jack said, his voice clipped.

'Excellent.' Jhala motioned towards the cavalrymen. 'We should be getting back.'

Jhala began striding towards the horses, hands behind his back. Jack walked alongside him.

'Come down to meet me in . . . shall we say an hour?' Jhala said. 'I will await your return and your decision.' He paused and stared hard at Jack. 'I hope you will have the right answer for me. If your people decline my offer, I will not be able to guarantee anyone's safety. Least of all yours. I'm counting on you. Make sure you do your very best.'

'We cannot accept such terms.' The Earl of Shropshire took a rattling breath, his eyes watering. 'It will mean the end of the crusade. The end of the state of Shropshire. I cannot countenance that.'

Jack placed his hands behind his back. He'd been expecting this reaction.

He was standing in the ruined hall once more, facing the earl, who was still slumped in his chair. Levin and Henry were also present.

'Is this the best offer you could get us?' Henry snapped at Jack. 'You told us you knew this general. You said he'd give us favourable terms.'

'What were you expecting, Constable Ward?' Levin said. 'Jack

has tried his best as far as I can see. The offer is in some ways a generous one. I expected worse.'

Henry seethed and flexed his fingers, but he remained silent.

'Whatever we think of these terms, we cannot accept them,' the earl said in a weak voice.

Jack cleared his throat. 'I understand, my lord. But we also have to face the hard truth that we cannot repel the enemy for ever.'

'The words of a coward and a traitor.' Henry marched across the chamber, jabbing his finger at Jack. 'You see how this man counsels despair. He wants us to surrender.'

'He is merely stating facts,' Levin said. 'The enemy have a far larger force than we have. And our supplies are limited. We cannot hold out for ever.'

'Then we will have to pray to God to save us.' The earl breathed with great difficulty and slumped further down in his chair.

'Aye, we should do that,' Jack said. 'But I'll have one last try to talk General Jhala around. I have another idea.'

'What is it?' Levin asked.

Jack paused for a moment, then said, 'Jhala might agree to allow those who want to surrender to leave the fortress.'

Henry growled. 'Let traitors leave? Never.'

'We can't force people to fight a battle we can't win,' Jack said. 'We have women and children and the elderly here with us. We can't make them stay.'

'What are you suggesting?' Levin asked. 'That we let those who want to leave hand themselves over? The rest stay here?'

Jack nodded. 'Aye. If Jhala agrees to it.'

'Won't those people be sent to East Europe?' the earl said.

'I'll try to avoid that,' Jack said. 'But I suspect that won't be possible.'

'I say women and children only should be permitted to go,' Henry said. 'We need every man for the fight.'

'These people came here voluntarily in the first place,' Jack said. 'We should let them leave if they want to.'

Henry squinted at Jack. 'You want us to fail, don't you? Those heathens have sent you here to weaken us.'

'Enough, Constable Ward,' Levin said. 'Your bleating is not helping.' He turned to the earl. 'My lord, what is your decision?'

The earl wheezed, went to speak and then appeared too weak to manage it. Drool escaped from one side of his mouth and dribbled down his chin. One of his pages rushed across to him and wiped his mouth clean, before the earl waved the lad away.

The earl took the deepest breath he could, then said, 'It is a difficult decision. But I believe Jack is right. Those who want to leave must be allowed to do so. And we must negotiate with the heathens to ensure their safety.'

Jack bowed his head. 'I will do it, my lord, as best as I'm able.'

He stood up straight again and, as he turned to leave, caught sight of Henry. The constable's face was almost purple and his eyes were burning.

⊰••⊱

General Jhala paced across the grass, his brow furrowed as if he were pondering an impossible riddle.

He stopped and looked at Jack. 'This saddens me. It saddens me very much.'

Jack coiled his hands into fists and fought the desire to punch Jhala in the face. He was standing out in the middle of the plains again, negotiating with his old commander.

Jhala shook his head slowly. 'Jack, Jack. I'm disappointed. I thought we had an understanding. I would be lenient, so long as you talked your leaders around. You didn't keep your side of the bargain. And now you come to me with this new suggestion. My original proposal was that all of you surrender, not just some of you.' He clicked his tongue. 'You are making things very difficult for me.'

'You can't kill women and children,' Jack said. 'Where's the dharma in that?'

Jhala pursed his lips and gazed up at the hill. 'Where's the dharma in betraying your oath to the army?'

Jack's face felt hot. He wanted to ask where was the dharma in forcing a man to hunt down his friend? Where was the dharma in threatening to kill a man's daughter? But, with a great effort, he held back.

Jhala sighed. 'Look at what has become of the two of us. This is not how it was ever supposed to be.' He looked at the ground and went silent for a long time.

The wind whistled across the flats and buffeted Jack, the cold seeping through his tunic and even the doublet underneath. In the distance, he could see the army making camp. The elephants had been led away and were being tethered to the ground with chains. Sappers were digging a defensive earth wall. Followers were wrestling with vast sheets of canvas and wooden scaffolding as they put up the Rajthanans' tents.

Eventually, after waiting for perhaps a minute, Jack said, 'So, what about our proposal?'

Jhala looked up at Jack again. 'You know, I was very pleased when I heard you were here. I came immediately when I got the message. I was looking forward to seeing you again. I know this situation is hardly ideal, but I felt certain that . . . that we could come to an arrangement. I offered to spare you. You could walk away from this a free man, and yet you throw it all back in my face.'

Jack went to reply, but Jhala held up his hand, saying, 'I haven't finished yet. You asked me what I think of your proposal. Ordinarily I would use that quaint English phrase: "Go to hell." But I won't do that. For you, I will show mercy. But only because you're an old comrade.

'Here's what we'll do. You can tell your people that whoever wants to leave may leave within the next hour. After that, my amnesty will finish. I will not make this offer again in the future.'

'Where will the people be sent? They should get safe passage. They shouldn't be sent to East Europe.'

Jhala shook his head. 'No. You know full well that is out of the question. I'm not playing games here. Anyone who surrenders will go to East Europe. That is already a remarkably good offer. General Vadula will probably question me as to why I'm being so generous. I will not budge on this. Your people have one hour to come down here and give themselves up. They will go to Europe, but they will live. I give you my word. That is my final offer. You understand?'

'I understand,' Jack said, his jaw tight.

'But Jack,' Jhala's face turned cold, 'this amnesty is open for one hour only. After that, I'm afraid it's war.'

22

⟫◆⟪

'No, Father.' Elizabeth's eyes glimmered in the grey light. She shook her head. 'I'm staying here.'

'As will I.' Godwin placed his arm about his wife's shoulders. He glanced down at Cecily, who lay swaddled in Elizabeth's arms, then looked up at Jack, raised his chin and placed his hand on the hilt of his longsword. 'We talked about this and decided. We cannot run away.'

Jack ran his fingers through his hair. He could have done without this problem now. All across the fortress those people who'd decided to leave were packing their things and streaming out of the gate. Elizabeth and Cecily had to go with them. Had to.

'Look,' Jack said. 'There's no real hope. We'll have a hard job holding back that army down there, and more and more of them are going to be arriving over the next few days. We'll be overrun.'

'Then why are *you* staying?' Elizabeth's bottom lip quivered slightly.

Jack stalled. Why *was* he staying? It was a good question. It was strange to think that four years ago he'd started off opposing the First Crusade. Back then, he'd believed it was pointless to resist, that there was no hope of success. And now, here he was – making a last stand, with the remaining rebels, in a fortress on top of a hill.

'I have to stay.' His voice came out hoarse. 'I can't give up on our dream of freedom.'

A tear welled in one of Elizabeth's eyes. 'Exactly. And neither can we.'

Jack's throat tightened and he had to blink back the tears. He couldn't argue with his family any more. They'd made their decision, and he would respect it.

——◆——

In all, around three hundred decided to leave the fortress and take their chances with the Rajthanans. Jack didn't blame any of them for going. As he stood on the east wall, watching the line of people wend their way down the hill and across the plains, he prayed for them all, prayed they could somehow make a new life for themselves.

The shadows were lengthening and the sun was lowering towards the Welsh mountains to the west.

'What time is it?' he asked Kanvar, who was standing beside him.

Kanvar drew out his watch. 'Five o'clock by European reckoning.'

'I make that an hour since I spoke to Jhala.' Jack stared out at the dark mass of the army encircling them. 'The amnesty's over.'

'It appears so,' Kanvar said softly.

'You stayed.'

Kanvar frowned. 'Of course. Did you think I would leave now?'

'You don't have to be here. This isn't your war.'

'No.' Kanvar stared out towards the hills. 'But it is Waheguru's will that I stay, I believe.'

Jack nodded slowly. 'I reckon it must be God's will that I stay here too.'

——◆——

Jack sat beside one of the five fires that had been lit in the camp. Night had fallen and now most of the inhabitants of Folly Brook had congregated about the flames.

Only a handful of villagers had chosen to leave during Jhala's amnesty. One of them was James. The farmer had looked sheepish as he bid farewell to Jack. 'I'm sorry,' he'd said. 'If I were on my own, I'd stay. But I can't put my family through it.'

Jack gazed into the flames. He prayed James and his family were safe, wherever they now were.

Saleem slid out of the shadows and sat with his knees drawn up to his chin.

'Your family all right?' Jack asked.

Saleem nodded. 'Better.'

Saleem's mother had been distraught earlier in the day. During the amnesty, Saleem had insisted she and his sisters leave. At first, his mother had agreed and even went as far as the gate. But then, when it came to it, she couldn't part with Saleem. She'd had a tearful argument with her son, then finally put her foot down and demanded to stay.

'Did you get a new musket?' Jack asked.

The barrel of Saleem's old firearm had split during an accident while Jack was in Staffordshire.

'Yes,' Saleem said. 'It's inside.'

Henry and his men had arranged for all the available weapons to be distributed throughout the fortress. Thankfully, plenty of firearms had been brought from both Clun Valley and Shrewsbury. Almost everyone who knew how to fire a musket had been given one.

Jack patted Saleem on the shoulder. 'I'm glad you stayed. We need all the good men we can get.'

Saleem's face went red, a broad smile crossed his lips and he gazed at the ground in embarrassment. 'I wouldn't leave. I decided long ago to fight for these lands, to become a knight.'

'As far as I'm concerned, you're a knight already.'

Before Jack could say anything further, someone shouted on the other side of the fire. He looked up and saw Sonali talking agitatedly to Elizabeth. Sonali was sitting down, with Cecily in her arms. Elizabeth stood over her, hands on her hips.

'What are you doing with my baby?' Elizabeth hissed.

Sonali's mouth dropped open. 'I was just—'

'Give her to me!'

Jack stood up quickly. The last thing the camp needed was Sonali and Elizabeth arguing again.

Sonali handed Cecily across to Elizabeth, saying, 'Mary gave her to me. I was just looking after her for a moment.'

Elizabeth scowled. 'Don't you touch my child ever again, you hear?'

Sonali shot to her feet, her eyes blazing. For a moment, it seemed she was about to shout at Elizabeth, but instead she ran off into the darkness.

Jack rushed round the side of the fire and stopped beside Elizabeth. 'What the hell are you doing?'

Elizabeth's eyes flashed. 'I don't want her touching Cecily.'

Jack's face went hot for a second, but all he said was, 'I'll speak to you later.'

Then he slipped away into the shadows, searching for Sonali. He found himself jogging through a forest of gnarled stonework and twisting creepers. Moonlit walls and arches loomed all about him. Solitary towers speared the night. At times, he saw campfires shivering in the distance, but otherwise the area was deserted.

'Sonali!' he shouted.

No one replied.

He stopped and gazed into the whorls of masonry receding in all directions. There was no sign of Sonali anywhere. He'd lost her.

Where would she have gone? She wouldn't try to leave the fortress, would she? That would be risky. She might be a Rajthanan, but she was also now a traitor – and there was no telling what could happen to her if she left.

Then he had an idea.

He ran on through the ruins until he saw the black bulk of the east wall rising ahead of him. He dashed up a set of steps and reached the walkway at the top. The last time he'd been here, there'd only been a handful of sentries. But now he found numerous detachments of artillerymen slouching beside an array of weapons. The serpent-headed guns peered like gargoyles out of the embrasures, their mouths open and ready to breathe fire and metal at any assailants. Tiger-shaped mortars crouched on wooden platforms.

He hurried along the wall, catching snatches of the gunners' conversations. It seemed sappers had been spotted in the hills to the east. No doubt the enemy were planning to dig gun emplacements, just as Jhala had said they would.

Jack ran faster. Where the hell was Sonali?

He finally found her leaning against the parapet on an empty stretch of wall. She was gazing out at the scattered, twinkling arc of the army's campfires. She turned as he arrived and he saw she'd been crying.

'You all right?' he asked.

She wiped her eyes with her shawl. 'I'm fine. Don't worry.'

'I'll talk to Elizabeth. She has to stop this.'

'No. Leave it. I don't want to cause any more trouble.'

'Elizabeth has to respect you.'

'Please. You talking to her won't help. I'll just keep away from her for now. I'll find somewhere else to sleep.'

'You can't stay somewhere else. It might not be safe.'

Sonali stared out at the enemy. 'Nowhere in this fortress is safe.'

Jack went silent as he tried to think of a response. It was out of the question for Sonali to sleep anywhere other than at the Folly Brook camp. At the same time, he would have to somehow smooth things over between her and Elizabeth.

He leant against the parapet and was about to try to convince Sonali to come back with him, when a gun nearby gave a sudden blast. The sound shook the wall, the parapet vibrating beneath his hands. Sonali yelped and jumped slightly.

Heart thrashing wildly, he spun round and peered along the ramparts. Further booms rippled along the wall as the gunners sprang into action. The men danced about the artillery, sponging out muzzles, ramming down charges, and lifting and loading the iron balls. The guns flashed, rocked back and vomited flame and smoke. Balls screamed away into the darkness, indistinct blots for a second before vanishing completely.

He stared into the hills. He could make out little, but here and there he spotted tiny lights that could be lanterns. The enemy must have moved forward and begun building earthworks. And the rebel gunners were clearly trying to stop them.

Sonali gasped and pointed to the north-east. Jack turned just in time to see a ball of blue flame streak up from the sprawling European Army camp.

'What is it?' Sonali asked.

Jack knew exactly what it was. He'd been injured by it once. 'Sattva-fire.'

The fireball arced high into the sky, then wailed as it hurtled down towards the east wall.

Jack grasped Sonali's arm. 'We'd better get out of here.' His voice was thick.

They charged along the ramparts, heading for the stairway. The sound of the fireball built to a piercing screech. And then the missile slammed into the battlements about a hundred yards away. The stones beneath Jack's boots quivered and Sonali was almost knocked off her feet. Blue-white flame rolled into the air and bled over the walkway. Globules and tendrils of fire spiralled down to the ground below.

Jack couldn't see whether anyone had been hit, but he heard screaming and shouting over the roar of the guns.

'Quick!' he shouted at Sonali. 'This way!'

The two of them sprinted on down the walkway, dodging past the labouring artillerymen. The gunners' faces were streaked with dirt and glistening with sweat. The men worked together fluidly, loading and firing, loading and firing. They must have been trained in the European Army at some point.

The guns flared and pounded the darkness, the sound so loud it shuddered in Jack's chest. It was as though he and Sonali were trapped in some vast, infernal mill.

Jack glanced to his right and spotted another fireball shooting up from the army camp. A second followed, and then a third. The missiles were being fired now in rapid succession.

Who the hell was creating them? Jhala had never had the power in the past. But perhaps, now, with the help of the Great Yantra, he'd managed it. Was that possible? Or were there other siddhas amongst the army forces?

The fireballs vaulted overhead, plunged into the interior of the fortress and blasted up pillars of flame and rock.

Jack whispered a Hail Mary under his breath.

He reached the top of the stairs, Sonali right behind him. Five gunners came scrambling up with an ammunition chest, and he stepped aside to let them pass. Out of the corner of his eye he spotted flickers across the hills to the east. When he looked harder, he made out a multitude of orange flashes winking on the slopes.

The enemy had begun firing their artillery.

Less than a second later, a storm of round shot was shrieking all about him. The balls appeared suddenly from the dark and whistled past like ghosts, before plummeting into the fortress. With a metallic crunch, one smacked into the battlements about thirty feet away. Dust and shards of stone jetted upwards, and three men cried out as they tumbled to the ground below.

'Down here!' Jack gestured at the stairs.

He and Sonali clattered down the steps. When Jack snatched a look across the fortress, he saw countless shadowy figures dashing in every direction. Campfires still blazed in many places, and added to these were the plumes of flame cast up by the fireballs hammering into the ground.

He reached the bottom of the stairway and, with Sonali at his side, raced into the ruins. They stumbled between meandering walls and gaping archways. He glimpsed fearful people rushing to find cover, and heard shouts and screams over the endless thundering of the guns.

A round shot hummed past in front of him and lopped off a finger of stone protruding from a building. A second ball punched through a wall just feet away from him, the brittle stone shattering into a cloud of dust and splinters. He held his arm up to cover his eyes as he charged through the dust, while Sonali spluttered and coughed as she scurried after him.

They came out at a courtyard and skidded to a halt. People were criss-crossing the open space as they raced to find some-where to hide. A swarm of round shot fell about them. Balls ploughed into the earth. Others plucked people off their feet and dashed them to the ground. Jack saw a woman's head knocked straight off, blood spurting from her neck as she fell. A man was blown apart when a missile pummelled him in the stomach.

Sonali whimpered and raised her fist to her mouth.

Jack wiped the sweat from his eyes. He was breathing heavily and his heart was battering in his chest. He desperately wanted to get back to the Folly Brook camp. He had to make sure Elizabeth and Cecily were safe. But, on the other hand, he and Sonali could be killed if they didn't find shelter soon.

He turned to Sonali. 'We'll find somewhere for you to hide. Then I'll head back to the camp.'

Sonali's eyes widened and shone brightly. 'Don't you dare. I'm coming with you.'

Jack knew better than to waste time arguing. 'Right, then.' He motioned to the courtyard. 'We have to get across that. It's the quickest way back.'

She nodded. 'Then let's go.'

They charged out into the open, weaving their way around the corpses. There were fewer people running across the area now – most had either escaped or been struck down. But the balls still battered the ground. They swooped down in front of Jack, a few bouncing away again. He heard them whistling all around him. He was certain he would be hit. There seemed no chance he would survive . . .

Then there was a deafening howl to his right. He looked up just in time to see a fireball moaning as it careered towards him. It was so close that the light stung his eyes and the heat scorched his face.

With his heart in his throat, he flung himself against Sonali. The two of them stumbled backwards and out of the path of the missile. The fireball thumped into the ground and a pulse of hot air seared the back of Jack's head, knocking him off his feet. He fell next to Sonali and flipped over in time to see brilliant flames erupting from the earth. The sattva-fire snarled and popped as it ran across the ground, setting the grass alight.

Jack saw a line of flame slithering towards him. He rolled to his side and yanked Sonali to her feet. They got out of the way just before the fire sizzled past.

Jack grasped Sonali's arm and dragged her towards the entrance to a walkway. As they plunged into the narrow passage, a second fireball pummelled the ground behind them. Jack glanced back and saw a fiery maelstrom boiling towards them. He charged on with Sonali and they escaped before the fire engulfed them.

They skidded round a corner and bounded across a stretch of paving stones. Finally, the crumbling palace of the Folly Brook camp stood before them. They were approaching the building from the rear and had to run round the side of the structure to get to the entrance. The final corner of the building appeared ahead. The entryway lay just beyond this.

They were almost there.

There was a piercing shriek nearby. Jack spotted a glint out of the corner of his eye, looked up and spied a shell with a sparking fuse streaking across the ruins. It pounded into a pile of masonry about twenty feet from him. There was a clap and a sheet of yellow flame roared upwards. Chunks of stone whistled through the air, and shell fragments skipped and hopped across the paving stones. A piece of shrapnel chirped as it stabbed the stone wall immediately in front of him.

He glanced at Sonali – her eyes were wide and glassy.

The two of them ran on, darted round the corner and found themselves in the open space about the entryway. More shells rained down. One smacked open in mid-air, scattering flame and musket balls. Another thumped into the earth and shot up a column of fire and clods. The sky teemed with shot.

Jack led the way along the wall, keeping as close to the building as he could in order to get at least a little cover. The five campfires were still burning, but all the villagers had vanished.

He reached the entrance and scrambled inside, Sonali pressing in right behind him. For a second, he saw nothing but darkness. But then his eyes adjusted and he found he was surrounded by the grey, wide-eyed faces of the inhabitants of Folly Brook. He spotted Mary, Godwin, Mark, Saleem and Kanvar. They were all crammed into the musty chamber.

Then a voice cried out. Elizabeth pushed herself forward and embraced him.

'I'm sorry,' she whispered.

'It's all right.' He patted her on the back. 'Don't worry.'

A shell exploded outside and musket balls and metal fragments screamed against the palace walls.

He dragged Elizabeth away from the entrance, then shouted at the villagers, 'Get back! Into the other rooms!'

With shells falling all around them it was too dangerous to stay near the entryway. Shrapnel could easily fly in.

Everyone shuffled back into the series of cave-like chambers formed by the fallen stonework. The ceilings were even lower here than in the first room, and Jack had to stoop to avoid hitting his head. He crouched down next to Elizabeth and Godwin. Elizabeth cradled Cecily in her arms, rocking and jiggling the child to keep her quiet.

Saleem struck a match and lit a tallow candle. The wavering light rendered everyone's features hollow and deathly.

'Should we go to the wall?' Saleem asked Jack. 'To defend it?'

Jack shook his head. 'Not at the moment. The army haven't sent troops up yet. They'll keep firing their guns and hope we give up. We'll stay here, unless we get word there's trouble.'

Henry had announced that, in the event of an attack, criers with bells would be sent to summon people to defend the walls. In the meantime, the best thing Jack and the others could do was stay alive.

The firestorm continued outside. Balls shrilled, shells blasted and fireballs howled. In the distance, people screamed as they were struck down.

Elizabeth shivered and Jack put his hand on her shoulder for a moment.

A shell burst immediately overhead. Metal fragments and balls scuttled across the stonework and rattled down through crevices and grooves.

A moment later, a fireball slammed into the roof. The impact shivered through the chamber's walls and floor. Jack could hear the flames sizzle as they poured across the masonry. Blue light licked through a crack in one corner of the ceiling.

Many of the villagers gasped. Several children whimpered and Saleem's mother sobbed. Cecily began grizzling, but Elizabeth rocked the child and she went silent again.

Jack studied the ceiling. How solid was it? He knew that in some places the stone lay several layers thick. But, for the most part, the roof was no more than the single layer of slabs lying directly above him.

He prayed they would hold.

Then the onslaught intensified.

A round shot pounded the roof, giving a metal chime. Everyone in the room jumped slightly, and dust trickled down from the ceiling.

A second shot struck the roof. Then another. A crack snaked across the ceiling and more dust gushed down.

Two more shells burst nearby, then further balls pummelled the stonework overhead. Many of the children were crying now, and several adults shut their eyes and covered their ears.

For a second, Jack recalled Jhala standing out on the plains earlier in the day. It was Jhala who'd ordered this attack, Jhala who was threatening them all.

Jack clenched his jaw so tightly his teeth ached. A cold determination flooded through him. One day, he would kill his old commander. He promised this to himself.

More and more fissures fanned across the ceiling and a central crack began to widen. Jack grasped the candle from Saleem and held it up to the roof. That main crack looked alarmingly large.

How much longer could the stone slab hold?

He handed the candle back to Saleem, saying, 'Wait here. I'm going to check something.'

Both Saleem and Elizabeth protested, but he ignored them, clambered over the crouching villagers and ducked back into the first chamber. He dashed across to the entrance, pressed himself against the wall and peered round the edge. A fiery blizzard raged outside. The sky seethed with sparks and flashes. Squalls of round shot flickered in the dark. Ahead of him, a minaret toppled over as balls battered it.

It was like a vision of hell.

There was nowhere nearby to take shelter, and he and the others couldn't risk searching further afield. It was too dangerous.

He darted back to the others and crouched down beside Elizabeth again.

'We'll stay here,' he said to no one in particular. 'Best place for us at the moment.'

Elizabeth nodded, and a few of the villagers muttered amongst themselves.

Then a series of balls smashed in rapid succession into the slab overhead. It was as if a giant were stomping on the roof. The stone groaned and the central crack yawned. A cloud of dust poured down and several people burst into fits of coughing.

Jack wiped the grit from his eyes. He shot a look at Sonali, who was crouching beside Kanvar and looking around like a cornered cat.

Thump.

Another ball struck the roof, loosening more dust. Most of the villagers were whimpering or praying now.

Thump.

The crack was getting dangerously wide now.

Thump.

The candle went out and someone started screaming. Jack grasped Elizabeth. Held her tight. Should he tell them all to flee now? Should they run out into the storm of metal and fire and take their chances?

He would wait for another few moments and pray that the roof would hold.

If he were crushed to death, at least he was with his family. At least they were together.

Thump.

23

◆

The man moaned, sobbed and clutched at the edge of the makeshift stretcher as Jack and Godwin carried him. Blood and dirt speckled his face, his hair was matted with what looked like innards and his torso was peppered with bullet wounds. The balls had ripped through his tunic and now dried blood encrusted most of his clothing. A shell must have exploded near to him and showered him with metal.

The pain seemed to come in waves. At times he lay still and quiet, but then he would shudder, gnash his teeth and cry out like one of the damned in hell.

Jack said a Hail Mary in his head.

Godwin, holding the other end of the stretcher, glanced back at the injured man at one point. But Jack muttered at his son-in-law to keep looking straight ahead and to walk faster. They had to get to the temporary hospital as quickly as they could.

Jack's eyes stung and his head felt as though it were in a vice. He'd barely slept during the night. Even when the bombardment had finally subsided, he'd found it impossible to rest. He'd lain in the dark, listening to the others snoring, and wondered how in the world he was going to keep his family safe.

Dawn had revealed a scene of devastation. Much of the stone-work inside the fortress had been smashed to piles of rubble. Fires smouldered where carts, supplies, tents and trees had been set alight. The smell of soot and burnt flesh drifted across the ruins.

Jack and the others from Folly Brook had gone to work straight away, hunting for those wounded who were still alive. Jack and Godwin had fashioned a stretcher from pieces of a broken wagon. Then they'd discovered the injured man lying beside a shell crater.

Now the large hall that housed the hospital appeared before them. The building had survived the onslaught during the night, but there were several gaping holes in its walls where the masonry had crumbled away long ago. People were carrying the wounded in through the various openings. Others limped into the hall, clutching themselves where they'd been injured.

Jack and Godwin carried the wounded man through what must once have been the building's main entrance. Inside, a scene of carnage confronted them. The wounded lay writhing on sacks on the floor. A man near the entryway was covered in blood, bellowing at the top of his voice and bashing his fist on the ground in agony. A woman lay next to him. She was covered in weeping burns and was trembling silently. Jack swallowed back vomit when he saw a small boy with both of his legs blown off.

Flies buzzed throughout the chamber, collecting around wounds and puddles of blood. Several people, including monks and friars, were nursing the injured as best they could. But clearly there was little they could do. It was unlikely any of them had been trained in Rajthanan medicine, and they had few supplies or pieces of equipment.

A monk in black robes bustled across to Jack and Godwin. As the man stepped into a shaft of milky light, Jack saw that it was Brother Michael from Clun Abbey.

'It's good to see you,' Jack said.

Michael looked dazed for a moment, as if he'd lost his mind, but then his eyes focused on Jack. 'Ah. You live.' His gaze flicked down to the man on the stretcher. He motioned to a corner of the hall. 'Put him over there. We will do what we can for him.'

Jack squinted past Michael, looking for Kanvar. The Sikh had headed to the hospital first thing that morning, saying he would use his healing power to save as many as he could. But Jack saw no sign of him now.

'Is Kanvar here?' Jack asked. 'The Indian with the beard.'

'He was here for a moment,' Michael replied. 'But then he left. He said he had to prepare himself for something. I heard he's over by the west wall. Someone saw him wandering about and raving.'

Jack frowned. Wandering and raving? Even for Kanvar that sounded strange.

After putting the injured man down, Jack left Godwin behind and set off on his own to find Kanvar. It was an overcast day and the clouds were motionless in the sky. He half expected to see a round shot whisk overhead or a fireball come screaming towards the earth. But, for the moment, the enemy had stopped firing.

Why wasn't Kanvar at the hospital? Why wasn't he using his healing power?

Jack wished he himself had some power with which he could treat the wounded. But the one healing yantra he knew, Great Health, could only be used once in a lifetime – and even then, you could only use it to cure yourself.

What the rebels really needed were Rajthanan doctors and medical siddhas. And there was no chance of any of those coming to the rebels' aid.

Jack found Kanvar in a courtyard on the west side of the fortress. The Sikh was sitting meditating in the shade of a hunched oak tree.

As Jack walked across the grass, he passed into a powerful stream. The grainy sattva coursed around him and the sweet incense tickled his nose. This was the only stream he'd come across so far inside the fortress.

Kanvar stirred and opened his eyes as Jack crouched down beside him.

'You all right?' Jack asked. 'Someone said you were walking around like a madman.'

Kanvar frowned. 'I do not understand why someone would say that. I was pacing about, but I was taking some measurements. Perhaps that is what this person saw.'

Jack snorted. The people in the fortress were likely to see almost anything Kanvar did as strange. 'What about your healing power?'

Kanvar put his hand to his forehead. 'I am preparing to use it. I must meditate for several hours. Sadly, though, I will only be able to treat one person per day at the most. That is, if I even survive myself.'

'You sure you want to do this?'

'I must help as best I can.'

'All right. I'll leave you to meditate in that case.'

'Wait.' Kanvar's eyes widened. 'I am glad you are here. This morning I made a discovery which should interest you.'

'What?'

Kanvar stared into the distance. 'You are, at this moment, in the Great Yantra.'

'Here?'

'Yes. The stream you are sitting in, if my calculations are correct, is within the yantra.'

Jack felt a flash of irritation. 'This is just a few hours from Folly Brook. You said the nearest point of the yantra was in Staffordshire.'

'That is what I believed. But when I met Takhat, we swapped the results of our surveys. I copied what Takhat had discovered onto my own map. I hadn't had a chance to study the map in detail until we got to this fortress. I started examining it yesterday, and then again this morning. And I now believe the Great Yantra covers a different area from what we Sikhs previously thought. I will show you.'

Kanvar reached into his satchel and unfurled a large chart. The wind tugged at one of the corners, and he placed a rock on the paper to hold it down.

The first thing Jack noticed was that a wide area of this map had few markings on it at all. Expanses around the edges were plain white.

'This is a map of Britain and Ireland.' Kanvar splayed his fingers over the central part of the chart, which was covered in the usual cryptic lines and squiggles.

He then waved his hand over a portion of the central area. 'This region is Scotland.' He pressed his finger on a large blue dot. 'Here is the centre, which you helpfully found for us.' He swept his fingers in a circle. 'And here are the markings of the Great Yantra itself.'

Jack noted the numerous blue lines that represented the sattva streams. 'It's not as complicated as I thought it would be.'

'No. As far as we have been able to tell, the design is not, in fact, as detailed as some yantras.'

Jack studied the map more closely. A strange feeling was creeping up on him, but he couldn't tell why. He had that odd sense of unreality he'd noted previously when Kanvar had explained the secrets of sattva.

'Now, here is the meeting point in Staffordshire.' Kanvar pointed to a blue dot towards the bottom of the map. 'You see some lines here that indicate where we Sikhs believed the edge of the yantra lay. But when I looked at this more closely, I came to see that, given Takhat's discoveries and the location of the centre in Scotland, it would make more sense if the edge ran along this axis.' He drew a line with his finger further down the chart. 'And, in that case, the edge would run directly through the fortress, exactly where we are sitting now.' He jabbed a point on the map with his finger.

Jack rubbed his eyes. He thought he understood what Kanvar was saying. But this seemed less interesting to him now. Instead, he was transfixed by the incomplete drawing of the Great Yantra. There was something about it that was almost familiar, but he couldn't put his finger on it. His eyes flickered over the chart, from Shropshire all the way up to Scotland and beyond.

He was surprised to see the blue lines extending up into the white space towards the top of the map. 'What is all this empty space?'

'That is the sea.'

'The streams run across the sea?'

'Oh yes. They run everywhere.'

Jack sat back. He hadn't considered this. But of course, if the streams could stretch over the ground, why not the sea? 'How do you map those, then?'

'By boat. It is difficult but possible. However, we've had to do less than you might think. You see, the design of the yantra is symmetrical. The pattern in one quarter is repeated in the other quarters.'

Jack stared at the map. The blue lines of the yantra seemed brighter and more vivid. He could see what Kanvar meant now – the design did seem to repeat itself.

'Almost all yantras are symmetrical to some degree,' Kanvar continued. 'The Great Yantra especially so. This has made our task much simpler . . . are you all right?'

Jack could well understand why Kanvar had asked him this question, because he was blinking furiously and trembling.

He'd seen something that couldn't be. Could not be true.

And yet there it was.

The blue lines representing the sattva streams seemed to glow with an unnatural fire and brand themselves on the back of his eyes.

'I know what the full design is,' he said.

Kanvar's forehead bunched into a frown. 'I do not think that could be possible.'

Jack pressed the paper with a shaking finger. 'I know it sounds crazy. But I do. I'm sure of it.'

'Jack, are you feeling well—'

'It's the Celtic cross necklace. The one Katelin always wore.'

'I do not understand what you are saying.'

'Listen.' Jack grasped Kanvar's tunic at the collar. Kanvar jumped and looked alarmed, but Jack continued gripping him. He knew he was sounding like a madman. But he couldn't help it, because he was caught up in a whirlwind now. 'I've seen the design of the Great Yantra before. Many times. It's exactly the same as the necklace my wife used to wear. She gave it to me, and now I've given it to Elizabeth.'

Kanvar swallowed. 'You are certain of this?'

'Yes!' Jack realised he was getting carried away. Perhaps he really was going mad. He let go of Kanvar, who straightened his tunic again.

'Look here.' Jack pointed at the map. 'It was when you told me the pattern repeats that I finally got it. See these two marks here.' He ran his fingers along two wide blue lines that stretched up towards the centre of the design. 'That's the bottom arm of the cross.' He gestured to the right side of the map. 'And here is another arm.'

'Yes, I know these.' Kanvar leant over the map. 'Those are what we Sikhs have referred to as the spokes. They reach out to the edge of the great wheel and then run towards the centre.'

'Exactly. They form a cross. All leading to that point in Scotland.'

Kanvar licked his lips. 'But a cross is not a circle. All the yantras are circular in design.'

Jack grinned. 'That's what confused me at first. The thing is, we're not talking about any cross – it's what we call a Celtic cross. It's an ancient design. A cross inside a circle.' He moved his finger around the edge of the yantra. 'You see . . . that's the edge, as you call it. That's the outer rim of the circle. And there inside is the cross, all four arms leading into the centre.'

Kanvar stared hard at the chart. He was completely still and his eyes didn't blink, although his pupils darted this way and that across the blue markings. 'I see what you mean. It is like a cross. We Sikhs have been describing it as a wheel, but a cross makes sense too.' He looked up at Jack. 'Extraordinary. You are certain the necklace matches this design exactly? In every detail?'

'Aye, I'm sure.'

'Incredible.' Kanvar stared into space for a long time, muttering to himself. Finally, he said, 'You must show me this necklace at once.'

'Right. Let's find Elizabeth. She should be back at the camp.'

Kanvar swept up his map and packed it away in his satchel. Then he and Jack marched back through the ruins.

Jack felt filled with a strange fire, as if a djinn had seized hold of him. The world about him looked sharp and distinct. Despite the cloudy day, the colours seemed bright.

Could it really be true that Katelin's necklace was moulded into the shape of the Great Yantra? It seemed impossible, but there was no other explanation for what he'd seen.

And did this mean that they now had the power and could use it to fight the Rajthanans? He felt giddy at the thought.

Then he heard a shrill whistling in the distance and his skin rippled. It sounded like round shot.

A second later, he heard a series of cracks and rumbles as several guns were fired.

It was starting again.

He glanced at Kanvar and, without either of them saying a word, they began running across the broken stonework. All around them, people were hunting feverishly for cover. Everyone knew what was in store for them now and wasted no time in finding shelter.

The grumble of the guns grew louder. When Jack looked towards the east, he spotted the dark specks of round shot swarming over the wall. The white smoke of the rebels' guns billowed across the battlements.

The firefight was growing hotter. He and Kanvar had to get back to the Folly Brook camp quickly.

A round shot shrieked out of the sky and slammed into the ground ahead of Jack. Another swung down from the left and smacked a pillar in half.

Jack and Kanvar clambered over piles of rubble, ducked through archways and charged across courtyards. More balls hailed down around them, clipping stonework, shredding trees and punching holes in buildings.

As they ran alongside a low, crumbling wall, Jack heard a familiar screech. When he looked up, he saw a shell plummeting towards him and Kanvar. It was already so close he could clearly see the black ball and the fizzing fuse. Blots of smoke trailed behind it.

For a second, the shell seemed to hang in the air – as if time had stopped. But then it smashed into the ground behind the wall, spitting up a puff of dust.

Jack's heart bashed in his chest. He knew the shell could detonate at any moment, and he mustn't be near it when it did. Both he and Kanvar charged forward, skidding on the shattered stones.

Jack felt as though he were wading through mud. Every step he took seemed intolerably slow. Why was it taking him so long to get away? Why couldn't he move faster?

Then he heard a cry behind him. He spun round and saw that Kanvar had tripped over and was now on all fours on the ground.

Jack's heart pounded. He shouted at Kanvar to get up.

Kanvar leapt to his feet and was about to run when the shell exploded. He was wiped out by a screaming wall of metal, stone and dust. Shell fragments whistled through the air. Jack flung himself to the ground, hands over his head in a vain effort to protect himself.

He lay still for a moment, panting heavily, heart racing. His ears rang so loudly he was deafened for a moment, but then his hearing returned.

He was still breathing. He was still alive.

He jumped to his feet again and saw a huge bulb of dust roiling before him. But there was no sign of Kanvar.

Christ.

He charged into the dust, coughing and spitting grit from his mouth. He scoured the rubble and finally spotted Kanvar lying half buried under the broken masonry that was all that remained of the wall.

Jack rushed across to the Sikh and squatted down. 'You all right?'

Kanvar opened his eyes. His breathing was shallow and there was blood on his face. He frowned slightly and stared up into the sky. 'I do not know.' He turned to face Jack, his eyes focusing again. 'I do not know if I'm all right.'

Jack's eyes strayed down to Kanvar's stomach. And then he felt as though the ground were sinking for a moment. A large chunk of shrapnel was poking out of Kanvar's abdomen. Glistening blood was pouring from the wound and soaking into his tunic.

Jack squeezed his eyes shut for a second and gritted his teeth. That injury looked bad. He doubted Kanvar could survive.

But he couldn't give up hope yet.

He grasped Kanvar's arm. 'I'll get you out.'

He began dragging the slabs of masonry aside. He quickly swept away the smaller pieces, but the larger chunks proved more difficult. Sweat burst on his forehead as he tried to shift the heaviest lump of rock. He grunted and pushed with all of his strength. But the stone wouldn't budge.

'Leave it,' Kanvar said in a weak voice.

Jack looked across at Kanvar. 'What?'

'There is no point.' Kanvar shut his eyes. 'I am departing from this world.'

'No. You hold on. I'll get you out and get you to the hospital.'

Kanvar opened his eyes again and shook his head. 'There is no hope for me. I can feel the life leaving me.'

A round shot tore past overhead and crunched into a building nearby. In the distance, a shell exploded in mid-air, blossoming into a red and yellow garland.

'I can't just sit here,' Jack said. 'I have to try.'

He glanced around and saw no one else in the area. He shouted for help as loudly as he could. But no one came to his aid.

Kanvar grasped Jack's arm. 'There is no need. I am happy.'

'Happy? What the hell are you talking about?'

'I followed Waheguru's will. I made the right choice in helping you. There is nothing to regret.'

Kanvar's eyes clouded over and slowly closed.

Jack shook Kanvar. 'Don't fall asleep, you hear me?'

Kanvar's eyes remained closed, but he was still breathing.

Jack scanned the surroundings again. The dust had faded, but he still couldn't see anyone. 'Help! I've got an injured man here! Help!'

'Listen to me,' Kanvar said suddenly.

When Jack looked back, he saw that the Sikh's eyes were open once more.

'You must try to use the Great Yantra,' Kanvar continued. 'You said you knew the design well. That might mean you know it well enough to hold it in your mind.'

'Don't worry about that now.'

'No. Listen. You must promise me you will try. If you gain the power, that could change the course of the war.'

'All right, I promise I'll try.'

'Good . . . Waheguru bless everyone.'

Kanvar sighed, then his head lolled to one side and his eyes went blank.

Jack shouted over and over again for help. He cried out so loudly that his throat hurt. But no one came.

And it wouldn't have done any good if they had.

Kanvar was gone.

24

The Great Yantra hung in Jack's mind, glowing white on a black background. With his eyes shut, Jack recalled every part of the design. He saw the outer circle, the four arms of the cross and the inner circle where the arms met. Each section was entwined with knotted Celtic patterns. In the middle, a whirlpool-like marking coiled into the very centre.

Kanvar had been right. Jack had found it easy to hold the yantra in his mind. He'd seen the design so often over the years, it was branded in his head.

He straightened his back and breathed in deeply. The material world began to recede. He heard the crack of shells exploding and the steady boom of gunfire. But none of this mattered to him. The battle was taking place far away, in a distant land.

He was approaching the purusha realm. A holy silence encased him and the air about him seemed still. He was outside time and outside his own body.

He focused all his attention on the Great Yantra, and the design circled slowly in the darkness.

And then, without him expecting it, the yantra locked into place and steadied. He bent all his thoughts towards it, blocking out anything else.

And suddenly it blazed into brilliant light.

In that instant, he knew, without any doubt, that Katelin's necklace was a yantra. Only a yantra would come alive in his head in this way. Only a yantra would blind his inner eye with light.

———◆———

Jack sat in a small chamber deep within the ruined palace. The other inhabitants of Folly Brook were huddled in the adjoining rooms, sheltering from the missiles that had been raining down on them for the past hour. Only Sonali crouched with him in the tiny grotto.

He held Katelin's necklace up, the ringed cross circling slowly in the light from a single candle. Before him, spread out on the floor, was Kanvar's map of Britain and Ireland. The chart had survived the blast – unlike Kanvar's spyglass and pistol, which had both unfortunately been destroyed.

Sonali's brow furrowed. 'It's hard to take all this in.'

'I know,' Jack replied. He'd just explained to her, as quickly as he could, everything he knew about the Great Yantra.

Kanvar was dead, and now it was down to Jack to make sense of what he and the Sikh had discovered just two hours earlier. Sonali was the only person he could talk to about all of this.

Sonali gazed at the map and then back at the dangling necklace. 'They do look the same. I can see that. The map is missing some parts. But otherwise it matches.'

Jack nodded. 'And just ten minutes ago, I managed to hold the design still in my mind. It's a yantra, without a doubt.'

'What I don't understand is why that necklace? Why would it have been made into the shape of this Great Yantra?'

'I've been thinking about that. The thing is, this necklace isn't one of a kind. There are lots of them in Wales. You see the design on shrines too. There are even a few in Clun Valley. It's all over the place.'

'How could that be?'

'I heard a theory once that the ancient Britons knew about the sattva streams. Jhala told me this, actually. The idea is that the Britons set up markers to show where the streams ran. They would put up standing stones, things like that. The markers were like a map. Maybe the Britons mapped out the whole Great Yantra.'

'That would be a huge task.'

'True, but they could have done it over time, couldn't they?' He placed the necklace gently on the ground. 'The thing is, I've been in the Great Yantra twice before – that I know about, at least. The first time was the meeting point under Mahajan's castle. The ancient Scots buried their kings in that exact spot. They must have known there was something important about it. The second time was with Kanvar, a few days ago. I was in another part of the yantra where a few streams meet. And that just happened to be in a stone circle. It can't all be a coincidence.'

A shell pummelled the roof directly above them. The impact made Sonali jump, and tremors coursed through the walls and floor. The shell burst a second later and metal fragments flayed the stonework.

Sonali brushed a stray lock of hair from her face. 'But, if the Britons knew the yantra, wouldn't they have used the power?'

'That's just it. I reckon they have used it. At least, a very few people did in the past.' He nodded at the map. 'I think this yantra is what we in Britain call the Grail.'

'The Grail? When you told me the story, you said the Grail was a cup of some sort.'

'I think the stories could be wrong about that. Or maybe whoever first told those stories was trying to keep the truth about the Grail secret. In any case, I reckon Galahad and Oswin both found out that the design could be used to release a power.'

'They learnt to meditate and hold it still?'

'Something like that. We Christians pray. That's a bit like meditating. Maybe they both just stumbled across the secret.'

A series of balls battered the roof and further lines of dust trickled down.

'So, you said you used the yantra.' Sonali fixed her gaze on Jack. 'That means you have the great power, then?'

Jack sighed and ran his fingers through his hair. 'I don't think so.'

'What do you mean?'

'I managed to hold the yantra still, and it worked. The yantra lit up. You know how it is. But nothing happened after that. I didn't get any knowledge about the power.'

'Ah. You think it's because—'

'Because I'm a blocked siddha, yes. That's the way it always is when you're blocked, isn't it? You can learn the yantra, but you can't use the power.'

Sonali nodded slowly. 'Unless you can use your special ability.'

'Exactly. If I could break the law of karma, my guess is I'd be able to use this yantra.'

'But, at the moment, you can't.'

Jack tensed his hand into a fist. 'No.' It had been a blow to realise that he was so close to gaining the power, and yet still couldn't achieve it.

'Perhaps someone else could try,' Sonali said.

Jack shook his head. 'There's not enough time. It takes months to learn a yantra. You know that. I'm the only one who's looked at this design enough to memorise it.'

Sonali lowered her gaze. 'That is true. If the yantra is to help us at the moment, it has to be you who uses it.'

Jack sighed again. He'd taken a big step forward, it seemed, but he still had a long distance to go.

And he was running out of time.

'All I can do is keep trying,' he said. 'Before he died, Kanvar told me to try. I won't let him down.'

Sonali went silent and stared at the ground at this mention of Kanvar. 'We will cremate him when we get a chance.'

Jack cleared his throat. 'Aye. When the firing stops. We owe it to him. All of us. He gave up everything to help the crusade, you know. His country, his people. Everything.'

Sonali nodded silently. 'And if you keep trying, Jack, perhaps you can gain the power. That is our only hope now, I fear.'

Before Jack could reply, Mark scurried into the cramped space. 'Master, the heathens have sent out a white flag again.'

Jack frowned. He now realised he hadn't heard shelling for several minutes. Clearly the enemy had decided to stop firing at the fortress.

But why would Jhala want to talk again? Whatever the case, Jack had to find out.

'Get my horse saddled up,' he said to Mark. 'I'm going down there.'

———✦———

General Jhala stood staring up at the hill for a long time. His eyes were slightly moist and a cold wind ruffled his tunic. With his weathered face, he had the look of a hunter, of someone who'd lived outdoors for much of his life.

Jack stood nearby, studying his old guru. He'd known this man almost as well as he'd known anyone. They'd spent months together in trenches, out on patrol, tracking enemy troops in the wilds, on the battlefield. There'd been a bond of some sort between them. Jack was sure of that.

But now all he wanted to do was to kill Jhala. The thought throbbed white hot in his head.

How would he do it? He had no weapons on him, and Jhala's entourage of five cavalrymen were sitting on their horses watching him from barely fifty yards away. If he tried to attack Jhala, they would set upon him in seconds. He doubted he could kill Jhala with his bare hands in such a short space of time.

What about Lightning? If he began meditating now, picturing the yantra in his head, he might be able to blast Jhala before anyone realised what he was up to.

Maybe.

But of course, all this planning was futile. He wasn't going to kill Jhala, because he was down here to negotiate. While there was still a chance of getting a better deal for his people, he had to hold himself back.

And more than that, even if he did kill Jhala, he would then be killed instantly by the cavalrymen. There was no hope of him using Lightning against all of them quickly enough. They would ride across and cut him down with their scimitars, or simply shoot him with their carbines from where they were seated, all before he had a chance to retaliate.

How would he help to defend the fortress then? How would he protect his family? How would he keep on trying to use the Great Yantra?

Jhala clicked his tongue as he gazed up at the fortress. 'The walls have held up well. I can see a bit of damage here and there. But, by and large, they've hardly been scratched.' He turned to Jack. 'Well built. Late-era English Caliphate, of course. You can tell by the battlements. Constructed for cannon.'

Jhala looked up at the fortress again. 'Of course, there are several breaches in those walls already, aren't there? And the gatehouse – no gates any more. That weakens the defences.' He faced Jack and smiled slightly. 'Makes my task a little easier.'

Jack's face was glowing and he could hear his heartbeat in his ears. For a second, he saw Kanvar lying dead beneath the rubble just a few hours ago. He felt the muscles in his face twitch at the effort of holding himself back from attacking Jhala.

'We have injured,' Jack said. 'Many injured. Women and children included. We can't look after them properly up there. We don't have the right medicines.'

Jhala sighed. 'If only you and your leaders hadn't been so obstinate. Then we could have prevented all this. There really was no need for it. It saddens me so very much.'

'I propose you allow the wounded to leave the fortress. We'll put them on carts and they can travel to somewhere else as best they can.'

Jhala scratched his nose. 'You propose that, do you? That is interesting. But you see, I don't think you are in a position to put forward proposals.'

'You can't just let those people die.'

Jhala sucked on his teeth. 'I would prefer civilians not to die. That is true.' He took a deep breath. 'I will therefore make a concession. This is not something I would ordinarily do. In fact, I can scarcely believe I'm doing it at all. Nevertheless, I will allow the wounded to come down, but only on the condition that *all* of you lay down your arms and come down too. All of you must surrender to me. The earl will be executed. The rest, as I said before, will go to East Europe.' Jhala looked at his boots for a moment. 'And you can still go free, Jack.' He looked up again. 'But this really is my final offer now. No more games. You must all surrender. Then this unpleasantness will all be over.'

Jack paused. Once again, his old commander had made what seemed a reasonable offer. But again, it was one the rebels could never agree to. He'd already spoken with the Earl of Shropshire, Sir Levin and Henry before coming out to meet Jhala. All had agreed they would remain in the fortress. They would fight, and they would never give in.

'My leaders can't agree to that,' Jack said. 'We will release the wounded. Everyone else wishes to stay.'

'I see.' Jhala nodded slowly. His eyes hardened. 'Once again, you throw my offer in my face. I offer to spare you, Jack, set you free. And you spit it back at me.'

'We can't accept—'

'What happened to you?' Jhala's cheeks were reddening slightly. 'You were my best disciple. A fine soldier. And now here you are, a traitor. Why?'

Jack felt a tidal wave engulfing him. He clenched his fists tightly. He almost couldn't breathe for a second at the effort of holding himself back.

With a strained voice, he said, 'You ask me why I joined the crusade? There's a simple answer – you. You threatened to kill my daughter. Why else would I turn against the empire?'

Jack hadn't meant to say these words. But now that he had, he was glad. How much more was he going to be able to get from Jhala anyway? Did it matter what he said now?

Jhala blinked. 'That is not fair. Your daughter had been arrested for aiding the enemy. She was only spared because of me. If I hadn't stepped in, she would have hanged.'

'You used her to control me. To force me to go after William.'

Jhala shook his head sadly. 'Jack, Jack. What has become of you? You seem to have lost your mind, like so many of your countrymen. William was a traitor. He broke his oath. He had to be captured, and I was merely giving you a chance to save your daughter. That is all.'

Jack trembled with rage. 'You should have spared her anyway. Without conditions.'

Jhala raised his chin and his eyes went dark. 'I see. That is what you think, is it? You believe that I, somehow, betrayed *you*. Well, in that case, you are very much mistaken. I saved your daughter's life the only way I could. I trained you to be a native siddha. Taught you the secret arts. I promoted you to sergeant.' His eyes flashed. 'I did everything I could to help you. I went far out of my way. My commander, Colonel Hada, said I was a fool to invest so much of my time in training natives, and yet I did. I staked everything on the scouting unit we built up. Everything.'

With a supreme effort, Jack forced himself not to punch Jhala in the face. 'I'll go back and tell my leaders what you've said.'

Jhala pushed up his bottom lip, his chin puckering. 'I am so disappointed. When I heard you were in the fortress, I was certain we would find a way out of this situation. I was certain we would make peace and save as many lives as we could. Now I see I was wrong.' His features darkened, as if a cloud had passed over him. 'You tell your leaders what I've said. And tell them this also – if they do not accept my offer, I will raze that fortress, and everyone in it, to the ground. You have not even seen a fraction of my powers so far.' Jhala paused and took a deep breath, his chest puffing up. 'You would not believe how powerful I am now.'

'I thought you were a blocked siddha.' Jack blurted this out without even thinking about what he was saying.

Jhala narrowed his eyes. 'I told you that, didn't I?' He stared into the distance. 'I was blocked, that is true. I used a power too soon. But that doesn't matter now. The rules have been broken. The laws have been cast aside.'

Jack went very still for a moment. Rules? Laws? Strange ideas bubbled in his head. 'You mean the law of karma?'

Jhala raised an eyebrow. 'Yes. I do mean that, in fact.'

Jack's thoughts whirled now and a tingle crossed his skin. A veil seemed to be lifting from his eyes. Suddenly, he understood.

He reached into his pouch and drew out Katelin's necklace. He hadn't yet had a chance to give it back to Elizabeth. He held the cross up, the metal spinning slowly.

Jhala frowned. 'What nonsense is this?' Then he froze and stared hard at the necklace. His eyes widened, and he looked as though he'd been slapped in the face for a moment. Then his brow furrowed and he locked eyes with Jack. 'You know about this, then?'

A smile crossed Jack's face. He'd surprised, even unnerved, Jhala. Perhaps he shouldn't be speaking about the yantra. And yet it had been worth it just to see the look on Jhala's face. 'Yes, we know about the Great Yantra.' And now he went out on a limb. Now he tried to confirm what he'd suddenly come to believe. 'The Great Yantra breaks the law of karma, doesn't it?' He waved the necklace. 'The yantra unblocks you.'

Jhala's expression soured. 'I see. You know it purifies, then.' He waved his hand dismissively. 'It matters little. We have many more siddhas on the way, and new weapons will arrive in days. How many siddhas could you have up there? No more than a handful,

I suspect. We will crush you. Even if you've learnt the secret now.' Jhala pointed his finger at Jack. 'You tell that to your leaders. Accept my final offer, or face being slaughtered. You have had only a small taste of what I will unleash on you. A very small taste.'

25

'But how did you know what the power of the Great Yantra was?' Sonali asked. 'You said you couldn't use it.'

Jack gazed up at the sky as he sat next to Sonali on the edge of the Folly Brook camp. The shadows were lengthening and the clouds darkening. 'It all just came together in my head. As Jhala was talking, I realised.' He looked across at Sonali. 'Jhala said he'd been able to learn new powers, despite being blocked. That's like me, isn't it? I've been able to do that a few times. Kanvar asked me whether there was any pattern to my special ability. I could never see one. It always seemed to just come at odd times. No rhyme or reason. But down there, with Jhala, I realised there has been a pattern after all.' He looked down for a moment. 'My dead wife, Katelin.'

Sonali looked at the ground as well. 'How could Katelin help you?'

'She didn't help me. Not exactly. Her *memory* did. My special ability only came when I thought of her. And when I thought of her, I always pictured her wearing that necklace. My ability came four times: during the Siege of London, in Mahajan's castle, at the spot where you used to bathe, and in the forest in north Shropshire. I thought about Katelin just before I broke the law each time.' He cleared his throat. 'I have this image of her in my head. She's lying on her bed, near death, and on her chest is the Celtic cross. It's the cross that did it. I'm sure of that now.'

'You mean, you thought of the necklace and that gave you the power? The power to break the law of karma and learn a new yantra?'

'Aye. It was as though I'd meditated on it for a moment. Just a split second, but that was enough.'

'That is very quick.'

'It is. But some yantras are quicker to use than others, aren't they? Kanvar explained that to me once. The Lightning yantra is very quick. You just think of it for a few seconds and then you can use it. The Europa yantra takes a lot longer. I reckon the Great Yantra is just very quick to use.'

Sonali gazed intently at the ground. 'But then, if you *did* use the power, why didn't the knowledge come into your head?'

'That is strange. The Great Yantra must be a different sort of yantra. It's not like the others, is it?'

'It is *very* different from the others, in that case.'

Jack shrugged. 'I don't know any more about it than what I've told you. But I'm sure I'm right about all this. Jhala said it himself. He admitted the necklace is the Great Yantra. And he also admitted that the yantra's power is to break the law of karma.'

'What about this last time you used the yantra, then? Just a few hours ago?'

'What about it?'

'Did you break the law of karma then?'

'I don't think so. But then, I haven't memorised any other yantras to try. If I knew any more, I'd try the Great Yantra right now. But it'll take me months to learn a new yantra.'

Sonali's eyes moistened. 'So, the Great Yantra won't be much help to us after all. You're the only one who can use it at the moment, and you don't know any other yantras anyway.'

Jack swallowed. He'd considered this as well. He stared up at the heavy clouds. 'Looks that way. And yet . . .'

'What?'

'There must be more to this. Two things still seem strange to me. For one thing, when I used the Great Yantra beside the Folly brook I felt this sort of lightness.'

'Lightness?'

'It's hard to explain. I felt a weight being lifted off me. Just for a moment. That happened at the same time as I managed to use a new power. I reckon that must be from using the Great Yantra.'

'What about the other times you used the yantra?'

'Those were all in difficult situations. I was dying or under attack. I might have felt the lightness, but I wouldn't have noticed it. There was too much else going on.' He paused for a moment. 'When I tried the Great Yantra earlier today, I didn't feel lighter. I was sitting quietly. I should have noticed it. But there was nothing.'

'I don't understand what this means.'

'I'm not sure either. It just seems strange. As though there is still something missing. Something I'm not understanding yet.'

'You think there's more to using the Great Yantra?'

'Could be.' He scratched the back of his neck. 'I don't know.'

'What was the second thing? You said there were two things that were strange.'

He rubbed his face. He was struggling to understand everything he'd learnt and to make sense of the many ideas coursing through his head. If Kanvar were still alive, he might have been able to offer some guidance. But the Sikh was gone. They had cremated him earlier, as was apparently the Sikh custom.

Jack and Sonali would have to make sense of it all without any other help.

'The second thing,' Jack said slowly, 'is that I can't see how breaking the law of karma could have helped Oswin and Galahad. All it means is that you can learn a new yantra if you've been blocked. How would Oswin and Galahad know any other yantras? Also, the Grail was always some sort of weapon in the stories. Or at least, something so powerful it could save the land at a time of danger. Breaking the law of karma is a powerful ability, but it wouldn't save a whole country straight away, would it?'

'No. It doesn't fit with the stories.'

'That's what I think. That's why I reckon there's more to this.' He paused. He was struggling to explain himself. So much of this was far beyond anything he'd ever come across before. 'Jhala said something earlier that's stuck with me. He said the Great Yantra "purifies". What do you think of that?'

Sonali shook her head. 'I have no idea. Purifies? It could mean many things.'

Jack nodded. 'But that's the word Jhala used. That exact word and not another. I reckon there's something extra we're missing. Some piece of a puzzle.'

Sonali stared glumly into the distance. 'I don't see how we'll solve the puzzle. We don't have much time.'

Far away, a gun clapped. Moments later, a round shot shrieked past over the fortress. Several further booms followed and a shell split open near the north wall, showering flame and metal over the ruins.

'It's started again,' Jack said. 'We'd better get inside.'

He walked across the grass with Sonali. Just as he entered the palace, she took his arm.

'One thing,' she said. 'If breaking the law of karma really is the Great Yantra's power, that means you're not so special after all, doesn't it? Anyone could do it.'

He smiled wryly. 'I always said I was just an old soldier. I was right, after all.'

———◆———

The missiles crunched over and over again on the roof of the ruined palace and the dust spilt down in endless streams. Jack sat huddled with the other villagers, Elizabeth to his left and Saleem to his right. With the bombardment worsening by the minute, none of them dared leave the building. The cracks in the ceiling groaned, but the stone slabs held firm.

Mark ducked into the room at one point and beckoned to Jack. 'Can I have a word, Master?'

Jack climbed to his feet and followed Mark into an alcove that was now serving as a storeroom.

Mark motioned to the barrels and sacks lined up against the wall. 'This is all we have left. Just a few days' food at this rate.' He patted one of the barrels. 'And only this of water, I'm afraid.'

Jack rubbed his chin. 'We'll have to ask around the fortress when we get a chance. Someone should help us.'

'I checked with Constable Ward's men. Everyone's running low. They've hardly even got enough water at the hospital.'

Jack paused. The fortress must have originally had a reservoir of some sort, but he'd seen no sign of one now. 'Right. We'll have to ration it out, in that case. A tankard of water a day for everyone, and half a bowl of pottage for each meal.'

Mark's face dropped. 'That will be difficult.'

'Aye. But we don't have a choice.'

A fireball thumped into the roof. The alcove shuddered and Mark flinched. Jack heard the flames snarl across the stonework overhead.

'Look,' Jack continued, 'we don't know how long we're going to be up here. We'll have to be careful what we drink and eat. The more we eke out our supplies, the longer we'll be able to survive.'

Mark nodded grimly. 'Yes, Master.'

<hr />

The missiles rained down on the fortress for almost twenty-four hours. Then, as night fell on the second day, they suddenly stopped. Jack and the others crawled out of their shelter and set about helping the wounded. The buildings had withered even further beneath the onslaught. The piles of rubble stood higher, and the places to find cover were dwindling. Fires still burned and a pall of smoke hung across the ruins.

After more than an hour had passed and the guns were still silent, Jack strode over to the east side of the fortress to investigate. Soon, the vast outer wall loomed ahead of him. It appeared to have survived the bombardment well. He spotted a few gouges in the battlements where round shot had struck, but Jhala's batteries were still too far away to do any serious damage to the stonework.

At the foot of the wall, Jack found a mangled gun lying on a heap of stones. The piece was bent almost in half and the smashed remains of the carriage lay scattered about nearby. A ball must have hit the gun and knocked it off the ramparts.

He climbed a set of stairs and found the gunners resting beside their weapons. Some slouched beneath blankets, while others lay asleep on mats placed between pyramids of shot and tin cases of bullets, known as grape or canister. The artillerymen had somehow kept the guns firing throughout the past twenty-four hours, and the enemy's bombardment would have been even worse without them.

Jack noticed a gunner leaning against the parapet and staring out at the hills through a spyglass. The distant slopes and ridges were dark, but they were speckled with tiny lights.

Jack walked across to the gunner. 'What's going on out there?'

The gunner grunted and handed over the glass. 'Take a look.'

Jack scoured the hills. For the most part, all he could see were shadows. Here and there, he came across glowing lanterns. The yellowish lights illuminated earthworks, gabions and lines of serpent-headed muzzles protruding from embrasures.

He lowered the glass. 'Why do you reckon they've stopped firing?'

The gunner shrugged. 'Getting some rest maybe. We're doing the same. Not a good idea for us to fire all our shot at them, unless they send a few back our way.'

Jack understood. The rebels would only have a limited supply of ammunition and would have to rely on reusing the balls fired into the fortress.

He leant against the parapet and gazed into the darkness. What was Jhala planning? What would he try next?

Jack stared at the great arc of shimmering campfires surrounding the hill. Off to the north-east, the camp of the European Army covered the plains in a glittering shawl.

Then his eyes strayed for a moment to the rocky hillside immediately below him. Large parts of it consisted of impassable bluffs, while the rest was smothered in scree and boulders.

He was about to lift his gaze again, when he stopped. Something wasn't right, but he couldn't put his finger on what it was. He'd been up on the wall many times over the past few days and had glanced at this scarp several times. It formed a key part of the natural defences surrounding the fortress.

But now it looked different somehow. What was it? The shadows seemed thicker and the hillside's contours smoother. The rocks in some places appeared blurred, despite being picked out by moonlight.

He lifted the glass, adjusted the draw tube and studied the slope more carefully. He could make out the crevices and cliffs and jagged boulders. And then he stopped, froze for a second. The thick shadow smearing one part of the incline was shifting slightly, inching higher and higher.

What the hell was causing that?

He shivered, despite the fact that it wasn't cold. Something wasn't right about that shadow.

He peered through the glass, focusing all his attention and his unnaturally good eyesight on the shifting darkness.

And then he saw it. Just for a moment. A figure creeping up the hill.

He blinked, rubbed his eyes and stared again. Now he could no longer see the shape.

'What is it?' the gunner asked.

'Not sure,' Jack replied.

He continued searching the shadow, trying to bore into it with his eyes. Then he spied another figure, followed by a third. He glimpsed them for only a moment before the darkness absorbed them once again. But he couldn't have imagined it.

People were sneaking up the incline. He was sure of it. But they were somehow remaining invisible.

And then he realised what was happening.

The figures were being hidden by a power – something like Kanvar's Night power. Only this was covering a much larger area.

He shoved the spyglass back into the gunner's hand and pointed down the scarp. 'The enemy are coming. They're climbing up over there.'

The gunner frowned, raised the glass and surveyed the slope. 'Can't see anything.'

'Look closely. You see movement?'

'Nothing.' The gunner lowered the glass and looked askance at Jack. 'Reckon you'd better go get some sleep.'

'Listen. I can see something. I swear it. I'm an old army scout. I know what I'm talking about. I'm going to get help. You need to get word to Constable Ward right now and tell him we're under attack. Tell him to send the criers out. We need everyone over here to defend this wall right now.'

The gunner widened his eyes and spluttered.

'Do it!' Jack snapped. 'Quickly!'

Jack dashed down the stairway and paused for a moment at the bottom to make sure the gunner had done as he was told. He was relieved to see the man scurrying along the ramparts, heading towards the gatehouse.

Jack then bolted into the fortress and ran towards the Folly Brook camp. Here and there, he spotted scraps of shell casing, along with spent round shot that hadn't yet been collected. Any corpses had been cleared away earlier and taken to the communal pit on the north side of the fortress.

Panting heavily, he arrived at the camp and found most of the villagers congregated about a cluster of fires.

He swallowed, caught his breath and shouted, 'Get your muskets and come to the east wall! We're under attack!'

The villagers sprang into action. Within seconds, they were crowding about him with their weapons. There were several women amongst the group, including Elizabeth, who held the firearm Jack had given her the week before.

Jack gripped Elizabeth's arm and dragged her to one side. 'You're staying here.'

Elizabeth's eyes flashed. 'I'm coming. You can't stop me.'

'What about Cecily?'

'She's with Mary.'

'You want her to grow up without a mother?'

'You want her to grow up without her grandfather?' She gestured to Godwin, who was now walking across to join her. 'Or without her father?'

'It's all right, sir.' Godwin was buckling on his longsword. 'Elizabeth wants to defend our people. I agree. We need as many fighters as we can get.'

Jack snorted. Godwin would agree with whatever Elizabeth said. But all the same, it was true that they needed people now.

'I've been practising,' Elizabeth said. 'I know how to fire a musket. What would you have me do? Sit around and wait to be killed, or fight to protect Cecily?'

Jack rubbed his forehead. What Elizabeth was saying made sense. It made sense, because it was exactly the sort of thing he would say himself. He stared at her for a moment. She was holding the musket in one hand, her chin was raised and her eyes flickered with defiance.

She was his daughter. She was just like him.

'All right.' He pointed his finger at Elizabeth. 'You stay close to me, though, and do as I say.'

He spun round and faced the rest of the gathered villagers. Mark and the apprentices stood together, with Sonali amongst them. Sonali didn't carry a weapon and presumably planned to fight with just her powers. She gave Jack a firm nod, but he could see the nerves in her eyes.

Saleem had retrieved Jack's musket from the storeroom and now handed it across. Jack slung the firearm over his shoulder and adjusted the knife in his belt. He then surveyed his troops. There were around sixty of them. Several had taken branches from the fires and now held them up as torches.

'Right,' Jack said. 'We're going to the east wall. The enemy are coming up the hill and we have to knock them back.'

With that, he led the way through the gloomy arcades and boulevards of the fortress. He spotted people huddled about campfires and was disturbed that none of them seemed to be preparing to defend the wall. They were all just sitting around, talking and cooking their evening meals.

And Jack heard no bells either. Henry had said he would send criers throughout the fortress in the event of an attack.

What the hell was going on? What was Henry playing at?

The east wall reared up ahead. The guns were still silent and the artillerymen, as far as Jack could see, were still sleeping or crouching beside their weapons. Jack had been expecting an army of rebels to be gathering to defend the fortress. But he saw only a handful of people milling about one of the breaches in the wall.

He marched across to the breach and quickly recognised Henry amongst the small group. The constable was speaking to the gunner Jack had sent off earlier.

As Jack approached, Henry turned to him and grunted. 'This all your doing, was it?'

Jack gripped the musket strap hanging on his shoulder. 'Get everyone up here. The enemy are just yards away.'

Henry's eyes narrowed. 'What enemy?'

'Troops. I've seen them.'

Henry snorted and walked through the opening in the wall, stepping over the slabs of fallen stone that lay half buried in the earth. He stood just outside the breach, hands on his hips and his cloak fluttering behind him. 'I see nothing.'

Jack strode through the opening and peered into the darkness. He felt a ripple of nerves when he saw that the shifting expanse of darkness was now less than fifty yards away. It was smothering much of the slope and spreading out as it approached the wall.

'Just there.' Jack pointed at the shadowy mass.

Henry growled. 'I still see nothing.' He turned to Jack, leaning in close. 'What game are you playing, Casey?'

'No game. Can't you see—'

'Out of my way.' Henry pushed Jack in the chest and brushed past. 'You've wasted enough time tonight.'

Henry clambered back through the opening and disappeared into the gloom, his henchmen following him.

Jack tensed his hands into fists. Damn Henry. The man was a fool and would get them all killed.

He gazed back down the hill and his skin crawled as he watched the strange shadow widening further.

The enemy would be at the wall within minutes. He had to do something fast.

He scrambled back into the fortress and stared at the worried faces of the villagers. Several still held burning brands, which hissed and spat sparks into the night.

'Listen,' he said. 'The enemy will be here any minute. No one is going to help us. Not yet anyway. So we're going to have to do our best on our own.' He gestured to the breach. 'Get your muskets loaded and take up positions around that opening. You won't see the troops at first. They'll appear suddenly out of the shadows. You won't have much time to shoot, so make sure you're ready.'

The villagers dutifully made their way to the breach. Jack swallowed hard when he noticed Elizabeth standing at the ready with her musket raised. He didn't like seeing his daughter in such a dangerous spot. But then, the whole fortress was a dangerous place. None of them were safe anywhere within the walls.

He would return and stand beside her as soon as he could. But first, he had to get more help.

He bounded up the stairway and found the gunner he'd spoken to earlier on the walkway at the top.

'Start loading grape,' Jack said to the gunner. 'The enemy are almost at the wall.'

The gunner's eyes widened and he raised his hand, as if to defend himself. 'You heard the constable. There's nothing there.'

'Can't you see it?' Jack pointed over the parapet. 'Look!'

The gunner's eyes turned to slits and his expression hardened. 'I take my orders from Constable Ward. I've listened to your babbling quite enough now. You need to go back to your camp and cool off a bit.'

Jack breathed in sharply. His face was getting hot, and he knew he was ranting like a madman. None of this was doing anything to convince the gunner to load the guns.

He snatched a look at the ground beyond the wall and saw that the dark, moving mass was perhaps fifty feet from the fort now, and one arm was advancing towards the breach where Elizabeth and the others were waiting.

Damn it. He couldn't waste any more time talking to the gunner now.

He charged back down the stairs and raced across to the breach, slinging his musket from his shoulder. He skidded to a halt beside Elizabeth and Godwin, who were crouching behind a slab of rock.

'What's going on?' Elizabeth whispered. 'We can't see anything.'

'You will in a minute,' Jack replied.

He poked his head up over the stone block and stared into the murk. Shadowy figures were moving quickly towards the top of the hillside. And as he watched, they came charging out of the darkness and into the moonlight.

They were European Army troops – hundreds of them.

And a large group of them were racing straight towards the breach.

26

Jack leant against the top of the slab, raised his musket and stared along the sights. He sensed Elizabeth and Godwin do the same beside him.

'Fire!' he shouted at the top of his voice.

The villagers peered out from their positions, saw the marauders bounding towards the opening and fired their muskets, virtually in unison. The muskets popped and crackled, smoke burst from the weapons' muzzles, and a blizzard of bullets whistled at the soldiers. Jack pulled his firearm's trigger and the weapon coughed and jabbed into his shoulder. Elizabeth yelped as her musket cracked. She slipped backwards and landed on her behind.

Jack looked down at her. He thought she said she'd been practising. 'You all right?'

She was on her feet again in a second, glared at Jack as if it were his fault and then quickly bit open a new cartridge. When Godwin tried to put his hand on her shoulder, she shrugged it off.

Jack stared through the fading powder smoke. More than a score of soldiers had been shot down, but hundreds more were still stampeding towards the opening. He could hear them snarling and bellowing now and make out their faces twisted with rage. Many of them had thick beards – they were probably French Mohammedans.

The villagers around him were already hurrying to reload their muskets, jabbing frantically with their ramrods. But Jack could see they were going to have a hard job shooting enough of the attackers. They needed more help.

He shut his eyes for a second and called the Lightning yantra to mind. In less than a second, he had it ready to use. He opened his eyes and raised his hand. But before he could voice the commands, Sonali leapt up on to a stone block and fired green lightning from her fingertips. The dazzling blaze forked across the slope and thumped into the mass of troops. More than ten men cried out as they were bowled over, knocking back those soldiers rushing up behind them.

Jack wasted no time now in uttering the command. He felt energy wriggle through his arm and brilliant lightning streaked from his fingers. The bolt pummelled the troops, knocking over at least a score.

The villagers blasted again with their muskets. A ramrod went corkscrewing through the air – someone had panicked and fired without removing it.

Mark and four of the apprentices joined Sonali on top of the stone slab and they all launched another volley of lightning. Jack could see a look of terror and astonishment on many of the lads' faces. They were using a power for the first time and facing their first battle.

Next to him, Elizabeth fired her musket and this time absorbed the kick of the weapon without even flinching. She glanced across at him and he nodded his approval.

So far, the villagers were doing well. But as they reloaded and the smoke cleared for a moment, he saw there were still several hundred men rushing towards the opening, replacing those who'd been struck down. And further off, a vast horde of troops were streaming up the hillside and racing out of the expanse of shadow. Several thousand at least must have joined the attack.

Jhala had launched a major assault.

Jack raised his hand and fired another bolt at the soldiers. A whole row flew backwards, as if an invisible hand had lifted them up and then flung them to the ground.

He heard shouts and the brittle crack of musket fire to his right.

He stepped away from Elizabeth and Godwin and stared along the wall. In the faint moonlight, he managed to make out activity at another opening further along the wall. Figures were pouring unopposed into the fortress. The rebel defences had been breached already.

He now heard bells ringing within the ruins. The peals started near the north wall, then spread like flames across the entire fort.

Finally, the rebels were mounting a resistance. He could only pray it wasn't too late.

A boom shuddered from the ramparts. He glanced up and saw that the gunners were loading the artillery. They angled the muzzles down and fired. The guns roared, rocked backwards and disgorged fire and grape at the attackers, the orange flashes leaving spots on Jack's eyes.

Jack whispered a Hail Mary. The artillerymen were finally responding.

Elizabeth was still firing her musket. She was doing well now, reloading quickly and efficiently. The other villagers were doing the same, and Sonali and the apprentices were flinging regular pulses of green lightning at the enemy. Jack reloaded his musket and was about to step back into the fray when he heard shouts from nearby. He stared back along the wall and saw European soldiers swarming from the darkness and bearing down on his small force.

He cursed under his breath. The troops must have come from the breach further to the south and decided to attack his party in the flank. He and the others were now facing foes from two directions.

He shut his eyes for a second and quickly brought the Lightning yantra to mind. He opened his eyes and was about to hurl a bolt at the soldiers, when a flash and a blast above him stunned him for a second. The artillerymen had circled a gun round and were firing grape down at the soldiers. The troops withered and fell back before the onslaught. A second detachment of gunners fired their weapon. The gun bucked, belched smoke, and then a deadly hail of bullets shrieked down at the soldiers. Scores of men dropped suddenly to the ground. The remainder retreated back along the wall, where their comrades were still spilling into the fortress.

Jack heard a scream. When he whirled round, he saw that a wave of attackers had got as far as the breach itself. Several villagers clicked out their muskets' knives and drove their weapons into the soldiers. One attacker jabbed back and impaled one of the apprentices on his knife. The lad fell back, blood foaming from his mouth. The soldier looked around wildly for someone else to stab.

Jack raised his arm, recalled the yantra and blasted lightning at the soldier. The blaze punched the man in the chest and hurled him back out of the breach.

The villagers managed to repel the assault, but still more waves of troops were charging at the opening, their yells echoing inside the fortress. Elizabeth and Godwin were still firing their muskets. Sonali, Mark, Saleem and most of the rest of Jack's group were still alive and fighting.

Jack thanked Christ they were all safe so far.

'God's blood!' someone shouted behind him.

He glanced over his shoulder and saw Henry marching out of the ruins, a party of around two hundred men striding behind him.

Henry's eyes widened as he saw the guns flashing on the wall and Jack's people defending the breach. He licked his lips, taking it all in for a moment. He locked eyes with Jack but said nothing. Instead, he turned to his henchmen and ordered them to split up. One force was to head to the south to defend the wall where the attackers were already streaming into the fortress. The rest were to stay to supplement Jack's party.

Jack resisted saying anything to Henry other than, 'I'm pleased you're here, Constable Ward.'

Henry's nostrils flared and his eyes shone. For a moment, he looked as though he were going to shout something. But then Jack spotted a ripple of flashes over Henry's shoulder, coming from within the darkened ruins. Jack knew instantly what it was. He didn't need to hear the dense crackle or see the ghostly puffs of smoke to confirm it.

It was musket fire.

Suddenly, he was caught in a thicket of bullets. The balls whispered all about him, screamed off stone, rattled against the wall and skimmed the ground, tossing up dirt. Missiles chimed and tinged against musket barrels and swords. There were a myriad wet thuds and cracks as the bullets struck flesh and bone. Dozens of Henry's men fell to the ground. One man near Jack gasped and collapsed, blood pouring from a hole in the back of his head.

Henry roared, scowled and stumbled towards Jack as if he were going to attack him.

Jack grasped his musket and was about to click the knife out to defend himself, when Henry coughed blood, sank to his knees and clawed at Jack's leg.

Jack looked up and saw many of Henry's men writhing on the ground. The rest were stumbling away towards the breach in an attempt to get at least a small amount of cover.

Christ. Enemy troops must have crept through the ruins to attack the villagers from the rear. He should have expected it.

He grasped Henry beneath the arms and dragged him back towards the wall. He had to get the constable out of the way before the enemy fired again.

He glanced behind him and saw that Elizabeth and Godwin were cowering, pressed against one side of the stone slab. They were hardly safe from the enemy bullets there, but they were at least partially protected. The other villagers were dithering. Some had now ducked behind the stonework to hide from the troops behind them. Others continued to blast feverishly at the soldiers still storming the breach. The villagers were caught in a desperate situation, with nowhere to run to.

The troops in the ruins fired again. A second storm of balls shrieked around Jack. A bullet plucked at the side of his tunic. Another shattered the musket stock of one of Henry's men standing nearby. The balls lashed the stones about the breach, spitting up dust. Several villagers were hit in the back as they tried to fight off the attackers outside the walls.

Jack's heart was crashing in his chest and his breath was short as he scrambled over to Elizabeth and Godwin. He hauled Henry alongside the stone slab and ducked down himself. He was still partly in the line of fire. But there was no point climbing further into the breach while the army were still rushing at the wall.

Godwin was raising his musket and firing at the enemy, but Elizabeth bent over Henry with Jack.

The constable was still breathing, but he seemed to have been hit several times in the back and blood was welling from his mouth. He stared at Jack and spoke in a cracked voice. 'You were right, Casey.'

'Forget that now,' Jack said.

'No.' Henry grasped Jack's tunic. 'You were right.'

Then Henry's head fell back and his eyes went cold as pearls. Jack searched for a pulse, but it was clear the constable was dead.

Damn it. The fortress was now without a commander – when it needed one the most.

Another volley of bullets blistered the air about Jack. A ball shrieked against the stone near Elizabeth's head, and she gasped and recoiled. Several more missiles were sucked into the ground.

The villagers were in a hopeless position and Jack knew they couldn't stay where they were. They were trapped between two sets of attackers and would soon be slaughtered.

He had to do something.

He scanned the ruins. Somewhere in the shadows the European Army troops were reloading their muskets and preparing to fire again. How many of them were there? It was impossible to tell, but it could easily be a hundred or more.

He raised his head and looked across the breach. At least a hundred of Henry's men had survived and were now crouching amongst the broken stonework, seemingly at a loss as to how to respond to the attack.

Jack knew what he had to do. He didn't want to do it, but he had no choice.

He grasped Elizabeth's shoulder. 'Stay here.'

Then he stood up and yelled across at Henry's men. 'Follow me!' He clicked the latch on his musket and the knife clacked out. 'Charge!'

Almost without realising what he was doing, he began sprinting towards the ruins, heading straight into the area where the muskets had been fired from. His heart roared and echoed in his head. Fire seemed to course through his body. There was a wild cry on his lips.

He would kill those bastards hiding in the shadows. Kill as many of them as he could. Because this was his people's fortress, his people's lands, his people's country, and he would show the enemy how the English fought . . .

He was vaguely aware that Henry's men were charging into the darkness alongside him. He could hear them cheering and howling.

Then the muskets started again. Small blots of flame jabbed the gloom. Jack found himself charging into a storm of whispering missiles. They hummed in his ears and one ruffled his hair. Crusaders cried out and fell all about him. He saw one man get hit in the forehead and topple over with blood and gristle dribbling down his cheeks. Another man caught a ball in his eye, a line of blood jetting out from his eye socket.

But Jack was invincible. He couldn't be hit, because he had to do this now. He had to defeat the enemy and save his family.

And then suddenly he was enveloped by the ruins and racing through an archway, into a chamber where the roof was largely intact. He skidded to a halt. It was almost pitch-black in the room

– the only light came from the faint moonbeams striking through the gaps in the ceiling. But it only took him a second to make out the European Army soldier crouching in a corner.

The soldier leapt to his feet, but Jack was already bounding over to him and jamming his knife-musket into his stomach. The blade ripped through cloth and skin and impaled the man deep in the gut. The soldier gasped, his eyes bulged and he clattered back against the wall.

Jack caught a flicker of movement out of the corner of his eye and turned just in time to see a second soldier lunging at him with a knife-musket. He saw a glint of steel as the blade slipped towards him.

He gave an involuntary grunt and dodged to the side, the knife missing him by an inch. The soldier was unable to stop himself and lurched past. Jack swung his musket like a club and battered the man in the back of the head with the stock. The wood thumped against the man's skull, and the soldier groaned and staggered forward.

Jack raised his musket. As his assailant spun round to face him, he pulled the trigger. The firearm flashed and spat smoke. The bullet caught the soldier in the middle of his chest and he stumbled backwards out of the opening Jack had just run through. He swayed for a moment, took a few more steps backwards and then toppled to the side.

Jack heard the sounds of fighting all about him in the ruins – shouts, groans and the crackle of muskets. The crusaders were battling with the troops, but he couldn't see anything in the gloom.

He turned to press on into the fortress, and then jolted when he found himself facing a soldier who'd crept up to a gap in the wall opposite and was now pointing a musket straight at him.

Jack reacted in a split second. He dived to the side just as the firearm burst and coughed smoke. The bullet whined past and flew out through the entrance.

He crunched on the ground, slid a short distance, then twisted himself round, raised his hand and scrabbled to bring the Lightning yantra to mind. The soldier clicked out his musket's knife and charged. But Jack had already grasped the yantra and now he barked the words of the command. His arm shuddered and went numb as the lightning coursed out from his fingers and thudded into the soldier's chest.

The soldier flew backwards out of the opening, disappearing into the murk. Jack rushed across to the entryway and saw the man lying motionless in the middle of the adjoining chamber, a trace of smoke rising from his chest.

Jack spun round, looking about wildly in all directions.

Where would the next assailant come from? How many of them would attack him?

But no one came. He could still hear the guns rumbling along the wall and muskets spluttering from the breach, but here in the ruins it was silent. He heard no further sound of a struggle.

Was that a good sign?

He gripped the musket tightly and darted back out through the entrance, heading towards the wall. As he came out into the open again, he saw a handful of Henry's men limping from the shadows.

'What happened?' Jack shouted to them.

'Got most of the heathens,' one of the group replied. 'Rest of them ran off.'

Jack grinned. This was good news. Perhaps there was still a chance of saving the fortress, after all. 'You lot stay here and make sure no one else attacks us from behind.' He gestured towards the breach, where the villagers were still battling. 'We'll hold them off over there.'

The man nodded and instructed his comrades to stay where they were.

Jack jogged towards the opening in the wall. His head felt strangely tight and heavy. He recognised the feeling – he was depleted after using Lightning several times.

Ahead of him, the ground was dotted with the dead and the dying. Most of the fallen were Henry's men, but a handful of European Army soldiers lay amongst the bodies. Several of the injured groaned and clutched at Jack's ankles as he rushed past.

He heard a series of cries coming from the breach. A phalanx of soldiers had burst through the opening and were now engaged in hand-to-hand fighting with the villagers. He saw Saleem jab a soldier in the stomach with his knife-musket. Mark despatched another by bashing him on the back of the head with a rock.

Jack ran faster. He had to get back to help his people before they were overwhelmed.

But he had only gone a few more paces before a scream coming from the edge of the breach brought him to a halt.

A woman had cried out. He knew that voice. He would recognise it anywhere.

Elizabeth.

He stared into the shadows at the foot of the wall. A gun on the ramparts thundered and the glare pushed back the darkness for a moment. In the livid glow he saw Elizabeth backed against the wall and surrounded by ten soldiers, all of whom were pointing their muskets at her. A figure lay on the ground nearby. As far as Jack could tell, it was Godwin.

He observed all this in a second before the light blinked out and shadow fell across the scene again. But he could still make out the dim outline of his daughter and the men threatening her.

His heart shot into his throat and he couldn't stop himself uttering a guttural cry. He struggled to call the Lightning yantra to mind. But it was taking so long. The soldiers would fire at Elizabeth at any moment.

Someone shouted from the edge of the breach. It was Sonali, standing on a block of stone, her arm raised and her hair fluttering like flames about her head. She screeched, and lightning blazed from her hand. It snaked towards the soldiers and bowled eight of them off their feet.

She drew breath and raised her hand to strike again. But the remaining two soldiers reacted quickly. They turned their firearms on Sonali and blasted before she had a chance to voice the command.

Jack heard the crack of the two muskets clearly, despite the ongoing booms of the guns and the shouts and cries coming from elsewhere in the fortress. The sound seemed to ring in his head as if echoing down a long tunnel. The white powder smoke from the muzzles blotted out the view for a moment, but then the haze tore apart and he saw what he'd been dreading – Sonali had been hit. She crumpled, fell off the slab and rolled on to the ground.

No.

Jack lifted his hand. The yantra was already hovering in the back of his mind and it only took him a moment to recall it. He voiced the command, his arm trembled and the lightning flew from his fingers. The blaze forked, snarled across to the soldiers and thumped them in the back. Both men flew forward and landed face first on the ground.

Jack started running. His eyes misted, but he blinked them clear.

He dashed across to where Elizabeth was crouching beside Godwin.

'Are you all right?' he asked.

Elizabeth nodded and he could see she was unharmed.

Godwin was sitting up now and rubbing his crown. 'I'm fine. Just got hit on the head.'

Elizabeth removed Godwin's hand and examined his scalp. She then crossed herself. 'Just a bruise, I think.'

Jack patted Godwin on the shoulder, then turned to look at Sonali. She was still lying on the ground, and Saleem and Mark were already crouching beside her.

Jack paused. He didn't want to go to Sonali's side, because then he would learn the truth. And that truth couldn't be good.

He didn't want to know, but he had to know.

He darted across, squatted down next to Mark and Saleem and looked at Sonali.

She lay on her back, her dark hair fanning across the earth around her head. She was breathing, heaving and biting her bottom lip. Her hand clutched her stomach and blood was oozing out between her fingers.

Jack felt numb and dazed for a moment, unable even to think.

Then he noticed her eyes had focused on him.

'Jack-ji,' she whispered.

His throat tightened and his eyes moistened. Why did it have to be Sonali who was struck down? Why couldn't it be someone else?

'Let me see.' He raised her hand and saw a bullet hole in her sari. The wound was weeping blood.

He put her hand back and lowered his head. It was as bad as he'd feared.

27

Jack felt as though he were walking through a dream. The darkened ruins about him, the black sky, the distant reverberations of the guns were not real. The Fortress of the Djinns had always been a figment of his imagination. He would wake up soon.

But then he looked down at Sonali lying on her back on the makeshift stretcher and suddenly he was back in the material world.

Sonali was dying. She looked pale and her skin was bathed in sweat. Someone had tied a length of cloth around her waist but it was doing little to staunch the flow of blood. Her eyes were open, but they were glazed and she stared at the heavens in silence.

He'd seen wounds like that before on the battlefield. Most soldiers shot in the abdomen would die within minutes. A few might survive for longer, if the bullet miraculously missed any vital organs. A very few might recover completely, if a Rajthanan doctor treated them. But here, in the fortress, there were no Rajthanan doctors.

Jack couldn't see how Sonali could survive. But he knew he mustn't think about that. He couldn't think about that.

He gripped the stretcher more tightly. Saleem was carrying the other end, while Mark and Elizabeth were scurrying alongside.

The villagers had held the breach in the wall and the rest of the crusaders, once they'd finally been roused, had managed to drive the enemy troops from the fortress. The remaining soldiers had retreated down the slope and returned to the European Army camp. The gunners on the ramparts were continuing to fire warning shots but, for the moment, the enemy were not responding.

The crusade was still alive. Jack's people had not yet been crushed.

But any happiness he felt about that evaporated when his eyes strayed to Sonali.

The hospital loomed ahead. It had largely been spared from the bombardment – the enemy batteries having concentrated their fire on other parts of the fortress. The glow of lanterns spilt out from the many apertures in the walls. In the dim light, Jack made out scores of wounded lying on blankets outside in the open. Many more people were swarming around the building or approaching from the darkness. And now Jack heard the chilling groans and cries of the injured inside the hall.

He swallowed hard and his skin crawled. When he glanced at Elizabeth, he saw that her skin was pure white and her eyes were glistening.

He and Saleem wound their way along a track through piles of rubble and finally drew up to the hall's main entrance. They only managed to go a few paces inside before they had to halt. The floor was completely covered in a mass of dying people. Their sighs, shrieks and bellows wafted through the giant chamber. The stench of rotting flesh struck Jack's nostrils. The monks were overwhelmed and clearly could do little beyond offering prayers.

A man lying on a filthy mat tugged at Jack's ankle, whispering, 'Water.'

Jack saw maggots crawling within the gaping wounds on the man's shoulder and chest.

Jack turned to Mark. 'We can't leave Sonali here.'

Mark was gazing at the tortured bodies sprawled about him, many of them clutching the air or scratching at the ground in their agony. 'Where will we take her?'

'Back to our camp.'

Mark seemed to shake himself from a trance. 'We have a dozen other wounded.'

'They can stay at the camp too. There's no hope for anyone in this place.'

Jack told Saleem to turn round, and they headed back out through the entryway and strode as quickly as they could away from the hospital.

Jack could still hear the screams long after he and the others had plunged back into the ruins and were well on their way back to the Folly Brook camp.

———❖———

A fireball slammed into the roof above Jack's head. The impact made the air quiver and Jack heard the flames hissing over the stonework. A tiny puff of dust wafted down from the ceiling.

Jhala had ordered the bombardment to continue. No doubt he would be enraged by the fact that the rebels had managed to repel his forces.

Jack crouched down beside Sonali. She was lying in a side chamber in the palace, along with the twelve other injured villagers. Mary was bustling between them all, tending to them as best she could and dispensing a drink of mandrake, which she said would ease the pain.

Sonali's face glistened with sweat in the candlelight. Her head was propped up against the wall using a rolled-up blanket. Mary had pressed a herbal poultice to the wound and tied a fresh length of cloth about Sonali's waist. Jack doubted the remedy would help, but Sonali had said she wanted to try it.

Jack took Sonali's hand. 'You stay strong. You'll get through this.'

Another fireball smacked into the roof and the floor rocked slightly. A larger trail of dust guttered down in one corner of the room.

Mark ducked through the doorway and gave Sonali a tight smile. 'The lads have asked me to tell you they're all praying for you, Lady Sonali. They're praying hard.'

Sonali's eyes moistened and she whispered, 'Thank you.'

Mark squatted down. 'Is there anything I can do for you? Anything you need?'

'I'm thirsty,' Sonali said.

Mark's eyes flicked across to Jack.

Jack knew what the lad was thinking. They'd all had their ration of water for the day. 'She can have my share for tomorrow.'

Jack's mouth was so parched it burned, but he didn't care. If Sonali needed water, she was going to have it.

'No,' Mark said. 'She can have my share.'

Jack smiled and patted Mark on the shoulder. 'Good lad. But give her mine first. She can have yours later, if she needs it.'

Mark nodded, retreated out of the door and returned a moment later with a tankard.

Jack helped Sonali to sit up and take several gulps of water. Once she'd finished, he eased her head back down and placed the tankard beside her.

'I'll be going, then,' Mark said to Sonali. 'If you need anything, you just call for me.'

Sonali nodded feebly and Mark stepped back out of the room. A round shot pounded the ceiling and a line of grit trickled onto his shoulder as he left.

Jack took Sonali's hand again. Her skin felt cold and she was shivering.

'I'm all right,' she said. 'It's not so bad.' She lowered her gaze. 'I've been through worse.'

Jack's eyes drifted to her arm. Her shawl had been removed and draped over her as a blanket. Her left arm hung outside the cloth and he could see the criss-cross of scars on the skin. Mahajan had tortured her. She'd hardly spoken about it and Jack had never raised the subject, although he knew she still had nightmares about it sometimes.

She seemed to understand his thoughts, because she said, 'I was sure I would die in Mahajan's castle. Everything that's happened since I got out has been an unexpected blessing. I've been so lucky.'

'And you'll carry on being lucky.'

She shook her head sadly. 'I'm not so sure about that.'

'Don't say that. You have to have faith. You'll pull through.'

'You know that's unlikely.' She took a deep breath. 'Listen, I might not have much time. I . . .'

A series of shells battered the roof and sent iron screaming against the masonry. Several of the injured lying nearby whimpered and one woman, who'd received a bullet in her chest, groaned and wept. Mary rushed to her side and dabbed her forehead with a cloth.

'It's noisy in here,' Jack said to Sonali. 'I could move you to the storeroom.'

She shook her head. 'It's all right.' She swallowed. 'Listen. I wanted to tell you that . . . that I think very highly of you. I wanted to make sure you knew that. In case anything I've said or done might have made you think otherwise.'

Jack's throat tightened so much it was hard to swallow. Tears brimmed in his eyes, but he kept them at bay. 'You don't need to say all this now. You're going to live.'

'Please. I have to tell you these things, in case I don't get another chance. You see, I've found it difficult . . . It's difficult for me to . . .' She frowned, seemed to search for the right words.

'It's all right. You rest.'

'You remember I said I ran away from my family?'

Jack nodded. She'd mentioned it to him once or twice, but had never gone into any detail.

'The reason I left,' she said slowly, 'was that I was due to be married. It was arranged, you see. I was to marry a rich old man. My parents believed it was a good match. Good for our family. I would be looked after, my father said. I didn't want to marry this man, but my father pressured me into it. On the day of my wedding, I climbed up onto the roof of my parents' house with my sister. I could see my future husband's wedding party coming up the road. And I couldn't do it. I couldn't go through with it. So I ran away. I ran to the nearest city, and I never went back.'

A round shot pounded the roof and she flinched, but then continued. 'Since that wedding day, I've found it difficult to . . . give myself over to someone. I'm always somehow holding back. I just wanted you to know that, in case you thought I didn't hold you in the highest regard . . . that I didn't . . .'

Tears welled in her eyes, and she struggled to continue.

He squeezed her hand. 'I understand. You mustn't worry. You just get better now.'

She nodded and blinked back the tears. Finally, she composed herself and gave him a slight smile. 'I have something for you.'

He frowned. 'What?'

'In my bag there.' She nodded towards a small embroidered pouch she often carried.

'What is it?'

'Take a look.'

He drew the strings on the bag. Inside, he found a silver box which he opened to reveal two paans wrapped in gold leaf.

He grinned at her. 'We'll share this later.'

'You have it now. You don't know when you'll get another chance.'

He fought back the tears. He didn't know how he was going to be able to speak, but somehow he managed it. 'When you're better, we'll sit in the sunshine and have these.'

He placed the box back in the pouch.

Then he heard a woman clear her throat behind him. When he turned, he saw Elizabeth standing in the doorway. Her face was pale and shone in the candlelight. Her cheeks were streaked with dirt and her eyes were glassy as they stared at Sonali.

She bit her bottom lip. 'May I sit with you?'

Sonali nodded weakly. 'Of course.'

Elizabeth crouched down. She met Jack's gaze for a moment, before looking back at Sonali. She lowered her eyes. 'You saved my life.'

Sonali frowned. 'I just did what anyone would do.'

'No. You risked your own life to save mine. I don't know how I can ever thank you.'

A shell roared overhead and the guns continued to pound in the distance. The other wounded villagers were sighing and moaning again.

Sonali shut her eyes and grimaced as pain racked her. Then she lifted her eyelids again and gently touched Elizabeth's hand. 'You don't need to thank me. You would have done the same for me.'

Tears streamed down Elizabeth's cheeks and she said in a squeaky voice, 'I'm sorry for what I said about you. I'm so sorry. I was wrong.'

Sonali raised her hand and touched the side of Elizabeth's face. 'Hush. I understand.'

Jack felt as though he were drowning. And yet he was happy. Elizabeth had apologised. She and Sonali were finally at peace. That meant he could be at peace himself.

He muttered a Hail Mary and crossed himself. He could have sat there for hours – days, even.

But Saleem scurried into the chamber, saying, 'There's a messenger here, Jack. The earl wants to speak to you. At once.'

※

The Earl of Shropshire sat propped up on a mattress that lay on the floor. He was covered by fine, embroidered blankets, although these were now speckled with dust and dirt. His long white hair was awry, and it stuck up like a bird's nest at the back of his head. An ornate Rajthanan oil lantern – a precious item – sat next to the mattress, providing the only light in the tiny chamber.

Jack crouched down beside the earl, while Sir Levin squatted opposite him on the other side of the temporary bed. Levin's features looked grim in the weak light, but the earl simply appeared dazed, like a child woken from sleep.

'You were with the constable when he died?' Levin asked Jack.

'Aye.' Jack nodded. 'He'd come to defend the wall. He passed away quickly.'

A fireball pummelled the wall behind Jack. The floor shuddered beneath his boots, and the flames sizzled and snarled across the courtyard outside. He was in a small chamber within the palace where the earl had set up his residency. It was one of the few rooms where the roof and the walls were still intact.

'Someone needs to lead the defence of the fortress,' Levin said. 'I would offer myself, but I haven't been a soldier for many years and I'm hardly fit to fight at present. We need someone with more recent experience in war. Preferably someone who knows the ways of the heathens, the way they fight.'

A shell struck the courtyard outside and fragments of iron screamed against the wall.

'Who do you have in mind?' Jack asked.

'You, of course.'

'Me? I don't think—'

'We have little choice.' The earl sat forward and seemed more alert now. 'You are by far the best candidate. Sir Alfred spoke highly of you, and that is recommendation enough for me.'

Jack bowed his head slightly. 'I will be honoured to command this fortress, if that is what you wish.'

The earl sat back and took a wheezy breath. 'Good. If you succeed in defending the fortress, I will knight you.'

At first, Jack thought this a ridiculous thing to say. A knighthood? What was the point of making such a promise? They would all be dead in days anyway.

And yet, at the same time, his chest surged with warmth. He was indeed honoured to be asked to lead his people – even now, in their final hour.

Jack took the earl's hand and kissed it. 'I'll do my best, my lord.'

Jack rode across the plains, holding a white flag above his head. To his right he saw the hills and the enemy artillery positions. To his left lay the battered fortress. And straight ahead stretched the expanse of the European Army. He could see the blots of the ambling elephants, the white dots of the soldiers' tents and, further off, the colourful flickers of the grand marquees of the Rajthanan officers.

More than a thousand army troops had been slaughtered during the night. The bodies still littered the slope outside the fortress. But Jhala still had thousands more men at his disposal.

Jack ached with tiredness and his clothes were caked in dust. He hadn't slept at all during the night and had spent most of his time beside Sonali. Now it was morning and, miraculously, she was still alive. But he had no idea how much longer she could last.

His mouth was painfully parched and he longed for a drink. Leaden clouds smothered the sky, and yet there'd been no rain for days.

If only it would rain.

Five riders, one of them carrying a white flag, appeared ahead. It looked as though the enemy were prepared to talk. Jack had waited until there was a lull in the firing and taken a chance in riding out. Jhala had already said he wasn't prepared to negotiate further. Jack had wondered whether he would simply be shot once he left the hill.

He met the cavalrymen out in the middle of the heath. The leader of the party was the same Rajthanan officer Jack had dealt with previously.

'General Jhala has agreed to see you.' The officer's voice was clipped and his moustache rigid. 'Get off your horse.'

As before, Jack dismounted and the officer searched him for weapons. By the time the Rajthanan had finished, Jhala was already riding out across the plains. A batman rode beside him, holding a parasol above the general's head despite the fact that there was neither rain nor bright sunshine.

General Jhala drew his horse to a halt and looked down at Jack. His face was serious and cold. He made no effort to smile as he had done before.

He sniffed, then dismounted and gestured for Jack to step away from the cavalrymen.

When they'd walked for about ten yards, Jhala turned to Jack and said in a crisp tone, 'What do you want?'

'We have many wounded—'

'Are you expecting me to be sympathetic?' Jhala scowled. 'You had several opportunities to surrender. You did not take them. It is hardly surprising you now have many wounded.'

'There are women and children. We can't look after them up there. They must come down.'

'They have been injured because of your own obstinacy. Their blood is on your hands.'

Jack was too exhausted even to be angry now. All he wanted to do was try to get safe passage for the injured. 'One of them is a Rajthanan.'

Jhala pursed his lips. 'What?'

'One of the injured is a Rajthanan. A woman. You must at least let *her* leave the fortress.'

Jhala narrowed his eyes. 'If true, that is very strange. Nevertheless, if she is up in that fortress, then she is a traitor. She will have to be treated in the same way as the rest of you.' He took a deep breath. 'No, I'm afraid the time for negotiations is over. Tomorrow additional forces will be arriving here. We have new weapons, beyond anything you will have seen before. You will not last long.'

'You really want the death of so many innocents?'

'They are not innocents. They are traitors. *You* are a traitor, Jack Casey. I once had faith in you English. I thought you were, in many ways, a remarkable people. Now I see I was quite wrong. You are merely ignorant natives. Nothing more.'

Jhala paused and gazed up at the fortress. 'Colonel Hada told me not to waste my time with natives. I should have listened to him.' He faced Jack again. 'Farewell. We will not meet again. And do not come down here any more. You will be shot, regardless of whether you have a white flag with you or not.'

Jhala turned on his heel and marched back towards his horse.

Jack watched his old commander and guru walk away. And he scarcely cared. Because he was tired, and his people were in danger.

And Sonali was dying.

28

The Great Yantra circled in Jack's mind, white on black. He held it steady, it blazed with brilliant light and then it faded again.

Nothing happened. Jack didn't feel the lightness he'd experienced previously. He didn't even know whether he'd used the power or not.

The Great Yantra remained impossible for him to understand. A mystery.

He sensed the powerful sattva coursing around him as he sat in the courtyard near the west wall. The familiar perfumed scent stroked his nostrils.

There'd been a lull in the fighting for the past hour and he'd come here to try the yantra one more time.

But now he heard footsteps. He slipped out of the meditation and opened his eyes.

Elizabeth and Saleem had entered the courtyard.

'What are you doing here?' Elizabeth asked. 'We were wondering where you were. We were worried.'

Jack sighed and rubbed the back of his neck. So far, he'd heeded Kanvar's warning and largely kept the Great Yantra secret. But what was the point of that now? There was no reason for him not to tell everyone about it.

'I was trying to use a power,' he said. 'I've been trying in different ways for two days now. But I still can't get it to work.'

'A new yantra?' Elizabeth asked. She and Saleem knew enough about yoga to understand what a yantra was. While neither of them was sensitive enough to sattva to become siddhas, they'd both learnt at least a little about these matters from Jack and the apprentices at the House of Sorcery.

Jack nodded. 'It's a yantra. But a very powerful one. I reckon it might even be the Grail.'

Elizabeth frowned. 'The Grail is a yantra?'

'I think it could be. You have Mother's necklace?'

Elizabeth nodded and drew the necklace out from under her dress. Jack had given it back to her after he'd shown it to Jhala.

Jack pointed at the glinting cross. 'That is the Grail.'

Elizabeth raised an eyebrow as she stared at the circling metal. 'This?'

'At least, that design is. It's a yantra. And if you keep it still in your mind and meditate on it, you can use the power.'

Elizabeth gazed at the necklace with a new reverence. 'It's hard to believe.'

'I've learnt a lot of things that are hard to believe over the past few days. But that's a yantra. There's no doubt about it. I worked it out with Kanvar just before he died.'

Elizabeth placed the necklace back under her dress and pressed her hand to it through the material, as if it could bless her just by touching her. She looked around the courtyard. 'But why are you trying to use it here?'

Jack sighed. He wasn't going to keep secrets from Elizabeth and Saleem now, but he also didn't have time to go through everything in detail. 'It's hard to explain, but this spot is like a part of the Grail.'

Elizabeth frowned and even Saleem looked confused.

'How can this place be part of the Grail?' Elizabeth asked.

Jack stood up. 'It's a long story. But it's as though the Grail is all around us here.' He lifted his hand and swept it through the bubbling sattva. 'As though we are touching it.'

'Touching it? Like Galahad and Oswin?'

'Aye. I was hoping it might make a difference. I thought if I tried using the yantra here, perhaps that would be the key.'

'And was it?'

Jack shook his head. 'Still nothing.'

He rubbed his eyes. He'd had little hope he would succeed. But he'd tried everything else he could think of. Since Kanvar had first explained to him what the Great Yantra was, he'd believed that somehow touching the Grail would release the power. The stories were so specific on this point, he thought it had to be an important part of the secret.

And yet, he'd failed once again.

A gun rumbled in the distance.

He searched the sky for round shot or shells. 'We'd better get back.'

As the three of them left the courtyard, Elizabeth said, 'Perhaps it's better you didn't get the yantra to work.'

Jack frowned. 'Why do you say that?'

Elizabeth bit her bottom lip as she walked. 'In the stories, the pure knight was always taken up to heaven when he touched the Grail, remember?'

Jack smiled grimly. 'Don't think you need to worry. I'm getting nowhere with that bloody yantra anyway.'

A second gun blasted and Jack walked more quickly. Would he really die if he managed to use the Grail? He hardly cared. He might be dead in days anyway. And at least, if he could use the power, he would have saved his people.

If the power even existed. If what he was hoping was actually true – not just a product of his desperate imagination.

<hr />

Jack strode along the east wall, staring out at the dark line of the army encircling the hill. After a full day of firing, Jhala's artillerymen had finally paused.

Jack had spent much of the past twenty-four hours up on the

ramparts with the gunners or reporting to Sir Levin. But every few hours, he'd returned to the Folly Brook camp to check on Sonali. Each time he'd gone back, he'd expected to be given bad news. But each time, he'd found Sonali was still alive. Elizabeth and Mary had been tending to her and she was clinging on.

But she couldn't last much longer.

Henry's deputies had accepted Jack from the moment the earl had appointed him commander of the fort. None had questioned Jack's authority.

Now the men were standing to attention next to their weapons as he paced along the walkway with one of Henry's sergeants, a grizzled old man-at-arms. The cold wind fluttered Jack's hair and he rubbed his hands together to warm them. Freezing winds often blew across the hilltop and up on the ramparts the men were exposed to them night and day.

Jack was pleased to note the walls had continued to withstand the onslaught. There were now numerous places where the parapet had been smashed, but so far the rest of the stonework had remained solid. However, he knew that couldn't last. Mahasiddha Vadula had powers that could bring down a wall – Jack had found that out during the Siege of London. If Vadula came to the fortress in person, Jack had no doubt the general would use his powers to destroy the rebels' defences.

Most of the artillery, Jack was pleased to note, had survived the fighting too. Several pieces had been struck by round shot, but the majority – around fifty guns and mortars – were still intact and lined up along the battlements.

He came to a halt and squinted in both directions along the wall. He noted there were several Mohammedans amongst the gunners. Most of the Mohammedans would have arrived in Shropshire as refugees during the past year. They'd remained loyal to the crusade, even when many Christians had abandoned the cause.

Finally, Jack turned to the sergeant. 'Almost all the guns are here on the east wall. We only have a handful elsewhere.'

'Aye, but we have to match the artillery over there.' The sergeant nodded towards the hills.

'Move an extra two guns to the other walls, in case there's another surprise attack.'

'We'll do that, sir.'

'Are the sentries still in place?'

'Aye, sir. All along the walls.'

One of the first things Jack had instructed his men to do was to set up watchmen, to keep an eye on the slopes at all times. The rebels had to be ready for whatever further tricks Jhala might throw at them.

'How are we doing for ammunition?' Jack asked.

'Plenty for the present time . . .' The sergeant's voice trailed off, because something over Jack's shoulder had distracted him. His face dropped and he said, 'You'd better take a look at this, sir.'

Jack turned and squinted to the north-east. At first, he couldn't see what the sergeant was talking about. But then, beyond the sprawl of the European Army camp, he made out what looked like a column of figures moving along the road.

One of Henry's men had given him a spyglass the day before. He raised this now and peered into the distance.

He shivered slightly. More troops were arriving. Many more. At the head of the column came European cavalry, and behind them marched European foot soldiers. Further back, hazy in the dust rising from the dry ground, he spotted the turquoise tunics and turbans of a Rajthanan battalion. He cursed under his breath. Indian troops were considered superior to Europeans – they were more disciplined, better trained and armed with the most recently issued firearms. These Rajthanan soldiers would no doubt be carrying the new rifled muskets, which were far more accurate than the smooth-bore firearms the European troops carried.

The train snaked away into the distance. Bringing up the rear, Jack saw horse artillery, swaying elephants and the beginning of the baggage carts.

He lowered the glass for a moment and did his best not to reveal his alarm to the men. There might be as many as ten thousand soldiers approaching, leaving Jhala with a force of around sixteen thousand.

Sixteen thousand.

And there could only be around a thousand uninjured people left in the fortress, some of whom would be too old or too young to fight. Could they really hold out against such a large force? It seemed an impossible task.

As Jack considered all this, he heard murmurs rippling between the men along the wall. The sergeant was speaking to one of his comrades and pointing towards the north-east.

Jack lifted the glass again and surveyed the approaching army. To the right of the main column, away from the dirt road, a gigantic form lumbered across the heath. It was blurred by a cloud of smoke and steam. For a moment, Jack couldn't make it out clearly. But then he spotted an iron thorax, jointed legs and a head dotted with stalks and rivets. Two green eyes glowed on the creature's crown.

It looked like the avatar from the forest.

Jack studied the beast's head carefully and identified several broken stalks. It seemed to be the same creature he and Kanvar had fought.

He lowered the glass and couldn't stop his face from dropping slightly. The avatar had been almost invincible when he and Kanvar had confronted it. Bullets hadn't harmed it. Kanvar's powers had barely done any damage to it.

The rebels would have a hard time fighting against this creature. And he'd seen what the avatar was capable of, seen the villages it had destroyed in north Shropshire.

Damn it.

Whichever way Jack looked at it, the chances of the rebels surviving were looking slimmer than ever.

PART FOUR

29

'Rao will come.' Sonali shivered. 'The treaty . . .'

Jack bent closer to her. 'Just rest. You mustn't use up all your strength.'

He'd already told her Jhala had dismissed the idea of the treaty, but there was no point repeating that now.

Sonali swallowed. Her face, as was always the case now, was bathed in sweat and her cheeks were hollow. Her eyes searched the roof of the chamber. 'Mahajan's here.'

Jack took her hand. 'He's not. You're not in his castle any more.'

She frowned slightly. 'Oh.' Her eyes focused on Jack again. 'Are we in Folly Brook?'

Jack held her hand more tightly. 'You must rest.'

'Oh.' She eased her head back and closed her eyes.

She'd been lying in this room for three days. All the other injured had died and been buried in the communal grave beside the north wall. But Sonali still clung on, lasting for longer than Jack had ever thought possible.

But she was slipping in and out of consciousness, often speaking about things that made no sense. Dreams and the past and the present seemed to be muddled up in her mind.

She opened her eyes again and licked her lips. 'I'm thirsty.'

Jack's eyes strayed to the tankard standing beside the sleeping mat. It was empty. She'd finished her day's water ration already and had even had his share. In theory, she would have to wait until tomorrow before she could have any more.

He grasped the tankard. 'I'll be back in a minute.'

He left the chamber and walked down the narrow corridor. A couple of shells burst in the distance, but the bombardment was lighter than it had been in previous days. He'd even been able to move around the fortress without feeling in great danger, as he had before.

Saleem stood guard outside the storeroom, a musket at his side. The food and water had to be protected at all times now to ensure no one took more than their fair share.

Jack waved the empty tankard. 'Sonali needs water. I'll take my ration for tomorrow now. She can have that.'

Saleem's eyes widened. 'If it's for Sonali, you could take some extra.'

'No.' Jack spoke sharply. 'No one gets extra, you understand?'

Saleem's eyes widened further and he stared at the ground.

Jack sighed and said more gently, 'Thanks for the offer. But we can't go breaking the rules for me, Sonali or anyone else. It's not fair on the others.'

Saleem nodded and stepped aside to admit Jack into the store-room. Jack walked across to the barrel, lifted the lid and gazed for a moment at the dark water. The light from the single candle danced on the surface. His mouth felt as though it were full of sand, and his throat was so dry it burned. He wanted to stick his head in the barrel and drink until it was empty.

He stood there gazing for perhaps too long, because he noticed Saleem watching him with concern.

He pulled himself together, plunged the tankard into the water, brushed past Saleem and went back to Sonali's side. He pressed the tankard to her lips and she drank until there were no more than a few drops left.

<hr />

When Jack saw the melee taking place near the gatehouse, he immediately clambered up a set of stairs that led to nowhere and stood at the top, as if at a pulpit. Below him two factions were pushing and shoving each other. A cache of food and water had been discovered in a shelter where the roof had collapsed, killing all inside. Two groups had already laid claim to it. They were arguing heatedly and would soon come to blows, by the look of it.

Jack raised his hand. 'Stop!'

At first, no one paid any attention to him. They were too busy fighting over the supplies.

Jack tried again. 'Stop! Now!'

The crowd calmed and the two opposing sides shuffled apart from each other. Everyone stared up at Jack. He was struck by how thin, drawn and dirty they all appeared. They looked like vagrants who'd been wandering the countryside for years.

He cleared his throat. He felt so thirsty black spots were circling before his eyes. But he had to say something now, had to rally his people.

He'd never been good at this sort of thing. For a moment, he thought of William. His friend had been a rebel leader and had inspired many to join the crusade. Jack had seen William give a speech in London before Vadula's attack.

What would William say now?

Jack raised his hand again. 'We should not be fighting amongst ourselves. The enemy are just outside these walls. We have to remain together if we're going to survive. We are all brothers and sisters.'

He motioned to the small collection of barrels and sacks that everyone had been fighting over moments before. 'These will be shared out evenly throughout the fortress. I will make sure of that. In the meantime, all of you need to be prepared to defend this fortress at a moment's notice. Keep your muskets and cartridges with you at all times. Be ready both day and night. Our situation might look difficult, but our people have faced many challenges in the past, and we will overcome the challenges we face now. We must all pray to God to deliver us.'

He looked about him at the gaunt but now hopeful faces staring back at him.

He raised his hand in a fist. 'God's will in England.'

'God's will in England,' the crowd murmured back.

⟡

Jack heard footsteps. Three people were approaching – two of medium height, and one shorter.

He opened his eyes and saw Saleem, Elizabeth and Mark walking through the archway in the east side of the courtyard. They were carrying muskets and Jack was surprised to see Elizabeth also had Cecily in her arms.

'Thought we'd find you here,' Elizabeth said. 'You trying the Grail again?'

'Aye.' Jack stood up, dusted himself off and picked up his musket. 'Still no luck.'

'I told Mark about the Grail,' Elizabeth said. 'Hope you don't mind.'

'Course not.' Jack gave Mark a tight smile. 'It's not a secret any more.'

Mark stepped forward. 'I thought I might try the yantra, Master, if you'll allow it. Elizabeth showed me the necklace.'

Jack rubbed his eyes. It felt as though he had grit in them. He'd only slept for a few hours at odd times over the past few days. 'You can try, if you like. But you won't have had time to memorise the design, will you? I would have mentioned it to you before, if I thought there was a chance of you using it.'

'I would still like to try,' Mark said. 'You never know.'

Jack nodded wearily. There was no harm in Mark trying. He gestured towards the spot beneath the oak tree. 'You'll be in the Great Yantra over there.'

Mark took the necklace from Elizabeth, walked across to the oak, sat down and crossed his legs. He held the necklace up before him, staring at it intently as if he could somehow lock it in his mind just through force of will.

Jack stood watching beside Elizabeth and said to her, 'You brought Cecily out.'

Elizabeth rocked the child. 'She hasn't been outside in days. I wanted her to see daylight again.'

Jack cast a wary look at the sky. 'Not sure it's safe.'

'There's been no fighting for more than a day. I thought I could take a chance. I can't keep her hiding in the dark for ever.'

Jack nodded stiffly. Elizabeth had a point. Jhala's artillery had been strangely silent for the past twenty-four hours. But all the same, the firing could start again at any time. He would have preferred Cecily to have stayed in the shelter of the palace.

Mark placed the necklace in his lap, shut his eyes and straightened his back. He sat like this for around three minutes before finally opening his eyes again. 'It's too difficult. I don't know the yantra well enough.'

'It's all right,' Jack said. 'We should get back now.'

'I'll try one last time. If you don't mind.'

Jack was about to say that he did mind and that they weren't going to wait around any longer, when he was cut short by the far-off clap of a gun and the faint whoosh of a shot.

'Right, we're going.' He grasped Elizabeth's arm. 'Now.'

Several more guns boomed and missiles began to whistle in the air.

Mark abandoned his meditation and Jack led the small group through the archway. Just as they came out in an open area that must once have been a garden, a shell bounced across from the left, struck a wall and came to a halt, spinning on a paving stone.

They all stopped and stared at the ball.

Jack felt the blood drain from his face. The bomb was less than ten feet away. It was circling, circling on the stone, making a scraping sound as it revolved.

Once it burst, the blast would catch him and the others, including Cecily. There was no chance of them escaping. The only thing he could do was throw himself on it and hope to block as much of the explosion with his body as he could.

His heart was beating hard. He was about to run forward and hurl himself on the missile when he noticed the fuse wasn't lit.

He felt the colour come back to his face. The shell wasn't going to explode after all.

Then he heard a second whistle coming from somewhere behind a ruined building. A moment later, another shell rolled across the ground and stopped about thirty feet away. As far as Jack could see, the fuse on this one wasn't lit either.

Strange. A fuse could fail to ignite in one shell. But two in such a short space of time? That was unlikely.

The shells hadn't been fitted with fuses. That was the only explanation.

'Come on.' Jack grasped Elizabeth's arm again and led the way across the open space, giving the shells a wide berth.

But Saleem suddenly stopped and pointed at the first shell. 'What's that?'

Jack paused and followed Saleem's gaze. And now he saw there was a crack running down the side of the ball. As he watched, a second fissure split the casing, making a metallic grating sound. The bomb was cracking like an egg.

Christ. Jack had never seen anything like it.

A third fissure snaked down the side of the shell and now Jack stared in disbelief as a set of iron feelers emerged from inside. The stalks flicked, swayed and then a head and a segmented body scuttled out of the crack. The creature looked like a centipede, although it was the size of Jack's hand and constructed of metal. It circled about the shell as a second centipede crawled out.

Elizabeth gasped. Mark muttered a prayer and crossed himself. Saleem grabbed the musket from his shoulder and pointed it at the beasts.

'Don't shoot,' Jack said. 'It's best we get out of here quickly.'

They turned to press on towards the Folly Brook camp, but quickly halted again.

Jack cursed under his breath. There were two further centipedes scuttling across the ground ahead. The creatures froze, raised themselves up on their hind legs and then shot across the ground towards Jack and the others.

'Back this way,' Jack said.

He led the group through the archway and back into the court-yard. But when he glanced over his shoulder, he saw the creatures were still rippling across the ground in pursuit.

Damn it. He could try shooting the beasts, but he didn't want to risk it. Not yet. Attacking them might draw more attention from any other creatures in the area.

He scanned the surroundings and spotted a ledge running along a building on the north side of the courtyard. It would be possible to climb up there and hide amongst the stonework.

'Follow me.' He led the others across to the building.

As they reached the other side of the courtyard, Mark suddenly cried out.

Jack spun round, whipping the musket from his shoulder. Mark was hopping along, grasping his ankle, his face twisted with pain. A centipede was clinging to his leg by its mandibles. It must have been hiding in the grass.

Jack grasped Mark's shoulders. 'Stay still!'

Mark stopped jumping up and down, and Jack studied the creature that had latched on to the lad's leg. The mandibles were lodged deep in the flesh, drawing beads of blood that soaked into Mark's hose. The creature made a soft clicking and hissing sound, its feelers swivelling on its head.

Jack didn't spend any time thinking what to do. He simply gripped the avatar at the back of the head and yanked it off. The creature came away more easily than he'd expected, but it twisted and writhed wildly in his hand. He quickly dropped it and stamped on it before it could dart away. It gave a final screech as it shat-tered beneath his boot.

When he looked up, he saw Elizabeth and Saleem staring at him, their faces blanched.

And now he heard more hissing behind him. The centipedes he'd seen earlier were racing through the archway and into the courtyard. Worse, he spotted another creature crawling over a pile of rubble where the yard's south wall had collapsed long ago.

The beasts were surrounding them.

He turned back to the building. 'Follow me!'

He grasped the edge of what must once have been a window frame and dragged himself up. The ledge was two storeys above him, but the climb was easy, with plenty of hand- and footholds along the way.

Elizabeth followed him halfway, then passed Cecily up to him before continuing. Saleem clambered up quickly, but Mark found it more difficult. His ankle clearly hurt from where it had been bitten, and he could barely put any weight on it. Jack had to reach down and help him up the last few feet.

They all sat panting on the ledge and watched as the centipedes below were joined by a steady flow of others. There were now around ten of the beasts patrolling the courtyard.

Jack stood up and gazed across the ruins. He was high enough to get a good view over much of the fortress. The guns had fallen silent again, but he could hear distant shouts and screams. Two people ran across the open space just beyond the courtyard's walls. A few seconds later, a wave of around ten centipedes wriggled past in pursuit. Several muskets crackled further off, nearer to the hospital.

It seemed the fortress was now infested with the creatures. He stared to the east, across the broken roofs. Somewhere over there lay the Folly Brook camp, the other villagers . . . and Sonali.

How would the villagers be faring? Would they be able to defend themselves against the avatars?

If he were alone, he would have tried running back to the camp.

But he couldn't risk it when he had Elizabeth and Cecily with him.

Mark groaned. The lad was now lying prone along one side of the ledge. He was bathed in sweat and his features were waxy. Jack crouched beside him, took out his knife and cut away the hose around the ankle. There were two punctures in the skin where the centipede had bitten. The small wounds no longer bled but they were now surrounded by a purple bruise that was spreading up the leg.

Jack didn't like the look of that.

He put away the knife and said to Mark, 'You hold on. We'll get you out of here as soon as we can.' Then he turned to Saleem and Elizabeth. 'Don't get bitten by those things.'

Both Saleem and Elizabeth nodded silently as they stared wide-eyed at Mark's leg.

A hissing floated up from below. Jack spied a centipede wriggling up the wall.

He slung his musket from his shoulder, considered firing at the avatar, but instead waited until it crawled up onto the ledge before crushing it with the butt of the musket. The creature squealed and shattered, a black substance oozing out of it. Jack kicked the remains back into the courtyard.

Elizabeth yelped and kicked away a second creature that came slithering over the lip of the ledge.

Jack looked down and cursed. There were four more creatures scuttling up the wall already.

Mark cried out in agony and began convulsing.

Jack gestured to Saleem and Elizabeth. 'Keep those things away from us.'

Then he bent down beside Mark. When he had cut the lad's hose open further, he saw that the dark bruise had seeped all the way up to the waist. Mark's face was pure white, his eyes rolled about in their sockets and foam was bubbling in his mouth.

Jack grasped Mark's shoulder. 'Stay awake, all right? Don't drift off.'

Mark's eyes focused on Jack for a moment and he managed to nod, but then his eyes glazed over and he shuddered so violently that Jack had to hold him down.

Saleem and Elizabeth were knocking away centipedes with their muskets. Elizabeth had placed Cecily down on the floor behind her. Jack wanted to pick the child up and protect her, but he also had to stay with Mark.

Mark's eyes rolled white.

Jack gripped the lad's shoulders. 'Stay awake!'

But Mark went suddenly rigid. His face twisted in pain and then went still. His lips turned blue and his eyes stared up lifelessly.

Jack searched frantically for a pulse. But he found nothing.

He lowered his head. Mark had been his apprentice for two years and had even helped to build the House of Sorcery. He'd told Jack several times that he was an orphan and that he'd never had a home.

'Well, Mark, you're home now.' Jack shut the lad's eyes and crossed himself.

Elizabeth gave a muffled shriek. Jack swivelled round and saw several centipedes crawling down the masonry above. One plopped onto the ledge and rattled towards Cecily.

Nerves shot through Jack's chest. He swept the infant up in his arms and stamped on the avatar, crushing it in the middle. The beast's head continued squealing and writhing for a few seconds, then slumped.

'There are too many of them,' Elizabeth said.

Jack looked around him. There were scores of avatars clambering up from the courtyard and ten or more descending from above. He, Elizabeth and Saleem were surrounded on all sides.

He heard a hiss near his ear and saw a centipede dangling from a vine overhead. The beast was inches from his face. He lurched to the left and the creature swung itself towards him. Then he dodged to the right, and the avatar again followed his movements.

Then he stood stock-still. The creature paused and its feelers flickered. It shrilled and rotated its head in different directions. Finally, it scuttled away along the vine.

Jack breathed out. He had an idea now. It was a risky plan, but it was the best he could think of at the moment.

He called across to Saleem and Elizabeth, 'Listen, these things can only see us if we move.'

Elizabeth swept a creature off the ledge with her musket. 'What?'

'They follow our movements,' Jack said. 'If we stay still, they won't be able to see us. They'll leave us alone.'

'You want us to just stand here?' Elizabeth said.

'We can't hold them all back. We have to try something else.'

'You sure that'll work?'

'No. But it's our only chance now.'

Saleem's eyes were wide. 'If you say so, Jack.'

Elizabeth's eyes glittered and she bit her bottom lip. Finally, she nodded her agreement.

Jack swaddled Cecily tightly in her blanket so that she was unable to move her arms and legs. Despite everything that was going on, she looked drowsy and even on the verge of sleep.

Elizabeth reached out to take Cecily, but Jack pulled the baby away. 'It's all right. I'll hold on to her.'

There was no time to discuss it further, because two centipedes dropped down and circled about on the ledge.

'Stay dead still,' Jack whispered. 'Don't move a muscle, or you're finished.'

They stood rigidly as more avatars poured over the lip of the ledge and scurried about their feet. Others fell from above, hit the overhang with a slap and then joined the writhing mass of creatures.

One avatar hung down right before Jack's face. He held his breath as he stared at the chewing mandibles and whirring gills.

325

A tiny puff of smoke wafted from the creature's side and its feelers swung about its head as it searched for any sign of movement.

Jack felt sweat running down his cheek. Would the movement be enough to alert the creature? He fought to remain as still as possible.

He mustn't twitch, mustn't even blink, because the creature was so close to his face it could strike him before he even had a chance to defend himself.

The avatar hovered before him, its legs coiling. Then, abruptly, it swung itself back up and clattered away along the wall.

Jack exhaled, but only felt a moment of relief because now he saw centipedes climbing up Elizabeth's dress and Saleem's hose. Both Elizabeth and Saleem were standing as still as they could, looking down in horror at the beasts clambering up.

It was all Jack could do to remain where he was. He wanted to lunge across and swipe the creatures off Elizabeth. But he knew that would only put her in even more danger.

Then he felt something on his ankle. He dropped his gaze and saw a centipede scrambling up his leg. It reached his knee-length tunic and scuttled over it up to his belt, where it paused for a moment, staring up at him.

The sweat poured off his forehead. One movement now and the thing would bite through his clothing and poison him in an instant. An unbearable itch developed on his nose, but he pushed the sensation to the back of his mind.

Then the creature clambered higher. Jack wanted to turn his head to check on Elizabeth and Saleem but didn't dare now. The avatar reached his chest and then crept onto his neck. His skin rippled and puckered.

The beast was walking up onto his face. He felt its cold, metal legs press into his skin. He could hear the faint whirring of the mechanism inside it. The creature's segmented body passed over one of his eyes and then crawled across his scalp. Finally, after what seemed like minutes but could only have been seconds, the avatar descended over his face again and began crawling down his chest.

He'd done it. The beast was leaving.

Then Cecily, who so far had been lying peacefully in his arms, began to whimper and shift her head.

Damn it. Cecily had been so still, he'd been hoping she would even fall asleep.

The avatar immediately swung round on his chest, squealed and dashed along his arm.

It was going to bite Cecily.

30

Jack's thoughts whirled. He had to act quickly if he were going to save Cecily. But if he moved, he would alert the avatars to his presence.

Cecily settled and fell silent again. Jack said a Hail Mary in his head.

The avatar paused halfway along his arm and turned its head first to one side and then the other, its feelers quivering as they sampled the air. The creature had registered movement, but now it couldn't see anything.

Jack prayed the thing would turn round and leave. Why was it staying poised on his arm?

Cecily closed her eyes for a moment. Jack willed her to go to sleep. But then she flipped her eyelids open again. Her face was bunching up and it looked as though she might be about to cry.

No.

Jack's heart hammered. The moment Cecily cried, her movements would give her away. She had to lie still. But that seemed to be the last thing she would do.

Then he had an idea. He remembered Katelin blowing on Elizabeth's eyes when she was a baby so that she would close them and drift to sleep. He was already staring directly at Cecily. He could blow and only make the barest of movements with his mouth.

As Cecily's face creased further and she looked set to burst into tears, he opened his lips a fraction and exhaled, just strongly enough for his breath to catch Cecily's face. She blinked a few times – this distracted her, at least.

The avatar on his arm made a sizzling sound and spun its feelers about its head. Its mandibles knitted and whirred.

Jack blew again, praying Cecily would close her eyes.

For a moment, Cecily fought against sleep. He could see she was exhausted but forcing herself to stay awake. She looked set to cry out, but then her eyelids drooped and finally shut completely.

A Hail Mary tumbled through Jack's head.

The avatar raised itself up on its hind legs, clicked loudly several times, expelled a tiny jet of steam from its side and then turned and ran back up his arm. It coiled about his chest for a moment, then scuttled down his leg and crawled away towards the courtyard.

Jack took a deep breath. He realised he hadn't been breathing for some time. When he looked across at Elizabeth, he saw she was largely free of avatars now. One still clung to the bottom of her dress, but it soon wriggled back to the ground and disappeared from the ledge.

But several centipedes were still entwined about Saleem, one of them crawling over his face. Saleem stood absolutely still, his eyes wide in terror. Finally, the creatures circled back down to his feet and scurried away.

Now Jack dared to move. He shifted his head enough to look down the wall. All the avatars had left, save for a couple still scouring the rubble to the south. He inched his head round and stared up. There were no avatars above him either.

His shoulders slumped and he breathed more freely. 'It's all right. Reckon we're safe now.'

Elizabeth and Saleem suddenly moved, statues come to life. Elizabeth sniffled, grasped Cecily and embraced the child. Saleem was panting and searching the ground below, seemingly unable to believe the creatures had gone.

Jack looked towards the east. In the grey light of the overcast day, the ruins looked peaceful and still. But then a bell began ringing somewhere in the centre of the fortress. This seemed to set off other bells, which now pealed from many different places.

Jack felt cold. On the one hand, it was heartening to hear this sound. It meant there were still some people alive in the fortress, that the avatars hadn't killed everyone. But, at the same time, the bells were ringing to sound the alarm.

The walls were under attack.

The centipedes must have been just the first wave of the assault, designed to soften the rebels up. Now the full attack was likely to begin.

Elizabeth shivered. 'We have to get back to the others.'

Saleem nodded, his hands shaking as he put his musket back on his shoulder. No doubt the lad would be thinking of his mother and sisters huddling together back at the camp. Just as Elizabeth would be thinking of Godwin.

And just as Jack was thinking of Sonali. He'd last seen her a little over half an hour ago and she'd looked alarmingly pale and weak. She'd only opened her eyes briefly to acknowledge him. The rest of the time, she'd lain as still as if she were dead.

Guns began firing. First, the enemy batteries grumbled in the distance, then the rebel artillery responded. Jack heard a series of blasts behind him. When he looked towards the west wall, he saw plumes of grey-white smoke drifting into the air. The small party of artillerymen stationed there were firing at something.

Christ. He could hear gunfire coming from the south, east and west walls. The enemy must be attacking on several fronts.

He scanned the surroundings. What was the best way back to the camp?

He noticed five avatars patrolling the open space beyond the courtyard. A man ran past, hurrying towards the south wall, but a centipede flung itself onto the back of his leg. The man cried out and slipped over, gripping the creature and trying to wrestle it off. But he was too late. The beast would have bitten him already, and he would be dead in minutes.

'Hold on for a moment,' Jack said to Elizabeth and Saleem.

He grasped a clump of ivy above him and scrambled up the wall. It was difficult to climb this part of the building – there were few handholds and the masonry was often brittle and crumbled away in his fingers. He almost fell at one point, when a small outcrop snapped off beneath his foot. But he eventually reached what must once have been a window and sat astride the bottom edge of the frame. From here he could see across much of the ruins. He took out the spyglass, scoured the immediate vicinity and spotted the dark flickers of centipedes everywhere he looked.

His grip on the glass tightened. It would be almost impossible to get back to the camp.

A gun boomed behind him, and now his eyes strayed across to the west wall. From this height he had a clear view of the battlements lying about a hundred yards away. He could make out the gunners labouring frantically to load and fire their artillery. Several of the men were positioned along the wall, facing in towards the fortress. At first, Jack couldn't understand what they were doing. But then he noticed they were jabbing with muskets and burning brands at any centipedes that clambered up the wall. They were doing a good job at fighting off the beasts.

As Jack considered what to do next, he realised that the safest place nearby was the west wall. At least there were enough people there to keep the avatars at bay.

Saleem called up to him, pointing into the courtyard. 'Look.'

Jack stared at the ground and saw that another centipede was scrabbling around in the grass. The creatures were returning and could climb up the wall again at any time.

He scrambled back down to the ledge and waved his hand towards the west. 'We have to get up on the wall.'

'What about the camp?' Elizabeth said. 'The others?'

'We won't make it,' he replied. 'Too many avatars about.'

Elizabeth tightened her jaw. 'We can't just abandon them.'

Jack paused. This was as difficult a choice for him as it was for

Elizabeth and Saleem. 'We're not abandoning anyone. They have each other. They have muskets, and the apprentices have their powers. They're better off than we are at the moment.'

Elizabeth's eyes gleamed brightly, but she finally nodded.

Jack went to the edge of the outcrop and peered down. The centipede was circling about the south side of the courtyard. Below Jack, to his right, lay an opening that led towards the west wall. Could he, Saleem and Elizabeth get down from the ledge and across to that opening before the centipede reached them?

It was risky, but they had to try.

He rubbed his eyes. His throat burnt with thirst. He would give anything for a drink, and felt slightly light-headed for a moment. But he pulled himself together.

He shot a final look at Mark's body, made the sign of the cross, and then said to Elizabeth and Saleem, 'Follow me.'

He climbed halfway to the ground and then jumped the remaining few feet. Elizabeth and Saleem followed, and all three of them darted over to the opening in the west side of the courtyard.

The centipede noticed their movements, hissed and hurtled across the grass towards them. It was moving faster than Jack had expected.

He stuck his head out of the opening and saw a wide boulevard leading all the way to the west wall.

He grabbed Elizabeth and shoved her through the archway. 'Get up on the wall. Hurry.'

Saleem paused, but Jack said to him, 'You too. Look after Elizabeth and Cecily.'

As Saleem and Elizabeth charged off down the boulevard, Jack slipped through the archway, hid round the side and held his musket with the butt pointing downwards. The avatar shot out of the entryway in pursuit and he slammed the musket down on it just in time, catching the last few segments of its back. The creature squealed like a pig and wrestled to free itself. But

Jack crunched on its head with his boot until it finally stopped moving.

He heard more high-pitched cackling and saw several more centipedes swarming across the rubble to the south. They must have noticed movement in the courtyard and had come to investigate.

He sprinted after Elizabeth and Saleem. He could see that the two of them had already reached the end of the boulevard and were disappearing to the right, following the giant west wall.

He ran faster. He hadn't wanted to part with Elizabeth and Cecily, but he'd had no choice.

He reached the end of the boulevard and skidded to a halt. A set of stairs about fifty feet away led up the side of the wall. Elizabeth and Saleem had already scrambled to the top. There were rebels spread out along the battlements, and many were looking down at Jack and urging him on.

He went to sprint across to the steps, but a group of around ten centipedes raced out of the ruins ahead of him, fanning across the ground.

The creatures were blocking his only escape route. And now he heard more clicking and shrilling behind him. When he glanced back, he saw a wave of at least twenty beasts rushing down the boulevard towards him.

He cursed under his breath. He turned back to the wall. He had to get up those stairs. Now.

He lifted the musket and went to fire at the centipedes immediately ahead of him. But then firearms spluttered overhead. The earth about the creatures rippled like water as the bullets struck. Avatars shrieked as they shattered, and tiny columns of dust pirouetted.

Jack glanced up and saw a row of around twenty rebels reloading their muskets in order to fire again.

'Hurry up!' One man waved down to Jack. 'Get up those bloody steps!'

Jack ran towards the stairway as another volley of musket balls rattled into the centipedes. More creatures splintered, while the others retreated before the onslaught.

Jack pounded up the steps and was greeted by Elizabeth and Saleem at the top. He embraced Elizabeth briefly and slapped Saleem on the shoulder. They'd all made it to the relative safety of the wall. That was something, at least.

A gun roared nearby, the sound shuddering through the wall beneath Jack's feet and making his ears ring for a second.

A gunner stepped up to him and bowed slightly. 'Master Casey, sir. I'm in command here.'

Jack was startled to see that the man was wearing a European Army uniform.

'Used to be in the army.' The gunner smiled. '3rd Native Heavy Artillery.'

Jack was strangely pleased to hear this. It was reassuring to know the man in charge of the west wall had been trained in the army.

'What's your name?' Jack asked.

'Patrick Fletcher, sir.' He cleared his throat. 'I was once a sergeant.'

'All right, Sergeant Fletcher, tell me what's going on here.'

An artilleryman touched a portfire to the vent of a gun nearby. The piece gave a pummelling boom, rocked back on its wheels and disgorged a cloud of sulphurous smoke that coiled along the ramparts and blocked the view for a moment.

Fletcher led Jack over to the parapet. The acrid smoke scratched Jack's eyes for a second before it was whipped away by the breeze. Now he could see the steep slope leading down the western side of the hill. Beyond this, the open countryside rolled away towards the hazy mountains in the distance. The enemy troops still encircled the fortress – he could see the line of them spreading out across the broken landscape.

Fletcher pointed down the incline. 'A few companies of heathens are hiding over there, behind those hills.'

Jack peered down. A knot of smaller peaks, mounds and spurs rose from the bottom of the western side of the hill. From this angle it was impossible to see the ground beyond.

Fletcher lowered his voice. 'That big demon was with them. Spitting fire and smoke, it were.'

'The giant avatar?'

'Aye, sir.'

Several more of the guns further down the wall blasted, the sound reverberating about the slopes.

'We were firing at them as they marched up,' Fletcher said. 'Can't see them now. We're just letting them know we're still here.'

Jack wasn't happy to hear the avatar was being moved closer to the fortress. That could only mean Jhala was planning a major assault. At the same time there was no point in the artillerymen wasting their ammunition. He was about to tell them to stop firing, when one of the gunners nearby started waving his arms and shouting.

Fletcher stared at the knot of hillocks. 'There's something there.'

Jack raised his glass and searched the collection of low peaks. At first, he saw nothing. But then he spotted figures slipping between copses and rocky outcrops. The soldiers had climbed up the far side of the hillocks and were creeping towards the fortress.

And now, as Jack stared, he saw the black bulk of the giant avatar lumber over the crest of one of the hills. Smoke swirled about it, and its green eyes blazed on top of its head.

He shoved the spyglass into his belt and turned to Fletcher. 'Train all the guns on that avatar down there. And tell anyone else with a musket to line up along this parapet. We've got a fight on our hands.'

'There are still those creatures.' Fletcher motioned to where one of the men was knocking a centipede off the wall. The beasts were still constantly scuttling up.

'All right,' Jack replied. 'Leave a few men to keep those avatars back.'

Fletcher blew a whistle he must have kept from his army days. Then he waved his arms about and barked orders to the men dotted along the wall.

Jack faced Elizabeth and Saleem. 'Get your muskets ready. The enemy are coming up.'

The three of them slung their firearms from their shoulders and Elizabeth placed Cecily down beside her feet.

Jack felt his eyes moistening. It wasn't right that Cecily was here, up on a wall, in the middle of what was soon to be a battle. But there was nowhere else he could put her. He couldn't tell Elizabeth to take Cecily down into the fortress again. There were too many centipedes about. There was nowhere else for any of them to go. They would have to stand here and fight and defend the child as best they could.

He glanced along the ramparts and saw the rebels lining up with their muskets. A few of them were loading their firearms directly from powder flasks – they must have run out of cartridges.

He shifted his gaze over to the south wall for a moment and made out figures congregating along the battlements. It appeared the army were approaching on that side of the fortress as well. The rebels were caught in a vice.

He turned back to the parapet and stared down the incline. The enemy soldiers were advancing into a saddle between the hillocks and the main hill. The avatar had surged ahead and had already reached the far side of the saddle, battering aside shrubs that got in its way.

Elizabeth and Saleem could see the beast clearly now. Elizabeth stared transfixed, while Saleem was breathing heavily.

'You both keep your heads,' Jack said. 'We can get through this, all right?'

Saleem swallowed and drew himself up taller. He'd been through the Siege of London and managed to keep his nerve then. Jack was sure the lad would do the same now.

Jack could hardly bear to meet Elizabeth's gaze. He wanted his daughter to be far away, somewhere safe. If he had been a better father, that's what he would have arranged. But he hadn't been able to do that, and so now she would have to fight alongside him.

Tears were brimming in her eyes.

'Empty your mind,' he said. 'Don't think about anything but firing your musket. And once you've fired, don't think of anything apart from reloading. If you think about anything else, you're lost.'

Elizabeth nodded, blinking away tears and pushing up her bottom lip, her chin puckering.

Fletcher returned to Jack's side. 'The guns are ready, sir.'

'Then fire,' Jack said. 'And keep firing. Don't let that thing get up here. And tell everyone else to be ready with their muskets.'

'Right, sir.' Fletcher bowed slightly. It almost looked as though he were going to do a namaste for a moment, but he stopped himself and instead began bellowing orders at the gunners.

There were only five guns along the west wall, but there would have been even fewer if Jack hadn't ordered more artillery to be moved here two days ago.

The artillerymen touched their portfires to the guns at almost the same time. The vents smouldered for a second and then the weapons punched in unison, the serpent-headed muzzles blazing like fire-breathing dragons. The snake eyes glared angrily as the pieces kicked back.

Balls swooped down from the wall. They overshot the avatar but battered the troops marching behind. When Jack peered through the spyglass, he saw several men lying dead in the grass.

The gunners were already sponging out the pieces, reloading and twisting screws to adjust elevation. But now the enemy came alive. Horns blared, drummers bashed on kettledrums strapped to their waists and a sergeant raised a standard. The soldiers, who'd been advancing cautiously up until now, roared and charged across the saddle, heading towards the final incline.

The change in the avatar was even more dramatic. Before, it had been ambling slowly. But now it expelled a jet of steam and bounded like a dog towards the west wall. It gave a high-pitched wail that sent shivers down Jack's spine. The cry seemed to unnerve the men along the ramparts, as many of them lowered their muskets and began muttering amongst themselves.

'Get ready to fire!' Jack shouted. 'Present!'

The five guns thundered again, spewing smoke and flame, and hurling balls at the beast charging up the hill.

Two balls struck the ground immediately in front of the creature and bounced over its head. A further three clanged into its rounded back, but glanced off, doing no more damage than denting the carapace slightly. The avatar howled, but it didn't even slow its pace.

Jack cursed under his breath. Kanvar had said the creature's armour was strong. But the beast had just been hit by three round shot and had barely been harmed.

The enemy soldiers had reached the edge of the saddle and were scrambling up the final scarp. But the avatar was racing ahead. It was now only around a hundred yards away from the wall.

Jack lifted his musket, stared along the sights and aimed at the creature. 'Fire! Fire at the demon!'

Jack's command rippled along the battlements as it was passed between the men. Jack waited for a second and then pulled the trigger. At the same time, the line of rebels along the parapet fired their muskets. The firearms popped and coughed, and bullets rained down on the avatar. Scores of balls rattled against its armour. But as the smoke cleared, Jack saw the creature was again undamaged and still charging up the slope.

The artillerymen were firing out of time now. One gun blasted a ball at the avatar's head, but the beast batted it away with its claw. Another round shot chimed against its side, leaving a small scrape but nothing more.

The beast screeched and raised its claws. It was close enough now for Jack to make out its whirring mandibles.

338

Jack joined the rebels along the wall as they reloaded their muskets and fired. The weapons flared and spluttered, and bullets teemed in the air. The hail of musket balls clattered against the avatar. But again, they did no damage.

Jack bit open another cartridge and reloaded his musket. He was feeling weak with hunger and thirst, but he pushed his discomfort aside. He was about to fire again, but then he realised there was no point. Because now the creature was just a few feet away from the wall.

Soon it would be at the fortress. There was no stopping it.

31

<hr/>

With an iron squeal, the creature leapt. It clattered against the wall about twenty yards from Jack, scrabbled to grasp the battlements and hauled itself up to the parapet. Its lurid green eyes, contorted head and flickering maw popped up over the crenellations. The artillerymen standing nearby cried out and abandoned their gun. The other soldiers fled along the wall.

The beast dragged itself over the battlements and kicked aside the gun, which rolled back, careered off the wall and cracked apart on the ground below. The creature slid over the parapet and straddled the walkway for a moment. It was so large that its abdomen hung outside the fort, while its front legs scraped at the inner edge of the ramparts. Then it launched itself off the wall and plunged down to the ground inside the fortress.

Jack cursed. The avatar would wreak havoc amongst the rebels.

He swung his musket onto his shoulder, shut his eyes and called the Lightning yantra to mind. In a second, he had the design glowing in his head. He flung his eyes open and raised his hand. The avatar was clambering up the side of a ruined tower, perhaps in an attempt to get a better view of the rest of the fortress.

Jack voiced the mantra and his arm shook as the lightning wriggled through it and shot out of his fingertips. The bolt snarled through the air and gave a metallic ring as it struck the avatar in the back. The creature jolted, bellowed and immediately swung itself back down to the earth. It circled round and charged back towards the wall, giving a deafening shriek.

It was bounding straight towards Jack.

Jack went cold for a second, but he composed himself and brought the yantra to mind again. He flung another bolt at the beast, smacking it just below its mouth. The creature skidded to a halt and shook its head, as if in agony. But this only lasted for a second, before it sprang forward, slammed into the wall and scrambled up the stonework.

The people about Jack shouted and ran along the wall to escape. Jack grasped Cecily and shoved the child into Elizabeth's arms, saying, 'Get out of here!'

Elizabeth backed away, but only a short distance.

Jack grasped his musket as the avatar's head leered over the top of the wall. It scratched with its legs as it heaved itself up.

Jack's heart battered in his chest. He was, once again, looking into the beast's eyes. Did it remember him? Was it determined now to kill him?

He lifted his musket. Perhaps he could hit one of those eyes and drive the creature back – for a moment, at least.

But before he could pull the trigger a pulverising blast sounded to his left. Fletcher had wheeled a gun round, and now fired at the avatar. The muzzle flashed, kicked and launched a ball at the creature. The round shot pounded the avatar in the head, snapping off a stalk and bashing a large indentation in the creature's crown.

Sulphur-scented smoke blurred Jack's view for a moment, but as it cleared he saw the creature groaning and shaking its head violently. Being pummelled at such short range seemed to have hurt it at last. It scratched wildly at the edge of the walkway, roared and thrashed about for a moment, then sprang down to the ground and bounded off into the fortress.

Jack breathed out sharply. His heart was still racing.

He glanced across at Fletcher, who was standing beside the gun.

'We got the bastard.' Fletcher grinned.

That was true, up to a point. But Jack saw that the creature was now charging down the boulevard towards the courtyard. In one claw it held a struggling man. It lifted the figure up high in the air, then snapped its claw shut. The man was severed in two.

Elizabeth gasped and Fletcher grimaced.

Jack tightened one hand into a fist. The avatar could easily slaughter hundreds of people, but there was nothing he or anyone else on the ramparts could do about that at the moment. They still had to defend the wall.

He spun round and stared over the parapet. While he'd been distracted by the avatar, the European Army troops had been pressing on up the hill. The vanguard was now no more than a hundred yards away.

'Fire at them!' Jack shouted to his men.

Elizabeth placed Cecily back down on the walkway and stood beside Jack. Saleem positioned himself on the far side of her and raised his musket. The three of them aimed and fired at the swarm of men rushing up the scarp. At the same time, the other rebels along the wall blasted with their muskets. The firearms crackled and spat, and smoke blurred Jack's view for a moment. When it cleared, he saw that scores of enemy soldiers had been knocked down.

But there were hundreds more still clambering up.

Jack, Saleem and Elizabeth reloaded and fired with the other rebels. Flocks of bullets battered into the enemy, cutting men down like wheat beneath a scythe.

A powder flask further along the wall exploded and went flying through the air. It must have ignited as someone reloaded.

The gunners began firing grape. The guns roared and sprayed the shrieking metal across the incline, flaying the soldiers rushing up. Men fell, surrounded by clouds of blood, but many more ran on fearlessly.

Jack guessed there were about three hundred soldiers still charging at the fortress, and he now noticed many of them were carrying scaling ladders.

'Keep firing!' he shouted. But he hardly needed to. The rebels were blasting round after round at the enemy, slaughtering many, but not enough to stop the assault entirely.

Jack noticed the splutter of muskets coming from the south wall. When he glanced across, he saw smoke smothering the southern battlements. The rebels there were fighting off a second assault.

He turned and fired again into the mass of soldiers below, but the first troops had already reached the wall. The enemy soldiers began raising ladders and scrabbling up.

'Get your knives out,' Jack told Saleem and Elizabeth.

The three of them clicked the catches on their muskets and the knives snapped into place. Jack studied Elizabeth for a second. She stood with her legs apart and her musket at her waist, the knife pointing towards the battlements. How could she hope to fight against trained soldiers? How had it come to this?

The situation was unreal, and yet there was nothing Jack could do about it. They all had to fight for their lives. Elizabeth was no exception.

The top of a ladder tapped against the battlements directly in front of him. He gestured to Saleem and Elizabeth. 'Push this away!'

The three of them slung their muskets on their shoulders and set about heaving the ladder away from the wall. Jack pressed against one side, while Saleem and Elizabeth pushed at the other.

Soldiers were already battering up the steps, and the ladder shuddered in Jack's hands. He ground his teeth, grunted and gasped. They had to get the ladder away from the wall before it became too weighed down with attackers.

Groaning at the effort, Jack managed to force his side of the ladder off the parapet. Saleem and Elizabeth only managed to shift their side slightly, but it didn't matter. Jack had done enough to send the ladder sliding sideways down the wall. The soldiers cried out and tumbled back down to the ground.

All along the ramparts, further ladders smacked into the wall. The enemy streamed up the rungs and the rebels struggled to shove the ladders away. Most of the attackers appeared to be European Mohammedans, but amongst them were a handful of Rajthanan officers wielding scimitars.

Jack raised his musket and fired at a line of soldiers climbing a nearby ladder. He hit one of the men, who toppled to the ground, clutching a wound in his chest.

Saleem and Elizabeth fired now as well, along with those rebels who weren't wrestling with one of the scaling ladders. The bullets pelted the soldiers below, knocking scores back to the ground.

The gunners angled their pieces down and blasted howling grape at the enemy.

Soldiers managed to clamber to the top of one ladder and jump down onto the walkway. Hand-to-hand fighting broke out, but the rebels soon slaughtered the attackers and finally heaved the ladder away.

Jack reloaded and fired several times, picking off soldiers one by one. He then flung a few lightning bolts at a group of attackers trying to raise a ladder immediately below him. A thick cloud of smoke suffocated the battlements so that he could see no more than a foot in front of him.

And then the muskets and guns fell silent. The smoke drifted apart to reveal the hillside was littered with bodies and broken ladders. A few of the soldiers squirmed on the ground and cried out in pain, but most were already dead. A single Rajthanan officer was limping about in a daze, swinging his scimitar at imaginary foes. A musket cracked on the wall and the man collapsed.

Now, not a single enemy soldier was left standing.

Fletcher punched the air and cried out, 'God's will in England!'

'God's will in England!' the rebels along the wall shouted back.

Jack embraced Elizabeth, clasped Saleem on the shoulder and bent down to check on Cecily. The infant gurgled and stared up at him with wide eyes. Did she have any idea what had just happened? Did she know she was in the middle of a battle?

He stood up again and surveyed the ramparts. There was no

further sign of an assault from the west, but when he looked back into the fortress he could see the fight was continuing elsewhere. Immediately ahead of him, many of the rebels were still struggling to repel the centipedes slithering up the wall. Further off, he glimpsed the giant avatar rampaging through the ruins. And to his right, powder smoke had completely blotted out the top of the south wall. Tiny dots of flame from the muskets jabbed the fog, while the guns continued to flash.

Jack turned to Fletcher. 'Turn the guns round. We have to be ready to fire into the fortress if the south wall is breached.'

Fletcher shouted the commands, and the four remaining guns were circled about. Jack considered locating the winch and moving the artillery pieces to the south. But that could take hours, and the centipedes would make the task almost impossible. Furthermore, there was always a chance Jhala would send yet another wave of attackers to the west side of the fortress. Someone had to remain to defend it.

Then Jack spotted a melee taking place at one of the gaps in the south wall. When he lifted the spyglass, he saw that a column of enemy troops had burst through the breach and were forcing their way into the interior of the fortress. Most of the attackers wore European Army uniform, but Jack also noticed several Rajthanan soldiers in turquoise tunics and turbans, along with officers carrying pistols and scimitars.

Rebels streamed down from the wall or rushed up from the ruins to confront the invaders. But the enemy troops fought back with knife-muskets and blades.

Then a blaze of green dazzled Jack for a moment. A second flash followed shortly afterwards.

Lightning.

Someone amongst the attackers was using Lightning.

Jack stared hard through the glass and spied a Rajthanan in a purple uniform flinging lightning bolts into the rebel defenders. The man was clearly a siddha.

Then Jack noticed a second man in purple. And finally a third man, half hidden by the haze, who was blasting bolts into the fortress. As this last figure strode out of the fog, Jack's fingers tightened about the glass.

It was Jhala. The general himself had joined the attack.

It was unheard of for a general to take part in a battle, but then Jhala had never been an ordinary officer. As a captain he'd been in the thick of the fighting, even when that wasn't entirely neces-sary. He'd been a champion wrestler and had even trained with his own European troops. Clearly, despite the years, he hadn't changed. He was still determined to lead from the front.

And, beyond all this, he was obviously confident that his forces were on the verge of taking the fortress. He wouldn't have risked joining the assault unless he was certain of success.

The rebels were now retreating from the breach and fleeing into the ruins. Jhala fired a couple more lightning bolts and then marched into the fortress, heading north, his troops filing behind him. The other two siddhas peeled off from the column and led a smaller force towards the centre of the ruins.

Jack lowered the glass. Jhala and the siddhas would be difficult to stop. The rebels faced defeat unless they could force the attackers back outside the walls. But that was looking less and less likely. Jhala and his men were advancing virtually unopposed.

Jack had to do something. Quickly.

He slung the musket on his shoulder and turned to Fletcher. 'Keep an eye on both sides of the wall.' He motioned towards Jhala and his men. 'And be ready to fire on that lot, if they come this way.'

Fletcher nodded. 'But you'll be with us, though, won't you, sir?'

'I'll try to be,' Jack muttered. Then he faced Elizabeth and Saleem, saying, 'You two stay here. I have to do something.'

Elizabeth frowned. 'Where are you going?'

'Just stay here,' he snapped. The words sounded harsh but he had to make sure Elizabeth didn't try to follow him. Then he gave her a tight smile and softened his tone. After all, this might be the last time he ever spoke to her. 'You need to look after Cecily.' He looked across at Saleem. 'And both of you need to help defend this wall. The enemy could try another attack. We don't know what else they could throw at us.' He gazed back at Elizabeth and grasped her arm. 'God's grace to you. Take care of yourself.'

Before Saleem or Elizabeth could protest, he pushed past the men crowding around the battlements and ran down the walkway, heading south towards Jhala.

<hr />

Jack jogged around the pyramids of shot, ammunition chests and milling rebels. Many men were still fighting off the centipedes with burning brands, muskets and even sponge staffs. But at least there seemed to be fewer creatures than before.

From time to time Jack scanned the fort for Jhala and his men. He couldn't see them amongst the ruins, but the occasional flickers of green lightning guided him.

When he was about halfway along the wall, he reached a set of stairs and plunged down into the fortress. A few of the crusaders behind him called out, warning him to come back, but he ignored them. He reached the ground, glanced around and saw no centipedes nearby.

He swallowed. His throat was painfully dry. He'd had half a tankard of water the day before, and nothing at all so far today.

He charged across to the ruins and ducked down an alleyway. Hearing shouts and the popping of muskets, he struck off in the direction of the sounds. He wound his way through a series of roofless chambers, ducked through archways and shattered apertures, then skirted a tower. He occasionally spied centipedes in the distance, but he always managed to avoid them.

He came out suddenly in a wide boulevard. A firefight was taking place ahead of him. Rebels crouched behind the broken masonry, blasting with their muskets at the attackers at the far end of the avenue. Bullets criss-crossed the air, screamed off walls and kicked up spurts of dirt from the ground. Several wounded rebels lay near Jack. Another was wandering about in a circle, clutching his head and moaning.

A bolt of lightning suddenly roared down the boulevard and battered into a group of rebels. The men were knocked backwards and flung to the ground. Jack could smell the burnt flesh and clothing from where he was standing.

The lightning had to have been fired by Jhala.

Jack squinted into the smoke. His old commander was nearby.

A musket ball shrieked against the wall near his head, chipping the stone and spitting grit. He ducked back into the ruins and cast his eyes about. He had to stop Jhala. The general might be a powerful siddha, but he wasn't invincible. If Jack could kill him, the assault might falter, or at least slow. That could give the rebels enough of a chance to fight back.

His eyes fell upon a small, domed building. It could have been a mosque at one time, although the stonework was so worn it was impossible to tell. From the roof of that building Jack guessed he would be able to see Jhala and his men.

Jack charged across to the structure and climbed up the side, thrusting through vines as he went. He stood on a ledge that encircled the dome and inched his way round until he could see down into the boulevard.

Jhala's men were hiding behind the stonework and firing at the rebels through a cloud of powder smoke. Most of them were European Army soldiers, but there were also several Rajthanan officers wielding rotary pistols.

And then Jack gave an involuntary hiss. He'd spotted Jhala.

His old commander was standing towards the rear of the party. But at intervals, he would step out from behind a block of masonry and fling lightning at his opponents. And each time he did that, Jack could see him clearly.

Jack had a clear shot at him.

He heard footsteps below him and spotted two Rajthanan soldiers running through the ruins nearby. He shrank back against the dome, but the two men would see him instantly if they looked up. Sweat crossed his forehead and he gripped the sling of the musket, ready to shoot if he had to.

But the two soldiers didn't pause for a moment. Instead, they ran on into the ruins, soon vanishing from sight.

Jack edged back round the dome and looked down into the boulevard again. He couldn't see Jhala, but the general was bound to step out again to use his lightning at any moment.

And then Jack would have his chance.

He thought of the Lightning yantra and left it dangling at the back of his mind. And then he waited. He kept his eyes fixed on the place where Jhala was hiding. He heard the cries and musket blasts, smelt the acrid scent of the powder smoke, sensed the bullets whispering in the air. But he ignored them all. Because now he had to make sure he killed Jhala. He might never get a chance like this again.

But Jhala didn't reappear. He remained in his hiding place for three minutes or more.

Sweat ran into Jack's eyes. His heart thudded in his throat and pounded in his ears.

Why wouldn't Jhala come out? What was he waiting for?

Then Jack heard a deep rumble to his left, loud enough to send dust trickling down the side of the dome.

He swivelled his head in time to see a giant, orange fireball boiling in the air on the other side of the boulevard. The flames crackled, snarled and coursed in veins about the ball. And underneath, with his hands raised to the heavens, stood Jhala.

Jhala swung his hand at Jack, as if throwing a stone. The fireball instantly shot across the boulevard, heading directly for Jack.

Jack cursed.

Jhala had seen him.

32

Jack leapt off the building and flew through the air.

The fireball pounded the dome where he'd been standing and flames hissed in all directions. He felt the heat scorching the back of his neck.

He landed on the ground behind a wall. He could no longer see Jhala or the boulevard, but he could hear the fight continuing.

How the hell had Jhala known he was there? His old commander must have spotted him climbing up the building, or perhaps used some power to sense him.

Whatever the case, Jack had to move quickly before Jhala and his troops came for him. He ran across a small courtyard and back into the labyrinth of the ruins. He charged through a series of arches and then hid behind a wall, gasping for breath.

He'd escaped. But what now? He still had to deal with Jhala. But Jhala now knew he was in the area. Jhala would be looking out for him.

He heard voices behind him, near enough to be audible over the continuing musket fire. He edged his head round the side of the wall and saw Jhala stalking between a set of pillars, three soldiers striding behind him.

Jhala was hunting for Jack personally, it seemed. And he was so sure of his powers that he hadn't even brought many men with him.

Jack scanned his surroundings and spotted a wall that had crumbled to about waist height. It ran parallel to the row of pillars, so he would be able to get a clear shot at Jhala from there.

He slipped across to the wall and ran along behind it, crouching low to keep out of sight. When he thought he'd gone far enough, he skidded to a halt. He took a deep breath, brought the Lightning yantra to mind and held it at the ready in his thoughts.

Finally, he raised his head above the wall.

He jumped slightly. Not only was Jhala now directly in front of him, he was much closer than before. He'd left the row of columns and was now heading straight towards the wall where Jack was hiding, with the three soldiers following behind.

Jack's eyes met Jhala's. For a moment, the two of them were staring at each other in surprise. But then Jack raised his hand, uttered the command and hurled a bolt at Jhala.

Jhala reacted more quickly than Jack had thought possible. Before the lightning reached him, Jhala had lifted his hand and voiced the mantra as well. The lightning forked from his fingertips and thumped into the bolt Jack had fired. The two streams of light smacked into each other, producing a pulse of snarling energy.

And then there was nothing. Both bolts had vanished.

Jack blinked. He hadn't realised lightning could be used defensively like that.

But he didn't pause to consider this any further, because the soldiers were already raising their muskets. He ducked back down behind the wall and scurried away. The muskets spluttered and bullets whined against the top of the wall, spraying dust. He kept running. Ahead, he could see an archway leading into a further chamber. If he could get through it, he might have a chance of escaping.

A pulse of lightning pummelled the wall, chipping off pieces of stone. A second volley of musket balls rattled over his head.

But then he was charging through the archway and scrambling through the maze of walls and broken doorways. He glanced about him, but he couldn't see his pursuers anywhere.

He'd lost them.

He ran on, avoided a couple of centipedes and then raced out of an entryway and into an expanse of open ground. Directly ahead of him, he saw a knot of crumbling walls, beyond which lay the mound of rubble on the south side of the Great Yantra courtyard. He could just make out the top of the oak and the rambling palace where he, Elizabeth and the others had taken refuge from the centipedes. To his right, the giant avatar bellowed and reared up above the buildings. But to his left, he now heard the click of multiple musket-knives.

When he turned, he saw five European soldiers standing with their firearms pointing at him, the knives jutting out from below the barrels.

He jolted, turned back and went to leap through the entryway. But then he saw there were two more soldiers and a Rajthanan officer approaching from behind him. And now, coming round a corner to his right were two further soldiers and Jhala himself.

Jack was surrounded.

He shut his eyes for a second, brought the yantra to mind and flung a lightning bolt at Jhala.

But Jhala casually lifted his hand, voiced the command and fired his own bolt. Once again, the two streams collided in mid-air, crackled and sparked as if they were tussling with each other, before vanishing.

Jhala shook his head. 'Jack Casey. I told you my powers were great. You cannot win. Give yourself up now.'

Jack lifted the musket and prepared to fire.

Jhala raised his hand again. 'I wouldn't bother with that. I can destroy your bullet just as easily as your lightning.'

The soldiers beside Jhala raised their muskets and trained them on Jack. No doubt the others encircling Jack were doing the same.

Could Jhala really stop a bullet? He would have to be unbelievably quick for that. But, on the other hand, it could be possible. Jack recalled that Mahajan had been protected by a magical shield that not even bullets could penetrate.

'I'll make you an offer,' Jhala said. 'Put aside your musket and fight me single-handed. No weapons save for our powers. Just you and me. I give you my word no one else will intervene.'

Jack narrowed his eyes and kept his musket trained on Jhala. 'Why would you do that?'

Jhala smiled. 'Because I am an honourable man. You know that. You are outnumbered. I could have you killed instantly. And yet that is hardly honourable. You and I have some scores to settle, it seems. We should settle them through a fair fight.'

Jack rested his finger against the trigger. He could still fire. Jhala's men would shoot him straight away once he did that. But perhaps he could hit Jhala before that happened.

Perhaps.

The giant avatar roared and lumbered across the far side of the open ground, kicking up dust behind it. Its footfalls were so heavy that the impact shivered through the ground.

A centipede slithered towards Jhala and his men but stopped as it came closer, then hissed and turned away. It seemed the creatures could detect who was an enemy and who wasn't.

Jack lowered the musket. What choice did he have? He would have to take Jhala at his word, would have to trust that Jhala would offer him a fair fight.

Jhala nodded slowly, his eyes moist. In a hoarse voice he said, 'I am so very sad it has come to this.'

Jhala took his pistol from its holster and handed it to one of his men. Then he unbuckled his belt, undid his cummerbund and lifted his tunic up over his head. He stood facing Jack, wearing just his undershirt, trousers and boots.

Jack went to lean his musket against the wall, but one of the soldiers grasped it from his hands and carried it away. Another soldier took the knife from his belt. The rest of the men backed away a few feet, leaving Jhala and Jack to face each other across an empty stretch of ground.

Jhala circled his shoulders and flexed his fingers. Despite his age, and his previous ill health, he looked well, strong. It was as if he'd grown younger since Jack last saw him. Jack was still almost twenty years Jhala's junior. But, at the same time, Jack was crippled by thirst, hunger and exhaustion. Added to that, he'd used Lightning so many times that he now had the strange sense of his head being empty. He'd used up much of his sattva.

And what about Jhala? Jack's old guru had used Lightning plenty of times recently too. How much more sattva could he have left?

Jhala crouched, as if to begin a wrestling match, and circled Jack slowly. Jack did the same. It was as though, for a moment, he were back in the training tent in the army, back learning from his commander how to fight.

'You should have accepted my offer,' Jhala said. 'You would have been far away from all this by now, if you had. None of this was necessary.'

'My family are here,' Jack replied.

Jhala raised an eyebrow. 'Why didn't you say? I would have spared them too.'

'I couldn't abandon my people.'

'Really? You'd risk your family's lives for a cause?'

As Jack prepared to speak, he was already recalling the Lightning yantra. It was difficult to talk while focusing on the design. He wanted to close his eyes to concentrate, but he managed to keep them open. 'I doubt my family would have agreed to leave. We're all committed to the crusade.'

Jhala snorted. 'Crusade? How can you call this mutiny a crusade? There have been no crusades in Europe for hundreds of years. You know that.'

Jack opened his mouth, pretending to be about to reply, but instead he raised his hand and spoke the secret commands. The lightning sizzled from his fingers and forked towards Jhala.

Jhala's face dropped and his eyes widened. He spoke the mantra quickly and lifted his arm. Lightning flew from his fingers just in time to block Jack's attack, but the collision caused a pulse of energy that knocked him back a few steps.

Jhala had managed to defend himself, but he looked ruffled. He composed himself and then squinted at Jack. 'You have advanced considerably.'

'For a native siddha.'

Jhala narrowed his eyes further, bent his knees and began circling again. 'You could say that.'

'You told me I could never learn anything beyond the Europa yantra.'

'That is what I believed, what I was told.'

And now it was Jhala's turn to launch a surprise attack. He pointed his fingers at Jack and blasted a streak of lightning.

Jack reacted instinctively. He dived to the side and managed to launch himself out of the way. But one prong of the lightning slapped his ankle. His foot felt as though a giant mallet had pounded it. It went numb for a moment, then throbbed with agonising pain.

He landed on his side and skidded through the dust before coming to a stop. He looked at his leg and saw that his boot had been burnt away. His foot was now scorched, the skin bright pink like boiled meat. The pain swamped him for a moment, but he gritted his teeth and lurched back upright.

Jhala was already preparing to fire lightning again. Jack tried to dodge to the side but realised this was pointless. The moment he put any weight on his injured foot, the pain overwhelmed him. He couldn't move fast enough to escape – his only hope was to use his own power in defence.

Jhala began to raise his arm. Jack quickly recalled the yantra and muttered the command. As Jhala's lightning streaked across the open ground, Jack's response struck it. The two streams crackled and then vanished.

Jack had found it easier than he'd thought to defend himself. The bolts of lightning seemed to attract each other, and he hadn't even had to aim in order to block Jhala's attack.

355

The giant avatar roared. Out of the corner of his eye, Jack saw the gigantic form lumbering closer.

Jhala's eyes darkened. 'Enough of these games. I don't have time for this.'

He leant down, grasped some dust and patted his hands. Then he charged straight at Jack.

Jack couldn't move any faster than a hobble. Instead of trying to escape, he braced himself and launched another lightning attack.

Jhala reacted with incredible speed. Even as he was running, he fired back with his own bolt and blocked Jack's lightning. He lunged forward and pounded into Jack's chest. With his injured foot, Jack couldn't keep himself steady. He tumbled over, falling on his back with a crunch. Jhala landed on top of him and punched him in the face.

A light flashed in Jack's eyes and his nose went numb. It felt as though warm water were pouring over his face.

Jhala raised his fist again. Jack brought the Lightning yantra to mind and prepared to strike, but Jhala hit him before he could hold the design steady.

Jack scrabbled to recall the yantra, but Jhala was already pounding him again. Darkness flooded across Jack's eyes for a second.

He couldn't let Jhala beat him now. Not after Jhala had threatened Elizabeth. Not after he'd forced Jack to hunt William. Not after he'd bombarded the fortress day after day, slaughtering hundreds of English men and women.

Jhala would have to pay for his crimes.

Jack bunched his right hand into a fist and was about to throw a punch, when Jhala suddenly stood up.

He beckoned to Jack with his finger. 'Get up. I'm giving you another chance.'

Jack clambered to his feet. He could feel blood coursing from his nose and running over his lips. His heart was beating hard and his face was growing hot. The pain in his foot, the roaring of the giant avatar, the shouts, screams and distant pop of muskets were all far away from him now. His sole focus was Jhala. And the only thing he wanted to do was kill his old guru.

He ran at Jhala, gritting his teeth and ignoring the pain in his foot as far as possible. Despite his limp, he moved faster than he'd expected and lunged at his old commander.

But Jhala had plenty of warning. He stepped to the side and struck Jack on the side of the head with his fist, so hard it made Jack's ear ring. But Jack had anticipated this move and elbowed Jhala in his undefended flank.

Jhala breathed out sharply, groaned and stumbled away.

Jack spun round and faced Jhala again. Pain welled in Jack's foot and the centre of his face. But he pushed all this aside.

Jhala had to die. Had to.

Jack summoned the yantra and blasted lightning. Jhala once again blocked the attack. Jack tried again, but again Jhala defended himself.

Enraged, Jack tried a third time and again Jhala parried the attack easily.

But now Jack saw black spots circling in front of his eyes, and his head was reeling. His mind felt drained, drawn. And he realised that he'd used up all his sattva. He was depleted and wouldn't be able to fire lightning again for some time. And even worse, he was on the verge of passing out.

He shook his head and pulled himself back from the brink. He glared at Jhala. He couldn't give up. He had to keep trying.

He raised his hand and attempted to hurl another bolt, even though he knew he would fail.

Then darkness passed over him. He fainted and fell backwards.

33

J ack woke to find Jhala standing over him, gazing down.

Jack spluttered. How long had he been out for? It felt like seconds but could have been longer. He could still hear the avatar raging in the background, as well as the sound of muskets. The battle was continuing.

But, for him, it looked as though the war would soon be over. Jhala was pointing his fingers straight at Jack's chest. Clearly Jhala was ready to fire lightning, and Jack was so depleted and weak there was nothing he could do to defend himself.

Jhala gave Jack a small smile and his eyes moistened. 'I'm afraid you have used too many powers today. I'm becoming depleted myself, but it looks as though I've been lucky enough not to have drained myself entirely.' He shook his head. 'It is such a great pity that it has come to this. I never wanted this to happen. You understand that, don't you?'

Jack clenched his jaw. Rage was burning in his chest. He struggled to get up. He couldn't give up yet. While he was still breathing, he had to do anything he could to fight against Jhala – even though the situation now looked hopeless.

He managed to sit upright, then clambered to his feet. He could barely put any weight on his injured foot, pain still welled in his face, his nose was still bleeding and clouds of darkness kept threatening to draw him back into unconsciousness. But he clung on and remained standing.

'Good.' Jhala nodded slowly. 'It is good you are standing. You will die honourably.'

Wincing at the pain in his foot, Jack lurched forward a few paces.

Jhala stepped back, still holding his arm up.

Jack's vision became blurry and he had to blink to make out Jhala properly. Why was his old commander delaying? Why didn't he fire a lightning bolt now and finish it?

Jack forced himself to take a few more paces forward. If he could make it over to Jhala, he could still attack him, still try to kill him.

Then a shriek erupted nearby. Jack looked past his old commander and saw the giant avatar looming no more than fifteen yards away. The beast was hunched over a mound of rubble, staring into a hole at the top. It reached down with its claw and plucked out a woman, holding her about the waist. The woman screamed, struggled to free herself and kicked her legs. But the avatar held her firm, lifted her up to its face for a moment, and then dashed her head on a rock. It threw her limp body aside, reached into the hole again and dragged out another woman, who wrestled furiously to escape, before the beast squeezed its claw shut and cut her in half.

Jack swayed as he watched the avatar. The beast was already bending over the opening and reaching in again. Jack thought he could hear the faint cries of people inside. They must have thought they'd found a good hiding place, but now they were trapped.

Jhala glanced back and took in the scene.

'Is that the dharma you've brought to England?' Jack's voice croaked. His mouth was so dry now, it was difficult to speak. 'That monster's killing trapped people. Women.'

Jhala frowned. 'That is not our concern now.'

'Isn't it? You're happy to let that go on, then?'

Another woman screamed as she was sliced in two.

Jhala pursed his lips. His men still stood to either side of Jack, all of them now gaping at the horror taking place just yards from them.

The avatar wrenched out a boy, aged about eight, and crushed him against a rock, blood streaming down the stone as if the beast were squeezing juice from a piece of fruit.

Jack felt bile rise in the back of his throat. He said to Jhala, 'You can't stand by while that happens.'

Jhala took a deep breath. Then, without acknowledging what Jack had said, he strode towards the creature. He raised one hand and barked commands in a language Jack didn't understand.

The avatar had already lifted yet another woman out of the hole and now held her by the neck. The woman kicked and writhed, but was unable to free herself.

Jhala held up his hand again, barked more words in the strange language, then shouted in Rajthani, 'I command you now to stop!'

The avatar turned and stared at Jhala. Its eyes throbbed brighter and the numerous layers of its maw slid open. It gave a hiss, exhaling hot, coal-scented air.

'Stop now!' Jhala called out.

The beast gurgled. The fire in its centre, just visible through the gaps in its armour, glowed more brightly. Then, in a single fluid movement, it snapped its claw shut, severing the woman's head from her body, while at the same time swinging its other claw at Jhala.

Jhala ducked and avoided the blow – he was still remarkably agile for a man of his age. Then he stood, voiced the command and launched a blast of lightning at the avatar. The bolt smacked the creature in the head and sizzled about its maw for a moment. The beast looked to the sky and bellowed.

'Run!' Jack shouted to Jhala. He knew the creature couldn't be defeated with powers. He'd tried himself, and so had Kanvar.

But Jhala either didn't hear, or he ignored Jack. Instead, he raised his hand to fire again.

The beast lowered its head and swung a claw. Jhala stooped again and the claw flew past. But now the creature responded by jabbing at him with its leg.

Jhala was caught off guard. The leg knocked him to the ground, where he landed on his back. He looked up in time to see the beast slamming its leg on top of him. He cried out, lifted his hand and went to shout the command again. But the creature stamped down, pressing its full weight on to him. With a sickening squelch, the leg crushed Jhala, popping him like a marrow.

A murmur passed through the soldiers standing about Jack.

'Shoot the thing!' a sergeant shouted.

The men lifted their muskets and fired at the beast, the muzzles coughing and spraying smoke. Bullets rattled against the avatar's carapace but did no damage at all.

'Reload!' the sergeant shouted.

As the men were biting open cartridges and pouring powder into the barrels of their firearms, the avatar growled and turned. It stared at the men, its eyes flickering, then it bounded towards the party.

Jack knew there was no point in him staying where he was. The creature had gone mad. The musket balls would continue to glance off it – and the soldiers would be butchered, if they remained where they were. He hobbled as quickly as he could towards the ruins lying on the outskirts of the courtyard of the Great Yantra. He half expected one of the soldiers to fire at him, but instead he heard the firearms blast at the creature. The bullets chimed as they bounced off its armour.

And then he heard shouts, screams and the squeal of metal against stone. He looked back once and saw that the beast had ploughed into the soldiers lining the wall, crushing several and scattering the others.

He didn't look back again but kept limping towards the crumbling walls ahead of him. If he could make it into the ruins, at least he would be able to hide, recover a little and decide what to do next.

A head poked out from a crumbling archway ahead of him. It took him a second to realise it was Saleem.

The lad was beckoning furiously and shouting, 'Run!'

Jack heard drumming on the ground behind him. He shot a look backwards and saw the giant avatar was now charging straight at him.

His heart jumped and he felt faint again for a moment, but he pulled himself together and pressed on. He lurched through the entryway and saw that Saleem was carrying Cecily in his arms.

Why did Saleem have Cecily? Why had the lad come down from the wall?

But there was no time to ask questions. The avatar gave a roar so loud that dust danced across the stonework and shivered to the ground.

'Over here!' Saleem shouted.

He led Jack through a second entrance, across a chamber and towards a wide archway, through which Jack could see the rubble on the south side of the courtyard. The oak tree rose from the far side of the broken stones.

As Jack ran, he slipped into the powerful stream. The sattva churned around him, forming eddies and whorls. Once again, he was within the Great Yantra.

Grimacing at the pain in his foot, he followed Saleem out of the entryway and then saw a strange sight on the other side of the rubble. Elizabeth was sitting cross-legged beneath the oak tree, her eyes closed, her back straight and her hands on her knees.

Jack grasped Saleem's arm. 'What the hell is she doing?'

Saleem looked at him with wide eyes. 'The Grail. She's trying to use it.'

'What?'

'She said she knows the necklace off by heart. She's been looking at it all her life.'

Jack stalled. He'd never considered this, but it made sense. Elizabeth knew the design of the cross as well as he did. She'd seen it hanging from her mother's neck since she was a child.

Could Elizabeth really use the power? She'd never meditated before, she wasn't sensitive to sattva, and she wasn't a siddha. And yet, maybe it could be possible. Maybe, after all, she would be the pure knight . . .

And if she really did manage to use the power, would that mean she would ascend to heaven? Would she die?

The ground seemed to drop an inch and Jack's head spun. Elizabeth could be in grave danger. But, at the same time, she might be on the verge of saving the crusade.

'She asked me to look after Cecily,' Saleem continued. 'Then I saw you over there, fighting those soldiers, and I came to try to help you. I didn't know what to do.'

Jack patted Saleem on the arm. 'You did all right.'

Then the ground shook and the air quivered as a rumble blasted to Jack's right. The giant avatar was lumbering round the outer edge of the knot of ruined buildings. It spied Jack and Saleem, gave a screech and charged at them.

Jack pushed Saleem, still with Cecily in his arms, back into the entryway they had just come through. 'Hide! I'll draw that thing away from you.'

Saleem opened his mouth, but Jack shouted, 'Do it! Now!'

Jack didn't stay to make sure Saleem did as he'd asked, because the avatar was racing towards him, mouth open in a scream. He tried to run but could manage little more than a jog. Each time he pressed his wounded foot against the earth, the pain streaked up his leg.

He ran across the open ground between the buildings and the rubble, heading in the direction of the west wall. He vaguely thought that if he could get closer to the wall, Fletcher might fire the guns at the beast and knock it back. But this plan was fraught with risk. In truth, all he was trying to do was to draw the beast away from Elizabeth and Cecily. It didn't matter if the creature killed him. He would accept his fate.

His breath was short and he was sweating at the strain of trying to run. A centipede patrolled ahead of him, but he ignored it for the moment. He heard the giant avatar gargling and howling behind him and then the crunch and scrape of metal against stone.

He swivelled round and saw, to his horror, that the creature wasn't pursuing him at all. Instead, it had bashed apart most of the wall beside it and was swinging its claws at Saleem. The lad, still holding Cecily, darted through another arch. But the beast sprang after him, smashing a second wall to pieces.

Jack shuffled back, dragging his burnt foot, desperate to move faster. After he'd gone a couple of yards, he could see deeper into the ruins and make out Saleem cowering against a wall. The lad was trapped, having run into a chamber with no exit. The avatar loomed over him, ready to strike.

Jack shouted and waved his hand in an effort to distract the creature. But its eyes were locked on Saleem and Cecily.

Saleem placed the infant on the ground, slung his musket from his shoulder and fired at the avatar. The bullet tinged against the creature's head, but it did no damage. Saleem clicked out the firearm's knife, but there was no way he would be able to defend himself with that.

Someone cried out from the courtyard. When Jack looked to his left, he saw that Elizabeth was standing now, although she was still beneath the oak tree. She'd seen that Cecily and Saleem were trapped, and her eyes glistened with fear. For a moment, he thought she was about to run across and attack the avatar with her bare hands. But then she stood very still, hung her head and sat back down on the ground.

Jack frowned. Was she going to continue meditating? Now? It seemed impossible, but that was exactly what she was doing. She'd already closed her eyes and placed her hands on her knees.

She'd abandoned Cecily.

Jack didn't waste any time thinking about this, however. He hobbled on, not sure what he was going to do once he reached the avatar, but still frantic to get there.

The giant creature raised one of its claws above its head and prepared to batter Saleem. The lad was jabbing with his knife-musket, but his efforts were futile. Cecily lay at his feet. Once the avatar swung its claw down, it would crush both Saleem and the child.

Damn it.

Jack had to run faster. But he couldn't manage it. The pain spiked straight through his body whenever he pressed down with his foot.

He wasn't going to make it.

Saleem and Cecily were going to die.

Then Elizabeth gave a high-pitched shriek. The sound was so unearthly that Jack thought she must have been attacked by a soldier or a centipede. But when he looked at her, she appeared unharmed. On the other hand, something strange was happening to her. She was standing now with her hands raised to the sky. A glowing aura surrounded her and her skin shone like the moon.

Jack felt the sattva spiralling about him. It seemed agitated, an ocean stirred by a storm. The sweet scent was stronger than usual.

Something powerful was smelting sattva.

He stopped dead still and stared at Elizabeth. Was she smelting? She couldn't be.

Then Elizabeth gave another piercing ululation and light suddenly blazed around her. Her hair fluttered about her head and a gale blasted away from her.

Sattva-scented air punched Jack in the face. The force of it knocked him to his knees.

His eyes watered as the powerful wind rushed over him. But through his tears he could see Elizabeth. She seemed to be burning with silver fire, so bright he could barely look at her.

The power of the Grail. It had to be. There was no other explanation for what he was seeing.

He felt a moment of sublime joy. Perhaps the rebels could succeed after all.

And then, a moment later, fear crushed him.

If Elizabeth were using the power, did that mean she would ascend to heaven? Did it mean this was the last time he would ever see her?

A whirlwind of light and air spun about Elizabeth and then seemed to detonate. The glare blinded Jack and knocked him backwards to the ground.

He could see nothing but brilliant light and hear nothing but the wild roaring of the wind.

He opened his eyes. He was lying on his back with spots from the brilliant light dancing before him. He felt sattva flowing about him, brushing against his face. But it was no longer agitated. The storm seemed to have passed.

Elizabeth.

He sat up with a jolt. He was still lying in the ruins and everything looked the same as before. The sky was still overcast, the rotting buildings were still standing. However, what he noticed the most was the silence. He heard no shouts, muskets or gunfire. For a moment, he even thought he might have imagined the whole battle.

But then he saw a centipede lying nearby. It was completely still, a line of smoke rising from it. He picked up a stone and threw it at the creature. The beast crumbled apart into metal fragments.

He looked up then and spotted Elizabeth stumbling through the rubble as if in a daze. She was dishevelled, and no longer glowing, but she appeared unharmed.

He leapt to his feet and staggered across to her. Her eyes flickered when she saw him. She gave a little sob and fell into his arms.

Jack blinked back tears and held her tight. 'Are you all right?'

'Yes.' Her voice was cracked.

'What happened?'

'I don't know. I think . . . I think I used the power.' She stepped away from him. Her eyes were focusing now and she seemed more aware of her surroundings. 'Where's Cecily?'

Jack felt the blood run from his face. He didn't want to find out what had happened to his granddaughter, but he had to.

He turned and saw the giant avatar towering over the ruins ahead of him. But there was something odd about the beast. It was completely motionless. It held its claw up in order to strike but was keeping it poised, hanging in the air.

Saleem cowered beneath the creature, still holding his musket at the ready. Cecily lay swaddled in a blanket at his feet.

Elizabeth gasped and rushed towards her child. But she only went a few paces before the avatar gave a deep groan. This was followed by the sound of scraping iron. A metal plate fell from the beast's abdomen and clanked on the ground. Then another plate tumbled off, along with several stalks. Finally, the raised claw dropped off its arm and clattered on the earth.

Saleem jumped as the claw struck the ground, grasped Cecily and dashed out of the way.

Now the whole avatar collapsed, fragmenting into chunks of metal armour that fell off, a piece at a time, making a series of groans and creaks. Finally, the beast was nothing more than a pile of iron with a trace of smoke coiling up from it. The fire in its centre had gone out.

Elizabeth ran across to Saleem and Cecily. Jack hobbled after her as quickly as he could.

Saleem was gaunt, covered in dust and shaking slightly. But he was alive. And Cecily lay gurgling in his arms, reaching up with her tiny hands to grasp her mother. Elizabeth stifled a sob and swept the infant into her arms.

Jack grinned at Saleem. 'You did well.'

Saleem swallowed and nodded, seemingly so shocked he'd lost his voice.

Someone gave a moan nearby. Jack scanned the area and spotted something moving in the broken ironwork that was all that remained of the avatar.

Christ. Was someone trapped underneath all that? Had there been someone else nearby when the creature fell apart?

He scrambled through the broken legs, claws and armour-plating. The metal was still warm when he touched it and the heat pressed against his face as he got near to what had once been the innards of the beast.

And then he saw a figure, a man, completely naked and lying in the midst of the wreckage. He was Indian, and short and slightly flabby.

Jack froze when he realised that he recognised the man.

It was General Vadula.

Jack sank to his knees. He'd seen many pictures of Vadula. The man before him had to be the general, or someone who looked exactly like him.

The man was covered in brass tubes and pistons. And as Jack looked more closely, he saw that these weren't merely surrounding Vadula, they were in fact piercing his skin in many places, jutting into his neck, legs, arms and abdomen. And yet these injuries weren't drawing blood. The skin seemed to have healed around the metal, as if the wounds had occurred a long time ago.

And finally it dawned on Jack. Vadula hadn't been near to the creature, or underneath it. He'd been inside it. Joined to it. Combined with it. Bound to it. And, no doubt, controlling it all along.

Jack had always thought there was something strange about this avatar. It had seemed far more intelligent than any he'd come across before. Now he knew the truth.

Vadula was still breathing, but he appeared weak and unaware even of where he was. His eyes focused on Jack for a moment. He seemed to be trying to speak, but there was a tube stuck in his mouth. As Jack watched, the life drained out of him and he gave a final sigh.

Jack checked for a pulse. But he already knew Vadula was dead.

PART FIVE

34

By the time Jack, Elizabeth and Saleem made it back to the Folly Brook camp, all those in the fortress who'd survived the attack were celebrating. Despite their exhaustion, thirst and hunger, people were managing to sing and dance. Because, although many had died, many too had lived, and they'd expelled the enemy from their walls.

The crusade was still alive.

As he'd limped across the ruins, Jack had heard snatches of stories from people. It seemed that suddenly all the avatars attacking the fort had died and crumbled apart. Jack could tell this was true, because he spotted numerous broken centipedes scattered across the ground. Furthermore, the enemy siddhas – sorcerers, as the rebels called them – had stopped using their devastating powers. Disorientated, afraid and without any clear leader, the army troops had faced a fierce attack from the rebels and had fled, despite their far greater numbers. They'd retreated down the hill and rejoined the forces that still encircled the fortress.

The army hadn't left. The siege continued. But at least the immediate battle had been won.

Godwin had survived, as had Mary, Saleem's family and many of the inhabitants of Folly Brook. But many had also died in the fighting. Half the apprentices had been killed defending the east wall, and around thirty other villagers had been slain as they fought either at one of the walls or around the ruined palace, where they'd faced a stiff struggle against the centipedes.

The apprentices also reported something strange to Jack. They'd noticed that their powers had all waned, despite the fact that several were certain they still had a plentiful supply of sattva.

As odd as it seemed, it was beginning to look to Jack as though neither powers nor avatars would work within the fortress any longer. And he could only think that had something to do with whatever it was Elizabeth had unleashed in the courtyard.

Finally, Godwin ushered Jack into the ruined palace and over to the small chamber that had been serving as the temporary hospital. Eight villagers lay in there now, newly injured in the fighting, as well as Sonali.

She was alive. Just.

Jack crouched beside her and took her hand. She felt hot, far too hot, and the sweat beaded on her forehead. Her eyes were glued shut, but when Jack whispered to her, she managed to open them. With what seemed a great effort, she lifted the corners of her mouth into a smile.

⊸◆⊸

'Are you all right, Father?' Elizabeth walked into the roofless chamber near the centre of the palace.

Jack had been standing here for the past fifteen minutes, staring up at the clouded sky. Kanvar had meditated in this spot just days ago. It seemed as though years had passed in that time.

Jack sighed and rubbed his eyes. 'I'm fine. Just thinking.'

Elizabeth stepped closer. 'I'm sure she'll live. She's strong.'

He lowered his gaze. 'Sonali, you mean?'

Elizabeth nodded.

'We can only pray for her.' He stared back at the sky. 'And the dead.' In his mind, he went through a roll-call of those who'd passed away over the last few days: Kanvar, Mark, the other apprentices and villagers, and even Henry.

Elizabeth looked down. 'I still don't understand what happened to me.'

'Neither do I.'

'I think I got the power to work. The power of the Grail.'

'Something happened, that's for sure.'

'It was strange. I was trying to keep the necklace in my mind, like you said. It was easy. I've seen it so much. But nothing happened. I thought I must be getting it wrong, but then I heard that big creature.'

'The avatar?'

'Yes. And when I stood up, I saw Saleem and Cecily.' Her eyes went moist and her bottom lip trembled. 'I wanted to run across to them. I didn't know what I could do, but I wanted to do something. But then I chose not to go. Can you believe that?' She stared at Jack. 'I decided not to fight for my own child. I decided to stay where I was and keep trying the Grail.'

Jack shook his head. 'You thought that if you could use the power, you would save Cecily.'

'No.' A tear bled down Elizabeth's face. 'I thought Cecily would die. But I still chose to stay and try. Just in case there was some chance . . .' Elizabeth wiped the tear away from her cheek. 'The strange thing is, after I made that choice, suddenly the necklace in my head seemed to glow very brightly. And then it felt like everything, the whole world, was spinning around me.'

'You did the right thing. You *did* save Cecily, after all.'

'But I thought I would fail.'

Jack gripped her shoulder to comfort her. But now thoughts were rolling around in his mind. It was indeed strange that the yantra had worked for Elizabeth after she gave up on Cecily.

Giving up. Abandoning. Leaving behind.

Could that be the secret? Could that be what he'd been missing?

He'd been able to use his special ability four times. Four times he'd been able to use the power to overcome the law of karma. Each time he'd thought of the Great Yantra. But he'd also learnt there had to be more to it than that. There'd been some other ingredient that had allowed him to use the power.

And when he thought about it, hadn't he made some sort of sacrifice each time he'd broken the law? Three of those times he'd been near death and just clinging on to life. And each time, he remembered now, he'd given up. He'd decided to stop fighting and accept his fate. He'd been prepared to give up on life itself.

And the fourth time, the time when he'd broken the law of karma while staring at the pool where Sonali used to have her morning wash? What had he given up then?

Of course, it had been Sonali herself. She'd travelled back to Dorsetshire and he'd accepted that she was gone and that he would never see her again.

His eyes widened and he muttered, 'That's it.'

Elizabeth frowned. 'What?'

He stepped away from her and limped back and forth on his wounded foot. For a moment, he felt like Kanvar, lost in his own world of thoughts. 'It's about leaving the material world. I should have seen it before. To use the Great Yantra you have to give up the material world. Give it up fully.' He stopped and looked back at Elizabeth. 'Jhala taught me that to use any yantra you have to move beyond the material world, see it for the illusion it really is. This Great Yantra, the Grail, is the same, just more so. We cling to the material world. We think it's all there is. But if we can stop clinging, then we can move closer to the spirit realm. When you gave up Cecily, you gave up something important to you. The most important thing to you. That was the secret all along.'

'You sure?'

'I reckon so. If Kanvar were here, he'd be able to tell us. But it makes sense. It all fits.'

Saleem appeared in the entryway. He'd cleaned the dust off his face, but he still looked exhausted and pale. 'You'd better come to the wall, Jack.'

Jack felt a tremor of nerves. Could the enemy be starting another attack already? 'What is it?'

'A white flag. The army have sent out a white flag.'

———◆———

Jack stood up on the east wall and stared through his spyglass. Down on the heath, in the middle of the plains, were six figures on horseback, one of whom was holding a white flag on a pole.

So, it was true. The enemy wanted to talk again. This was surprising. Their leaders might be dead, but there were still thousands of them encircling the hills – and they could request much greater numbers of troops, should they need them. They could still crush the rebels eventually, or simply wait for them to die of thirst and starvation.

Jack studied the faces of the riders, searching for any sign that might give away their intentions.

And then he froze. He couldn't stop his lips curling into a smile.

One of the men on horseback was Captain Rao.

———◆———

Jack rode across the plains, holding a makeshift white flag high above his head. The mare had somehow survived the battle, the centipedes, and the lack of food and water. She seemed as strong as ever.

He drew to a halt beside the riders. Rao gave a small shout of delight and swung himself down from his horse. Jack dismounted and Rao embraced him, patting him on the back.

Rao stepped away and put his hands on his hips, looking Jack up and down. 'Praise be to the Innocent Lord that you're safe. When I got here and heard there'd been a battle, I feared the worst.'

Jack grinned. 'I'm not dead quite yet. But what are you doing here?'

Rao frowned quizzically. 'The treaty, of course. You remember?'

'Aye. I remember. I didn't know whether to believe it or not.'

Rao drew a sheet of paper from his satchel. 'This is a summary. I got the message at Leintwardine two days ago. I came as quickly as I could.'

'So, you Rajthanans want to make peace? Now?'

'Al-Saxony is in flames. Another uprising has started in the Napoli Caliphate. The whole of Europe is teetering on the brink. The Maharaja wants a deal with England. Immediately.'

'England would be a protectorate?'

'That is the offer.' Rao waved the piece of paper. 'Is the Earl of Shropshire still alive?'

'He is.'

Rao handed across the page. 'Get him to sign this, and the army will withdraw from Shropshire. I give you my word on that. The Maharaja has agreed for me to start by negotiating peace in Shropshire. We'll get the rest of the earls and the regent to sign after that.'

'The earls must decide who'll be regent. The Earl of Norfolk has to go.'

'That is acceptable.' Rao pressed the piece of paper into Jack's hand. 'But you must get this signed first.'

Jack took the page. 'I'll talk to the earl. I'll do my best. In the meantime, we have many wounded, including Sonali. She took a bullet in the stomach.'

Rao drew his breath in sharply. 'Ah. That is bad news. Send the injured down here. They can go to the hospital tent.'

'The army would do that? For traitors?'

'So long as you get that piece of paper signed, anything is possible. Do that, and I'll have no problem getting them all treatment.'

'Right. We need water too.'

'I can send some up.'

Jack took a deep breath. It was hard to believe it, but it seemed the battle – and indeed, the whole crusade – could finally be over. 'Right, then. I'd better get back up there.'

Rao scratched his nose. 'Before you go, the army siddhas wanted me to ask you a couple of questions.'

'What?'

'General Vadula is missing.'

'He's dead.' Jack gestured towards the fortress. 'Up there.'

'Ah. That is as everyone suspected. We request that you send the body down for cremation.'

Jack nodded. 'I'll do it. He was inside that thing. That avatar.'

'Yes, I believe that is so. It's a very strange story. It's been a secret up until now, but the siddhas told me just an hour ago. It seems he was in possession of some great power.'

'The Great Yantra?'

'Something like that. Not my field, as you know. But Vadula had become more powerful than he'd ever been before, and some of the siddhas seem to think it had gone to his head. He'd gone a bit mad in the past few months, they say. In the end, he decided to use his new powers to create that avatar and seal himself inside it. No one has ever heard of anything like it, but there it is.'

'He was inside it all the time? From a few months ago?'

'I believe so.'

'That avatar was prowling around north Shropshire even before the army got here.'

'Yes, it seems he'd gone quite mad. He was no longer himself, they say. He'd become as much a machine as a man. He was no longer even commanding his troops. The other generals had taken over. It was all kept secret, though, until now.'

'That is a strange story.'

'Indeed.' Rao cleared his throat. 'The siddhas also instructed me to ask you about a light they saw up on the hill during the battle. It was as bright as the sun, they said. After that, all their powers stopped working. Do you know anything about that?'

'A little. I don't understand it all, but I have a few theories. Can I speak to these siddhas?'

'If we make peace, I'm sure it can be arranged.'

'Good. I'll tell them what I know. I have a few questions for them myself.'

'Very well. Just get the agreement signed, Jack. And then all this will be over.'

———◆———

'Can we trust them?' Sir Levin asked.

Jack stood with his hands behind his back in the Earl of Shropshire's residency. The earl was, as always, slumped in his chair. The courtyard was littered with spent round shot, shell fragments and burnt ivy leaves. Many of the walls had been reduced to rubble and cracks fanned across the paving stones.

'I believe we can trust them,' Jack said. 'The negotiator is a friend of mine. He wouldn't betray us. I'm certain of that.'

The earl took a wheezy breath and examined the sheet of paper Jack had handed to him. 'We have little alternative. We are weak. Many of us are dying. I cannot see how we could withstand another assault.'

'That is true,' Levin said. 'At least if we see them withdraw from this area, we'll know it's safe to come down. We could always return here, if we find this is all some sort of trick.'

'Very well, then.' The earl motioned to one of his attendants. 'Bring me my pen.'

The attendant left the courtyard and returned with a Rajthanan pen and an inkwell on a silver platter. The young man went down on one knee beside the earl, who took the pen, dabbed it in the ink and scrawled his signature on the piece of paper.

'There is no sand.' He handed the page to the attendant. 'Blow on it.'

The attendant took the paper, blew on it until the ink was dry and then handed it to Jack.

'Well, Jack Casey,' the earl said, 'it seems you have successfully saved this fortress. As I promised, I will knight you.'

Jack bowed his head. 'It's a kind offer, my lord. I'm grateful. But I have another request.'

The earl frowned. 'Oh?'

Jack looked up and met the earl's gaze. 'I would prefer it if another were knighted in my place. He's served the crusade since the beginning. He's fought bravely in many battles. He's given everything for the cause. And he saved my granddaughter's life. He deserves to be knighted more than I do.'

The earl raised an eyebrow. 'A strange request. You are certain of this?'

'I am. It would please me more than anything.'

The earl sat back. 'Very well. I will offer you a bargain. I will knight your comrade, but only on the condition that you allow yourself to be knighted as well. Immediately.'

'My lord, there is no need—'

'Do you want your friend to be knighted or not?'

Jack hesitated. 'Yes, my lord.'

'Then stop your bleating and step forward.'

Jack could see there was no point in refusing. The earl was determined.

And yet, Jack still felt reluctant. At first he didn't know why – but then he realised.

William.

It was William who should be getting the knighthood. He was the true rebel leader. Jack hadn't even supported the crusade at first and he'd betrayed his old friend. He didn't deserve to be knighted.

But then he remembered what William had said to him four years ago: 'You were in a tough spot. I understand.'

William had just learnt that Jack had been sent to hunt him down. And yet, even at that stage, he'd been prepared to forgive.

Maybe Jack had to start forgiving himself.

He walked forward and went down on one knee. One of the

earl's pages approached with an arming-sword. The earl lifted the blade and tapped it against the side of Jack's neck.

And with that, Jack was dubbed a knight.

———◆———

Jack delivered the signed document to Rao, and the wounded were transported down the hill using the remaining vehicles.

Jack rode alongside the mule cart carrying Sonali, following it all the way to the hospital tent. And, after the doctors drew the bullet out, he stayed at her side as she lay on a cot. He stayed there all night, until the doctors could tell him with certainty that she would survive.

When he returned to the fortress, he found Saleem and brought him to the earl's residency. The two of them stood before the earl in the courtyard. Sir Levin was also in attendance, along with two of the earl's pages, one of whom carried the arming-sword.

The earl sat forward slightly, narrowing his eyes as he peered at Saleem.

Saleem licked his lips, swallowed and shot a fearful look at Jack.

Jack couldn't help grinning. The lad thought he was in trouble. He had no idea.

Finally, the earl leant back in his seat. 'Saleem al-Rashid.'

Saleem bowed his head. 'Yes, my lord.'

'Your friend Jack has told me much about you. He has praised you very highly. You are a Mohammedan and yet you have fought bravely, along with several others of your religion. For too long the Mohammedans have been regarded with, shall I say, suspicion in our country. It is time that ended. The war against the Caliph was two hundred years ago. You, and your comrades, have proven yourselves in this and many other battles during the crusade. Therefore, I have decided to knight you and to request that you return with me to Shrewsbury to serve in my forces.'

Saleem's mouth dropped open and he glanced at Jack.

'Jack tells me you have your mother and sisters with you,' the earl continued. 'They will also be provided for in Shrewsbury.'

Saleem went to speak, then couldn't seem to find the words.

The earl frowned. 'Well? What do you have to say for yourself?'

Saleem shot another look at Jack, his eyes wide and glassy.

'Go on.' Jack nodded towards the earl. 'Say something.'

Saleem looked at the ground, his cheeks going a deep red. He smiled slightly and said in a voice so soft it was barely audible, 'I would be honoured to serve you, my lord.'

'Very well, then,' the earl replied. 'Step forward.'

Saleem walked across to the earl and went down on one knee. The page handed the sword to the earl, who lifted it and, with a shaking hand, tapped Saleem on the side of the neck. He handed the sword back to the page, then said in a wheezy voice, 'I bid you arise, Sir Saleem.'

35

The celebration took place on a Sunday night, in the field just outside Newcastle-on-Clun. Everyone from the surrounding area attended. Candle lanterns were hung from the trees, minstrels were summoned and pigs were stuck on spits over a series of fires. A huge bonfire blazed in the centre of the field and the sparks floated up into the black night.

The people of Clun Valley felt as much sorrow as joy. So many had died, so many more were badly injured or missing. And yet, the people were free. The native state of Shropshire had been returned to its earl, and the Rajthanans were arranging for the other earls of England to sign the treaty.

The Earl of Northumberland had been appointed regent and would rule until Prince Stephen came of age.

The minstrels played their drums, lutes and pipes frenetically and the young people danced wildly about the bonfire.

Jack spotted Elizabeth standing alone, holding up Katelin's necklace and gazing at it as it glinted in the firelight. So far, few people knew what had happened to her up in the Fortress of the Djinns. But eventually the word would get out.

He walked across to her. 'So, it was you all along.'

She lowered the necklace. 'What do you mean?'

'Turns out you were the pure knight. You were the one who would use the power to save us all.'

She frowned. 'It's hard to believe. Are you sure?'

'I spoke to the army siddhas before we came back here. I had a long talk with them. They were suspicious of me at first, but they wanted to know what I knew. It seems that when you used the Great Yantra, all yogic powers stopped working and all avatars fell apart. Not just in the fortress, but across the whole of England. Reports have been coming in from all over the place, apparently. Powers don't work any more in England. They're fine in the rest of Europe, but not here.'

'Everywhere in England?'

'Seems so.'

'I did that?'

'Aye.' He grinned at her. 'I reckon it was the same for Oswin and Galahad. Remember the old stories. Galahad freed England from enchantment. That's what you've done, isn't it? You've stopped powers from working.'

'I suppose so. What about Oswin? I thought in the stories he used the Grail as a weapon.'

'The stories just say the Grail released a power and that meant the Caliph was defeated. No one knew what that power was. I reckon it was the same – it stopped powers. Magic, if you like. One of the reasons the Caliph was so powerful was that he had siddhas, or something like them. The English were trapped up on a hill, just like we were. When the power of the Grail was released, the Caliph's siddhas would have lost all their abilities. That must have tipped the balance in favour of the English.'

'It makes sense. It's all so strange, though.' Elizabeth gazed at the figures cavorting about the flames. 'Still, if the power of the Grail stops powers from being used, why could people use powers in England up until a few days ago?'

'That is a mystery. When I talked to the siddhas, they seemed to think the effect is only temporary. It'll wear off at some point in the future, no doubt, but probably not for many years.'

Elizabeth mulled this over for a moment, then said, 'There's something I still don't understand. You used the necklace, the Great Yantra, yourself. Do you know why you didn't release the power?'

'I talked about this with the siddhas. No one is sure about this, but it seems the key to the yantra is that it "purifies". Jhala said that to me at the fortress, but I didn't understand what he meant at the time. I'm not sure I even understand it now. But the siddhas told me that when you use the yantra on yourself, it purifies you. That's why you can then break the law of karma. You see, normally, using a power makes you impure. It tangles up spirit and matter. But the Great Yantra untangles all that and makes you pure again.

'What happened to you is a bit different. You weren't trying to use the power on yourself, you were trying to use it to save England. That meant England was purified, rather than you.'

Elizabeth shook her head. 'It's a lot to take in.'

'Aye. Not sure any of us will ever fully understand it. But whatever the case, you did it. You were the one who touched the Grail. You are the pure knight.'

'I don't feel like anything special.'

Jack put his arm around her shoulders. 'You're special to me. But perhaps you don't need to be anything other than a normal person to use the Grail. You knew the design of the yantra, you touched the Grail by sitting inside it and you made a sacrifice and so moved away from the material world. You unlocked the secret. That's special enough.'

Elizabeth was silent for a moment, then said, 'I thought I was going to die when I did it.'

'I thought you were too.'

'I had a choice.'

'A choice?'

'When it happened, when there was all that light around me, I had a strange feeling, as if I could give up everything and everyone. I could float away if I wanted to. Like going up to heaven. But I realised I could pull myself back. I didn't have to go away.'

Jack kissed Elizabeth on the top of her head. 'Thank God you didn't let yourself float away.'

'Oswin and Galahad must have chosen to go up to heaven.'

'That must be it.'

Elizabeth smiled. 'They were purer than me, then. I wasn't ready to say farewell yet.'

Jack found Rao gazing at the bonfire, a mug in his hand. He'd ridden down to Clun with Jack and agreed to spend a night in the valley to join the celebrations.

'You're not drinking ale, are you?' Jack asked.

Rao smiled and lifted the mug. 'It's not bad. One could get used to it.'

'You still riding to Leintwardine tomorrow?'

'I must. The Maharaja is expecting a report from me. I must post it to him.'

'And after that?'

'I will return to Andalusia and Reena. We have a marriage to arrange.'

'I'm pleased for you.'

Rao smiled. 'It's all worked out in the end, hasn't it?'

Jack cleared his throat. 'I've a lot to thank you for. All these people here might be dead, if it weren't for you.'

Rao laughed nervously and looked at his boots. 'Well, I don't know. I simply tried my best to do what was right. You got me thinking when we were in Scotland. I was lucky enough to be able to act on my convictions. To make a difference.'

Jack patted Rao on the shoulder. 'Whatever the case, I can tell you, everyone here is grateful to you. We'll always remember what you did.' He looked towards the flames. 'Another thing. I've decided to ride with you to Leintwardine.'

'Oh?'

'It's on my way to Dorsetshire.'

A smile spread across Rao's face. 'I see.'

It was easy for Rao to understand Jack's motivation. Sonali was in Dorsetshire. Once she'd recovered enough to be moved, she'd been transported back to her aunt's estate, where she would be recuperating. Jack hadn't had a chance to speak to her before she was taken away. It had happened suddenly – when he'd gone to the hospital for a second time, he was told she'd already left.

'The doctors told me she should make a full recovery,' Rao said. 'I'm sure she'll be pleased to see you.'

Jack rubbed his chin. 'Hope so. I don't know what she'll have to say when I show up there.'

'My impression is that she will be happy to see you.'

'She was happy spending time with me here in Shropshire, but it'll be different in Dorsetshire. She's a Rajthanan and I'm an Englishman.' He looked down. 'She might be ashamed to see me.'

Rao's moustache rippled on his top lip. 'Somehow, I don't think so. But you will have to take a risk. As a friend, as a brother, I urge you to go and find out what she has to say. That's the only way you'll know.'

In the morning, it turned out that Jack and Rao weren't the only people leaving the valley. Saleem and his family had packed their few remaining possessions in a mule cart and were setting off for their new life in Shrewsbury. Saleem drove the cart, while his mother and sisters sat huddled in the back. Rao and Jack rode alongside as far as the point where the road forked near the town of Clun.

They all paused at the split in the road.

Jack nodded to the northerly route. 'That's the way to Shrewsbury. I'll come to see you soon.'

Saleem looked at the ground, his face reddening. 'I hope I'll still be there.'

Jack frowned. 'What are you talking about?'

'I'm not a real knight, am I? It must be a mistake.'

Jack shook his head. 'No, you're a real knight. You always were.

Enough moping now. You have a new life to be getting on with, Sir Saleem.'

Saleem looked up. 'You will come, won't you? Soon.'

'Of course. In a few weeks. Now go.'

Jack slapped the rump of the mule and it lurched forward along the north road. The cart rattled away, wisps of dust rising behind it, until it finally disappeared round a bend.

36

On his way south, Jack stopped at the cemetery where Katelin was buried. In the past, he'd come here often with Elizabeth, but since he'd gone to Shropshire he hadn't been back once.

He walked between the graves, a bunch of wildflowers in his hand, and found the simple cross of wood and brass that marked where Katelin lay. He placed the flowers on top of the grave and knelt for a moment, praying.

'Sorry I haven't been back for a while,' he said. 'I'm sure you understand. I'll come back more now the country's at peace. Elizabeth's eager to come as well.' He stilled a quiver in his voice. 'I'm so sorry you aren't here to see Cecily. I know you would have loved being a grandmother. But I'm sure you're looking down on us and watching over us all. I'm sure you understand everything I'm trying to say to you now.'

He took a deep breath. 'And I'm sure you'll understand and forgive me for where I'm going next.'

He was in a strange mood as he left the graveyard. On an impulse, he left the mare tethered to a tree and instead crossed the road and walked across to the edge of a forest. He scoured the ground for some kindling and a few larger branches, which he used to make a small fire. Once the flames were crackling and consuming the wood, he stepped back and bowed his head slightly.

He didn't know why he was doing this. But he couldn't help himself, and it somehow seemed right – or, at least, necessary.

'General Jhala,' he mumbled, 'you didn't get a funeral. No one found your body. No one was all that interested. So, I've lit this fire for you at least. In the way you Rajthanans do. You don't deserve this. But I'm doing it anyway.'

He raised his eyes and stared at the flames for a moment. He didn't know the words the Rajthanans said in these situations. And he wouldn't have said them, even if he did. It was enough that he'd lit this fire.

And yet, he found that he had a stone in his throat.

'You betrayed me, sir. But at least you died honourably. You tried to stop that creature, Vadula, from killing innocent civilians. I'll remember that.'

He drew himself up taller, pressed his hands together in front of his chest and bowed slightly. 'Farewell, sir.'

Then he stamped out the fire, turned and walked back to the road.

The steward at the house of Sonali's aunt was perplexed when he saw the guard from the gate leading Jack up the corridor.

'No, no, no.' The steward waggled his finger. 'He can't come in here. Only blessed servants allowed.'

Jack understood instantly. The inner sections of a Rajthanan home were sacred and only a handful of specially chosen and ritually blessed servants were allowed in. This steward, an old Englishman with white whiskers, would know he risked losing his job if he let Jack through. Jack had been able to talk the guard into leading him this far, but the steward presented more of a challenge.

'I'm here to visit Kumari Sonali Dalvi,' Jack said. 'I believe she will want to see me.'

Jack was far from certain Sonali would want to see him. She might not want to have anything to do with him. She might be embarrassed that he'd come to find her here.

The steward raised an eyebrow, looked Jack up and down and sniffed. 'Kumari Dalvi has said nothing to me.'

'Perhaps you could tell her I'm here. I'll wait.'

'She is recuperating. She has been injured. She is not to be disturbed.'

'I've come a long way, sir. And I'm sure—'

'It's out of the question,' the steward snapped. 'You must leave now.'

Then a woman's voice called down the hallway, 'Steward? Who's there?'

'It's no one, madam,' the steward shouted back. 'I'm getting rid of him.'

The voice called again, 'But who is it?'

Jack recognised that voice. He was certain it was Sonali. 'It's me,' he called out.

He thought he heard a gasp and then Sonali shouted, 'Steward, bring him in here!'

The steward stiffened. He glared at Jack, his nostrils flaring, then turned on his heel and led Jack to the end of the corridor, where a door stood slightly ajar. He opened the door and admitted Jack into a room that smelt of jasmine, lotus and rose water. Light streamed in from a large set of windows that opened on to an inner courtyard garden. A brightly coloured parrot squawked in a cage hanging just outside the windows.

And lying in a bed, propped up by several pillows and brocaded cushions, was Sonali. Her hair was awry and her face was thin and gaunt. But there was a huge smile on her face and her eyes glowed.

'You can leave us alone,' she said to the steward.

'Are you sure, madam?' the steward asked.

She beamed at Jack. 'I am.'

The steward bowed, left the chamber and eased the door shut.

Jack walked across the room and sat on a stool beside the bed. 'How are you?'

'Much better. They say I'll be up and about soon.'

Jack crossed himself. 'I wasn't sure I should come.'

She smiled quizzically. 'Why do you say that?'

He cleared his throat. 'I wasn't sure ... When you were wounded you were talking a lot. You said you had difficulty . . . I can't remember how you put it.'

Her eyes became tearful. 'There's no difficulty now. Why don't you kiss me?'

Jack paused for a moment.

And then he leant across and kissed her on the lips.

Acknowledgements

I would like to thank my agent, Marlene Stringer, for representing me so well over the past four years, and my editor, Carolyn Caughey, for giving me the opportunity to write not only *The War of the Grail*, but the entire *Land of Hope and Glory* trilogy. Thanks also to Francine Toon and everyone at Hodder & Stoughton for all the work they have put into this book.

I am grateful to Dilraj Singh Sachdev, Mihir Wanchoo and Vandana Gombar for advice about various aspects of Indian history and culture. Thank you also to Nicole Hughes for information about battlefield injuries. I must emphasise, however, that any mistakes in the text are solely my own responsibility.

Thanks to Belinda Tobias, Simon Tobias and Edward Stone for designing and producing my website. And thanks to Gail Tatham for reading and commenting on the draft versions of all the books in the trilogy.

Finally, thank you to my family and friends, who have done so much to support and encourage me over the years. I wish I could mention everyone specifically, but the list would be very long. I hope this all-encompassing thank you will suffice.